Robert Hillstrom enjoyed a distinguished legal career
in major litigation, including the field of libel. A
native of Minnesota, he currently divides his time
between Montana, Florida and New York.

Nothing But the Truth

Robert Hillstrom

First published in 1992
by HEADLINE BOOK PUBLISHING PLC

First published in paperback in 1992
by HEADLINE BOOK PUBLISHING PLC

A HEADLINE FEATURE paperback

10 9 8 7 6 5 4 3

ISBN   0 7472 3980 0

Printed and bound in Great Britain by
HarperCollins Manufacturing, Glasgow

HEADLINE BOOK PUBLISHING PLC
Headline House
79 Great Titchfield Street
London W1P 7FN

FOR PATRICIA
and
In memory of Sara Ward Leake

Disclaimer

Because there are readers who knew me and my associates in the practice of law it is inevitable that some will try to see real people in my characters. None of them are based on any real person, or composites of real persons, alive or dead.

With specific reference to the major characters, I know of no person upon whom the characters of Gunnar Larson, Eddie Kerr, Tony Djilas, Holly Tripp, Al Bergdorf, Dov Levy or the employees of the *Times–Journal* could be based. They are all totally fictional and products of my imagination.

As to the characters in Florida: I know of no person alive or dead upon whom the characters of Ralph Ek, José Kelly, Loren Cressik, John Koronis or Chucky John Waycross could be based, nor am I aware of any facts indicating that any police officer or other public officials have engaged in the acts attributed to these characters in this novel. They are totally fictional and products of my imagination.

The same is true of the legal cases that make up the story. The fact–situations, parties, witnesses and proceedings are entirely fictional and are not based on any actual cases or composites of actual cases.

Any resemblance to real people or actual cases is entirely coincidental and beyond the intent of the author or the publisher.

Acknowledgements

Earl Gray and Stephen Bronis, distinguished criminal lawyers, who provided answers to difficult questions.

Richard Craven, Living Unit Director of Stillwater State Prison, who spoke to me from the inside.

Roy Doliner and Sara Leake who made me believe I could write a novel.

Marlene Fanta Shyer and Roy Doliner, professionals, whose encouragement kept me going.

Anne Williams, whose keen editorial eyes opened mine a little wider.

BOOK ONE
QUESTIONS

The heart has its reasons which reason knows nothing of.

Pascal

1

'Honey boy, when you grow up, stay away from women who make your heart beat faster,' Grandpa once said to Gunnar Larson.

Grandpa was a talker and he stood at the ready with bits of advice. Most of it Gunnar didn't understand, at least at the time, and Grandpa died when Gunnar was fourteen. His parents had given him Grandpa's name. 'Gunnar the runner', kids teased.

'Honey boy,' Grandpa had said more than once, powerful voice dampened in secrecy, 'you're the one in this family that's going to amount to something. You know why? Cause you're smart. There's no substitute for brains.' Grandpa had spent most of his life in America digging cesspools, leaving his hands coarse as broom-finished concrete. Yet, he quoted from the Constitution and played the best whist in Estherville, the county seat where he lived. He claimed to have duked it out on a back street in Oslo with Roald Amundsen, who went on to lead the first expedition to the South Pole in 1911.

Grandpa was fond of Milky Ways. As reward for his attention, little Gunnar got half, and in the thirties a nickle Milky Way was something to sink your teeth into, not the two bites you get now for a quarter or more. When Gunnar was five, he thought God must look like Grandpa – huge jowly face with serious, faded blue eyes underhung by wrinkled pouches. Below a noble Nordic nose, the silver mustache trimmed to short stubble tickled Gunnar when Grandpa kissed him. But God surely didn't chew Copenhagen, of which Grandpa exuded a faint fragrance twenty-four hours a day. His massive head might have effected his demise. No big-enough hat suited him, so on the coldest days of winter he went without. Now, a half-century later, Gunnar thought the old man's head would have been perfect for Chief Justice.

3

When Grandpa came to visit, the two Gunnars swung slowly for hours, Grandpa gently pushing the porch swing with his hickory cane. Little Gunnar recited nursery rhymes and knew the states of the union and their capitals.

'Nevada?' Grandpa would say.

'Carson City,' said Gunnar.

As evening light waned, they counted the headlights passing over the Madison Highway bridge in the distance. Although Grandpa's last car was a '25 T-model, the new all-steel bodies and hydraulic brakes fascinated him. By the time Gunnar was eight he knew all the neighbors' cars by make and year. Olson's '39 Studebaker Commander was the only hard one. The rest were all Fords and Chevys, and one '36 Plymouth. Right after the war, Olsons got the first new car in the neighborhood, a white four-door Buick Roadmaster. Kids from six blocks away came to look, some adults too. Grandpa said it was a sign of the new order, that ordinary people like the Olsons could acquire such a fine automobile. It was about then he warned Gunnar about women. He said each man was allotted just a certain number of heartbeats, so you should stay away from women who made your heart beat faster.

Not long before pneumonia got him, Grandpa had counseled young Gunnar one last time. 'Honey boy,' he said, 'remember this: It's no better to have the right answers, if you've got the wrong questions, than to have the wrong answers to the right questions.' He finished with a dip of his head lest Gunnar miss the gravity of his caveat.

'What do you mean, Grandpa?' Gunnar asked.

'Someday you will understand,' the old man said, adding something in Norwegian, as though Gunnar knew more than *please, thank you, hello* and *goodbye* in the language of the old country, as Grandpa called it.

It had taken forty-one years for Gunnar to understand. But now it was clear. A good man might still be alive had Grandpa's advice not been hidden away so remotely two years ago when Gunnar met Holly Tripp and, later, when he confronted the decision of whether or not to take her father's case. A river of tears might have been dammed at the source if Gunnar had asked the right questions from the beginning.

4

Maturity had brought Gunnar Larson the broad shoulders and deep chest of an athlete and, in his fifties, he still carried himself well – with just a slight stoop in the shoulders that gave him a fatherly look standing before a jury. Receding dark blond hair had become half-gray and from the back, in bright light, his scalp showed through on top. Bound together with the legacy of the name, Grandpa's heavy Nordic brow and straight well-cut nose gave Gunnar's face a stern look in repose. Years had turned the corners of his full-lipped mouth down, but smiles brought all the textured flesh into play, almost closing his eyes. A row of good teeth, grown some darker, drew you back if you were put off by the forbidding face of a second before. From under the shelf of his brow, wreaths of redundant skin gave his blue eyes a smallish look. Jurors had been persuaded, and witnesses frightened, by the fire in Gunnar's gaze. As Grandpa had predicted, little Gunnar had amounted to something. Many said he was the best trial lawyer in this part of the country.

It was a Tuesday morning in late May when Gunnar Larson read the newspaper article that would spill like a load of gravel across his life. Breakfast while watching the water was a special pleasure. Through the broad dining-room window, far across the bay, a ribbon of deep green dappled with specks of human habitation separated water from empty sky. Earlier that morning, he had walked down to the shore to investigate a floating object near the end of the dock – a northern pike, agate eyes clouded, apparently dead of old age, easily over twenty pounds and the biggest fish he had ever seen in these waters.

Twenty-two years ago in 1964, Gunnar and his wife Anne had joined the cabal of city dwellers bent on transforming this land of farms and Indian mounds into sanctuary for the terminally busy. Their home crouched among the hardwoods on Preacher's Bay, near the spot where, when he was fifteen years old, Gunnar had caught a five-and-a-half-pound largemouth. The first house was much smaller but ten years later – when money began to flow in quantities beyond any expectation – they added a guest room, a panelled den, a third bath and a rustic family room with a fireplace of stones the four of them had gathered along the lake shore.

Gunnar and Jack, his son, had fished the bay together in the sixties, especially in May and early June when the walleyes spawned in shallow water. The best spot was a drop-off straight out from their dock. In the ten years since Jack died, Gunnar had taken his rod and reel out only once or twice. Sometimes the urge to get back on the water returned, but there was no time.

Breakfast finished, Gunnar scanned the front page of the *Times-Journal*. Only on Sundays did he venture beyond page one. The Challenger disaster still dominated the news. In the center of the page, below a two-column picture of a smiling elegant man, a line of vivid black type declared: TONY DJILAS WASN'T SMILING YESTERDAY. Gunnar had seen the face before, in a spread in the society section on Holly Tripp's wedding, last summer. Tony Djilas was Holly's father. From the end of the dock, Gunnar could see the newlywed's boathouse across the bay.

Gunnar had never met Djilas, nor did he think any of the sixteen lawyers in the firm had done business with him. But Gunnar *had* met Holly, last fall, just after the first snow.

On Sunday mornings Gunnar walked through the countryside for exercise and private thinking time. Upon overtaking someone, he hello'd, lengthened the long stride afforded by his lean six-foot frame, and quickly passed.

That raw day, dry leaves mixed with fine white powder swirled around her boots and puffs of frosty breath emerged from within the hood of her bulky parka. A few big flakes flew randomly black against the gray sky, suddenly white when they fluttered below the naked tree tops. Gunnar's hello was met with a smile that must have shown a hundred teeth. Her face, colored by the biting air, made him search for other words, and for a few moments he found none.

And then: 'Cold enough for you?' Had he actually uttered such an inanity?

'I guess so,' she said, apparently far more self-possessed than he. 'But the chick-a-dees are having a fine time.'

Gunnar matched her pace. About thirty, she had the wide-eyed open look of a high-school girl. He had seen her before, from a distance, as she passed on the other side of the road with another woman, but up close was different. Her face, framed with soft brown curls and the dark fur trim of the hood, made his heart beat faster. Even in the cold, she smelled of summer orchards.

'I'm Gunnar Larson,' he said, pulling off his leather chopper.

She stopped and took his hand firmly. 'Holly Tripp,' she said.

'I know. I saw your picture in the paper when you got married.'

'You remember? That was way last summer.'

'I have a memory for certain faces.'

'That bad, huh?' she said.

'Yeah, that bad,' he said. 'You want some company?'

'Why not?'

And away they went, crunching along, the ghost of a sun barely burning through the autumn mist. The friendly smell of burning wood drifted down from a chimney on the hill and from somewhere among the throng of trees came the frosty ring of a shovel scraping ice-encrusted concrete.

Now, most of a year later, he took a swallow of coffee, and began to read the piece about her father. He'd heard that the *Times-Journal* had been making momentous accusations, and knew that a series of five articles, in preparation for more than a year, had been run that previous week, but he hadn't taken the time to read them. Gunnar had learned that the press needed little fuel to kindle fire, that they often tried to produce heat from only smoke. This time they were homing in on the methods by which contractors and developers were selected to do business with the city.

DEVELOPER'S PAST BLOWS PROJECT the headline read. Under the byline of 'Ward Chapin and Suzie Cline' the article went on:

On Monday, the City Council, based on revelations of Anthony Djilas's past criminal activities in these pages last week, killed the proposed project of the group headed by Djilas to develop Block 13 of the New City renewal district. The project contained a 40-story convention hotel, a 44-story office tower, an atrium shopping center and an 800-car parking ramp. The estimated total cost was over $200,000,000.

7

Criminal activities. Holly had said nothing. She must have known about the earlier articles, but she hadn't given the slightest hint.

Last winter, after a couple more chance Sunday meetings, Holly had started waiting along the road near the same horse pasture every Sunday morning, until Gunnar came along. The three-mile circuit of country road brought them back past her lane where she would say goodbye, leaving Gunnar to walk the last mile alone.

His weekly walk took on new importance.

She was on the road every morning, she said. One Sunday in early February she shivered with the horses until Gunnar came. The temperature was eleven below zero. That was the day she had slipped on a patch of ice, and he grabbed her arm and held on as she spun toward him and reached out to his shoulder to catch herself. He was the first to look away from the soft gray eyes.

The walks were their only contact. They discussed the beauty of the countryside. Certain birds and animals tended to appear in the same places along the way. In the spring, cardinals whistled at them from a grove of maples guarding both sides of the road. And often, in a tiny circular marsh, a muskrat sat alone: a curl of brown fur sunning itself on the side of a lodge poked up among broken reeds. Sometimes they talked about themselves, though they both avoided asking questions, as if they didn't want to know the answers.

Two bass fisherman in a small boat, casting shiny lures toward the end of the dock, caught Gunnar's glance. Then his eyes returned to the front page.

Mayor Steven Carpenter, a close friend of Djilas, expressed 'great disappointment' at the Council's action. Helen Wilson, Council President, said that in view of last week's media revelations concerning the past associations and activities of Djilas, the City Council was no longer interested in doing business with him. She conceded that the Djilas group's proposal was clearly the type the city wanted and that, had the information regarding Djilas not surfaced, the Council would have proceeded to negotiate with the group.

The revelations about Djilas were made in a series of five articles, in preparation for more than a year, published last week in this newspaper on the method by which the city chose contractors and developers.

They better have their facts right or this guy is going to sue their nuts off, Gunnar thought. The dollars are so big even these arrogant bastards at the *Times-Journal* would not take any chances. Holly must be suffering. Not one clue. Didn't she know he cared about her?

By January, Holly had told Gunnar her husband Davey had a drinking problem, concealed from her prior to their marriage. Secrets shared beget secrets and Gunnar surprised himself when he revealed that a wall had risen between himself and his wife Anne since their son had died. Holly's parents had lived apart for a long time, she said: her mother in Florida; her father, a real estate developer, here in the city. She had grown up in Florida; she loved boating and swimming, and was happy to be living on the lake.

When the weather warmed in late February, Holly appeared in sweater and workout tights. Gunnar saw a figure to complement her lovely face – long slim legs and wonderful breasts. Sometimes he felt compelled to hold her hand as they walked, but he thought better of it. The frequent soft eye-contact would have to do and when she zapped him with the hundred-tooth smile his heart quickened.

A couple of months ago when they parted she had said, 'Next week?' And he'd said sure. They both knew it would be about eight-thirty, and last Sunday when she said it again, she reached out and took his hand.

Gunnar's coffee cooled in the cup. The article said that Djilas had bitterly accused the *Times-Journal* of being out to get him. Their accusations were all lies, he said. Gunnar's eyes followed the story down the page.

Anthony Djilas was born in the northern part of this state where he attended high school in various small towns. He came to the

9

city in his senior year and graduated from Southeast High in June of 1955. In 1958 he obtained a real estate broker's license and spent the next ten years working as a salesman for several different real estate brokers, among them Emanuel Zilman. In 1969 Zilman moved his operations to Broward County, Florida. In 1970 Djilas turned up working for Zilman in Florida as a licensed real estate salesman. Djilas refused to speak to reporters during the time the articles in question were being prepared. The reporters were unable to locate Zilman.

Djilas should have talked to the reporters. Gunnar wondered how hard they had tried to find Zilman. Talking to *him* might have spoiled a good story. Why no mention of Tony Djilas' family, especially since Holly was married into the Tripp money? One thing for sure: if Holly had wanted him to know about this, she would have said something last Sunday. They had taken an extra hour on their walk. Overgrown with spring grasses, a cart path led off into the woods. Holly suggested they explore it. There were no 'No trespassing' signs. It petered out in a hay meadow near an old barn that stood, sturdy and square, weathered gray like a watercolor. Nearly hidden in the new growth, a concrete foundation was all that remained of the accompanying farmhouse.

Gunnar followed her through the meadow and past an old hay rake that lay rusting in the tall grass like the brown bones of an extinct mammal. They sat down together amid a chorale of bird songs. She spoke of good times with her only sister, Marvel, still living in Florida. They talked on the phone almost daily, she said. Holly could easily have broached the subject of her father's problems, but she mentioned him not at all. She must have been aware of the story. And if she hadn't seen the newspaper surely husband Davey would have told her.

Gunnar neared the end of the astonishing allegations.

As reported last week, in 1973 Zilman was investigated by a Federal grand jury, but though suspected of various smuggling, drug and conspiracy offenses connected with the procurement

and sale of large quantities of marijuana, he was never prosecuted. The *Times-Journal* discovered that the grand jury
investigation of Zilman in 1973 led to evidence that Djilas
was involved in marijuana trafficking. Although the statute
of limitations for the prosecution of Djilas has long since
expired, the *Times-Journal* is entirely satisfied that the dope
trafficking did indeed occur, and if necessary to provide hard
evidence to that effect, it could. Pierce Pentecost, one of
Djilas' competitors for the City Council contract refused to
comment . . . .

Gunnar felt somebody looking over his shoulder.

'Daddy, let me see that.'

'Good morning Katie, dear. Are you going to be late for school
. . . hi, babe.' Anne stood in the doorway, pink tank-top soaked
with sweat. Except for the age difference, Anne and Katie, made
a matched pair: tall, slim, short blonde hair.

'Have a good jog?' he said to Anne.

'Dear, I've told you, I don't jog, I run.'

'OK sweets, whatever.'

Katie sat down at the end of the table.

'Did you cover libel in your torts class?' Gunnar asked.

'Yes Daddy, I know all about New York Times *v. Sullivan*,
and *Gertz*. Daddy, do you know that now, to recover against a
newspaper, the *Hepps* case makes any plaintiff prove the stuff was
false? *Plus* that it was published with actual malice.'

'But don't forget honey, if they knew it was false or should
have, that's malice, right.' Gunnar had handled his share of
libel cases.

'Right, Daddy.'

'I wonder what it will be like to live with two lawyers?'
said Anne.

'Mom, I promise I'll move out if I'm ever admitted to the
Bar.'

On the way downtown a few minutes later, Gunnar considered
calling Holly, but it was not for him to disturb the fragile
framework of their secluded little Sunday-morning world. She
had taken his hand, if only for a second or two. But he knew

better than to deal in fantasy. After all her father hadn't died. Of course, to some, missing out on four or five mill might seem worse than death. Gunnar saw images of bodies hurdling through the air after the stock-market collapse of '29, three years before he was born.

2

On Thursday afternoon at one-thirty, two days after he had read the accusatory newspaper article, Gunnar Larson's secretary, Shana, handed him a note. Leo wanted to talk to him as soon as possible.

In his sophomore year at State, Gunnar had found a job officiating intramural basketball games for five dollars a night. He and one other student handled three thirty-two minute games in the steamy cracker-box gym. One night he worked with an unusual guy who gave the impression he was ready to take on anything. Gunnar liked him immediately. Bouncing up and down the court, steel-rimmed glasses, curly black hair, blasting on the whistle, he loudly proclaimed the fouls: 'You blocked him! . . . Reaching in! . . . Pushing off!'

In the third game a fraternity played a team from the campus YMCA. The first half was a brawl. The fraternity, a mass of thick bodies and flying elbows, played without regard to the rules against physical contact. They overpowered the smaller Y team. Even with their growing lead, the fraternity brats bitched at every call. Attempting to maintain some control, Gunnar and his partner whistled the fouls, one upon the other. At the half-time break the frat-house team led by fifteen. For a buck and a half it seemed like a lot of shit to take.

During the rest period Gunnar's new colleague said, 'Say pal, what do you say we teach these smart alecks a lesson?'

'If we call them any closer we'll be here all night,' Gunnar said.

'That isn't exactly what I had in mind; I think these Greeks could use a little humility.'

13

'You want them to lose? They're ahead by fifteen!'

'With your help, they're gonna lose a squeaker.'

In the second half whistles blew for every fraternity infraction. The YMCA could do no wrong, and when they obviously did, Gunnar and Leo didn't seem to notice. The fraternity lost by a couple of points, and the association of Leo Lawson and Gunnar Larson began.

Thirty-three years later, they sat together in Leo's corner office in Lawson and Larson's suite on the nineteenth floor of the Finance and Commerce Tower – downtown's prestige address. Early afternoon sun filled every corner of the room. Eighteenth-century furniture was grouped around two central pieces: in the rear, a Chippendale sofa covered in a blue chintz print; in the front, Leo's desk. He leaned way back in the chair behind it, fingers interlaced on the back of his head. His black wing-tips were crossed and resting on the cherrywood wood top. In the Sheraton style, with fluted legs and brass-handled drawers, it was an exact replica of the one President George Washington used. Two narrow, finely crafted shelves elevated above the top extended the full length along each side.

Leo's face had accrued a line or two. There were flashes of gray in his tightly trimmed dark hair and he had cultivated a neat mustache which ended at the short curved creases bracketing his mouth.

'You see the article about Tony Djilas?' Leo asked, in a passing-the-time-of-day tone. Steady brown eyes with a hint of humor gleamed behind dark-rimmed glasses.

'Tough stuff,' Gunnar took a sip of Leo's latest gourmet decaf.

Leo got up and walked over to the plate glass window, holding the handle of a steaming cup with tapered fingers, perfectly manicured. The summer sky looked cool and clear, belying the year's first ninety-degree day. 'Make a hell of a case if it's not true . . . think?'

'Are you suggesting it's not true?' Gunnar asked.

'That's strange coming from you,' Leo said. 'You never believe a word you read in the paper.'

'True enough, especially those bastards.'

'I've met Djilas. You know, I kind of liked him. Sure didn't seem like a crook . . . and the mayor's his close friend. You're pretty high on the mayor, aren't you, Gunnar.'

'Suppose so. I trust him. That's saying something for a politician.' Gunnar's quiet response lacked conviction.

Leo peered into his cup, as though he expected to find something floating in the coffee. 'Do you know Djilas?' he asked.

'I never met him. Heard the usual talk. Supposed to have some big-buck backers.' Leo didn't know about Gunnar's Sunday-morning walks with Djilas' daughter.

'I was taking a steam this noon, and Al Bergdorf sat down next to me.'

'I hope he had a robe.'

Leo laughed. 'No, as a matter of fact, he was jack naked. He must go three hundred.'

'Aaaagh.'

'Anyhow, partner, he talked about you.'

'Nothing good, I trust.'

'*Au contraire*. He's Tony Djilas' lawyer you know.'

'I guess I didn't. Then Bag and Rat will lose a bundle of fees if Djilas doesn't get the New City development deal.' Gunnar referred to Bergdorf and Ratner, Al's firm.

Leo turned away from the window, 'Al wants you to sue the *Times-Journal* for Tony.'

'Not a chance in hell.' Gunnar's answer was pure reflex in full courtroom voice. The image of Bergdorf squeezed any thought of Holly from Gunnar's mind.

'Can we at least talk about it?' Leo asked.

'I'm sorry, old friend, but I don't want to get involved with Al Bergdorf.'

'Talk?'

'When have I refused to talk to you?' Gunnar reverted to the respectful tone.

'He promised he'd have nothing to do with the case, beyond what you asked, and he didn't think you'd ask.'

'Remember, counselor, you can discount anything he says – including good morning.'

'Hear me out. He says Tony knows the reporters blew it. He says they couldn't have found anything because there was nothing to find. Tony was doing fine in real estate and he left Zilman as soon as he got a whiff of the drug business. The DEA just talked to him once . . . only about Zilman.' When Leo sought to persuade, his smooth low voice moved up the register. 'He was never even under any kind of suspicion according to Bergdorf. Remember, they took him out of a two-hundred-million-dollar deal. The damages are horrendous . . . millions.' Leo paced to the back of the room, behind Gunnar. 'You've always wanted the real big score. This could be it!'

Talking money with Leo disquieted Gunnar. He wasn't a gambler. To him, money represented time and security. His parents had taught him the security part; father on the same job for forty-five years; mother accounting for every penny, managing to build their savings, even in the Depression. But to Leo, money was power and a way to keep score.

Just after they had gotten started, Leo had asked Gunnar to join him in a deal, a chance to get in on a contract for tearing the streetcar tracks out of the city streets. It took thirty-five thousand. Leo arranged for a loan with a client bank, but, with the bids running less than the out-of-pocket costs to remove the rails, Gunnar didn't want to take the risk. You had to make it all on the resale of the steel. After Gunnar opted out, Leo borrowed the whole thirty-five himself and pocketed over a hundred thousand clear when the steel was sold. That was a lot of dough in 1960, and the beginning of a golden snowball for Leo.

He walked back toward the glass wall and turned, facing Gunnar, the top of the city spreading out behind him. 'I think they'd stand still for a fifty-per-cent contingency. If Djilas would advance the costs, the only downside would be your time.'

'Yeah, just my time.' Gunnar blew out a puff of air. 'Why me?'

'Come now. You know damn well why you. You've kicked more than one butt at Bag and Rat, not to mention all over town. They know you defended Grunwold Pharmaceutical and Tompkins, the two high-profile defamation cases. I just saw a cite to Tompkins in the *American Bar Journal*. Plaintiff took nothing both times.

16

I'm sure they think you'll defend the *Times-Journal* if you don't represent Tony.'

'No way. I'd go back to drunk-driving cases before I'd work for that newspaper. They're all alike, sneaky little bastards. Investigative journalists, my ass . . . Opportunists . . . greedy little opportunists.'

Leo had been edging toward Gunnar's chair until his compact frame hovered over his larger partner, his dark brows arched like the wings of a gliding gull. 'That's the point! Here's your chance to teach them a lesson.' He whacked Gunnar's shoulder.

Gunnar, sitting on his spine, straightened up. 'Look, I can't say it doesn't feel good to have these guys want me; and you might be right, it could be a career case. And the defendants *are* schmucks of the first water, but I just don't want to get involved with these guys. It's that fucking simple.'

They were both silent for a full minute: Leo back at the window looking across the city; Gunnar forming a tent of his finger tips.

'Anyhow,' Gunnar said, 'it's gotten next to impossible to beat a newspaper in a libel suit.'

With his back still turned, Leo played his last card. 'Tell you what partner, you take this case and you can keep the whole fee. I'm sure Djilas will advance all the costs. I'll get the partners to agree. You're everybody's hero, and it's been a long time since I've asked them for anything. Now is that a deal, or what?'

When Leo turned to face him again, an expectant look on his face, Gunnar felt like a fish contemplating a worm, sure there was a hook in it.

'Ah, the filthy lucre is tempting, but we all must draw our lines.' As he spoke Gunnar reached both arms straight out, like a traffic cop, palms pushing toward Leo. 'Count me out this time. I don't want to inflame anybody, just tell them I'm busy, and that's no lie.'

Leo shrugged, 'What more can I say? I have a three-thirty at the bank. Remember the way we used to grub for clients. That guy you knew, whatshisname, convinced you we should never turn down a case. And we didn't for years. Now they come crawling, and you turn 'em away. High principles. Maybe that's why I love ya.' He smiled, grabbed a file and was gone. From the hall he called back to Gunnar. 'I'm surprised you helped me fix that game.'

Back in his own office, Gunnar's juices still simmered. Leo was right. It might be a bonanza case and Gunnar could use the dough. With his problems at home, it could give him some room to maneuver. What about Holly? Innocent as it was, the delicate balance of their relationship might be upset by a wrong word or the wrong question. After all, she *was* a newlywed. Getting involved with her father could wreck everything. Especially in a losing cause. Especially if the charges were true, as they might well be. For the first time since Jack's death, something in Gunnar's own life seemed as important as his cases.

He had surprised himself at the stonewall stance he'd taken on account of Bergdorf. The issue hadn't come up before. It was the old absurdity. How do I know what I think, until I hear what I say? It had to be more than the one time Bergdorf had double-crossed him. He broke a handshake deal and forced Gunnar to trial six months before they had agreed. Gunnar had beat the bastard anyway.

Bergdorf's trespass was ten years ago, maybe fifteen. Others had done the same to Gunnar, and worse. He had forgotten some of their names. Why had he reacted so fast – so sure of himself, without reservation. No one doubted the quality of Bergdorf and Ratner's professional practice. Al's father, Simon, was a legend – an immigrant who had reached the top in more ways than one – a man of unquestioned integrity and stature. Yet at the mention of his name, Gunnar's first thought was 'Jew' – then all the rest. Gunnar had been trained in a relentless school.

As a child he was introduced to the word 'Jew' as an expletive used to characterize people his father despised. In the forties the family listened to 'The Sixty-four Dollar Question' on the radio. Phil Baker, the host, would introduce contestants, mostly New Yorkers, as 'Mrs Rose Green' or 'Mr Michael Levin'. Carl Larson would immediately say 'Jew' in the same tone as he might have said 'traitor'. Uncle Floyd had used the word as a verb. 'Hold for your price, Carl,' he would say to Gunnar's father, 'don't let them jew you down.' When he bought a used car that turned out to be a lemon, Uncle Floyd said he had been 'jewed'.

'Is Mr O'Leary a Jew?' Gunnar had asked.

'Of course not, he's Irish,' Uncle Floyd said. 'I wouldn't buy a car from a Jew.'

As bright as Gunnar was, it still confused him. He asked Uncle Floyd, wasn't it true that Jesus was a Jew? 'No,' he was told. 'Of the twelve tribes, Jews came only from Judah.' And one of the proofs of this astonishing statement was that if you extended a straight line north-west through two corners of the Great Pyramid of Cheops it exactly bisected the British Isles. The whole thing seemed kind of convincing at the time, but Gunnar was only thirteen. Grandpa said Uncle Floyd was as full of shit as a Christmas turkey. But Grandpa didn't like Jews very much either. Even Gunnar's mother suggested that Gentiles couldn't really trust them.

'Are we Gentiles?' Gunnar had asked.

'Of course,' she said. To add to Gunnar's confusion, when they couldn't find what they wanted at Sears, Roebuck, his parents almost always ended up buying from Jews. Gunnar got his first suit from Abe Gold, and most of his other clothes came from Kaplans.

At State, Gunnar became a freshman liberal. Took to arguing about prejudice and discrimination with his father and Uncle Floyd. At the Jazz Society he enjoying hanging out with young Jews, even a few blacks. Gabe Sussman was a hell of a pianist. He could make the box sound like Art Tatum or Errol Garner, or Mead Lux Lewis, if you were in the mood for boogie. But there wasn't one Jewish partner, associate or support employee working for Lawson and Larson.

Gunnar put the idea aside. Why did Leo want him to take the Djilas case – to the point of making a deal on the fee that was unheard of, not just at Lawson and Larson, but anywhere in the law business? And was Gunnar's own reaction to Al Bergdorf just an excuse to avoid meeting Djilas? Gunnar wanted to maintain the status quo with Holly Tripp. Actually, it was past wanting. To get from week to week, he needed the taste of her presence on Sunday morning. Still, what a hero he would be if he could work a miracle for Holly's father.

19

3

On Sunday morning after Leo's midweek sales pitch for Tony Djilas, Gunnar stood on the end of the dock watching a hen mallard swimming purposefully past in the green algae forming on the surface. Her near-adult family, close to a dozen, tagged along behind in single file. Distant white caps blended into the calmer waters of the bay, dotted with sails and powerboats on apparent collision courses. Tony Djilas had called for an appointment but didn't get past Angela, the receptionist. Gunnar took Al Bergdorf's call. He had begged off, quite gracefully, he thought; he was, he had said, swamped with files that weren't settling as expected. Of course, Al knew it wasn't true, but he had feigned belief and expressed genuine gratitude at Gunnar's promised refusal to defend the *Times-Journal*. Even Mayor Carpenter had called, extolling Tony's uncommon qualities as citizen and patriot. Leo hadn't mentioned the case again. Gunnar looked at his watch, and headed for his walk with Holly.

Sunday mornings had become pivotal in his week. Walking nimbly through the woods on the curving lane leading from the lake-shore properties to the main road, he tossed scraps of orange peel into the underbrush. July branches, crossing high above, grasped at each other. Ragged dollops of white light connected by silver wire filigreed the damp gray loam underfoot. The stiff breeze from the lake couldn't find its way through the tall trees, and beads of sweat quickly formed on Gunnar's hairy torso.

At the blacktop he waited to avoid a pickup truck travelling north. Then, crossing quickly, he headed south-east along the shoulder, giving oncoming traffic a wide berth. Less than a half-mile later, before the road disappeared over a hill, he turned

20

straight west on a narrower blacktop, Preacher's Bay Road, that wound ahead of him up a long hill like a stripe on a snake's back. At the top, he looked out over the bay from the South. His own house, sheathed in cedar, peeked through the trees on the east shore, the little matching gazebo on the lawn in front.

He turned south on still another blacktop through a dense stand of oak and maple and then out into the open between two rolling pastures. On the left, a lone stubby oak stood like a shepherd on a knoll surrounded by a herd of black and white cows. The pasture on the right, fenced with white board on stout posts, enclosed several Arabian mares with their foals, mostly grays. Like Rosinante, a poor old gray gelding stood far to the side, eating purple clover blossoms. A white salt-box house was stationed on a rise behind the horses.

He was never sure until he saw her, but each Sunday she was there. Only once had he needed to wait. Holly quietly spoke to one of the mares. A foal poked its head through the fence and tore at the long grass in the ditch.

'Hi, Holly Tripp.' The mare and foal took off across the pasture in full gallop.

'Oh, the body beautiful,' she said.

Her breasts were trying to squeeze their way out of a white tube top. The heat had stripped them both down to the current requirements of conventional modesty. Embarrassment at her comment mingled with a sense of satisfaction.

'Look who's talking,' he said, crossing the road in the fulgent sunlight.

'Hi ya, Gunnar!' The smile zapped him.

He held her extended hand for a few seconds. They marvelled at the day, the countryside, the charm of the horses and their new babies. Her gray eyes held steady on his as they spoke, and he felt compelled to look away at times – so unlike the way he talked to clients, witnesses and others from whom he sought the truth or, at least, their version of it. As the mares and foals edged curiously toward them en masse, he didn't resist the impulse to look at her chest. She caught him at it and smiled even wider, if that was possible.

'Gunnar, I can't make the hike today. Libby Cochrane needs a substitute partner for doubles. She's been so nice to me I couldn't turn her down. I'll really miss our walk, and our talk.'

'No problem,' Gunnar said. He was painfully disappointed.

'Next Sunday,' she said, 'for sure?'

'For sure,' Gunnar said.

'I gotta run. Bye now.' She playfully tugged on a tuft of his chest hair, and quickly turned and walked back toward the lake.

He felt the flow of blood to his face. The conversation had passed so quickly that he hadn't considered the opportunity of walking back with her to Preacher's Bay Road, but his eyes followed her. The tan skin on her long legs contrasted with the white tennis shorts. A hundred yards down the road she turned for a moment and waved, as though she knew he would be watching. Another week would pass before she would have the chance to raise the subject of her father's trouble. But, clearly, her face had betrayed no concern. She had seemed happy, perhaps more than ever before. Gunnar clicked his tongue at the twenty-odd equine faces staring at him. Then, he crossed the road and walked on in the sun.

Anne pushed her way into his thoughts. They had made their most recent try at sex a week ago. He remembered the sadness in her eyes when he gave up, looking at her futilely in the dim light, then nestling his head in the hollow of her shoulder, the muffled gong of his heart palpable in both bodies. Anne had stroked his hair and covered his face with the gentlest of kisses – wordless assurances – but he didn't believe her anymore. It wasn't OK for him or her. Other times she would go down on him and there would be flickers of response – then the ebbing, and the gripping embarrassment, but in the end it was fear and anger prevailed.

It had begun after Jack died. At first, the passing of time was healing, but the intervals became longer – weeks, then months. Now it seemed it would never happen between them again. His inner capacity for softness subsided along with his penis's capacity for hardness. He was quicker to anger. He criticized Anne for meaningless little things. His sense of humor ebbed, and his concentration was affected. His fleeting erections could be costly to clients.

His predicament demanded careful analysis. Gunnar's habit was to bounce issues off Leo, or one of the other lawyers, or his clerks. That was one of the few pleasant aspects of trial preparation. Most of it was drudgery. Who could he bounce his impotence off? Reading medical journals only increased his anxiety, but he had learned it must be a psychological problem. The mechanism was still there, workable. Often in the night, or upon awakening in the morning, his penis was staunch, ready for action, as though he had been having an erotic dream immediately lost to memory.

Why should a boy's dying make love more difficult for his father and mother? Jesus Christ, would it ever get better? Ten years. Time heals all. But some things didn't heal. Gangrene sets in, and you have to amputate. Was that it? Did he have to cut himself away? Cut the good from the bad. Start over? He barely noticed the cars whooshing on the narrow road six feet away. A maroon Jaguar honked. Someone he knew perhaps.

The shadow cast over the marriage grew darker. It was as though there was no day. Dusk followed immediately upon the dawn.

He had handled some divorces, only major cases where the marital assets were in the millions. Impotence had never been an articulated issue. Usually the husband had left for another woman, invariably younger. He owed Anne better than that. She had committed more than thirty years to him. Yes, he owed her. Or did he? Are you responsible for another person – an adult person? Surely, debts accrue. But maybe she would be better off. Maybe he would be doing her a favor. Of course, that would be her call. She had never indicated anything of the sort. Divorce was not an option to Anne. She would never consider it. Maybe that was the flaw. Maybe she *should* consider it.

White paint peeled from the little house on the left-hand side of the road that hid behind an untrimmed weeping willow. As Jack ran along this same route when he was in high school, a German shepherd had sprung from beneath the willow and bit him in the butt. Jack bought an aluminum canoe and a two-horse outboard with the money Gunnar got from the dog owner's insurance company. The joke was that he would run by again that winter, when he was ready for new skis and boots.

Now, Gunnar didn't know the occupants. Most of the others in its class had disappeared, replaced by elegant colonials and Georgians built by the equestrian set who had settled in the wooded hills of Preacher's Bay Township.

Already, the sun felt oppressive on his uncovered head. It was a question of priorities. Up to now, the cases had come first. They had taken all of his time. How could he find room for personal problems, no matter how cataclysmic? A week from tomorrow morning the Miracle Mills trial began. It was routine, but it would last for weeks, maybe months. He was defending them in a class action brought by a group of franchisees operating as Creamy-Sweet Cones under an agreement with Miracle Mills, giant food conglomerate, and longtime client of Lawson and Larson. The ice-cream dealers alleged that Miracle Mills was not living up to its promotional agreement. For Gunnar, the big difference in this case was that Eddie Kerr was assisting. He didn't like working with Eddie, but on this one Gunnar needed the best brain he could get, and Eddie was available. The first time he had worked with Eddie he had promised himself never again.

Eddie Kerr's attitude had fostered an impulse in Gunnar to drive out of his way on a trip up north just to see the turf from which such perverse attitude might spring. A local grocer, remembering him as 'Pudge', said he always kept to himself; his older brother, Fred, was much better known. The father was still around. He had worked all of his life as a watchman at a lumber operation, and Gunnar could tell the grocer didn't like the elder Mr Kerr.

Today, as he drew near the lane leading him home, Gunnar's mind found its way back to its comfort zone, the practice of law. He focused laser-like on preparing to win the Miracle Mills case, the next trial on the horizon, the first in an endless chain of new cases.

4

Behind the giant walnut desk, Al Bergdorf subsided into the oversized chair. His office and its contents were scaled to his bulk. Tony Djilas, not a hair of silver waves awry, paisley pocket silk and all, sank into the spongy fawn sofa under a ten-foot wide Jackson Pollock. Renowned for their expertise in real estate development law, Bergdorf and Ratner were almost as well known for the twentieth-century art acquired by Al's ninety-year-old father, Simon. Though totally blind by now, he still came to the office two or three mornings a week.

'OK pal, what'so damn interesting to get me down here this early on Monday morning?' Al was putting Tony on. Like most lonely men, he came in early every day.

'You won't believe this Al, but we might have another shot at getting Gunnar Larson to handle my case.'

'It'd be a miracle. Even your buddy, the mayor, got nowhere. And he tells me Leo Lawson doesn't think there's a chance.'

'Holly knows him,' Tony said.

'Your daughter?'

'Yeah, Holly.'

'I haven't seen her since that blast you threw at Maple Hills last summer when she married Davey.'

'Cost me twenty-seven grand,' said Tony.

'She's some looker.' Al clipped the tip off a six-inch cigar as thick as his thumb. 'How does she know Gunnar?'

'She meets him on the road when she walks around the neighborhood. You know they live out by the lake.'

'Start at the beginning. Why did she bother to tell you she knows him?'

'They had me out there for dinner last Friday night,' Tony said.

'I go out about once a month. It's really nice out there this time of year . . . right on the bay.'

Al watched the blue smoke from his cigar curl toward the ceiling. He remembered times at the lake with his son and wife years ago, before his family had just sort of fallen apart like a cheap piece of furniture when the glue gets old.

Tony continued, absently tugging at a hair in his ear. 'We talked about my case. Davey was half in the bag, but he agrees with us. He thinks Gunnar's the guy. Anyway, I told them it was no soap. He just wouldn't do it. He's too fuckin' busy.' The last Tony said in a smirky mimic.

'I told you he didn't like me,' Al said. He knew what he said was true, but he didn't know why.

'Now listen to what I'm saying,' Tony said. 'That's when Holly told me she knew him. When I was talking to her on the phone last night, she mentioned she had seen him again yesterday.'

'So, did she mention the case?'

'Hell no, she's never said a thing,' Tony said. 'She said she didn't have time to talk to him yesterday, but she wouldn't have anyway. I think she's kind of embarrassed by the stuff in the paper.'

'How often does she see him?'

'On Friday night when she was talking in front of Davey, it seemed like she just knew him, you know kinda casual like, but on the phone I got the idea she sees him almost every Sunday morning.'

'Maybe little Davey wouldn't like that so well,' said Al.

'He's been a schmuck. He's drunk all the time and, you know, he must have gained thirty pounds since they got married.'

'Fat people aren't all bad,' Al said with a straight face.

'He was off the booze for two years. She never saw him drink 'til the night at Maple Hills. He was too sloshed to fuck her on the wedding night . . . not that he hadn't before.'

'He ain't the first, correct?' Al asked.

'No, she's been married before, or same as. I thought it might be different with Davey, he's really heavy in the green, big important family and all that stuff.'

'Tell me about it. Those brokers been cleaning up ever since the movie actor took over.' Al thought of Ronald Reagan as an affliction the people deserved, like a glutton with gout.

'Not only that, he's got a trust fund from Grandpa, and more bucks from Momma and Poppa. But his drinking has pretty well fucked up the marriage. He's drunk from about seven-on every night.'

'So, what does Papa have in mind?'

'Maybe *she* can get Gunnar to take the case.'

Through the window, the gothic façade of the City Bank Building he was sitting in reflected back at Al from the glass wall of the Finance and Commerce Tower across the street. 'I never heard that he was into pussy,' he said, 'but who isn't, I guess. We never socialized. I know Leo pretty well. But that bastard only listens. He never tells you anything.'

'I didn't mean she'd sleep with him.' Tony seemed offended.

'I didn't either. Don't get your shit hot. It was just a manner of speaking.'

'Well . . . what do you think?' Tony's good nature returned.

'What do you mean, what do I think?'

'Ain't that what I pay you for? Should I tell Holly to take a shot?'

'She's your kid,' Al said. 'And I can't help thinking he's not the only lawyer in town.' But Al knew, for sure, Gunnar Larson was the best trial lawyer he had ever come up against. Juries loved him. 'Do you think maybe he'd rather steer clear of you if he's got eyes for your kid. Don't forget this guy's a big man in town, ethics committee and all that shit, and he's married. And your kid's married. Could work against you.'

'May be, but I'm not ready to give up on Gunnar. I want to make those schmucks pay some real money.'

'Goniff.' Al threw back his head and guffawed, his huge body shaking. As he calmed down he leaned to the side, snuffed, and hocked an enormous gob of amorphous matter and tobacco juice into the wastebasket. 'If you want him so bad, give it a shot,' he wheezed. 'There's nobody better.'

Gunnar took her call mid-morning. Sunday's sun had stayed over for Monday, and downtown was heating up for more July.

'It's Holly Tripp,' she said, in a tone like maybe he had forgotten her. He visualized her smile.

'Good to hear from you,' he said. In his chest, he could feel his heart pumping.

'I hate to bother you. I know you must be busy.'

'Don't be silly. Call any time. I suppose you made the circuit this morning.'

'Yes, it's a beautiful day out here,' she said, her voice smooth and soft like a child's, 'but, it's warming up fast.'

He agreed that it was another beautiful day and that it was going to get too hot. The lake was the place to be. He felt a bit bold telling her he had missed her company on Sunday. She told him she had already spoken with the horses.

'Gunnar, I need to talk to you.'

'Sure,' he said. It must be about her father. Was it going to be pressure to take the case? 'Let me check my schedule. Maybe you can come down this afternoon.'

'I'd rather we meet by the horses, like always,' she said.

'Do you want to tell me what it's about?'

'When I see you,' she said. 'I need to talk to you . . . professionally, I guess you'd say.'

'Fine, but professionally it might be better here in the office.'

'Could you make an exception this once?'

'Of course.' He thought of the conferences scheduled for late afternoon and evening, today and tomorrow, all week really. They were in the last days of preparation for the Miracle Mills trial.

As he hesitated she spoke again. 'Gunnar, this is really an imposition. If you're too busy I'll understand.'

He didn't want to push her to come downtown when it was obvious she was uncomfortable with the idea, and it did sound inviting, taking an extra walk this week. 'No, no way could I be too busy to talk to one of my best pals,' he said, 'how about we meet by the horses at six Thursday afternoon.'

'I'd really appreciate it.'

'It's a date,' he heard himself say. After the goodbyes, he swung the swivel chair back to face the desk and there stood Eddie Kerr. Silent Eddie, little blue eyes glittering in a face modeled in bread dough. The idea of Eddie Kerr listening to Gunnar's end of that conversation, however innocent, angered him. How long had the little bastard been standing there? When someone was as closed up as Eddie, it was only natural to stay closed yourself. There was nothing, absolutely nothing on a personal level between Gunnar and Eddie.

'I didn't hear you come in.'

'I thought you might want to talk about Miracle.'

'Are the summaries all ready?'

'They're in word processing, and Wes is finished with all the direct. He's got it in folders, indexed.'

'That's the good news,' Gunnar said. 'The bad news is we must have forgotten something. We can't possibly be ready a week ahead of time.'

'Winnie's still labeling and indexing exhibits. I'm meeting with the judge's clerk and a bunch of the lawyers to put together the stipulations on Wednesday. You making any new offers?'

'I think the board wants it tried,' Gunnar said.

'We could lose big,' Eddie said.

'Not to worry,' Gunnar said. But Eddie would worry. Worrying and overkill were major weaknesses. He didn't know when to shut up, or when to stop writing. Now he just fixed Gunnar's eyes with a Doberman stare that said, you're wrong, but it's your funeral. Why in hell did they ever hire Eddie?

Eddie Kerr had graduated from law school at State in the top ten per cent of his class. Even with his dubious personality traits, he could have hooked on with most of the good firms in town, and many in other cities. When Leo and Gunnar had interviewed him, Eddie's intelligence had overcome Gunnar's instant aversion. It would never happen again. Ignoring their established policy and agreeing there was no substitute for brains, Leo and Gunnar had hired him on the spot after he'd told them he would take the job if offered.

Eddie's worst problem was his fear of being wrong. Clients were billed heavily for the time Eddie spent in erudite flights through the treatises to make sure he came up with the right answer. The stakes in most cases didn't justify such profligate expenditure of lawyer's time. Pressure from the partners had little effect and adjustments had to be made to protect clients at the time of billing. At a partners' meeting five years ago, Len Pettibohn, resident practical-joker, had presented Eddie with a yarmulke. In spite of his Lutheran background, Eddie should wear one because he approached his cases like a Talmudic scholar, Len said.

But for Gunnar at this point Eddie's status in the firm was like having a house you had gotten so used to living in, it just wasn't worth moving, even though you hated the view.

Despite his minor irritation with Eddie Kerr, Gunnar kept the soft sound of Holly's voice with him in his office all afternoon.

5

Eddie Kerr, in baggy gray pinstripe, lips in a tight little bow, slouched into the offices of Lawson and Larson at nine-thirty on Tuesday morning. His daily late arrival passed without comment by management because he rarely left the office before nine-thirty in the evening. In five years no one had come within two hundred hours of Eddie in billable time.

No good mornings were exchanged with Angela as he picked up his call slips from a slot on her desk. His face aimed at the blue carpet, his belt tight over his swelling belly, he marched to his office – the only shareholder without a window.

'Good morning, Mr Kerr,' a young woman said evenly from her gray module outside his office door. Winnie Slaught had just started as Eddie's secretary, his fifth in the five years he had rated one of his own. Not new in the firm, the office joke was that Winnie had drawn the short straw.

'Yeah, save the good mornings,' Eddie said, his small blue eyes a little too close together and fixed on hers for a millisecond. 'I can't stand morning.'

'Both Mr Wilson of Pratt Express and Frieda Gaulk want to talk to you real bad. I'll have your mail in there in a minute.'

Eddie's domain never changed. In front of a run-down black chair, a desk with an uncommonly large top dominated the small room. Hundreds of pages filled with various quantities of typed text, open and closed books, Manila folders, russet-brown file jackets, scribbled notes in tiny hand on flimsy four-inch white squares, pink telephone call slips, lined yellow legal pads, and a partially opened umbrella randomly covered the desk like a sanitary land-fill. Directly behind it a waist-high bookcase partially covered the wall. A few maroon-bound volumes of state and federal statutes, a thick green *Black's Law Dictionary,* and a copy of Arthur C. Clarke's *2001*, still in its dust jacket, were the only books. Loose papers, folders, and sheaves of much larger documents rolled together and bound with rubber bands filled the remaining shelf space. Except for an occasional smudge, the off-white walls were blank. After years of begging him to tidy up, the executive committee had asked Eddie to keep his office door closed, and he usually complied. He met clients in one of the conference rooms.

On the seat of Eddie's chair a note from Leo urged him to call Wilson at once, and asked him to sit in on a one-thirty conference with Bob Braxton, a young venture capitalist the firm was courting. A 'p.s.' directed him to bring his time records, presently two and a half weeks behind, up to date.

As he dropped his ample backside on the beat-up cushion, the phone began to buzz, buttons blinking frantically. Angela announced a call from Dan Blackmer, president of Commuter Computer, one of the firm's oldest and most important clients, and surely Eddie's weightiest responsibility. Dan and his colleagues were enormously impressed with Eddie's work. In telephone calls to Leo, at two-or-three-month intervals, Blackmer extolled Eddie's efforts on their behalf. An annual letter, usually just before Christmas, formally memorialized Commuter Computer's satisfaction with Eddie. He responded with religious dedication to their interests.

'Kerr here,' Eddie said in a low voice, almost a mumble. 'Yeah Dan, I hope to get it out by the end of the week,' he said more distinctly. 'Sure, I know it's important . . . . You don't need to change that. State law already requires it . . . Our compliance paragraph covers that.' As the conversation went on, Winnie – willowy, with short brown hair and just a hint of a bosom – bounced into the room and dropped a neat stack of mail in the middle of the disarray on the desk. 'O*K*,' Eddie said, with emphasis on the '*K*', as he hung up nine minutes after the conversation had begun. He grabbed a legal pad, scratched what appeared to be the date at the top, and in tiny barely legible printing he wrote, *Computers lease 1/4.* And the phone buzzed again.

'Mrs Gaulk wants to talk to you right now. She says it's urgent and you haven't returned her earlier call.'

'I can't talk to her. Tell her anything.'

But after Eddie had dictated answers to four letters, the intercom buzzed once more.

'It's Mrs Gaulk again,' Angela said. 'She demands to be put through.'

'*OK*,' he said. Then, 'Good morning, Mrs Gaulk,' as he gingerly picked up the receiver. He was greeted with a harangue on the legal system, the government in general, the gall of some people, the good faith and patriotism of Mrs Gaulk, and the failure of Lawson and Larson to take her case seriously.

When she had finished her tirade six minutes later, punctuated with an occasional 'Uh-huh' from Eddie, he said, 'I can't reasonably do anything until their lawyer has had a chance to look at the facts and reply to my letter. I mailed it just last Friday, five days ago, including the weekend. I wouldn't think I would get a reply for a week or more. I wouldn't want me to be unreasonable? I really must go. Thank you for calling.' On the pad he scrawled, *Gaulk TC 1/4*.

He filled out time slips for the letters and then called up Dan Blackmer's lease on his screen as Angela's voice announced a call from Craig Thibodeau, the attorney representing the estate in a will challenge Eddie had sued out. 'I'm trying to set up a date-certain deposition, Eddie,' he said. 'Faulck and Simmons can make next month on the seventh, how do you look?'

Eddie dragged his appointment book out of the litter. 'Sorry, Craig, I'm booked on the seventh and the eighth. How about the ninth?' Thibodeau was booked on the ninth so he suggested the fifteenth which was OK with Eddie.

'I'll get back to you when I've talked to Faulk and Simmons,' Thibodeau said.

Another buzz.

'Lawrence Carlson is calling from Seattle,' Angela announced.

Eddie picked up the phone, 'Kerr here,' as he rummaged through the papers on the desk, 'hello, Mr Carlson,' eventually pulling out a sheaf of letter-sized typewritten pages stapled together in one corner. 'Yes I have the contract. We made the changes and sent it over to their office.'

Turner is holding from New York was written on a piece of lined yellow paper Winnie held in front of his eyes.

He covered the mouthpiece and shook his head as he said, 'I'll have to call him.' Into the phone, he said, 'I have no reason to believe it will not be accepted in its present form. I spent an hour with one of their attorneys yesterday. As you know they won't give on the non-compete or the trade secrets, but they were good about the money and the special medical insurance for Candy.' Eddie closed the conversation, 'I'm looking forward to meeting you when you get to town.' He ran his fingers through his wavy hair; a strand of gray was mixed with the clumps of dark brown left in his comb that morning.

Carlson empl K 1/4.

The next two hours differed little from the first. In between calls he managed to make the necessary changes in Blackmer's lease and sent it through for a final draft on the laser printer. He grabbed a slice of pizza on the street around one-fifteen and got to the meeting with Leo and Braxton a couple of minutes late. They were already seated at George Washington's desk. In the distance dark green parks surrounded quiet blue lakes. After offering his limp hand to Bob Braxton, Eddie sat down beside him.

Braxton, barely thirty, was the epitome of the aspiring entrepreneur. He spoke with force, moving quickly from one subject to the next, occasionally chiding the lawyers about all the money they were going to make on his innovative and complicated investment schemes. Eddie inferred from Braxton's manner and jokes that the business was theirs. Their first job was the securities work on a private placement for a franchised auto-parts operation. Both lawyers knew they were looking at ten thousand a month in new business. In situations like this, Leo had long before ordered Eddie to express no opinions, and only answer questions put to him directly. No questions were being directed to him today. He listened carefully and made his usual notes, readable only to him.

Near the end of the session Braxton completely changed the subject. 'One of the bankers I have been working with in New York has a kid who's in some kind of jam here in the city.

Apparently he tried to sell some stolen bonds. I told him you guys could take care of it. Somehow, the kid got a public defender. The cops picked him up three days ago.'

Eddie had handled a couple of felonies when he first started practicing, but it had been about five years ago. He did do an occasional drunk driving case because he was the workhorse, and almost all of those cases were bargained out.

Leo's smile faded. His hands, on their own, squared up one of the several neat piles of papers on his desk top. He asked Eddie the direct question: 'What do you think about handling a case like that, Eddie?' The brown eyes, through the dark-framed glasses, told him what the answer had to be.

'Do you know if the kid's got a record?' Eddie asked.

'Negative. The old man was astounded. He passed it off as some kind of play for attention,' Braxton said.

'In that case it shouldn't be a problem. I think we can plead him to something inconsequential and he'll get probation. Perhaps get the record expunged if he keeps his nose clean for a year. But, you know, we can't really tell anything without talking to the kid and getting an idea what the government has . . . . Where is he?'

'I don't know if he was bailed out or what, I do know he is staying with a friend on the university campus. I have his number.' Braxton handed Eddie a small slip of paper.

Eddie replied with his trademark 'OK.'

'Don't forget this is quite important to me, guys,' Braxton added.

'Don't worry, we won't,' Leo said.

6

Sagging into the chair with the computer keyboard on his lap like a commuter settling down to a long train ride, Eddie Kerr worked on a revision of Dan Blackmer's lease. His suit jacket was thrown over the raincoat on the chair, his collar unbuttoned, tie knot slid partway down. In an hour he was meeting Dexter Epstein, the bond thief from New York.

When Eddie's day was over and he finally got to his little apartment, he would read or watch television until he fell asleep, completely spent, at one-thirty or two. Every night was approximately the same. Either a book or the TV obviated any need to look at himself with loathing. He had always loathed himself or at least ever since he realized his father loathed him. Just this past year his mother had begun telling him how his father was bragging about how Eddie had made partner at Lawson and Larson. But Eddie was sure she was making it up. She had always tried to make him feel better. But then on a trip north last Christmas, one of his old teachers told him the same thing, and Eddie began to believe it. Although his father had said little to him on his two-day stay, he had asked a couple of questions about the practice, had even treated him with a modicum of deference. His father might actually come to view him as a man, maybe even call him 'Eddie' instead of 'Pudge', the name that his older brother had stuck him with when he was eight.

'Mr Kerr, Mr Epstein is here,' the voice of the night girl announced.

As he was the only lawyer still in the office, Eddie led Dexter Epstein into the main conference room. The black-glass table was a full fifteen-feet long tapering slightly at the ends. Fourteen black leather swivel chairs surrounded it. The sun, sinking toward the horizon, shone through the gray translucent drapes. Eddie dropped his yellow pad at the end of the table nearest the door, and invited his client to sit on the chair across the corner of the table. Dexter sat down with his back to the sun. Eddie, though even baggier than in the morning, had knotted his tie and donned his jacket.

'This is very embarrassing for me, Mr Kerr,' Dexter said. His voice had a feminine singsong rhythm. He was slightly built, short, with shoulders thrust forward protecting his puny chest. He wore a pink sports-shirt with wide collar. Black unruly hair cried out for a comb.

'I can imagine,' Eddie said, wishing he had thought of a better opening line. After the normal small talk, squinting slightly into the bright sunlight, he said, 'Suppose you give me a rundown on exactly what happened.'

After asking if it was all right, Dexter lit a cigarette, took a deep drag. The beginning of his story was accompanied by trails of smoke from nose and mouth. 'I had gotten a summer job at Shearson. I thought I was going to be able to learn something worthwhile, but I soon realized it was going to be little more than janitor work. I was supposed to help keep the place straightened up and do errands for the brokers and the back-room guys. It turned into all clean-up work because another guy got to do the errands. He knew the brokers, and had been working around there a few months.' He sucked hard on the cigarette. 'So, I . . . .'

'What hours were you working?'

'At first it was eight to five, like everybody else, but a couple of weeks after I started, they switched me to noon to eight-thirty at night. That's when I started feeling like I was a janitor.' Dexter said, 'Anyway, to make a long story short, this one guy, Peterson, had stuck a stack of bonds in a Manila folder in his file drawer. I was standing right behind him when he did it . . . right after I started working there.'

'What kind of bonds?'

'Bearer bonds, telephone.'

'How many dollars?'

'About thirty-four grand.'

'OK,' Eddie said. 'Go on.'

'Anyway, after I started working nights I kept checking that drawer. It was always locked. About the fifth or sixth time I tried, it opened. The bonds were still there . . . in the folder, with some stock certificates.' Dexter stopped as though he thought Eddie might say something. He didn't. 'I decided to clip 'em,' Dexter said.

'Why?'

'I needed the bread.'

The answer must be a lie. The kid's old man was a big-shot banker, but for the moment, Eddie decided, not to argue with Dexter.

'What for?' Eddie said.

'School, a car, stuff like that.'

'How did you get them out?'

'I put 'em under my shirt when I walked past the guard. It went smooth as silk.'

'It could have been smoother.' Eddie didn't resist the opportunity for sarcasm.

'I got news fer ya. That isn't how I got caught. Nobody figured me for the thief.'

'What was the fatal flaw?' Too late, Eddie thought he should have dropped the sarcasm. Braxton might not like it.

But it escaped Dexter, and he took the question seriously. 'This guy I know works at Merrill Lynch. I called him and I go, "My dad gave me some bonds I want to cash," and he goes "Give me the numbers and I'll call ya." He called me the next day and told me to bring 'em in. The cops were waiting when I got there.'

Eddie scratched out several more notes, then looked directly into Dexter's eyes, 'Now tell me why you really needed that money. If you won't tell me the truth I can't help you.'

Dexter's little hazel eyes opened wide, his eyebrows arched like live caterpillars. 'But I am telling you the truth!'

'Have you got a habit?' Eddie asked.

After cross-examining his client for an hour, Eddie established that Dexter had a one-hundred dollar a day cocaine habit of which his parents were unaware, except that they knew he used occasionally, that both of his parents were users, that he had committed several other thefts in New York, undetected as far as he knew, that a search of the room where he lived would reveal several grams of coke, and that he simply couldn't get rid of his stash totally. He had to have it.

Eddie, giving no assurances, sent Dexter home to await his arraignment the following week.

7

At six on Thursday afternoon Gunnar kept his appointment with Holly. They hiked back to the meadow they had found on their last walk together. It would be a nice private place to talk, she said. In the shade of a grove of cottonwoods, looking toward the weathered barn, they sat a foot apart on the rough foundation of the vanished farmhouse.

When they had finished talking of the heat, and the smell of new-cut hay in a nearby field and the wild flowers, a breeze crept across the meadow and cooled Gunnar's face.

'Mmmm, feels good,' Holly said.

Gunnar hated the tracks of sweat crawling down his skin. But his shirt was the only concession to the attorney-client nature of their rendezvous. He felt compelled to leave it on.

'Yeah, thank God for a little air,' he said, smiling at her, and getting the hundred-toother in return. Moisture shined on her face, surrounded by clusters of brown curls.

She had brought a huge beach towel to fold for a cushion, and a can of insect repellent. Gunnar's growing affection for her made him believe that she was simply ingenuous, but he did consider the possibility she had deliberately sought a beguiling setting. A washed-out moon emerged from behind the trees like a perfect hole in the hot white sky. Bees circling purple clover blossoms made the only sound.

'I suppose you wonder why I called this meeting,' she said in an officious tone, garnished with the smile.

'I think I might know,' he said.

'My dad?'

'I thought maybe.'

'You've read the papers?'

'More than that. I've been approached.'

'Approached?'

'Yes. His lawyer talked to my partner, then me.'

'My dad talk to you?'

'No.'

'Would that have helped?'

'Not really.'

'Why did you turn the case down?'

He didn't want to say anything about Bergdorf. But he didn't want to lie to her. 'I can't tell you all the reasons,' he said, 'but I am very busy, and libel cases against newspapers are hard to win.'

'You mean it's hopeless?' She held his eyes every second.

Her voice conveyed more than the words. He was suddenly suffused with a sense of adventure – a feeling retrieved from boyhood – even as he recited the rudiments of the protection afforded newspapers under the First Amendment.

'Well, I know what they said is false,' she said. 'And there would be no reason but a malicious one for them to print what they did.'

Her eyes narrowed with the last remark, the first time Gunnar had ever seen anything but a kind cast on that incredible face. It was hard to believe she didn't believe. And living with Tony Djilas during the time in question she should have known, but maybe she was too young. She couldn't be much over thirty. In 1973 she would have been sixteen or seventeen. She could not know for sure that the *Times-Journal's* allegations were false. She could only know for sure if they were true. That was something: at least she didn't know they were true. As Gunnar pondered, he had looked away. When he turned back, the gray eyes were waiting, the face again kind. Even in this idyllic place, now cooled by the soft evening breezes, she was here on serious business, and he must treat it so. An owl blew a hollow 'whoo' at them from somewhere in the woods.

'Holly, are you asking me to take your father's case, or do you just want to talk about his chances?'

'He's been told you're the best. His chances are best with you. All these walks we've taken . . . for all I knew, you were some kind of an accident attorney, or divorce, or whatever. My dad says

41

you're the best there is. He mentioned your name when he was out for dinner last Friday night. I told him I knew you.'

'That's nice of him to say, but there are many good trial attorneys.' He really didn't think there were that many, but how else could he put it. In fact there were damn few he would want to have represent him, especially in a quixotic joust with the First Amendment.

'As good as you?' she said.

'Let's talk about the facts a little more,' he said.

And they did. She told him about growing up with her family. She said she was close to her dad. She knew very little about Manny Zilman. Her memory was vivid. Or her imagination, he thought. Asking a question from time to time, he listened to her story as carefully as if she were sitting across his desk.

When the light drained from the sky they needed the repellent. Even so, the tiny tormentors whined in their ears. The full moon sprayed between the shadows of the trees. Her face was just visible, but he knew she could see every little mark on his, and he knew now that he could kiss her, and he wanted to as much as he had wanted to kiss anybody for a long time. But now was not the moment, if ever there was to be a moment. There must be no question of a contract or further consideration or value received. Now, he mustn't even touch her.

'Holly,' he said, 'even though we have spent so many hours walking together, I have never really felt I knew you. I know we have exchanged some very private thoughts, but I'm used to hearing private thoughts from people I barely know. The difference is I've told you some things I've told only one or two other people.'

'I know,' she said, her face still enshrouded in shadow.

'I'm not sure getting involved with your father's litigation won't somehow hurt our friendship. I wouldn't want that.'

'I wouldn't either,' she said.

'Then, it's completely up to me?' he asked.

'Completely up to you,' she said.

She really means it. He stood up and walked a few feet away, so that when her face followed him she was looking up into the moonlight. For a moment Gunnar wished he could see her eyes in the light of day, but the softly lit face tilted up to his couldn't lie to him.

'Holly, do you know anything, anything at all, that causes you to question . . . even a little . . . whether your father might have done any of what they've accused him . . .'

'No Gunnar, of course not. I wouldn't get you involved if I had any doubt.' Her brow crinkled with concern and she reached out for his hand.

He took it and sat back down. For a minute or two neither spoke. The crickets became a roar in his ears. What was left if he couldn't trust her?

'OK my dear, I'll talk to your Dad. I can promise nothing beyond that. And you must let me call his attorney, first. There's some protocol involved. And it will have to wait until the trial I am about to start is over. It could take weeks.'

He knew she would carry the message, but it didn't matter. His contact with Bergdorf was purely a question of form. The immediate reward was the moonlight on her face.

'I'd really appreciate it,' she said.

'It's getting late. Your husband will worry about you walking these roads after dark,' he said.

'He's been asleep for at least two hours. It's the same every night.'

'Didn't he know you were meeting me?'

'Nobody did . . . How about your wife. Won't she worry?'

'I think she figures I can take care of myself,' he said. But he wondered what Anne would think if she knew where he was.

8

Behind George Washington's desk, one side of his face bathed in light, Leo clapped his hands loudly. The lean lined face behind the dark-rimmed glasses split, showing even teeth and a flash of gold. He stood up, continuing to applaud.

'Happy Monday,' Gunnar said.

'Happy, indeed!' Raising his coffee cup high, 'To the defender,' Leo said, 'to the miracle of Miracle Mills.'

'Just a routine settlement,' Gunnar said. 'But it's nice to know one's appreciated.'

'Hardly routine,' Leo said, 'General McKormick called me at home this weekend. He's very pleased.'

Four-star General-retired, combat hero, and high-placed Republican mucky-muck of the early seventies, Malcolm McKormick chaired the Miracle Mills Board. As was often the case with Leo's mystical methods of attracting business, his twenty-odd year relationship with the General evaded Gunnar's understanding.

'How in the world did you pull all of those lawyers into line?'

'It was fucking frightening,' Gunnar said, 'After two and a half weeks of Judge Wendell Watkins, we all knew we were shooting dice. In this case, you can't just say that he's a bad judge, he was lost at sea. It was pitiful.'

'Another of Kettle's appointments,' Leo said.

'Of course. Asshole governor, asshole judges. When he was forced to rule, it was invariably wrong. We all knew . . . if we ever got through the case, there would be a new trial on appeal. He didn't have the foggiest notion of what the evidence meant. So we settled it. McKormick is happy because I used two million less than my authority.'

'That should keep Miracle in the fold for a while,' Leo said.

'I suppose you have figured out how *we* did over the long haul.'

'We grossed $613,000 on the Miracle Mills case.'

'The good news is I get to take it easy for three weeks of summer,' Gunnar said.

'Then maybe you can take another look at Tony Djilas' case,' Leo returned. It hadn't come up since their original discussion.

'Is your offer still good?'

'On the fee? Of course.' Leo took off his glasses, silver-black brows lifted. 'Of course the offer is still good,' he said.

'Tell Bergdorf to send him in. Alone.'

'Mind if I ask what changed your mind?'

'Mind if I ask why you wanted me to take it so bad?'

'You first,' Leo said.

'Let's face it, I'm not getting any younger; I can use the money, and I thought perhaps I reacted too fast . . . . I talked to some people. He may be telling the truth . . . and thinking about it . . . it's not hard to remember that *you* are not often wrong. Usually I ask for your advice. When you offer it, maybe I should listen . . . . Your turn.' Gunnar hoped he wouldn't ask whom he had talked to.

'I'm thinking of quitting,' Leo said.

'You're not serious . . . Jesus Christ. Why?'

'I'm fed up,' Leo said, 'my advice is obsolete days after I give it. Good old-fashioned judgment takes a back seat to technicalities and bureaucratic games . . . . The fun's going out of it. It's not exciting like your trial work, and the money, which I don't really need, isn't that great. I can do better with my investments.' There was weariness in Leo's face.

'Remember, just like Miracle Mills, you originate most of these big-buck defense cases,' Gunnar said. 'But what has all this got to do with Djilas?' He spoke the words, but the Djilas case was lost in a whirlpool of feelings. He wasn't ready for Leo to go. He never would be.

'I don't want to leave you in the lurch. I thought the fee might give you quite a nest egg.'

'I can take care of myself,' Gunnar said, not as sure as he

sounded about a future without his pal, the overseer at the Lawson and Larson plantation for twenty-six years.

'I know, I just want to help. We've always been a team,' Leo said.

'Couldn't you just cut back? Do you have to hang it up, completely?'

'Sarah and I are going to take the Concorde to Europe and browse around a few months. I'll decide for sure when I get back. There's some great opportunities in Florida and we would both like to get away from the winters.'

'God, I'll miss you!' Gunnar said. 'But whatever you want, I want you to have. You're my idol, you know.'

'You're the idol, mine and everybody else's,' Leo said.

They talked about the fun of getting the whole thing started; they recalled some of the high points, and a couple of the low points. Leo left no real doubt about his meaning. The partnership that had brought them closer together than most husbands and wives had reached its end. When they parted they wrapped their arms around each other and held on.

Minutes later Gunnar stared down into the glass top of his desk. He hadn't noticed before how the flesh hung way out from the bones of his face when he held his head in that position. The boyish good looks people talked about were suddenly absorbed in the deep folds of skin. A tear splashed on the glass. Then it got away from him, and he dropped his face into the cradle of his arms. His shoulders shook to the rhythm of spasms deep within.

For decades, Leo and Anne had been there, his last fall-back line. Seldom had he needed them, but knowing they were there was enough. For the last ten years it was only Leo. It wasn't that Anne wouldn't or couldn't, Gunnar just didn't give her the chance. Five years ago a favorite little spaniel, Casey, had been killed by a car. Then, too, he had lost control. A host of doubts and disappointments, and confusion about his life had exploded from hiding. Now, with Leo gone, there would be no one left. Ten years trying law suits back to back, you don't make new friends, at least close ones, and old ones slip away.

But one day in these holes of self-pity was the most you could afford. He sucked in long breaths to quiet the trembling within. He stared at his treasured Mondrian hanging above the sofa, no system to his thoughts, just letting himself ease back to the moment, find a starting place. Tomorrow, he would come out swinging. It was his life to live, with or without Leo. Maybe his new young friend was what he really needed – and maybe she wasn't.

Twenty-four hours later, Gunnar was back in his office looking over the city, steaming in another blast of humid air that, according to the weatherman, had found its way more than a thousand miles north from the Gulf of Mexico. The colors of summer dresses dotted Corum Park. Knowing Leo was leaving was like knowing someone was going to die. To make the pain go away he thought of calling Holly for a midweek walk, but he quickly rejected the notion. A voice in his head kept telling him to walk down the hall, sit down in front of George Washington's desk and make the case for changing Leo's mind. An hour ago he had walked halfway before abandoning the idea. It was Leo's decision to make. For him, the idea made sense. Gunnar's argument would be solely in his own interests, selfish and cynical. Leo rated better.

Gunnar thought of a noontime walk through the park, something he'd done many times in the past when he was without a lunch appointment. It was just too hot and sticky. Then, Anne thrust her way into his thoughts. In the very beginning he had wanted to share every thought, every feeling, every experience, with her.

After they had met in college, he had literally run the two miles to her house nightly, to study together, they said. Everywhere they went, in cars or buses, or just walking across campus, or in the student union, even when the professor darkened the room for a movie in the biology-class they had together, he needed to touch her, every minute. Kissing her was as important as breathing. But Anne didn't seem to understand his urgency.

It had been clear; he would accomplish nothing more until she was utterly committed to him, as he to her. She tried to tell him in nice little ways that, not yet nineteen, she wasn't ready. She didn't conceal letters and telephone calls from other young men. Undaunted, he acted as if it were decided; they would marry, raise a family. Only, first, they must become lovers. Sex had dominated Gunnar's thoughts since he was fifteen. He understood the current aphorism that an eighteen-year-old boy would fuck a brush pile in hopes there was a snake in it, yet, his shyness, far more than his Christian compunctions had preserved his virginity. Now, there was no need to put it off. Marriage, family, that sort of thing required planning, time, changing circumstances. The consummation of his passion must be now. For a time she fended him off. The church, sin, her parents, her need for self-respect: none of it shook his persistence.

From the way it eventually happened, it was clear that Anne had considered carefully, and then taken a stand. This was the way she was to live her life – take a stand; stick to it. Nothing was more important to her than loyalty, to people *and* ideas.

One evening, one eye on the only stairway leading down into the pine-panelled basement where they studied, Gunnar had begun moving his hands on her body as he always did. This time as he approached her breast, she didn't resist. She just pressed her soft lips harder on his, and his hand reached its destination. As he gently caressed, first one, then the other, she seemed to welcome it, and he felt blessed by the most high. Through the fine cashmere he found her nipples. Awkwardly he pushed her down on the sofa, forgot about the stairway, and, lying on top of her, he ejaculated in his pants. Something intruded on the silence. It was his future mother-in-law's heavy leg on the second-from-the-top step. Gunnar leapt up and immediately moved to the end of the sofa, a book covering the wet spot on his light gray slacks. Anne turned over, her face buried in the pillow under her long blonde hair.

Mom reached the bottom step. Only a flimsy pink nightgown concealed part of her great bulk. 'How can you read that book with the light off?'

'Oh, I was just thinking,' he said. 'I guess Anne has fallen asleep.'

'I thought it was getting a little quiet down here,' she said. She crossed to the end table, leaned over him, revealing much of what the nightgown was intended to cover, and turned on the lamp. As Mom laboriously climbed back up the stairs, Anne giggled into the pillow. In the weeks that followed, sex with Anne became the centerpiece of Gunnar's life. Usually he coerced her, in the back seats of cars, even once under the spreading branches of a fir tree in the park – with mosquitoes jabbing his ass as he pumped his seed into his reluctant sweetheart. On St Patrick's Day, the one time it was her idea, she became pregnant with Jack.

Three months later they married in the rectory of St Andrew's Roman Catholic Church. Although Gunnar eagerly submitted to marriage instructions from the curate, he was not permitted to be married in the church because he was not a Catholic. His mother had raised him Methodist. If Anne had made his conversion a condition of the marriage, he would not have hesitated. The mating accomplished, Gunnar was ready to return to his studies.

Jack was born in the dead of winter. The new family was cozy in a Quonset hut, originally set up to house World War Two married veterans. Gunnar earned all the money for their meager living from part-time jobs during the school year, and he worked long hours all summer. Student loans paid his tuition. Sometimes the two of them talked far into the night, then slept naked in each other's arms. In bed, last night, thirty-five years later, they hadn't spoken and they hadn't touched.

The distancing had begun soon after Jack's death. Gunnar couldn't positively identify the feeling. There was no question of fault, yet there was guilt. Their son had been a mutual joy, but somehow his death was not a mutual sorrow. They each clung to their own hurts. A scene from only a month back crept into Gunnar's mind, stark contrast to the passion of their youth. Anne had asked him to have a lemonade with her in the gazebo on the shore of the bay. In fading summer light they'd walked down the slope to the lake. The grass was springy and damp, the scent of lilacs in the air. A giant orange sun ducked behind the trees on the opposite shore. Anne's dark-blonde hair was short and softly wavy with streaks of white from time and running in the sun. Soft and tan, her skin had coarsened some, more from the weather than age. She was more beautiful, past fifty, than when he'd met her at eighteen. Her eyes, fixed on his, brown with little flecks of gold, pupils dilated in the twilight, were set more deeply than she would have liked.

'What's up?' Gunnar had asked. They needed to spend some time together, she said, and it was so lovely by the lake at sunset. He knew the worry around her eyes wasn't for herself. She simply had never been into self. Her concerns were the children, Gunnar, and the children of the world. And, it seemed to him, the whole damn universe. Her concern for self dealt only with her soul, her spiritual self, a concern which, despite her drift away from the Catholicism of her girlhood, was still the driving force of her life.

That night in the gazebo, she had reached across the small table and gently placed her hand on his. Purple veins stood out on the back. Her nails, unpolished, were trimmed short for a chic woman, her breasts prominent under a simple white T-shirt. It wasn't lost on Gunnar that her veneration of God had in no way inhibited her desire to be a graceful woman in the context of their lives and, most importantly, to be beautiful for her husband.

'My darling Gun,' she said. 'We have so much to talk about.'

'It's no use, Anne, we've tried,' he said.

'But it has been so long.'

'I know.'

'I don't think we can keep letting it slide.'

'I don't expect you to,' he said. 'You must live your life just the way you want.'

'But that's with you, only closer than it's been.' Her voice was strained, hoarse.

'I can't be a real husband,' he said. He withdrew his hand from under hers.

'Doesn't thirty-five years count for anything?'

'Sure,' he said, 'I'm willing for everything to go on just as it has been.'

'But I think it might be so much better, my sweet.'

'I know, you deserve more. You are so good,' he said, his voice just above a murmur.

'Oh darling, I don't want to lose you.' Tears welled up in her eyes, now just visible in the deepening shadows, and spilled out to trickle down her face. 'It's still Jack . . . it's been almost ten years.'

He sat dumbly, looking out across the bay. She sniffled and rubbed her wrist across her nose. The evening star and lights from the houses on the far shore reflected in the lacquered surface below the receding band of light in the West. Two Canada geese, in long-necked silhouette, swam slowly by.

'But the fact is plain,' said Gunnar, pronouncing each word individually, as though it were a complete sentence, 'I can't make love to you any more.' His throat constricted in anguish. 'I try not to think about it, let alone talk about it.'

'There's more than that to us.'

'I know,' he said, 'but we're too young for passion to be gone from our lives.'

'Oh Gunnar, love isn't sex. And there may be some things we can do.'

'I don't know, Anne, I just don't know,' he said. He got up and opened the narrow screen door and walked up toward the house in the dark.

The gazebo scene was on a record run in his head. It would play seven days a week until he squarely faced the issues between them. But how the hell could he just pack up and walk? Maybe, if he did nothing, she would do something. But everything he had accomplished in his life had resulted from planned aggressive action. Those who let themselves be buffeted about by circumstances not of their own making stood forth clearly in Gunnar's mind as deserving unmerciful fate.

Gunnar's thoughts returned to the present. He decided to skip lunch. He had already skipped breakfast that morning. Perhaps he really needed another big case. Contrary to what he had told Bergdorf, everything *was* settling. There were no trials until October. In the intensity of the Miracle Mills case, like so many before it, he'd thought of nothing else: not Jack, not Holly, not Anne, just the fucking case.

The principle of cause and effect: Jack's death had made him the intense litigator he had become. No question about it. He had

51

learned that work could, block out grief and mask some of the torture of loneliness. As fast as Leo romanced the clients, Gunnar and his litigation department consummated the relationship with superlative lawyering. Of course Leo was great at his end, too, counseling the prime movers of society, but if trials were your game, Gunnar was your man.

Now, if Tony's story held up tomorrow, his case would move to center stage, and Gunnar could get on with what he did best: solving other people's problems.

9

'Have we met before?' In the waiting area, Gunnar Larson reached for Tony Djilas' hand.

Each silver wave perfect, golfer's tanned face, broad smile – Tony assured him they hadn't. Except for Gunnar's friend Fleet, athlete *exceptionale* and Captain of Detectives, Tony squeezed Gunnar's hand as hard as anybody ever had.

He took a chair in front of Gunnar's desk and Shana, within days of delivery, handed Tony his coffee.

'Gunnar, I take it you are ready to make 'em pay,' Tony said.

Of course, the familiarity should have been obvious. The silver hair and prominent nose dominated Tony's image, but it was Holly's face – the same gray eyes under dark brows.

'We have a lot of ground to cover,' Gunnar said.

Though camouflaged by the gray mustache peppered with dark, the mouth, too, was Holly's – wide, full-lipped and quick to smile. 'Shoot your best shot,' the mouth said.

'Suppose we start at the beginning,' Gunnar said. 'The very beginning. Tell me where you come from . . . how you got here. Something about your family . . . . Summarize your life from as far back as you can remember; I may interrupt from time to time.'

'S'a big order, Counselor. I'm no spring chicken even though I might look like one.' Tony laughed loudly. 'Matter a fact, I just turned fifty-one.'

He waited for a moment, apparently expecting a comment. Gunnar smiled to keep the light mood, but said nothing.

'Anyway,' Tony said, 'I was just starting high school when I moved here with my mom.'

Gunnar interrupted him. 'No Tony, the beginning, the very

beginning . . . . Where were you born? Where did you grow up? What was your life like then?' Gunnar had to know the inside of this man. Misjudging him could be deadly.

'You're the doctor . . . . I was born in Iron City. We moved all over up north. The old man wasn't much of a provider. Hit the booze pretty hard. Used the dodge of getting four-five months behind in the rent, then moving. Kept the cost of living down. Course, it worked better if he moved from town to town before the landlords got wise. Usually made it about a year in each town . . . . My mother worked her ass off, mostly cleaning up in restaurants or chambermaid in motels.'

Between every two or three sentences, Tony sucked on a cigarette, inhaled deeply, and expelled most of the smoke with the next spate of words. When Gunnar held his gaze, Tony was the first to look away.

'I had three sisters. Two of 'em still live up in that country. One, Helen, lives here in the city. I didn't think much of my old man, and he didn't have much time for me.' Tony stopped without explanation.

Gunnar waited.

'When I think about my old man it doesn't feel so good,' Tony said. 'We hardly talked after I got outta high school in '54. He died in '59.'

Gunnar thought of his own father who'd died fifteen years ago. They were best pals.

Tony went on without prodding. 'I met Ila, my wife, when we moved back to Iron City. I was about thirteen, but I didn't marry her until after I moved here and got out of high school. We were nineteen. Teenage marriage is a mistake.'

Tony lit a second cigarette and stared out the window. Under low-hanging rain clouds a commercial jet made its final approach. From the dark sky, rain pelted into downtown, leaving long streaks on the wall of glass.

'Nothing very memorable happened as I was growing up. I played a little ball for a Legion team the summer before we moved here. By then, my mother had given up on the old man, but she never divorced him. They never lived together after we moved here in '50, not long before Christmas.'

'Any trouble with the law, growing up?' Gunnar asked.

'Not much.'

'Is there a file?'

'I thought they were protected, or sealed or whatever they call it.' His mouth still showed good humor, lots of teeth, but fear flickered just briefly around the eyes.

'Hopefully, that's true,' Gunnar said. 'But I hate surprises. Our best chance in this case is I know everything.'

'Whatever you say,' Tony said. 'I had a couple a scrapes.'

'Involving?'

'While I was still up north we took a ride in a guy's car; "unauthorized", I guess the term is.'

Car theft, at fourteen.

'And I was with some guys that got caught derailing a train, just for fun,' Tony said.

Just for fun, a fucking train. Gunnar made a note.

'They transferred my probation file when we moved here.'

'Any trouble here?'

'A couple of breaking and entries. We stole liquor and beer. I was kind of wild as a kid. Not much discipline at home . . . Mom was working.'

'How about after you turned eighteen.'

'Clean as a whistle . . . . Surprised?' Tony laughed.

'Should I be?' said Gunnar.

Some of Tony's laughter was nervous; his eyes betrayed the lack of humor. Gunnar noticed the little curved sword barely visible on the glen-plaid lapel. He imagined Tony in a maroon fez. He scratched a note: *Shrine*. Could be helpful with a jury.

'You were very reluctant to take my case,' Tony said.

Gunnar let it stand in the form it was voiced: statement, not question. 'What happened to you after you moved here?'

Tony lit his third cigarette, then recounted substantially what the *Times-Journal* had written about his vocational endeavors in the city. He added stories about his courtship and marriage, and the birth of his two daughters; 'the oldest' and 'the youngest', he called them.

Gunnar asked him how he met Zilman.

'I answered an ad in the paper,' Tony said. 'Through most of the last half of the fifties and the first half of the sixties I had been selling houses, both used and from models, for builders. I saw all the money guys were making in the apartment business in the mid-sixties, so I jumped at the opportunity to catch on with Manny. He built close to a thousand units around here in the sixties, some partnership stuff, but most for his own account.'

'Seems odd that he would take off for Florida with everything going so well,' Gunnar said.

'Not really. He wasn't giving up what he still owned here, and the apartment building was slowing down toward the end of the sixties . . . . And he was getting a lot of bitching from some of the investors he sold buildings to . . . he wasn't exactly known for quality. Course, as it turned out he might have had other things in mind when he left. If he did, I didn't know about it.'

'You sound almost kindly toward the man,' said Gunnar, 'when it appears he has created much misery for you.'

He had learned that clients and other witnesses seldom testified at trial exactly as their lawyers expected. Lies or sudden changes in perception no longer surprised Gunnar, even when uttered by the best of people. They couldn't seem to help it. You could never be sure which version you heard was the truth. Fact issues often were not black or white. Witnesses, especially the aggrieved plaintiff or the wary defendant, tended to try too hard and make last-minute guesses, often incorrectly, as to what might impress judge or jury. Lawyers had certain ethical obligations if they knew a witness had lied. But it wasn't easy to tell. You were seldom sure.

Cross-examination was supposed to expose the false testimony, and sometimes it did – Gunnar had high regard for his own technique on cross. But he had said to friends, just half in jest: if you want to see people lie, spend a day in court. Most importantly, the witness must *appear* to be honest. Gunnar had developed a trial principle of his own: honest people, in error, were more likely to be believed by a jury than liars telling the truth.

Early in his career he had defended drunk drivers. The money was good, and it was a way to get courtroom experience. At the initial interview he asked the anxious defendant's weight. Then, with the aid of a table he kept on his desk, he told them the maximum number of drinks they could have consumed over a given period whilst still within the limit for blood alcohol. Of bankers and teachers, doctors, lawyers and housewives, and even one minister of the gospel, Gunnar couldn't remember any who had testified that they had more drinks than the number he had told them the table permitted.

Now, he had to evaluate how a jury would see Tony: a consummate salesman, good humor. Tone down the dress a little and he should sell well. His slightly roguish personality was attractive. And the jurors wouldn't have as close a look at his eyes as Gunnar did this morning. Gunnar would have to slow down Tony's lightning-like responses that, half the time, amounted to interruptions.

As the day pressed on, Gunnar warmed to the man across the desk. Tony's story of life in Florida differed little from Holly's. He had been interviewed by a Drug Enforcement Agency investigator, name forgotten. Although they'd grilled him pretty good, the questions focused on Zilman. I had done nothing wrong, Tony said. He wasn't even aware of Zilman's involvement with drugs, other than that he knew Zilman smoked grass on occasion.

'Did you testify before a grand jury?' Gunnar asked.

'Yeah, I told 'em the same things I told you today,' Tony said. 'As you know, they didn't indict anybody.'

'Any idea why they didn't indict Zilman?'

'No, but they must have made that decision a long time after I appeared. I steered clear of Manny after that.'

Complete sudden estrangement didn't ring true with Gunnar. 'Didn't you have any discussion with him about his involvement . . . and business in general?'

'His attorney wanted to know what I was going to tell the grand jury; beyond that, we didn't cover much, just small talk. I decided to come back here.'

He said he had returned because he thought he had learned enough about commercial development to get a piece of the downtown renewal of the seventies, and Zilman's problems had hurt his Florida prospects.

'And as I understand it from Al Bergdorf,' Gunnar said, 'you have no idea what happened to Zilman.'

'I've heard nothing in years.'

57

'How many years?'

'Ten, twelve, and then only that he'd left South Florida for points unknown.'

Beyond the glass, the dirty sky pressed down on the city as though the day had skipped afternoon, and a dismal dusk was setting in. Summer thunder bellowed through the clouds. Headlights reflected from the wet asphalt.

Gunnar started a new tack. 'Did you demand a retraction promptly after the articles appeared?'

'Yeah, Al Bergdorf wrote them a letter less than a week later, but they said they stand on the story. They even mentioned our request in the paper . . . said that they were confident of their facts.'

Tony started patting his pockets for cigarettes just before noon. Exposing his most haunting doubt, Gunnar posed his last question for the day. 'What makes no sense to me,' he said, 'is the risk the *Times-Journal* has taken if they were not absolutely drop-dead certain that their facts were correct.'

'That's easy,' Tony said. 'Those reporters maybe think it's true, but the reason that story appeared was to wreck my deal. We're talking serious dollars – the biggest project in city history. Axing me is worth many millions to whoever ends up with the contract.'

After Tony had left, Gunnar sat staring at the Mondrian. Ethically, he had the right, within reasonable bounds, to believe his client. Heroic investigations weren't required. But experience had taught him to probe beneath the upper layers. Big money had blinded colleagues he had respected in the past. Not just big money: women, bad associates and even nagging wives had colored otherwise sound judgment. Gunnar had served on the ethics committee for years and on a Presidential Commission investigating failing public confidence in our institutions. He was the Larson in Lawson and Larson. The simple fact remained: when Tony Djilas testified he must tell the truth, nothing but the truth. Otherwise Gunnar would back away – Holly or no Holly. Suddenly he realized that neither he nor Tony had mentioned her name once all morning.

10

The bell rang again and again, nine or ten times, even more. It was a fire drill. Eddie Kerr tried to get down the stairs, but the crowd shoved him aside, and back. A huge circular blade ripped through wood, screaming in the same frequency as the bell. He was scared. He had to pee. He sat up straight in bed. Sunlight slipped in around the edges of the dark drapes. The phone on the bed table continued to ring. He looked at his watch. Something after seven. Nobody ever called him this early, not even Dan Blackmer. It kept on ringing. 'All right,' he said. Then, into the phone: 'Kerr here . . . Dexter, I'd rather you call me at the office . . . . How in hell, never mind, I'll be down there before noon.' Dexter Epstein had called from the county jail.

On opposite sides of a wooden table, Eddie and Dexter sat in a windowless cubicle, about five by seven.

'They picked me up in my roommate's car about three this morning,' Dexter said. He wore the same pink sports-shirt as he had at their first meeting, his black hair snarled even more. He needed a shave. Two weeks back, the judge had continued the arraignment to give Eddie more time to prepare to make a plea on the bond-theft charge.

'Why did they stop you?'

'My dumb fucking roommate didn't renew his license plates.'

'They wouldn't bring you in for that.'

'The cop claimed he smelled burning grass, and then he found a baggie under the front seat.'

'Jee-sus,' Eddie said. 'We may have a problem.'

'I got news fer ya,' Dexter said. 'There's coke in the trunk.'

'How much?'

'Too much.'

'Did they find it?'

'They didn't open it while I was there.'

'You can be sure they opened it.'

'Can they?' Dexter asked.

'I'm afraid so,' Eddie said.

'That's bad.'

'Probably,' Eddie said. 'I'll be in touch. Want me to call anybody?'

'Not yet.'

'O*K*,' said Eddie.

Gunnar lunged with his forehand at the yellow ball skipping out of the ad court at a thousand miles an hour. It glanced off the end of his racquet into the floor-to-ceiling net dividing their court from the next, falling harmlessly to the floor, settling down in a series of tiny bounces. 'Seven-five!' Gunnar yelled. 'Time to quit anyway.' It was the second tie-breaker Fleet had won in the past fifty-seven minutes, both with service aces.

'When we play an hour on Thursdays I'm ready to quit,' Fleet said. 'And at the end on Mondays, after an hour and a half, I'm still just ready to quit.'

'God always grants your black ass just the strength you need to beat me by a hair,' Gunnar said, his heart pounding, his lungs sucking for more air. They walked down the long hall to the men's locker room.

'Do you know, you won all five sets this week? I think that's a first.'

The big brown man grinned. 'I'll mark it on my calendar.' His basso profundo was impossibly smooth.

'If you'd just hit that serve like a normal human being I could beat you more often,' Gunnar said.

'Your competitive ass probably wouldn't enjoy it as much,' Fleet said.

He was right. When Gunnar did beat him, it was a genuine accomplishment. And when Gunnar returned a first serve with a winner, it was almost as sweet as when a juror winked at him. It happened with about the same frequency, once every couple of years.

Fleet's talents were legion. He played a mean jazz piano, never forgot a name, and he drew photo-realistic pencil portraits of his friends and, when needed, of his enemies – some of the scumbags he encountered in his rôle as Captain of Detectives. A promising career with the Philadelphia Eagles had ended before it started – in training camp. His knee had exploded on impact against the rock-hard shoulder pad of Chuck Bednaryk. The crack-back block afflicted Fleet all his life, and when he first hooked on with the police department as a patrolman, the knee almost kept him off the force. Properly braced, he adjusted to it and remained active. It didn't seem to bother his tennis game but, on rare occasions, he complained about pain.

Fleet's dad had worked for the school board as a janitor from the early thirties, and in 1944 he was killed in action in the Battle of the Bulge. His outfit, the 755th Field Artillery Battalion was all black with white officers. Fleet's mother, Barbara, a waitress at O'Brien's, the city's nationally known steakhouse, had raised Fleet and his two sisters with little outside help. In the late thirties the Fleethams never missed any of Roosevelt's fireside chats, and when Fleet was born in 1939 he was named Franklin Delano.

He had become, unquestionably, the city's best-known cop, often accused of rough tactics by the liberal City Council. Gunnar speculated that, had Fleet been white, he would have been fired from the department long ago. He had been instrumental in cracking several highly publicized murder cases over the past fifteen years. One thing was certain, at six-five, two-seventy-five he couldn't work undercover.

In 1977, after Gunnar had settled into his twelve-hour days, his body softened. Tennis might take advantage of his aggressive nature and keep him in shape as he immersed himself in his trials. At the front desk, the Southeast Tennis Club kept a list of members looking for games. After trying about a half dozen players on the list, Gunnar hit on Fleet. They were eventually able to secure permanent court-time on Monday evening and Thursday morning. Except for interference from Gunnar's trials, they had been playing together for the eight ensuing years. With their wives, they met for dinner about three times a year and occasionally visited each other's homes. Rose Fleetham and Anne kept contact on the telephone, and got together a few times for special women's events. The Fleethams had two grown children: Franklin Jr, trying to make a mark in professional baseball; and Shirley, a heart-stopping beauty, who had arrived as a model.

The two friends, stood in the spray of the tennis club's common shower. 'I need a favor,' Gunnar said.

'Shoot,' said Fleet.

'See what everybody's got on Anthony Harold Djilas, d-j-i.'

'I know how he spells it.' The ceramic walls accentuated the deep resonance of Fleet's voice.

'Do you know anything else about him?'

'Just what I read in the paper. Off the record, some of the boys and girls on the City Council got pretty interested in the guy lately,' Fleet said.

'They find anything?'

'I don't get involved with that crowd much, but I heard he was clean? Nobody's got better access to the mayor.'

'Except you.'

'I'll see what the FBI's got,' Fleet said.

'Check Florida too,' Gunnar said, 'and DEA.'

'It may take a couple days. Can I ask what's going on?'

'I guess it's privileged,' Gunnar said. 'One more thing, it could be helpful if you keep an eye out for inquiries related to Djilas from any newspaper guys, and what they find out, if anything.'

Twenty-four hours after Tony Djilas had left the office, Gunnar sat at his desk picking pieces of raw onion out of a salad that Angela had sent out for.

'I have your call for Mr Davis on 76,' Angela said.

Davis was an assistant US Attorney in Miami.

'Mr Larson, I checked our files on Anthony Djilas. Anything we had would have been presented to the grand jury. Federal law makes it confidential.'

'Can anybody get it out of your office?'

'Assuming there was anything to get,' he said, protecting his ass, 'nobody could get it.'

'Assuming there was, and they somehow did,' Gunnar said, 'could they use it?'

'For what?'

'In a trial.'

'In a civil case?'

'Yeah.'

'I guess you know more about that than I do,' Davis said.

'Of course.' A twinge of embarrassment brought heat to Gunnar's face. The line remained quiet for several seconds. 'Mr Davis, could you put me in touch with any cops or agents who might have anything at all on Djilas?'

'First, you're talking more than ten years back. We have a drug calendar down here like Macy's basement. Those involved in it probably have some kind of touch with four or five hundred new names a year. Ten years . . . you're talking four-five thousand. You're talking a needle in a haystack. And that, assuming that Djilas was a target and not just a witness, if he was anything; and I'm only assuming, remember, based on what you're telling me. And then you're talking this office. There's Fort Lauderdale, and Tampa and Jacksonville and Orlando, and the whole damn country.'

Gunnar fell all over himself with thank-yous, and Davis said he could call anytime. Next, Gunnar contacted an information broker to search the Miami newspapers for 1972 and 1973, and any other public records that might exist, for anything with reference to Djilas or Zilman. They told him they couldn't get back to him for two weeks. Tony wouldn't wait for ever. Gunnar had to decide. The retainer agreement would allow him to withdraw if the story unravelled. Any in-depth investigation on Gunnar's part would need to be based on facts and clues uncovered in pre-trial discovery proceedings. In the next couple of days he would have somebody interview Tony's neighbors in

Fort Lauderdale, if they could be found. And Tony would get his answer sometime next week.

Gunnar pulled a clean yellow pad out of the black laquered credenza behind his desk, drew a line down the middle of the page and penciled a (+) at the top on the left and a (−) at the top on the right. On the plus side he began the column with 'Money, 1,000,000+'. Gunnar hadn't saved the money people thought he had. Income tax had eroded much of his handsome salary and bonuses. He hadn't invested in tax shelters as Leo and many of his other colleagues had done. Gunnar was busy trying lawsuits. With his pension plan and various stocks and bonds, he and Anne had accumulated something over a million in assets, plus their home. And a big score in a case like Tony's could give him the security he needed. On the plus side he also wrote, '*Times-Journal*' and then 'Leo'. On the minus side he wrote 'Bergdorf', then 'Uneasy', then 'Holly', but he quickly drew a line through 'Holly'. Minutes went by while he wrote nothing. Yesterday's storm had given way to cool blue. Perfect summer. Somebody was beginning to set up a big red and white tent in Corum Park.

He wrote 'Time' on the minus side, then 'Need' on the plus side. Let's face it, the money *is* big. The time is big. What if he got the costs up front and a retainer? That would be stretching it, and it would really kill off the justification for demanding fifty per cent of the action. Of course, Holly wanted him to take it. This time he penciled her in on the plus side.

Civil trials never bring lawyers much limelight, but *Djilas v. Times-Journal* could have the aura of a major criminal case. One thing was certain: nothing else on Gunnar's agenda compared as to potential money in his pocket, or notoriety, or challenge. All he had to lose was time. Even that was a long shot. He would likely learn his weak spots before the other side did, and he could exact reasonable tribute from them to settle – saving face and getting paid, both. He must get a tight settlement-provision in his deal with Tony. It was nice to have bargaining power. Although he didn't write it down, the probability of the newspaper checking the facts carefully in view of the potential damages nagged Gunnar. It belonged under 'Uneasy'. As an afterthought he scribbled 'Likable guy' on the plus side, then tore the page off the pad and threw it into the wastebasket in a ball. The red and white tent was now fully erected. Gay Pride Day promised a big weekend in Corum Park.

11

Nobody in the criminal justice system had noticed Dexter Epstein's other file – the bond theft – so Eddie Kerr was able to get $10,000 bail set on the drug charge. Epstein Senior, persuaded by Dexter over the telephone that the money was needed for the defense of the bond case, wired sufficient funds for the bondsman and Eddie's additional fees. With his client on the street, and Dexter's future liberty in the hands of two different prosecutors in the same office, the time was right for Eddie to obtain Dexter's consent to a strategy designed to minimize the time he would serve in state prison.

Dexter leaned against the lobby wall of Lawson and Larson. Something in or on his skin had penetrated the fabric of the pink shirt collar to form a border of yellow-brown where it touched his neck. Somebody had taken a shears to his wiry hair.

'You said we had to talk. Did you get the check I sent you?'

Eddie thanked him for the money and offered his apologies for the unavailability of the conference rooms, then led the way into the debris of his own private office, a scene few clients would ever see. Settling in, they looked like looters combing through the bombed-out store of a Beirut stationer.

'A week from tomorrow we have to make a plea in the bond case,' Eddie said.

Without asking permission, Dexter lit up. 'What's your idea?' he said, carefully extinguishing the match so as not to ignite a major fire.

'We must deal with both of your problems at the same time. Even with a clean record you're going to do some time. I've gone

66

over the sentencing guidelines. We might have gotten probation on the bonds, but, along with your checkbook, they found eight ounces of cocaine in your briefcase. The clincher is having it divided into small bags. They've made you as a dealer. The best we are going to do is three years.'

'Shit, I don't want to do any three years.'

'You'll be out in two.'

'Oh, boy!' Dexter said.

'You took some god-awful risks,' Eddie said, thinking that in prison Dexter might get treatment for his addiction.

'Should I get another opinion?'

'I already have. This firm has a connection with Barry Busch. He's the last word in criminal law in this state. He says it's at least three years on any deal. They're hard on dealers.'

'How about, I plead Not Guilty, hope for a break with the jury.'

'Busch says the only people who hate dealers worse than the cops and the prosecutors are jurors. You could end up with two trials and consecutive sentences and do eight years.'

Dexter's face puckered in frustration. 'Make the deal,' he said.

'OK,' said Eddie.

Across the street in the City Bank Building, Tony Djilas and Al Bergdorf had convened in the big office, Al behind the massive desk, Tony slouched into the couch under the Jackson Pollock painting. They agreed the cool weather was welcome, and OK'd a tee time at Maple Hills for Saturday morning.

'Carmine Castillo, my old neighbor in Fort Lauderdale, called me at home Sunday night. Said some private investigator wanted to talk to him about me on Monday. Said he represented Lawson and Larson. Carmine wanted to know if he should talk to him.'

'So what?' Al couldn't imagine how Tony would expect anything different.

'I thought Gunnar was on my side?'

'Not yet,' Al said. 'He's on his side.'

'Is this kinda shit kosher?'

'Shows how smart Gunnar is. He doesn't want your case if he isn't gonna win some money.' Al said, 'Anyway, didn't he get the name from you?'

'Yeah, but he didn't say he was going to call them.'

'I suppose he thought the info might be a little fresher, if you didn't talk to them first . . . . But you got nothing to hide.'

'That's exactly right, Counselor, I got nothing to hide.'

'I hope so,' Al said.

'Carmine won't say anything to hurt me, but I don't know about those other neighbors. I haven't talked to them for years. I don't even know if they're alive.'

'What can they say?' Al asked.

'Nothing . . . nothing,' Tony said. 'There's another little development maybe you oughta know about.'

The pungent cigar smoke Al blew across the desk drifted to the ceiling before it reached Tony on the sofa. The big lawyer, interested, straightened up in his chair. Apprehension tightened his mouth.

'Holly . . . you know Holly, my daughter. I think she really likes this guy.'

'What does that mean?' Al asked. 'You said in the first place that she liked him.'

'But I think it's different, Al. I mean she really likes him . . . like he's something special.'

'Oh-oh,' Al said, 'she better not start liking him too much. She ain't sleeping with him, is she?'

'She wouldn't tell me if she was.' Tony said, 'Don't forget, I'm her old man. But she's seen him more than once since I asked her to help, and she doesn't seem like she wants to answer the questions I ask.'

'Like what?'

'I just want to know when he's gonna make up his fucking mind.'

'I doubt if she knows,' Al said.

'Something's different. That's all I'm sayin'. I don't know how it cuts.'

'Wake up, Dad,' Al said. 'He wasn't even thinking about taking this case until she talked to him. Did her name come up when you were in his office?'

'No, I don't think it did.'

'Patience,' Al said, 'if you don't hear tomorrow, I'll call Leo Lawson on Friday. But leave Gunnar alone. OK.'

'You're the expert,' Tony said.

That afternoon Gunnar took a call from Wyman Farmer, former FBI agent, now retired in south Florida and Lawson and Larson's man when they needed information in that part of the country. In spite of his seventy-three years, many law firms relied on Wyman Farmer.

'What you got for me?'

'Gunnar, this guy Castillo thinks your man Djilas is the second coming. I got nothing from him. A couple of times I thought Mrs Castillo was about to say something of interest, but old Carmine cut her off. I don't know if it was calculated, or he was just a butinski. Anyway, by the time Carmine was through, and I asked her directly, she said Carmine had covered everything she knew.'

Wyman should have talked to them separately, Gunnar thought, but that might have been difficult. 'What about Rosen?' he said.

'He's dead since '79. She moved back to New York City to be near her daughter. I got a guy who can talk to her there.'

'Forget her for now,' Gunnar said. 'Did you find Crossman?'

'Yes. They moved to Boca Raton. You wouldn't believe the house. Gotta go three, four million. Right on the beach.'

'They remember Mr Djilas?'

'They know the whole crowd. Mrs Crossman still sees Mrs Djilas on rare occasions. I don't think she likes your man, but Peter Crossman himself wasn't making any judgments. He talks matter-of-fact. He's used to having people listen to him.'

'He know what was in those articles? We telexed them,' Gunnar said.

'Sure, I took them with me, but Crossman knew all about it. He didn't tell me how he knew. He just ignored the question.

He thinks Djilas and Zilman were very thick, but he said Djilas never talked about his business with him . . . Crossman, that is. Crossman said he always thought that was a little odd because, I guess, Crossman was a big real estate investor. I think he's out of it now, although he doesn't talk that way. I think he's older than I am.'

'Isn't everybody down there?'

'Not hardly.'

'How about the boat? Did you ask him about the boat?'

'He said your man didn't use it much, but it was gone a lot. Apparently Djilas lent it to somebody, Crossman didn't know who.'

'Did the reporters from the *Times-Journal* ever talk to any of them?' Gunnar asked.

'Never, not once, not a phone call,' Wyman said.

'That was a mistake,' Gunnar said. 'Any chance these people will come up here and testify?'

'Of course, you'll have to talk to them, but I don't think you could keep Castillo away. I think the other guy'll come too, his life doesn't seem that exciting, but we may want to interview him in greater depth.'

'For sure,' Gunnar said. 'The other side will take their depositions when they get our witness list.'

'I'll type something up and send it out within a week,' Wyman said, 'but to summarize, I really didn't learn anything to help you much.'

'I guess that alone helps,' Gunnar said, 'thanks for the quick action. Hey Wyman, just as an afterthought, maybe we ought to check see if any of these people has a record.'

'I'll do it,' Wyman said. 'Might take a couple of days.'

Gunnar decided not to wait for Wyman Farmer's call or anything else. Holly had told him again that it would be nice if he took her dad's case, but it was up to him. He could tell she didn't want him to think she was pushing too hard. They were still walking every Sunday, but she didn't talk about her father unless Gunnar brought it up. Oh, how that lovely face would glow when she heard he was taking the case!

'Get me Al Bergdorf on the line,' he said to Polly, his temporary. Yesterday, early in the morning, Shana had delivered an eight-pound boy with black hair four-inches long. They named him Gregory Gunnar. It had been a while since anything made him feel quite like that did.

12

Gunnar liked the rich aroma of Al Bergdorf's Havanas but, mixed with Tony's cigarettes, breathing could become a serious issue before the morning was over. They sat in the two chairs across the glass desk top from Gunnar. He had asked Al Bergdorf to represent Tony in the negotiation of the retainer agreement. Gunnar had also warned Al that more answers were needed. The meeting in the lobby had been cordial with firm handshakes and compliments about the offices.

'You said you had a few more questions for our man here,' Al said.

'I'd like to start with the boat,' said Gunnar.

Tony's eyes narrowed. 'What boat?'

'You owned a boat when you lived in Fort Lauderdale.'

'Sure. What the hell has that got to do with anything?'

'You kept it in the canal behind your house?'

'Yeah,' Tony said.

Al Bergdorf listened with the unreadable visage of a poker player.

'The boat was gone a lot?' Gunnar said.

'Some, I guess.'

'Who had it?'

'Friends.'

'Zilman?' Gunnar led him with a guess.

'Sometimes.'

'How often did Zilman borrow your boat?'

'Gunnar, it's been thirteen, fourteen years.'

'Try.'

'Few times a year,' Tony said.

'Was he using it in the drug business?'

'I hope not; he used it to take clients out on the ocean.' The big smile appeared for the first time this morning. The eyes didn't join in.

Gunnar took him back through his relationship with Zilman, point by point. Tony agreed to find what records he could of his own real estate deals of the period. He said his banking records and tax returns were long gone. Gunnar began a new tack.

'Why did you refuse to talk with the reporters from the *Times-Journal*?'

'I didn't.'

'They state at least twice in print that you did,' Gunnar said.

'They state a lot a things in print,' Tony said. 'I wasn't willing to see 'em at their convenience. I had no idea that they were out to knock me off.'

'Did you tell them you were willing to talk to them?'

'Sure. We just never connected on the times.'

'How often did they try?'

'I couldn't say for sure . . . a few times.'

'This could be important,' Bergdorf said.

Gunnar ignored him. Al's chin rolled down to the knot in his polka-dot tie. Finding clothes to fit must be a problem.

'You will be cross-examined on this point, and every detail about your relationship with Zilman,' said Gunnar. 'If you don't refresh your memory, you may find yourself in hot water.'

'How much time will all this take?' Tony had a look of pained impatience.

'Your deposition alone could take weeks,' Gunnar said.

'Don't we have any control over that?' Tony asked.

'None that I will likely exercise,' Gunnar said.

Another August thunderstorm soaked downtown. Corum Park looked lush, but empty.

Tony had no idea who might be plotting against him, but he doggedly insisted the articles were calculated to accomplish what they had. The pieces might fit, he said, when they saw who got the contract, but even that wouldn't prove anything. The guilty party might not succeed, or there might be a well-disguised front man. In a couple of months they might know more. A developer should be picked by 1 November. Making these points, Tony used

73

his hands, sometimes gesturing dramatically; once, even getting up and pacing the room.

Gunnar stopped the questions by asking Tony if *he* had any.

'Just one,' he said. 'Are you takin' the case?'

Gunnar told them he wanted to talk about the law. Whether Tony was a public figure was vital. To Tony's protestations that he was not, Gunnar hoped that they could prove it. A search of the *Times-Journal* for 1985 and 1986 had uncovered nothing beyond routine articles that named Tony among several others as a potential developer of Block Thirteen, and the piece on Holly's wedding. There, it was the groom's celebrity that prompted the coverage. The information broker had also found Tony Djilas on the contributor's list of several major political figures, including, of course, Mayor Steven Carpenter.

Another possibility, Gunnar said, was that the New City contract might be considered a public controversy. If Tony was a figure at the vortex of the controversy, he would be a public figure as a matter of law, and therefore required to show actual malice on the part of the *Times-Journal*. Gunnar could withdraw, the retainer agreement provided, should the court make a preliminary finding that Tony was a public figure.

'But wouldn't it be malice if they did it just to knock me off?' Tony said.

'If they knew it was false, or thought it was false and didn't check thoroughly, it might,' Gunnar said.

Tony surprised him by saying they might be able to prove that. When Gunnar asked how, Tony said someone would have to know, and secrets were hard to keep.

Gunnar ignored the uneasy flutter deep inside. 'If we overcome the public-figure problem,' he said, 'and the malice question, the principal problem will be proving the alleged libelous statements were false.'

The US Supreme Court, just recently, had imposed that burden on all plaintiffs suing newspapers. He reminded them that all of this law that worked against them was supposedly designed to maintain a free and unfettered press as provided by the First Amendment to the US Constitution.

'It's like, if we had some ham, we could have some ham and

eggs, if we had some eggs,' Tony said. The eyes joined the grin this time.

'Aptly put,' said Gunnar.

The air-conditioning system was losing to the cigars and cigarettes. Gunnar called for more coffee, then shifted focus, 'If you decide to execute the retainer agreement, I want you to deliver with it your Federal Tax returns for the last five years – along with all of your business and personal checking account records and checks for that period. Further back too, if you have them. And this office will need to have full access to all of your business records, including any personal financial records.'

'What could that have to do with this case?' Al Bergdorf broke his long silence, the blue smoke accumulating over his head like an active volcano.

'Before it's all over the judge will allow the other side to see them. They may be relevant to our damage claim. Besides, I want to know as much about my client as any one in the world.'

'Fair enough,' Al Bergdorf said.

'One last thing,' Gunnar said. 'When you get back to me, I'll need a written statement identifying everyone who had any part of the action in the proposed New City deal – financial, joint venturers, partners, whatever. Remember, no surprises.' But there would be surprises. There always were.

Gunnar handed them each a copy of the retainer agreement. 'Take this with you and study it. You pay all out-of-pocket expenses monthly. That means everything this firm spends on this case other than salaries to lawyers and other regularly employed personnel. It also provides that when, and if, we achieve a settlement or a judgment, this firm will collect, for its fee, fifty per cent of all proceeds. These two items are not negotiable. Any of the details regarding my discretion to withdraw, and our rights to payment if we withdraw, I'm willing to discuss.'

'How much are we talking about on costs?' said Bergdorf.

'Could be well into six figures.' Gunnar said, 'Tony's making a substantial gamble.'

'What's it all for?' Tony asked.

'Discovery and investigation. Mainly investigation. We will have a full-time investigator, maybe two or more at times, working from now until we have put together a winner. Could be right up to the trial. We want to know everything about those reporters and anyone else involved in the decision to publish the articles.'

'What are my chances?' Tony asked.

'I can't say,' Gunnar said. 'But remember my time is worth more than the investigator's, and you're not paying for it unless we collect from the defendants. You might look at it this way: you are not going to show a return until we have collected close to half a million, but if we convince the jury that you have been libeled, and get over all of those hurdles we've been talking about, this case should hit seven figures.'

'I know,' Tony said. 'If we had some ham . . . .'

'OK now, cut the comedy,' Gunnar said, allowing himself the big smile that closed his eyes and showed the row of even teeth.

When the laughing died down, Al Bergdorf asked if they had covered everything. Gunnar told them he had no more for today, but they would be doing a lot of talking for a long time. He didn't think Al would need to be involved after the decision was made on the retainer agreement, but he assured him that he would be glad to answer any questions that might come up. What else could he say? He hoped there would be none, but he suspected that somewhere down the line this walrus of a man would play a bigger rôle than Gunnar might like.

Gunnar had planned to take a walk to give his lungs the fresh air he had been promising them all morning, but the rain was still coming down steadily. In the lobby, Al said Gunnar would be hearing from them this afternoon or first thing tomorrow. Just before leaving, he pumped Gunnar's hand and held on longer than you would expect. His dark eyes, like black grapes in his formless face, asked a secret question. Gunnar was the first to look away.

13

In the morning sunlight, with his playing partner, Mayor Steven Carpenter, riding beside him, Al Bergdorf bounced along in the rough toward the eighteenth green at Maple Hills. Across the fairway, Tony Djilas drove another cart with passenger Davey Tripp III. Late yesterday afternoon, Al had Tony's agreement to retain Gunnar Larson hand-delivered to Lawson and Larson, without change or further question. Tony was jubilant; getting Gunnar's commitment to represent him was a coup, money in his pocket. Al wasn't so sure. The courts made it tougher every year to beat a newspaper, and there was something missing. He'd had the feeling before. Sometimes the roof fell in; sometimes not. He hoped this time his apprehension proved false. But, without any question, Tony had landed the best man to do the job. Al only wished Gunnar liked him better.

In colored T-shirts, three of them waited for Tony to putt. The Spanish style clubhouse, partially hidden among the towering maples, overlooked the scene. In front where the tall trees thinned out, several players intently knocked balls around the practice green. Tony lined up his nine-footer. If he sunk it, he and his son-in-law would be four hundred dollars richer. Unsure of Carpenter's ability to lose that kind of money, and hating to lose himself, Al hoped Tony would miss. He wondered if Tony saw the slight break to the left just in front of the hole. Tony crouched over the ball, knees moderately flexed. He drew the putter back slowly, low to the smooth bent-grass surface, and stroked. After the crisp click, the head of the putter followed the ball, rolling toward the hole on a course that would miss on the right side by an inch or two, but a foot in front of the hole it bent to the left just a trifle and dropped out of sight. Tony flashed the wide grin. In unison, Al and Steve dutifully said, 'Nice putt,' as Davey slapped Tony on the back.

Minutes later, the four of them surrounded a table in the men's lounge. It was a familiar routine. Several times every year, Tony and Al invited Steve and Davey to play at Maple Hills. Reciprocal matches were scheduled in between at the aristocratic Toonawana Club, Davey's home course. Steve had a membership and maintained a handicap at Francis Leland, a city-owned links, named after one of Steve's predecessors as mayor. Hundred-dollar bills lay in little piles in front of Tony and Davey. Intent on rehashing the match, particularly Tony's spectacular shot out of the sandtrap on eighteen, followed by the pressure putt, they didn't seem to notice the view out over the sea of green, speckled with flowerbeds, the fairways defined by tall old trees and squat pines and firs.

'Sorry fellas,' Steve said. 'Now that you have all my money, I've gotta go. I have a meeting with Helen Wilson at one-thirty.' After shaking hands all around, the tall politician headed for the locker room.

'You know guys, I'm afraid these games may be getting a little rich for Steve's blood,' Al said.

'No lie,' said Davey.

'He likes it,' Tony said.

'But he's been losing lately, especially when he plays against you, you sandbaggin' goniff,' Al accused. He burst into a loud hacking laugh as he clipped the tip off one of his contraband Havanas.

'You know my game, you fat fart. We play three times a week. You're gonna get Davey, here, doubting my veracity.' Tony said the last three words in an affected Harvard accent.

'Speaking of Davey, you better tell him about that little list we had to give Gunnar,' Al said.

'Oh yeah, the list,' Tony said, turning to Davey. 'I told you that we had gotten signed up with Gunnar for my case against that fucking newspaper. Part of the deal was he wanted a list of everybody who had any interest in our New City proposal. I had to put your name on it. No chance of talking him out of it, right Al?'

'No chance,' Al said.

'Shit!' said Davey. 'The old man'll find out.' He took a sip of his Chivas on the rocks. His face perpetually flushed, little purple lines etched his pug nose.

'I don't think he will from Gunnar,' Al said, 'but it could come up in the trial I suppose. You didn't put any of your firm's money in the deal.'

'That's right,' Davey said, 'but the documents commit me to later.'

'We didn't give him the documents yet,' Al said. 'This newspaper shit floored me. Up 'til then we had the votes counted.'

'Nine out of thirteen,' Tony said, 'all three of us have got a ton of time in that deal. And if I don't win this suit, I may be finished in this town, or any town. Maybe even if I win.'

The waitress set Al's plate of pork chops and baked potatoes in front of him. He asked her for some more sour cream.

Clear summer morning mutated to dreary downpour in the afternoon. Under the canopy, partly out of the weather, a kid checked the oil while the gas tank filled. From his inside jacket pocket, Gunnar pulled the letter he had found that morning at breakfast. He read it for the fourth or fifth time. Anne's handwriting, once near perfect, had become scrawly and almost illegible.

Dear Gun,

By the time you read this I will be on my plane heading for Jackson Hole. You surely must remember the times we spent in that part of the country. Studying the Grand Teton through your big telescope and admiring the reflection of the mountains in Jenny Lake in the evening when the surface is glassy smooth. I'm sure you are wondering why I left without telling you. I just had to get away and think about a lot of things, mostly us. The retreat I am going to at Wind River Ranch may be just what I need, and I will get a chance to do some riding in the mountains. You know how I love it, and Father Cleanth Hughes is the leader. I have read three of his books.

I just couldn't try to talk with you before I left. We never seem to get any place talking, and although I must be somewhat at fault, I think you are the one preventing us from dealing with our problem. I suppose I should say *problems*. I love you more than anything in the world, more than my own life, more than anything in this world. You must know that. But I don't think you love me any more. I have never said that to you before. Perhaps I should have. As you lawyers say, that's my case in chief. Simply that. You don't love me any more. Now it's up to you to tell me, or better yet, show me I'm wrong, if I am. If you don't I guess the verdict will be clear.

You need to take some quiet times, too. I haven't ever told you what you <u>should</u> do, or what I think you need, but I am telling you now. It is crazy to give your life completely over to the cases and the trials. Where has it gotten you? You seem unhappy much of the time. You must know now that it can't possibly take the place of friends and that wonderful lost son. Your anger and grief is killing you, or at least, us. What good does it do? Maybe you should face it. Jack wasn't drafted. He did everything he could do to get the appointment to the Academy, and we all helped him, although, God knows, I didn't encourage him. I was scared to death. Even with the war winding down I thought of all the boys who had died in that stupid war, and for what? I didn't want him to go. I prayed he would change his mind. But he took the responsibility himself. It wasn't you or me, it was him. If you can come to believe that, as I do, you may be able to accept our boy's death and go on with your own life as I know he would want you to.

I'll call and let you know when I get to the ranch. Don't worry about anything around the house. Katie will take care of everything. I'll be back a week from tomorrow evening. Katie will pick me up.

I Love You,
Anne

Leo's connections with Senator Winthrop got Jack that appointment. Nothing else understandable entered Gunnar's head. Thoughts ran in all directions. Her having to write made him feel somehow ashamed. What could he expect of her that she hadn't delivered on? To avoid the answers, best not try to define the questions. And now Holly Tripp was a factor.

On their walk last Sunday morning when they'd come to the abandoned road to the meadow, Gunnar had taken Holly's hand for the first time. He hadn't planned it. The moment simply took over on its own. They walked hand-in-hand to the clearing. She acted as if nothing had changed, but Gunnar felt as though Katie or Anne might suddenly step from behind one of the birch trees along the path. In the shadow of the square old barn he stopped and faced her. She looked up at him, a serious expectant expression in her eyes. He leaned over and kissed her so lightly he barely felt her lips. He could go no further.

She reached behind his neck with both hands and pulled his lips hard against her open mouth. She leaned against the wall of the barn and held on. With their bodies pressed together, he felt his penis thicken. Gunnar finally pulled away, and she smiled the hundred-toother.

'We've got to talk,' he said. 'And walk.'

'Sure, let's talk,' she said. 'And walk.' She took his outstretched hand.

'Are you laughing at me?' he asked honestly.

'No, no, why would you think that?'

'I guess I'm not brimming with confidence. And you're almost a newlywed, and your father's my client, and your friendship is very important. I don't want to spoil it. And I'm married, and, Jesus Christ, there's no end to the reasons why I shouldn't . . . .'

'I need you,' she said.

That was all he needed to hear. He held her hand tightly as they walked back to the main road with summer flies fizzing in their ears.

'Oil's all right sir.'

Gunnar had forgotten he was in a service station. He handed the kid a credit card, then folded Anne's letter and slid it in his coat pocket.

Elated about the retainer agreement, Holly had called that morning. I knew you would help us, she said. But there was more on her mind. She needed to see him again soon, and she

81

had asked him if he wanted to see her again, other than just for the Sunday-morning walks. He said he did.

'How about tonight?' she said, 'On the lake. I've got a twenty-six foot Bayliner. I'll anchor just off the rocks around the point at ten.'

'I can't . . .' he tried to interrupt.

'I'll leave the lights on. Come any time after ten.'

Had she somehow heard about Anne's trip? He hadn't even put their runabout in the water this year, but he had a fourteen-foot aluminum fishing skiff with running lights. He needed a little more time to think – to settle on the idea.

'Give me a couple of days. I haven't had the boat out once this year. I don't know if the motor will start,' he said.

'OK,' she said. 'Ten on Friday. I'll be waiting.'

Sitting on the rear seat, right hand on the tiller of the small outboard, Gunnar guided the little boat across the bay through the dusk. A planet hanging just above the band of failing light at the bottom of the western sky marked his heading for the spot where Holly's boat was supposed to be anchored. The buzz of the outboard motor blocked out all sound except the small waves slap-slapping the aluminum. Over his shoulder, an ascending moon, slightly flattened on one side like an incandescent egg, held off the night. Lamp-lit windows, appearing much closer then they actually were, surrounded the bay. Other boats on unknown missions, only their running lights visible, tooled along in the murk. Jesus Christ, he thought, there's still too much light.

The graceful silhouette of the cabin cruiser had been easy to find. Bright white light atop a short chrome mast at the rear, red and green bow lights, it was anchored a few yards from a buoy marking a pile of rocks barely visible above the surface.

The stern running light illuminated her face as she looked into his – her hands, fingers interlocked, resting on the back of his neck, an impish grin between little words of appreciation that he had kept their rendezvous. A much larger cruiser plowed by, not a hundred yards away.

Gunnar's mouth went dry. 'Where does your husband think you

are?' He was edgy, unsure of himself, inclined to get the hell out of there.

'He's sound asleep, or passed out, really. How about your wife?'

'She's out of town.'

'Oh my God,' she squealed, 'you can stay all night!'

'No, no, not on your life. You've got to get back before you're missed. And Katie will wonder what I'm up to.'

Holly pulled his lips down to hers. It was all so fast, but he was ready. There was a pad on the deck like the kind used on an outdoor chaise lounge. Coming across the lake he had wondered if he could perform. He was nervous, limp. He remembered an off-color comedian telling about his girlfriend, the tease. She had rubbed his crotch and French kissed him all the way home in the cab; then, ensconced on the couch in her living room, she had said she was tired, the time wasn't right. 'Man, it was like a piece a steel,' the comedian said, 'and it was two in the morning and she said the time wasn't right!' Maybe not a piece of steel, but now Gunnar was more ready than he had been in years.

The deck felt cool and damp beneath his bare feet. Since he had met her that cold fall day almost a year ago, he'd wondered if they would ever become more than Sunday-morning friends. She had never given him a signal. Now, his hands slid up under the back of the terry-cloth robe, barely long enough to cover her crotch when she stood. His fingers glided across silky skin. Her breath played on his neck. He was ready. God, was he ready.

His shorts were off and she laid the robe on the pad and knelt on it, her mouth level with his erection, and she sucked him hard. He felt little jabs of pain from the sharp points on her teeth. Knowing it would be over in seconds, he pulled away, and pushed her down on the pad. She guided his rigid penis into her. He resisted the spasms building to ejaculation, all else gone from his mind save the concentration of his will to head off an early end to the moment. He held perfectly still and let the muscles in his ass relax. He sensed that she detected his effort. They waited. The time came when they could move together gently; it was going to be the way he wanted it to be. And then he gave his passion some head under a taut rein, loosening for moments, but then checking it in. She didn't restrain hers. She bucked under him and dug her fingers into his back and he covered her loud sounds with his open mouth. And when she was free, she told him to let go, 'Come, do come now,' and he let it all go. An accumulation of months, in some ways years, burst forth in rhythmic waves. And then he was dead still, his whole weight pressing on her. He couldn't move. His prostate burned.

'If I die,' he whispered. 'Dress me, and set me adrift.' The tremors of her giggle passed osmotically through their skins. 'Am I too heavy?' he asked.

'No.'

'Was it too fast?'

'No, no, no, *no*, it was perfect.'

The distant humming of boat motors had him on edge again. He got up and sat in a deck chair. She leaned her head on top of his knees.

'I better go,' he said.

'Not yet, it's only a quarter of eleven.'

'It takes me twenty minutes to get back with that little boat.' He felt as though somebody would materialize out of the dark and demand an accounting of his transgressions.

'Just a while,' she said.

He let his fingers work through her dense curly hair. 'You never let me know what you felt,' he said.

'Neither did you. I didn't want to intrude on your life, and I guess I was afraid you didn't want me . . . . I think I love you.'

'You hardly know me.'

'I've always loved you,' she said, 'since I was a young girl. I knew you were someplace. Exactly you. And I loved exactly you, and I finally found you.'

Her profession made him feel warm, but at the same time, worried. He already felt responsible for her. 'I better go,' he said.

'Can you believe the moon, and the breeze?' She sounded ecstatic.

'Aren't you afraid?' Gunnar asked. He was.

'No, I'm not afraid,' she said. 'Oh, I am afraid you might go away and not come back, I guess.'

84

He said he wouldn't. He still had his fingers in her hair, her head in his lap.

'When's Anne coming back?' She spoke as though she knew her.

'In a week.'

'Then you can come again . . . soon.'

'I don't know.'

'Don't worry about me talking,' she said, as if she had read his mind. 'I'm a big girl now,' she said. 'I won't tell, if you won't tell.'

'Scout's honor?'

'Scout's honor.'

Later he pulled the little boat up on the beach. The house was dark. Relieved that he was alone, he decided to sit in the gazebo a while. What if Anne should find out? Where would they go from here? She was too smart to be fooled very long and, in any event, he didn't think he could sustain the deceit indefinitely. Where did these things end? Who the hell could he discuss it with? Leo? Never. But what difference did it make? Tony didn't need to know about him and Holly, and even if he did, what difference did it make. It *had* been like a piece of steel, and as hard as he worked, and as good as he had been to Anne, didn't he deserve a shot? But didn't Anne deserve something other than his fucking the Queen of the May? Having taken the ayes and nays, he knew he would be going back for more of what he had found on that boat tonight.

The egg of a moon, having soared away from the trees, became smaller, but brighter. He could see the blossoms on Anne's rosebushes up by the house. A lone mallard, chattering to himself, made a V in the midnight calm just off the end of the dock. Guilt oozed through Gunnar's every muscle. It sprung from the hiding not the doing, he told himself. But the feeling of excitement even exceeded the overwhelming trepidation that had shared his little boat on the ride across the bay.

BOOK TWO
PRE-TRIAL

Make no little plans; they have no magic to stir men's blood.

Burnham

14

Gunnar's favorite season was fall. The Corum Park maples were turning yellow and scarlet and the sun hung lower in the South at noon. He had served Tony Djilas' libel complaint on the *Times-Journal* Company and the two reporters, Ward Chapin and Suzie Cline. The *Times-Journal* reported the suit in detail on page one of the second section.

Gunnar had claimed $10,000,000 in compensatory damages and $10,000,000 in punitive damages. 'Compensatory damages' included damages presumed by state law to rise out of harm to reputation, and actual damages which must be specifically proven at trial. 'Punitive damages' were assessable like a fine against a defendant who had acted with malice.

Defendant's answer denied a libel had occurred, and if one had, various constitutional and statutory privileges protected them. The articles were true, it said, truth being an absolute defense to libel. To Gunnar, most interesting was the signature at the end: Terrance J. Wood, of Ransome, Randall and Wood, counsel for defendants.

Gunnar had always admired Terry Wood, and secretly felt somehow inferior to him. Wood's father had been a federal judge. Terry had taught in the law school at State for several years, and had even been seriously considered as a candidate for governor at the Democrat convention one year, long before the Kettle era when the party had fallen into the hands of fools and miscreants.

Upon the filing of the complaint, the case was assigned for trial to Michael O'Boyle, veteran judge of the District Court. Gunnar was pleased to draw Judge O'Boyle. He ran his court like a German U-boat captain. That could only help Gunnar,

89

because nobody understood the operation of the U-boat better. Gunnar sent copies of the answer and the notice of assignment of judge to Tony Djilas and Al Bergdorf for their comments.

Anne had come home from the ranch, her face tanned more than she wanted, she said. But she looked rested, relaxed around the eyes. She told Gunnar the retreat had gone well. The meetings had been stimulating, and Father Hughes had spent some time with her alone. Gunnar detected some of her old serenity. She didn't mention any of their problems. In bed that first night, there had been no touching and they had talked only incidentally since, and touched not at all. He was committed to the Djilas case as he never had been before, Gunnar told her. She couldn't imagine how he could be *more* committed than he had to some of the others. He would be at it night and day for months, he said. It could pay off big. She smiled and wished him well and wondered out loud if any amount of money was worth such devotion.

Tony's case had not completely taken over Gunnar's consciousness. There was still room for Tony's daughter. On a brilliant autumn Saturday, with Davey playing golf all day, Gunnar and Holly had driven to the river bluffs. She had been there before and found a favorite hidden spot for their picnic. Every time she looked at him as they climbed the highest hill, she turned on the smile and her curls fluttered in the gusty wind. The climb made him sweaty and breathless, but he felt good and light-hearted, and easily kept pace with his much younger guide.

Near the top, Gunnar looked back down across the green velvet hillside to the gravel road they had followed up from the River Drive. A clump of white cows had gathered near the fence by Gunnar's car, far below and tiny. He caught up to Holly at the summit. Spread out before them the river widened into Lake St Joan, reaching at least twenty miles to the South down the luxuriant river valley. Fall pigments adorned the bluffs and hillsides as far as you could see.

It was as though Jack was beside him, looking out over the Hudson at West Point. Then, Gunnar saw himself, with Jack, paddling a canoe down the middle of this same Lake St Joan, maybe twenty years back. It had been an outing for Explorer scouts. He stood there alone with the feeling, as Holly, the lunch basket swinging in her hand, ran ahead down the open gentle slope. Not daring to confront it any further, he pressed the regret and sadness back where it came from and he took off with big strides across the grass, the plaid blanket tucked under his arm.

A clump of stunted trees grew out of a patch of tangled brush pressing tightly against the hill. Gunnar found Holly on the other side, standing on a flat notch in the hillside. It looked as if some pioneer had long ago sought to hew from the hill a piece of ground on which to build a small structure. If so, he had given up early in the game, because the level earth on which Holly stood measured only about ten by ten. But sheltered from the wind by the foliage on the West, and with the view of the lake and valley, it was perfect for a secret picnic.

Gunnar spread the blanket on the grass. After they'd eaten the lunch, she lay in his arms. Content with the sound of the wind in the branches behind them, neither spoke for the time it took a river boat coming into view far down the lake to reach the water directly below them. It had a paddle wheel at the stern and people in bright colored sweaters gathered on the deck like a funeral of flowers. You could hear the faint melodies of a Dixieland band wafting up on the warm air currents of afternoon. She wanted to go for a steam boat ride soon, before it got too cold, she said. Maybe, Gunnar said. But he wasn't ready for any public appearances yet. Already, her reliance on him was palpable. Gunnar rolled over on his back and watched a lone little cloud sneak by. He thought of Anne and wondered how she was spending the afternoon.

'It's a perfect day,' Holly said.

With a complication or two, Gunnar thought.

Two hours later they cruised northward with a rubbery whine, whistling car windows cracked to crisp autumn. A red disc sun lingered low over pale golden wheat stubble and green cornfields turning to brittle buff. Even as he was excited by the pact he had made with her, Gunnar questioned his sanity. Holly had a friend living in the woods on the bay in a big estate just west of the Tripps. They played tennis every day, and Holly had held her hand through a recent divorce. Gunnar knew them by name only – Cochrane, downtown department-store money. Libby Cochrane would allow them to use the guest house located in a dense stand of trees a couple of hundred yards from the main residence. Whenever they wanted. He promised to meet Holly there the following Tuesday night.

Eddie Kerr and his client, Dexter Epstein, stood for sentencing before Judge Thomas Trowbridge, red-faced bald head sitting on top of the black robe like a tomato. Moments earlier the prosecutor had asked Dexter a routine list of questions, the answers establishing the elements of the crime to which Dexter was pleading guilty: felony possession of a controlled substance. Under the plea-bargain agreement, the bond-theft charges were dropped. Now, the judge was to complete the ritual.

Wetting his thumb, Trowbridge flipped through several pages like a truck driver checking a bill of lading, then let his gaze, over very narrow reading glasses, stop on Dexter's face for an instant, before returning to the text before him. 'Dexter Epstein, it having been determined in open court on the record that you are guilty as charged under 479.77 of the Criminal Code, and pursuant to your plea of guilty thereto, I hereby sentence you to serve three years in the custody of the State Department of Corrections.'

They would send Dexter to the state prison at Watsonville. Both Eddie and Dexter shook their heads in negative response to the judge's offer to either one of them to make further comments on the record. After asking the deputy for permission to talk with Dexter for a few minutes before he was taken into custody, Eddie led him out the back of the room, while another target of the criminal justice system and his lawyer settled in at the counsel table.

They stood in the hall near the railing overlooking the crowded atrium floor, eighteen stories below. Tears streaked Dexter's cheeks. He wore a freshly pressed gray blazer and the pink sports shirt had been laundered. His mother and father hovered wordlessly twenty feet away in the company of the waiting deputy. Eddie held his own tears back. Criminal law wasn't his game. He had grown fond of his skinny little client; they were more alike than he wanted to admit. And he had heard horror stories about the prison life of inept little con-artists like Dexter. His cocky attitude, a mask crudely devised to cover his self-loathing, had disappeared. His mouth hung partly open, the what-do-we-do-now look of earlier this morning was replaced by pathetic blankness.

'The time will go fast. You'll see,' Eddie said.

'Sure.' Dexter sounded unconvinced. 'I'll catch up on my reading.'

'Great, I'll send you some books I just love, great science fiction,' Eddie said.

'I'll give 'em a try.'

Eddie grabbed his hand, 'I'm sorry I couldn't have accomplished more for you.'

'No . . . no, I was stupid. There was nothing more you could do,' Dexter said.

'Listen,' Eddie said, 'I'll drive up and see you; you can count on it.'

'That'd be real nice,' said Dexter.

'OK,' Eddie said. 'Bye for now.' He walked away as Dexter's sobbing mother threw her arms around her son's neck. Worried, Eddie wondered if they would give Dexter adequate medication to cope with his withdrawal.

On Tuesday evening a cool autumn soaker drenched the countryside. The narrow lane led to Cochrane's guest house through a grove of maples and birches. To clear the road, someone had cut a section out of the long straight trunk of a tree felled by the wind years after its death from the Dutch Elm scourge. The Lodge, as Libby Cochrane called it, cloaked in weathered cedar siding, stood in the forest unnoticed, except by the occasional boat positioned to look straight up the alley cut through the trees to provide a view of the water.

He stopped behind Holly's Mercedes. Narrowing his eyes against the chill raindrops, only partially blocked by dense foliage above, Gunnar ran around the end of the building to the front door.

'I'm so glad you came.' She kissed him long and hard.

'I'm glad you're glad,' he said, nervous and self-conscious.

Isaac Stern played Mozart's Third Violin Concerto in the background. She had built a small fire, and laid out hors d'oeuvres on the low table in front of the huge fireplace. A quart of some kind of sparkling fruit-juice chilled in a silver-plated ice bucket set in a stand. He picked up a pudgy sausage, noted that it was bursting with fat. He chided himself for worrying about the nuances of his diet while his thirty-five year marriage disintegrated.

A carafe of coffee warmed over a candle flame. One glass eye stared at him out of the side of a black bear's head, the skin made into a rug covering the floor between the table and the stone fireplace. A wire screen obstructed tiny firebrands impelled by miniature explosions in the burning cedar, their sound punctuating the pleasant patois of rain on the roof. Water, flying before random sweeps of wind off the lake, sprayed across the window glass like brushes on snare drums. Stern's fiddle fitted in perfectly.

She deftly pulled the knot in his tie loose, then trailed her full lips lightly across the furrows of his forehead.

Gunnar was apprehensive. 'Will you draw the drapes . . . please?' he said.

The one big juicy sausage devoured, he sank back into the soft fabric of the sofa. He expected Anne to burst through the door at any moment – or Davey.

'Where does Davey think you are?'

'He said he'd be late at the club. I suppose somebody will have to bring him home.'

Wouldn't it be nice if they could stay in the lodge all night, she said, and he agreed, it would be nice.

'But Davey probably wouldn't like it,' he said.

They cleared a place on the table and put their feet up and she laid her head on his shoulder, her soft brown hair brushed his neck and the line of his jaw. They watched the fire for an hour or so, polishing off most of the sausages and some of the rest. The talk was small. He felt warm and stirred, in no hurry. But Anne spent the evening there on the sofa with them.

During the month after the hill climb, Gunnar and Holly had met at Cochrane's lodge every Tuesday and Thursday. The reawakening of his sexuality begot new tensions. The exquisite pleasure of the moment drew him back for more, but the hangovers of guilt dulled the high. He told her that the regularity of their meetings exposed them to greater risks. She didn't seem to care.

15

'The best news I've had in a long time is that you're not ready to give up your office.' Gunnar smiled at Leo, sitting behind George Washington's desk. Tomorrow was to be his last day.

'I figure by the time we get back from Europe I'll know what to do with my furniture.'

'I hope it stays right where it is,' Gunnar said.

'With rents what they are, that would be an awful waste,' Leo said.

'One last opinion?' said Gunnar.

'Shoot.'

'I'm considering using Eddie Kerr on the Djilas case.'

'You can't stand him.'

'He did some nice work on Miracle Mills. I kinda got used to him.'

'Do it then,' Leo said. 'Have you talked to him about it?'

'Not yet, but he'll help me if I ask,' Gunnar said. 'Don't forget, nobody else around here likes working with him either, and Eddie likes the big stuff.'

'Better set some ground rules,' Leo said.

'Right, I was sorry I hadn't done more of that in Miracle,' Gunnar said.

They discussed some of the conditions that should be spelled out to Eddie, especially in view of the fact that the firm wasn't going to share in the fee. Eventually, Gunnar changed the subject. He was concerned about Len Pettibohn's ability to fill Leo's shoes. Even though their professional corporation was based on democratic principles, Leo was a true Chairman of the Board. He had always gotten his way. It was a case of respect, and knowing which side your bread was buttered on. Several of the partners had been invited into Leo's investment deals. Others were waiting their turn.

'Len will do a great job,' Leo said, and he assured Gunnar that no one had a higher regard for him than Len Pettibohn.

Back in his own office, Gunnar speculated on firm politics with Leo gone. He thought of last year's merger attempt, that had finally failed when Leo and Spike Rafferty, of Rafferty Wilson and Smead simply could not agree on the name of the new firm. Leo insisted on Lawson and Rafferty, or as a compromise, Rafferty, Lawson and Larson. Spike wanted only two names, his first. He reasoned that their firm was more than three times the size of Lawson and Larson. Leo remained unpersuaded. Gunnar and a majority of the other shareholders backed Leo's position. Realistically, everyone involved knew, regardless of the alignment of the voting shareholders, the merger would fail on the name issue if Leo was unsatisfied.

Later that year, the Rafferty firm did merge with Caulfield and Holden, a firm about the same size as, and with a practice similar to Lawson and Larson. The Rafferty firm name was adopted by the new firm in its exact form. The very week the merger was implemented, eleven shareholders of the Rafferty firm, including two of their top trial guys, walked out to form their own firm with several large corporate clients in tow. They didn't like the order of the names on the letterhead. Gunnar was relieved that their own merger hadn't taken place. With Leo gone, he was afraid he might sink in the quicksand of law-firm politics.

Al Bergdorf had called Gunnar early that morning and asked him to have dinner at Maple Hills to talk about Judge O'Boyle. After telling Tony and Al not to get up, and exchanging the usual greetings, Gunnar sat down at the table covered with white linen and fine china, two candles burning in the center.

Al smeared butter on a popover the size of a Chihuahua. 'This O'Boyle thing worries me,' he said.

'Me too, Counselor,' said Tony.

'I gathered as much,' Gunnar said. 'But actually, I was tickled with the draw. Of course, if you've got a problem we better talk about it.'

After they'd ordered, Al described his general dislike of O'Boyle and mentioned an incident twenty years before when he said O'Boyle had welshed on a settlement deal and Al had called him a cocksucker to his face. Then, Tony told the story of a much more recent crap game, when a drunken O'Boyle had tried to fade him by throwing a wallet on the table. When Tony'd made his point he'd emptied O'Boyle's wallet of cash. Later O'Boyle had accused Tony of taking a hundred dollars more than was owed on the bet. The two hadn't spoken since. Gunnar listened without interruption, a frown fixed on his face as he saw another obstacle blocking the path to a big verdict. When Tony had finished, both he and Al joined in asking Gunnar to opt for a different judge.

'It could be worse,' Gunnar said.

'Not much,' said Al.

'Yeah, I think quite a bit,' Gunnar said. 'At least O'Boyle's a known quantity. I've tried three cases in his court.'

'Come on, Gunnar,' Al said, 'he hates Tony's guts, not to mention mine, and he's a pompous schmuck.'

'I don't think we have to worry about how he feels about you, Al,' Gunnar said. 'You won't be appearing.' And any judge that knows Al isn't going to like him, Gunnar thought. 'And as for Tony, let's talk about our alternatives.'

'It ain't good, Counselor,' Tony said.

'I know, but as I said, it could be worse.' Addressing Tony, Gunnar glanced at Al enough not to be offensive.

'How?' Tony said.

'That prick Kettle has been in office almost eight years. He's appointed fifteen judges in this county, maybe more,' Gunnar said. 'Caligula's horse to the Roman Senate was a better appointment than most of Kettle's judges.'

'I know he's been pretty political,' Al said.

'That's not the word for it,' Gunnar went on. 'He has a penchant for incompetents, either his pals, or friends or relatives of his pals, and women and blacks just because they're women and blacks.'

'Doesn't that cut both ways?' Tony asked.

'No, it doesn't cut both ways,' Gunnar said. 'It increases the element of chance in your case. If you have a winner, it increases the possibility that something unforeseen can turn it into a loser

. . . such as a stupid evidentiary ruling by the incompetent judge.'

'Fuckers,' said Al.

'For example,' Gunnar said, 'we could draw Elaine Witherspoon-Johnson. The only way Kettle could get her out of the commerce department was to appoint her to the bench. She's an open Sandanista sympathizer, and she gets good press from the *Times-Journal*.'

'Shit!' said Tony,

'Then there's Peter Penn, son of Freddie Penn, one of Kettle's favorite ward heelers; he suffers from paranoia among a variety of other mental disorders. And Bracken, I forget his first name, handsome guy, likes to intimidate lawyers. Fact is he knows no law, and couldn't function in any job that demanded a modicum of talent. By the way, he's fucking the Honorable Rose Anderson, that tall redhead, one of Kettle's first appointments. So they may be deciding important issues in your case with their heads, or whatever, together under the sheets. Or Carol Kelly, the public defender, now judge because her brother is Kettle's campaign treasurer; she's worse than what's-his-name, Bracken. No, it doesn't cut both ways. These yo-yo judges tend to be levelers. You do a good job, you might not get the benefit.'

'But we *know* O'Boyle doesn't like Tony,' Al said.

'I also have never known him to be unfair,' Gunnar said. 'And he's been off the sauce for at least two years.'

'He won't forget that he was drunk at the crap game.' Tony was not to be deflected.

'No,' Gunnar agreed. 'But he knows evidence; he was a good trial lawyer in his day.'

'I'll give you that,' Al said.

'We could draw Merton Liscomb,' Gunnar said. 'Walks around the court house acting like a judge, every place but in the court room. Or Jane Franchette, she's screwing one of the bailiffs.'

'With or without her robe?' Al said, starting on his second popover.

'Or we could draw Arnold Wilson whose brother is a political consultant to Kettle. Arnie's bright as hell, but he has no patience. If a trial takes more than three days he starts to roll his eyes up in his head at every question. Like who the hell are you to take up all of this time in my courtroom. This case is going to take weeks, maybe months.'

'Shit,' said Tony again.

'Frankly, guys, I'm glad you didn't have anything worse to tell me about Mike O'Boyle,' Gunnar said. 'I was happy as hell to get him.'

'But Gunnar, he's actually not on speaking terms with our client,' Al said.

Gunnar didn't like the sound of *our* client but he ignored it. 'We need a real judge on this case,' he said. 'If we win, we want it to stand up on appeal. If we have a good legal point we want a judge who can understand it. Most of Kettle's fools don't know the meaning of relevance or materiality. Another thing – our enemy is the newspaper, the only one in town. O'Boyle's established, self-confident. He won't toady to the press. Some of these other assholes will do anything to get the newspaper to say something good about them. And another thing, the way O'Boyle runs his court the case will take half as long to try. Most of the others are piddlers. They don't know how to rule. So they let counsel argue the law on every objection.'

'You win,' Tony said. 'But don't ever forget, that bastard's been looking daggers at me for four years.'

'Let's hope some of that's your perception,' Gunnar said. 'Have you ever really tried to talk to him since the crap game?'

'Not really,' Tony said.

'If you should run in to him again,' Gunnar said, 'just give him a hello Judge, or good morning Judge, nothing more, nothing less, agreed?'

'Agreed,' said Tony.

'I still don't like it,' Al said.

Tough shit, Gunnar thought. I'm not crazy about it either, but you go with what you know. Cut your losses. Don't get greedy.

They started on their steaks as the waitress poured wine for Al and Tony. Gunnar had turned his glass upside down. 'You know,' he said, 'what's really inexcusable is the bar association. One thing they could do is at least make responsible comments on Kettle's appointments, but they assign some pal of the new judge to write a glowing report in the *Journal*, telling how wonderful they are – ignoring their pathetic law-school performance, their total lack of trial experience . . . and that their main qualification is that they are related to somebody, or did something to benefit Kettle. In seven years Kettle's done more damage to the courts than all the rest of the governors before him.'

'Yeah, like that hyphenated broad,' Al said. 'I heard plenty to clean up the mess she made in her department at the capitol.'

'But the mess she made there can be cleaned up; much of the mess she makes in the courthouse we're stuck with. For ever,' Gunnar said. 'Praise the Lord for juries!'

'Amen,' said Al.

'The sad part,' Gunnar said, 'is that many of our best trial lawyers would happily take appointments to the bench – including some outstanding women. One of the best lawyers I know is Victoria Nolan, last year's bar association president. She would accept a judicial appointment and there's others like her, blacks too.'

'Including you?' Tony smiled at him.

'Maybe even me,' Gunnar said.

'More likely my pal Al here will get the nod from Kettle,' Tony said, laughing out loud.

Al's big, smooth beard-shadowed face sagged in an expression of discomfort. Gunnar suppressed any reaction by taking a swallow of ice water. Jock humor, even directed at Al Bergdorf, turned Gunnar off.

16

Dov Levy could shorten the odds in the Sisyphusian task of beating a newspaper in a libel suit. Tarnished ball-bearing eyes drilling you from under lean-tos of flesh furred with tangled brows you could hide a pair of cufflinks in was memory's image. Dov's uncomely face looked closer to fifty than the forty-three on his passport. But complex convulsions of muscles as fast as a Hasselblad shutter brought forth a puppy-dog expression that could extort love from an Auschwitz guard. One of Gunnar's four-woman, two-man juries wanted to reach out and pet Dov when he testified in a will contest three years ago.

Searching desperately in England for a witness named Williams and a letter mailed in 1949, Gunnar had been referred to Dov by a connection of Leo's in the CIA. Dov found Williams, and the letter, in Liverpool. It led to three more letters that Gunnar didn't know existed, and finally to a safe-deposit box in a Coventry bank. A losing case became a winner. And Dov got no cooperation. All of the documents were obtained using sophisticated listening devices and tedious surveillance. Gunnar even suspected burglary, but the issue never came up at the trial. Williams had too much else he wanted to hide.

Born in London's East End during the war, Dov never saw his father – a West End internist turned ship's doctor who went down with all hands near Gibraltar. From the time he'd first heard the term 'Jew boy', Dov had wanted to emigrate to Israel. His resourceful mother, a surgical nurse, made his dream come true in 1954 when Dov was eleven. They lived in a kibbutz in the Galilee. In 1963 Dov married Carolida, a girl born in Brooklyn. She and their little boy had been killed by a terrorist bomb in 1965 and Dov's mother had lost an eye in the blast. His own daily reminder was a keloided scar the shape of a boomerang that had recently been completely unveiled by the hair receding from his left temple. He had the habit of touching it as though he were checking to see if it was still there.

By the end of 1966 Dov had a commission in the Israeli Army. The next summer the Six-Day War ended his days as a soldier when he leapt from a helicopter in the dark, assuming they were hovering three feet above the desert earth, not the twenty he fell. The damaged hip socket produced a limp that grew worse with time, and dreadful recurring lower-back pain. After trying army intelligence, then chasing war criminals for a few years with Simon Weisenthal, Dov had opted for free enterprise. He'd set up an international investigative service, Levy Searches Ltd, in London, the city of his birth.

In between, Dov studied in some of the technical disciplines related to intelligence work, as well as Romance languages. He'd spoken English in school in London. And besides the Hebrew, Yiddish and Arabic that he'd learned growing up in the Galilee, he was classified fluent in French, Spanish and Italian.

When Dov had come to town to testify in the will contest, Gunnar was captivated. Over a long dinner, Dov promised that if Gunnar ever found anything interesting enough, he would come running. And Gunnar hadn't forgotten Dov's affinity for beautiful women. In town for only four days, he had bedded Angela, the receptionist who had since married, and his eyes followed every woman who walked through the room as they dined. Dov's presence in the witness box had been professional and self-confident. The jury was out only two hours before returning the verdict Gunnar had asked for, a seven-million-dollar bonanza for his clients. Although delighted with Gunnar's work at trial, they considered his selection of Dov Levy as their man in the UK a true stroke of genius. Gunnar had neglected to mention that he really had had nothing to do with it.

On this fall morning on the North American plain, Dov, in a bulky black sweater, sat across the glass-topped desk from Gunnar. His thick black hair, further back in front than last time, leaving a longer widow's peak, dribbled over the back of his collar.

'So you think this reporter Suzie Cline is a hot pants, eh?' Dov said.

'Just a rumor,' Gunnar said.

'She a Jew?'

'I doubt it, she spells it C-L-I-N-E,' Gunnar said. 'A cop friend of mine will get you a picture. I'm told she's attractive.'

'Bugger the luck,' Dov said. 'I love those Jewish girls and they love me.'

'I think you'll do fine regardless of race, creed or color,' Gunnar said.

'One doesn't forget one's roots, you know.' Dov's brush brow closed his right eye in a wink that radiated ripples like a stone landing in still water. Gunnar eyed him pulling at the big mustache with his lower lip.

'Don't worry about the mustache, it comes off tonight, and I'll get a nice neat haircut in the morning.'

For the next two hours Gunnar explained in great detail the nature of the proof he was after. He hoped Dov could help him find what he needed to prove malice – a motive for undermining Tony Djilas in the contract process. They would need to discover everyone who stood to gain by Tony's loss of the New City deal, and any possible connection between them and the *Times-Journal*. Past or continuing indiscretions of the two reporters, Ward Chapin and Suzie Cline, might interest a jury and could therefore help make the case; the same for other employees of the paper, especially those in management and editorial positions.

'My personal focus for now is proving falsity,' Gunnar said. 'My young partner Eddie Kerr is handling damages. The first issue in a libel case is the truth or falsity of the allegations. Because defendant is a newspaper, the burden of proving falsity is on us.'

Dov got out of his chair, limped over to the window and looked out at the wind blowing through downtown. Dov remembered everything you told him – down to minutia. He even seemed to know it before you told him. In deep thought, he ignored an inquiry from Gunnar about the problem hip joint. The logical difficulty of proving falsity wouldn't escape Dov. All proof was positive. It was a logical impossibility to prove something hadn't happened. It could be done indirectly by proving positively that something did happen that is entirely inconsistent with the event you sought to prove didn't happen, such as an accused establishing an alibi. But alibi evidence couldn't exist for Tony Djilas. Beyond being confined to an iron lung or being in prison, no alibi could cover you for a period of months, even years. Gunnar had his own ideas, but now he waited for Dov to drop back to earth.

Still looking through the glass, Dov said, 'Of course you know you can't do it.' He turned around and gave Gunnar a scrunch of wrinkles and dimples that made you think of Albert Einstein in a dark wig. 'But you wouldn't have brought me across the Atlantic to tell you that.'

'The standard is clear and convincing evidence,' Gunnar said. 'I think we can satisfy the court.'

'I take it there's no police file on this chap, at least concerning dope smuggling, eh?' Dov ended his questions with a grunting oral question mark.

'We are aware of none,' Gunnar said. 'We'll know more when defendants have answered the interrogatories we submitted with the complaint. They must have some police evidence on Djilas, or they would have been the worst kind of damn fools to run the story.'

'Can he get law-enforcement people in the area to testify. They would have known if he was suspected of dope dealing, eh?'

'I think so, a highly placed cop from Fort Lauderdale, as well as a detective from Broward County,' Gunnar said. 'Perhaps others, and, of course, Tony himself, maybe some friends and neighbors who had an opportunity to observe him closely during that time . . . and his wife. I'm hoping that the court will at least consider that kind of testimony as prima facie proof of falsity. Short of that we lose.'

'How about testimony as to his good character?'

'Plenty,' Gunnar said, 'if the judge lets it in. The mayor here; and Robert Goodspeed, the evangelist.'

'That *is* impressive. He's well known, even in Britain. But I'm not involved in that phase, at least to start with, eh?'

'Right, I need you to prove the defendant's knowledge of the falsity; that's the key to the counting house,' Gunnar said.

'I'm going to have to edge up real close to these people,' said Dov.

'Real close,' Gunnar said. 'I have found the best access to the dark side of the corporate conscience is a former employee. Or, if you are real lucky, a pissed-off present employee with an axe to grind, or some kind of an emotional complication.'

'We caught an old camp guard a few years back, bloody sadist, SS,' Dov said. 'He lived in France for thirty-four years with this widow – in the country – in sight of the Pyrenees. Safe as can be. Then, this younger neighbor was widowed, well into her fifties. So, Herr Kraus, already in his late sixties, decides he's got to fuck her.' Dov shook his head as if he was hearing his own story for the first time. 'The first widow called us directly, spilt all the secrets of lover-boy's past and the local police grabbed him in the midst of his last piece of ass.' Dov's face exploded with the wrinkles and dimples, and a flash of the ends of his teeth under the mustache. 'Funny thing, he'd been whipping the shit out of the first widow for years, even broke her arm and a couple of ribs.'

'We understand each other,' Gunnar said. 'You need to get started. You must never come here again. When you need to talk to me from time to time, call and tell me that Schwartzkopf is in town. I'll give you a time, and then you call me at this number.' Gunnar handed him a card. 'This is not a criminal investigation, so you have broad latitude in your methods. If the other side makes you as one of us your usefulness will be over.'

'I understand completely,' said Dov.

'It wouldn't do for you to compromise either me or my client.' It was no trouble for Gunnar to maintain a serious expression. Unless he smiled his face always looked like Cotton Mather catching his wife in the kip with a pilgrim.

'I get the picture,' Dov said. 'You barristers are all alike. You would never do anything questionable. That is, unless you must in order to win.'

Gunnar laughed out loud. 'Very funny, Mr Levy. But, all joking aside, you must never cause me to cross the line between questionable and illegal, and for that matter I don't much care to roam around very much in questionable.'

Again the wrinkles and dimples. 'If the Iraqis had caught me in

Baghdad they would have cut off my fingers one by one whether I gave them the right answers or not. Then they would have shot me and put my head on a stick in the prison yard.'

Gunnar reverted to his serious mode. 'I trust you, Dov. I got the feeling the first time we met. It's not necessary that I know everything you do, nor do I want anyone else to know. Nobody. OK? I want you to be able to testify honestly that I never asked you to do anything illegal.'

Dov stuck out his hand.

Gunnar eyed the thick stubby fingers as he reached for it, and stopped, without thinking, when he noticed the pinky was cut off at the first knuckle.

Dov held it up close to Gunnar's face with just half a grin. 'It wasn't an Arab axe or anything else exciting. I lost it in a blasted table saw . . . just after I saw you the last time.'

Dov lowered his hand and Gunnar grabbed hold, squeezed hard and got a firm grip back.

Holding on to Gunnar's hand, Dov said, 'Where I'm concerned Gunnar, you have nothing to worry about; except, of course, the evidence you are looking for may not exist. If it does I'll do my best to find it.'

'Do you think you can manage alone?'

'Perhaps. But Christine, my assistant, might be able to get closer to this young Chapin. She's in her thirties, and quite attractive, eh?' Dov handed a snapshot to Gunnar.

She resembled Holly: wide sensual mouth, slim-waisted. 'An understatement,' Gunnar said.

'She can get here with a day's notice,' Dov said. 'But for now, I'll get on with it.'

Gunnar handed him an envelope containing two floppy disks. 'Everything we have so far that might help you is on here,' Gunnar said.

'*Shalom.*' Dov dipped his head slightly.

'*Shalom*,' said Gunnar for the first time in his life.

Eddie Kerr was due in fifteen minutes for their eleven a.m. meeting to discuss the discovery schedule and the division of labor on the Djilas case. When Gunnar had approached him yesterday, he had seemed willing, even failing just slightly to suppress signs of enthusiasm.

As Gunnar waited, he admired his Mondrian hanging across the room. He had obtained the original oil as part of the fee arrangement in a case involving the liquidation of a manufacturing corporation. At first the stark black lines and vivid right-out-of-the-tube reds and blues had put him off. Over the years he had grown fond of it: a statement of the essence of form.

Eddie plopped his fat frame in the chair Dov had left.

'Who's going to be playing in the World Series?' Gunnar asked.

'Boston and the Mets,' Eddie said,

'Care to take 'em both against the field?' Gunnar said.

'Sure, make it five bucks on each,' Eddie said.

'You're on,' He handed Eddie a copy of the case plan for *Djilas v.* Times-Journal *et al.* 'Our proof in Tony's case, like most, falls generally into two categories,' Gunnar said, 'liability and damages. And the damages category divides into three more.'

'Actual, punitive and presumed,' Eddie said, without having looked at the case plan.

'Very good, Counselor,' Gunnar said, 'To start with I want you to plan our proof and discovery on actual and punitive. You know the drill on both. I'll work on the liability.'

'Good luck,' Eddie said, with a tinge of irony.

'Don't think we can do it?'

'What do I know,' said Eddie.

'I want to put it all together in six months,' Gunnar said. 'You'll work closely with Tony, and his staff and architect, to establish his lost profit on the New City deal. You'll also need to plan testimony proving that his group would have gotten the contract. Mayor Carpenter will help you with that. You know what you'll need from the *Times-Journal* and those reporters for a basis for punitive damages. Complete financials and so on. Apparently, the reporters are being indemnified because Terry Wood is representing all the defendants.'

'I'm not going to have much time for anything else,' Eddie said.

'I know, but Pettibohn has promised all the extra help you want from associates,' said Gunnar. 'I think the firm feels the publicity value of this one is worth the inconvenience and the concessions it has made on the fees. Of course, your time will be covered like any other case.'

'How about Henry?' said Eddie, referring to the firm's investigator.

'You can use Forbes if you need him,' Gunnar said, 'but I'm getting outside help. I don't want to tie Henry up on one case.' Gunnar was glad Eddie rarely asked for information that wasn't volunteered. Eddie didn't want to let anybody know that such things made any difference to him, and Gunnar wasn't ready to tell him about Dov.

One side of Eddie's little thin-lipped mouth moved up just a trifle, to give notice to you of his superior perspicacity. 'Dan Blackmer is expecting a lot of me over the next few months.'

'Help me pull this off,' Gunnar said, 'and there's a twenty-five-grand bonus in it, assuming we cover the costs.'

'*OK*,' said Eddie, with even more than usual emphasis on the 'K', and a peek at his two little front teeth.

Gunnar went over the schedule he had prepared, with depositions to begin in mid-October. He planned on moving for a date-certain trial in May based on the argument that with these accusations hanging over him, Tony was prevented from finding other development opportunities. Eddie said it was ambitious, nothing else.

As he was leaving, Gunnar called after him. 'I don't think I ever thanked you for all of your help on Miracle Mills. We would never have gotten that settlement without you setting them up.'

Eddie almost smiled as he turned and walked through the door.

Just before noon, Angela announced a call from Mrs Hogan, Holly's code name.

'Eight-thirty?'

'Make it nine,' Gunnar said.

'I love you.'

'Bye,' Gunnar said.

* * *

Tony's case could mean real money in the bank. Dad and Mom had taught him to be ready for the rainy day – and maybe a way out. There wouldn't be time to dally away at Cochrane's Lodge. Anyway, Davey Tripp was planning on taking Holly to Palm Beach from Christmas on, but she was thinking of not going. Did they keep that trail into the Lodge free of snow in the winter? A way out of what? Jesus Christ.

17

Suit, dark blue, double-breasted with a subdued dark tie; hair, freshly trimmed; upper lip, naked: Dov Levy picked a stool at the bar just to the right of the waitress station. One block down Eleventh Street from the main entrance to the *Times-Journal* Building, the Three-O Club had catered to newspaper people for fourteen years. Business types and lawyers in pinstripes and fast-talking, skirt-chasing salesmen in wrinkled sport jackets completed the complement of barflies. Spending last night sipping Scotch and sodas, Dov had learned the make-up of the clientele. Mainly regulars, many enjoyed the petty ego trip of having the bartender serve their first drink without need of asking their choice – clearly a watering hole for serious drinkers. Men outnumbered women four to one. The dark red mahogany bar, twenty feet long, took the shape of an oval race-track. An infield of colorful booze bottles stood under an assortment of stem-ware glasses suspended from a rack above.

Two male bartenders in long white aprons stayed busy. The noise level wasn't bad. Six large booths occupied one wall. An open door led to a dining room with a half dozen or so small tables where they served spectacular hamburgers – thick ground sirloin grilled to order, with great gobs of fried onions. They also served at the bar. Captain Fleetham had accurately described the Three-O.

Dov had stopped at the downtown precinct to see Franklin Delano Fleetham. Gunnar's name had had a magical effect on the big cop. And when Dov outlined his mission as investigator on the Djilas case, Fleet promised to help him if he could. He gave Dov a mug shot taken by the cops when Suzie Cline, then editor of *Campus Voice*, was arrested for lying down in the path of a truck transporting National Guard troops to the airport – and on to south-east Asia or some foreign place. Ward Chapin's arrest on suspected drunk driving produced another photograph.

On Friday night at seven o'clock Suzie had bellied up to the bar escorted by a tall blond man with a German accent. She put away four glasses of white wine while the German got sloshed on stingers. Perhaps Italian, she looked better than the old mug shot. The sharp nose of a predatory bird came to an edge on the bridge like a dull axe. Prodigal dark hair, tamed at the back with a loose ribbon, flared out over her shoulders. Perhaps thirty-five, she wore no make-up, maybe lip gloss. Your eyes lingered on the lips, sensually thick, suggesting a Negro genetic influence, like those beautiful Indian girls from the Antilles.

Dov waited. Within ten minutes he felt her eyes on him. After another ten, he allowed quick contact, then looked away, uninterested. A little later he settled on her eyes again, dancing dark brown. She wouldn't look away. The German rattled on. Dov allowed himself a smile. She smiled back, a knowing look around the eyes. Then Ward Chapin sat down next to her. Dov never looked back at the group, and he left a few minutes later. The next time he met those eyes he would hang around until they talked.

Now, only twenty-four hours later, was the next time. And she came in alone. For Christ sake, she was coming right up to him, no fooling around.

'Back again, I see,' she said.

'I'm flattered you remember,' Dov said. But who could forget Dov's face.

'You're not one of us,' she said.

'It shows, eh?'

'Hardly a midwestern twang,' she said. 'European?'

'Soldier of fortune, here and there, mostly Brit; of course, of the brethren, currently Coventry.'

'Suzie Cline,' she said.

He squeezed her warm moist hand. 'Jesse Katz, shall we take a perch?'

'By all means.' On the stool, her black leather skirt hiked

up on her thighs. Black nylon encased thin legs. 'What brings you here?'

'The Scotch,' he said.

'No silly, I mean to the city?'

'In search of the Holy Grail, or you, whichever comes first.'

'Pu-leeze.'

'You don't believe me, eh? How about, I call on Miracle Mills for my office in London – international grain brokers.' Gunnar had worked out the cover with the head of the grain-trading department at Miracle.

'White wine,' she said to the bartender.

He covered his half-full glass with his hand. 'A lonesome calling, an ocean, and half a continent away from home on Saturday night,' he said.

'Not necessarily,' said Suzie Cline.

By ten, she had brought him home. Settled in the couch in Suzie's high-rise condo, The Grateful Dead bombarded Dov's ears while she mixed him a drink – a specialty of hers, she said. She suggested a tape of soft music and she set the dark-colored mixture in an Old-Fashioned glass on the low bronze table inches from his knees. He smiled his assent. Soon the melody of 'In the Still of the Night', full orchestra, filled the room and she sank down in the couch with him, hip to hip. Without having asked one question, he had learned her complete educational background, the details of her family and an early failed marriage, the pleasure she took from her job as an investigative reporter with the *Times-Journal*; and her utter contempt for the Republican administration in Washington, especially the President, to whom she referred as Ronald von Reagan.

Dov sipped the Black Russian.

'Like it?'

'People get drunk on these, eh?'

'Promises, promises,' she said.

She was in heat. No doubt. He had to decide whether to wait. What if some assignment later took her away, abruptly? It could blow the whole deal. Tonight was the night.

They each had the second Black Russian. Dov had dumped most of his first in the kitchen sink while Suzie was in the bathroom. Kissing her wonderfully soft lips required little further motivation, but careful accommodation for two heroic noses needed to be arranged. Montovani's orchestra played softly on the tape.

Her breasts were so small as to obviate any need for a bra. His thick fingers found her nipples through the silk. But Suzie Cline was master of this ship. He let her push him down on the sofa, his head resting on the softly padded arm. You Europeans, she said as she fumbled with the buttons on his fly. He sprang hard into her hand and she licked the head of his circumcised cock. Dov's fingers searched among the roots of her mass of thick hair.

'Come to my bed, Jesse,' she said.

At least eight full-sized pillows cased in a pale-blue print spread across the king-sized bed in a double row. Dov dropped his clothes on a chair and slid beneath the comforter. When Suzie was naked she whipped the comforter off, and crawled on top of him. Her nipples stood out from the brown circles on his almost flat chest like rubber erasers on pencils, and she pushed them into the rug of black hair on his chest. Her big lush lips pressed on his as their heads were smothered in an opulent envelope of hair. Could he be working, and getting six hundred quid a day?

Suzie Cline was the quintessential blow-job artist. She drew him into the warm tube of her throat where he could feel the muscles of swallowing, and then she emitted a choking sound as the reflex tried to push him out. Her choking scared him and threatened his erection. She came up for air.

'Are you all right?' Dov asked,

'Don't you like it?'

'Of course,' he said.

'Don't worry about it,' she said. 'It's just the gag reflex, you're big, you know.'

'Isn't it dangerous?'

'No, no,' she laughed.

Not much later he came in a gusher in her mouth. He felt a series of exquisite electric shocks between his anus and the base of his cock, and he thrust hard toward the ceiling, hoping after each spasm for another. He subsided to a state of suspended animation.

After the sucking and the swallowing, she loomed above in the dim light with a little Mona Lisa smile from within the feathery cape of hair. 'That's not the end?'

'Only the beginning,' he said. His face reassembled into the lovable puppy.

Across four continents and thirty years he had met three other Suzie Clines, girls to whom fucking and sucking was a sport like amateur wrestling, with an arcane scoring system known only to aficionados. The first was a girl in the Israeli Army. In 1967, before and after the war, he must have fucked her fifty times in a couple of months – in a camp near Herzlia, and after the war, in Gaza. Naomi would laugh and yell when she came, and scream when she felt him squirt inside her. Ten years later he ran into her in Tel Aviv. She was married, three children, contemplating divorce, missed the Army for Christ sake.

After Naomi, it was Verna in Rome, just briefly in the fall of '73, and a couple of times again in the summer of '74. Fucking for the sheer love of it, nothing to do with attachments, or tenderness, or commitment, or romance. Just the physical drawing together of two people, at least one of whom was supercharged with desire for the other's body, and the eventual coming apart, maybe after a dozen times, as with Verna, or much longer as with his Israeli soldier, or maybe they would never stop as with Christine, whom he liked to call his junior partner. She managed the office in London, and on rare occasions helped him in the field. She was the other Suzie; he'd met her at an art fair in the street in Brighton. They couldn't wait to get to her flat. Seven years later she still yelled with joy and revelled in fucking him, but they both had other friends of the opposite sex and didn't wish to merge their lives any further than they had. But, no doubt, there was more tenderness between him and Christine than with the other Suzies, but wasn't that true, too, between friends who didn't fuck each other, or even friends of the same sex.

Now, he would make the most of the current Suzie. If she had information that he could use, he would get it in the days to come, in this bed or somewhere, as they lay waiting for his prick to rise again. Suzie Cline could have her will with him. Maybe the Black Russians would oil the machinery of recollection.

At three-fifteen a.m. Suzie's breathing was deep and regular with a little whistle. Time to explore. Still naked, he painstakingly eased to the side of the bed on his stomach. He dropped his knee over the edge until his foot, pressing into the carpet, could support his weight with just the slightest assist from his hands pushing down on the mattress. He stood beside the bed, the pain in his hip flaring up. The musky smell of sex was in the room. Suzie still breathed in an even series of faint whistles.

The kitchen light was on. Dov looked over the light fixtures, the phone, the cabinets and the appliances, sizing up the possibilities for planting a bug. As he opened the cabinet door above the broom closet, he felt a movement on the floor behind. Resisting the impulse to whirl around, he turned slowly. Suzie stood naked before him, a quizzical look on her face, her eyes offended by the bright light from the ceiling.

'I just wanted a drink,' he said. 'Sorry I disturbed you.'

'What the hell are you doing in the cabinet?'

He sensed she wasn't as angry as the words. 'I thought I'd put a little Scotch in it,' he said.

'It's in the cabinet over the sink,' she said. 'Didn't those Russians do the trick?'

'Sure,' he said, 'but when I can't sleep, I drink.'

'If that's all that's the matter,' she said, 'give me another try before you drink anymore.' She dropped down on her knees on the hard white linoleum, and took his cock in her mouth until it started to come to life. Then, she led him back to the bedroom.

18

Over the years since Jack's death, dreaming the dream, Gunnar had cried out in his sleep, and when he awoke Anne would be sitting up in bed trying to comfort him, as his mother had done when he was a little boy. If the dream came early in the night, sometimes in an hour or two he could get back to sleep. But when he was awakened at four or five, Gunnar knew it was hopeless to try. He always awoke at precisely the same point. This time it was nearly five, and he eased out of bed in the dark, pulling on his clothes quietly, hoping not to disturb Anne. She was breathing evenly, unaware of his torment.

Jack was alive. They were driving cross-country in an old car. Gunnar could never be sure, but he thought it was a '37 Ford coupe, with the old-fashioned gear-shift lever – a round black Bakelite knob on the end, protruding up from the floorboards between driver and passenger. In the dim beam of the headlights the highway got narrower and narrower until it was only a dirt-road. It came to an end in a field, and he told Jack they would have to turn around, that they must have missed a turn, but he could not remember where there had been any options. He backed the car into tall weeds, and somehow the rear wheels sunk into a snowdrift. When Gunnar tried to drive forward, the wheels spun, sliding sideways, at the top of an incline.

'Careful, Dad,' Jack said, 'don't let it slide down the hill.'

'Take the wheel, I'll push,' Gunnar said, and he got out of the car, and walked around the back through knee-deep snow, and then yelled, 'Go ahead!' The wheels spun and Gunnar pushed, but the car continued to slip over the brink, and he was unable to hold it. But Jack was alive in the car; and even though it was hopelessly stuck, just at the moment he awoke, he knew Jack was alive. It was all vivid, real. In the instant of awareness of bed and pajamas, the darkness in the room and Anne beside him, he experienced the reality of Jack's death all over again: the hopeless sinking, the emptying out of everything within him. Until, like a lost-wax bronze casting of a man, rendered on the outside in meticulous detail, he was completely hollow on the inside.

Exactly ten years before, the day had unfolded, as a day of victory: Tuesday, 21 September, 1976. On the afternoon before, he had delivered one of his finest summations. For five days witnesses for both sides paraded to the stand. Gunnar drew a finely detailed portrait of a vital teenage girl, slaughtered by a drunken driver just as she set out on the adventure of life. His opponent, defense lawyer Malcolm Harris, foolishly relying on a century of cases limiting parent's recovery to purely pecuniary loss, reconstructed Lu Anne as mediocre, a shamefully inadequate high-school student and lethargic pot-smoker, doomed to a lackluster life – all to disprove her value, her pecuniary value. Gunnar sensed the disgust of the jurors at the mauling of the dead girl in view of parents, brother, teachers and friends. He chafed to make his final argument.

'It saddens me that Lu Anne Thrush had to die only a few short months after graduating from high school,' had been his opening line. 'And it saddens me that defense counsel acting for that same driver who crushed her body inside of her brand new car, the pride of her young life, had to come into this courtroom and mutilate her all over again.'

Gunnar barely paused as the judge overruled Malcolm Harris's objection. 'But,' he said, 'sad as I feel, I am glad that you, members of the jury, must now feel a tiny bit of the pain that these parents, and this brother . . . .' Before the jurors' eyes, Gunnar held his thumb and index finger a fraction of an inch apart. 'Just a little of the pain they feel . . . so that you can multiply that feeling a million times to get an idea of their pain.' He turned to face the family. 'And then, members of the jury, you can see to it that Mr Harris' client, Frank Willis, pays these people for their loss, in an amount appropriate to the devastation Mr Willis has wreaked upon them.'

From that opening, he reviewed the testimony of each friend, each teacher, his expert economist, the parents and the brother – thirteen witnesses in all.

Speaking to the issue in the most recent case, the State Supreme Court had broadened the concept of pecuniary loss, opened the door a crack for a case like this one, and Gunnar meant to sneak through. He approached his conclusion. 'Mr Harris has skillfully pointed out how hard it is to attach a dollar-value to Lu Anne's lost life. But that doesn't mean it can't be done and, I believe, the court will tell you that you may assign a value to the parents' society with their child, a value to the relationship as a whole.' He neared the end. 'As you do this, think of what a child is to a parent, or a brother.

'A child,' Gunnar said, 'is someone to talk to. Someone to play with . . . . Someone to sing with and someone to dance with. Someone to go to the movies with . . . . Someone to have Christmas with. Someone you are proud of and someone who is proud of you . . . . Someone to comfort and someone to comfort you. Someone to share with . . . . Someone to laugh with and someone to cry with.' In rehearsing this coda Gunnar had been unable to hold back the tears, but in front of the jury he knew his tears would evoke feelings for him rather than his client, and all he let them see were his glistening eyes. 'And, someone to hug, and someone to hug you.' He stopped and drew in a deep breath. 'And most of all, someone to love . . . and someone to love you.' Two women jurors sobbed openly. A man used his handkerchief.

The following afternoon, Tuesday, 21 September, 1976, the clerk called. The jury had awarded Gunnar's clients $1,250,000, more than three times the next highest verdict for the wrongful death of a minor child in the history of the state. With his upper arms covered with the goose flesh of singular elation, Gunnar called Lu Anne's family.

Minutes later, Angela announced that a Colonel Jimmy Ray Starkweather wanted to see Gunnar on a personal matter. In the lobby, he spotted the silver eagle on the shoulder. The gray-haired colonel was accompanied by a bald captain, officers' hats tucked under their arms. When Gunnar saw the two of them and their faces, he guessed their mission. He stopped breathing and a faint shaking possessed his body. The hoping began. Maybe it was just a serious injury – they wouldn't send a bird colonel to see him about a serious injury. God, there was no war on. Jack was in Germany. He shook their hands by rote. And they followed him to his office where they declined a seat and the two stood facing him. Colonel Jimmy Ray Starkweather, his face disfigured with pain, said, 'There has been a helicopter accident outside Stuttgart. I regret that your son, Lieutenant John Larson, has died in the crash, along with three enlisted men.'

Someone to love, and someone to love you.

Ten years later, walking alone in the dark house, having dreamed the dream, he looked again into Colonel Jimmy Ray Starkweather's eyes – the moment of realization that he had relived much more often than he had dreamed the dimly illuminated events leading up to the old coupe stuck in the snowdrift. Though he had probed desperately for years, any special meaning the dream might have was lost on Gunnar.

He walked across the lawn in the faint gray light with a casting rod in his hand, a plug dangling from the tip. The air was damp and cold with a smell of rotting fish from the shore. He laid the rod in the aluminum skiff and shoved it into the dark still waters of the bay. In the early morning gloom he rowed the boat along the south-west shore, quietly dipping his oars so not to disturb the bass. Stopping from time to time, he flicked the plug toward the shore and reeled it in slowly, now and then jerking the tip of the rod to entice a strike. First light fell upon autumn leaves in the trees along the shore, mostly yellow, some reds and orange. Many already lay on the ground waiting for winter.

He hadn't fished for a blue moon; it felt good, and soothing. Once a small bass splashed, passing at the plug, but the only other movement in the water was the dipping of his oars and the plug gurgling as it approached the boat, breaking the surface tension of the still water. From the trees on shore came the cries of awakening birds.

He wished Anne were there in the boat, beside him. She loved sunrises and sunsets; and she remembered them and compared them. The champion, she said, was a sunset they had pulled off the road to watch for a half hour in the Snake River country of southern Idaho. Gunnar had glimpsed it in the mirror and he surprised her by turning into a side road so she could watch and remember. She said it was an army of ancient Romans in chariots charging into battle in another world.

With chilled hands he pulled on the oars to reposition the skiff. Tripp's blue boathouse clung to the bank down the shore. A soft rush of warm air began to blow from the clouds. The glassy surface broke into a delicate ripple. A shudder shook Gunnar's whole body, and he remembered the childhood admonition that someone was walking across his grave. The red disc slowly slid up from behind the forested hills, and, for a second, balanced on the tip of the tallest. When it lifted free of the earth it was again a blinding yellow ball, and he had to avert his eyes, dried of their tears by the light September wind.

As he approached his own yard on the route back, pulling easily on the oars, Gunnar looked over his shoulder. Katie, slim and blonde, in one of his baggy old red sweaters, waited for him on the end of the dock.

'Hi, Daddy,' she said.

'Kinda early for you on a Sunday morning?'

'I heard you go out,' she said.

'Oh, I'm sorry, I was tippy-toeing,' Gunnar said.

'No harm, I was awake already. It's been ten years for me too, you know.' She bent down to grab the skiff's bow line.

'Of course it has, Kate,' Gunnar said. 'I know how you miss him.'

She asked him if he would sit with her a while in the gazebo. Mom had gone to an early mass at St Martins, she said. She had brought a carafe of hot coffee down from the house and some English muffins spread with peach jam.

'Doesn't it ever get better for you, Daddy?' Her blue eyes were moist.

'Only when I occupy my mind with something that seems important to me, like work, and the excitement of the trials,' he said. '. . . The coffee's great.'

'I'm concerned about Mom. I sense she's kind of sad all the

time. It's something different, not Jack. She doesn't talk to me about it.'

'I know,' Gunnar said, passing the temptation to plead ignorance.

'Is something going on with the two of you?'

'In a way,' he said.

'Daddy, I lost my big brother. I can't lose my parents. I need my parents to be real parents . . . together!'

'We'll always be your parents, honey,' he said. 'You don't have to worry about that, and really, Kate, you're a grown woman now.'

'I need you two as much as I did when I was five, Daddy.' Her face had gone rose-petal pink and she bowed her head like a cut flower, too long in the vase.

Gunnar reached across the table and held her hand. He groped for the right words. 'I love you, Katie,' he said, 'I'll never do anything to hurt you.'

Looking into his eyes, she narrowed her brows and moved her head side to side. 'I don't even know what it means to be a grown woman. I'm still just a little girl. I don't feel any different on the inside than when I was in grade school.'

'You'll always be my little girl, Katie,' he said.

'Daddy, I remember when I was really a little girl, and I was playing on the lawn, and you and Grandpa and Jack had been fishing out in the bay. I was standing right up there, by the back door, and I saw the boat coming in and Jack was standing up in the bow. He must've been about thirteen, and he was holding this big fish up in front of him as the boat came up to the dock. And I ran down to meet you and he had this huge smile on his face, and so did you and Grandpa. Oh, Daddy! Do you remember?'

'I remember,' he said. The knot in his throat permitted nothing more.

'It's not fair, Daddy,' she said.

'No, it's not fair,' Gunnar said. Looking at her in her misery, he couldn't say it, but it was no different for him. Inside the noble trappings of a big city trial lawyer, he was just a small boy too. But he had to act like a man, an important man.

19

In his room at the Downtown Hilton, twenty-six stories above the street, Dov Levy made notes in tiny meticulous script. Hebrew served as a code against most intruding eyes and whenever he left the hotel he deposited his case log in a lock box provided for guests. This Monday morning, still in his robe, Dov wrote down everything that had transpired during his weekend with Suzie Cline, without presently judging its relevance.

He had awakened alone in the bed around nine on Sunday morning to the aroma of brewing coffee. He hoped the coffee would cure the dull ache the Black Russians had left in his head. He knew nothing but bed rest would help the pain in his lower back. Naked at Suzie's bathroom sink, he gargled – trying to rid his mouth of the taste of having served as roost for a flock of starlings. In the mirror his incipient beard looked menacing.

'Who rolled the stone away?' said Suzie, standing in the open bathroom door, naked, abundant hair in wild disarray. 'This'll help.' She handed him a steaming cup.

'Thanks,' Dov said. 'Another speciality, eh?'

'For similar considerations,' she said. Stepping closer, she thrust her pelvis forward, smooth skin against hairy belly.

His cock reacted as expected, and they spent the rest of Sunday morning in her bed, a reprise of the night before. When she had her fill, at least for the nonce, they talked for an hour, finally reaching the investigation of Tony Djilas. Again, Dov asked no questions beyond what kind of assignments she covered. She had brought it up in the context of getting sued.

'It's only the second time I've been sued by somebody looking for money,' she said. 'The other time the case was dismissed right off the bat. I've been involved in cases where people have tried

123

to prevent us from writing about some particular thing, or where we have gone to court to get access to information and public meetings and the like. But in this Djilas thing the guy apparently thinks he can collect a bundle.'

'Can he?' Dov stared at the bedroom ceiling.

'Truth is supposed to be a perfect defense,' she said. 'I learned that in journalism school.'

'What's the guy's point?'

'His suit alleges that what we said was false. Our lawyer says Djilas has to prove it's false. There ain't no way he can.'

'Why?'

'Cuz everything we wrote is true.'

'Sounds like he's wasting his time.'

'That's what I say,' Suzie said, 'and ours, too.'

'So, apparently there's no real problem, eh?'

'The lawyer says Djilas' lawyer is the best there is, and he wouldn't fuck around with it if he didn't think he had something to go on.'

'I've been told your barristers will do anything for money.'

'That's always been my impression, but our guy says not so with this Larson. To me, a lawyer is a lawyer.'

'Whatever, Mr Djilas must be bloody upset to go to all the trouble and expense.'

As they lay side by side their fingers laced together, Suzie told him the story of the investigative work she and Ward Chapin had done on City Hall and the developers, and particularly Tony Djilas; but nothing she said indicated that she or anybody else had reported anything but facts. When she had finished her story, she rolled over and looked at him with a wide smile, her hand on his cock. 'You're good,' she said. 'I believe my body, and it tells me you're wonderful. I hope you're not in a hurry.'

She fed him smoked salmon and he didn't leave until after four, Sunday afternoon. They agreed to get together on Tuesday night. He assured her he would be in town for at least a month.

Now, in his hotel room, Dov read back over the notes he had made. He had learned nothing, absolutely nothing to help their case. It read like the memoirs of Fanny Hill. But there would be other opportunities.

* * *

Al Bergdorf, alone with his Jackson Pollock, reread the letter he had prepared for Gunnar Larson.

> Dear Gunnar,
> Following is the list you asked me to prepare of the only serious competitors for the Block 13, New City contract. Steve Carpenter agrees that this is the complete list. As you know, neither Tony, Steve nor I have any idea which might be the culprit, if indeed there is one.

Developer	Contact
Quentin Industries	Raymond Flis, Ruth Renken
Djilas Ventures	Anthony Djilas
New City Partners	Ford Freetack, Arnold Decker
Val-Con Inc.	S.K. 'Bud' Lonsborg
Four Flags Ltd.	Pierce Pentecost

> Best Regards,
> Al

Al wanted to help, but if it had been solely up to him he wouldn't drag the mayor into this minefield. Still Tony was as close or closer to Steve Carpenter, and he meant to use every possible resource in nailing the *Times-Journal*. The seven names on the contact list and their closest associates would be the targets. Al was skeptical about the whole idea, but Tony was sure something sinister was going on – and it was his case, and his money.

Ah, that redhead, whenever Ruth Renken's name came up, Al remembered fondly – it must be twenty years and a hundred pounds back, before his life had gotten complicated – meeting her at a state Democrat convention up north, and getting one of the rides of his life. She was just out of college. He wasn't much older. That was some broad. She'd liked him then, but if she saw this gut now, she'd puke. He took the last bite of his second Danish and reached for a Havana.

*   *   *

Gunnar started Monday morning by returning a call to Wyman Farmer in Miami.

'Gunnar, you'll remember my FBI search came up empty on those neighbors. Now I finally found something kinda by accident,' Wyman said. 'The DEA does have something on Djilas' neighbor, Castillo. He was arrested on 11 August, 1973. Their report says his thirty-three-foot Chris Craft was identified as a boat seen accompanying another boat in US territorial waters – get this – being used by one Emanuel Zilman, a known smuggler. They got a warrant and searched Castillo's boat moored in the canal behind his house. Came up with a few seeds in the vacuum-cleaner bag. I guess they had bigger fish to fry and decided not to prosecute.'

'Did you find anything on Zilman?'

'No, I suppose it's all part of that grand jury record, and as long as they didn't indict we're not going to get a look at it. Incidentally, Crossman and Rosen, the next-door neighbors, are squeaky clean on the record. Of course you'll remember Mr Rosen is dead, and I haven't interviewed Mrs. She's in New York.'

'Send me a copy of that report,' Gunnar said.

Castillo's arrest and connection with Zilman produced a sinking sensation in Gunnar. Knowing about the arrest, he would have to object if Terry Wood asked Castillo the right question, or make a motion *in limine* to protect him, and that would get his opponents sniffing around in areas they might not even have thought of. Wyman had discovered earlier that the neighbors had not been contacted by Chapin, Cline or anyone connected with the *Times-Journal*. Better not use Mr or Mrs Castillo as a witness. He still had the next-door neighbor, Crossman. What if Crossman knew of Castillo's arrest? It would come out on cross-examination. Of course, Tony Djilas must have known about the arrest, but that wasn't an absolute certainty. Tony's got to get it through his head that he can't hold anything back. The jury can bail out on him on just one surprise. Obviously, Holly hadn't heard about it, or could she have forgotten?

Turning to the mail, Gunnar was pleased to see that the answers to his first set of interrogatories to the *Times-Journal* had arrived. Scanning the first page, he wasn't surprised they listed no witnesses because there was nothing they needed to prove. It rested on Gunnar to prove the case: simply put, that the articles were false, and the newspaper knew it. Only then would the *Times-Journal* have some proving to do. Fully half of all libel cases were dismissed before the defendant was compelled to prove anything. Of course, they had plenty of witnesses in mind should they need them.

On page two, Gunnar had asked them to identify everyone interviewed in preparing the story on Tony. Gunnar recognized several names in city government. Regarding the Florida people whose names Gunnar so eagerly awaited, the newspaper claimed the reporter's privilege not to reveal sources of information obtained under a guarantee of confidentiality. He might be able to get the court to order them to divulge the names. If not, Gunnar might not discover their identity until they were needed as rebuttal witnesses, assuming that he made a believable case of falsity. As Tony said: If we had some ham, we could have some ham and eggs, if we had some eggs. But nobody ever expects these cases to be easy.

On page three, he had demanded the identity of any documents relied on in preparation of the articles. They identified a series of monthly bank statements for 1973 from Bank of the Indies in Freeport, Bahamas and they attached copies. Jesus Christ, January 1973, four deposits: $26,700; $33,440; $25,800 and $41,000. February 1973, two deposits: $18,000 and $66,300. Each month was similar, deposits aggregating about $100,000, with checks written out of the account leaving a year-end balance of about $200,000. In July there was a deposit for $200,000. He had told Tony he hated surprises. 'Anthony Djilas' was printed across the top of each statement. His pal Castillo into smuggling. A million a year going through a foreign bank account. Could be, this case was already over.

Late that afternoon Angela's voice came over the intercom: 'Mr Larson, there's a man on the phone who won't give his name. He says he has something to tell you about the Djilas case.'

Gunnar took the call.

'You, Tony Djilas' lawyer?' The voice was weak and whiny, perhaps someone trying to conceal his identity.

'Yes, who is this?'

'I can tell you some interesting things about those articles on Djilas and those other developers.'

'I'm interested,' Gunnar said.

'It'll cost you twenty-five thousand.'

'Obviously, you will have to identify yourself if we are to do any business.' Gunnar said.

'In time,' the voice said.

'What have you got?'

'If I tell you, I won't get the money, now will I?'

'If you have information that proves the paper knew those allegations about my client were false,' Gunnar said, 'I have no objection to your price. I'll give you my word on the money.'

'What if somebody with the paper had a personal reason they wanted Djilas out of that New City deal?'

'That could be helpful,' Gunnar said.

'I'll get back to you, soon,' the voice said, and the dial tone came on the line.

Inside of an hour the foreign-bank deposits and now this strange call. Proving those articles were published to harm Tony the biggest problem in a libel suit – and then finding out they were true would be the ultimate irony. Gunnar remembered his reaction when Leo had first suggested he take the case. He had to find out if his client was lying to him. *Now*.

'Mr Djilas' secretary says he's out of town until Wednesday,' said Shana. 'He will call you as soon as he gets back.' It was her first day back on the job since the baby was born.

'OK,' said Gunnar, 'I trust Gregory Gunnar is prospering.'

20

Tonight the startling face, more beautiful each time he beheld it, withheld its smile. Mother-of-pearl, white translucent skin revealed fine veins, faintly blue. He moved to pull her to him. She backed away.

'You're late, I expected you an hour ago.'

'Sorry.'

'I wish you'd called.'

'Sorry, I should have.'

'Out of sight, out of mind.'

'Eddie never goes home. I was going over some proof with him on your dad's case.'

'Out of sight, out of mind.'

'And I'm subjected to those stares. If he disagrees, and then you don't immediately see the light you get the goddamn stare.'

'I wish you'd called.'

'But I'd be dead in the water without him.'

'Goddamnit, you should have called. It's after ten.' She whirled and marched into the kitchen.

She had built a fire and shadows danced above the open beams. He dropped into the sofa, and put his feet up on the table. As usual, the bear stared at him with one eye.

Five minutes passed. She didn't come out of the kitchen. He wanted to stay stretched out, eyes closed. The hell with it. The heat felt good. It had been chilly out, stray snowflakes in the air.

Another five minutes. He felt drowsy. He'd better keep his eyes open or he would fall asleep. Sleep would be such a release.

'I'm just your fuck!' From the kitchen, she was in good voice.

Back at her: 'Jesus Christ, I said I was sorry.'

129

'You could have called!'

A broken record. He kept his mouth shut, but any inclination to sleep had disappeared.

'You could have been lying on the road somewhere!'

'But I'm lying here on this nice soft sofa,' he said, not loud enough for her to hear the words distinctly.

It worked. She charged back into the room, a bottle of catawba juice in her hand. 'I don't want to be just somebody's fuck! What did you say, before?'

'Never mind,' he said.

'I want to know what you said!'

'Into every life a little rain must fall.' Why did he say that?

She flung the full bottle of catawba at the fireplace and it shattered on one of the andirons. Coals hissed, as the juice splashed over the blaze. The grape's sweet redolence mingled with the burning cedar. She sat down in a leather wing-chair in front of the bear's face. He resisted the comments fluttering through his mind. She stared into the fire. Started to cry. He decided to get up. Changed his mind. Decided to tell her he was really sorry. Changed his mind. She whimpered into a handkerchief.

'Why don't you come over and sit down with me,' he said.

'Do you know what it feels like to be somebody's fuck?' Sobs interrupted her words.

'I've never heard you talk like this,' he said.

'Well that's how I feel. Libby said this afternoon that she'd give her left tit to have an affair with you.'

'Why not both?'

'You bastard! That's all it is to you – an affair.'

'Jesus Christ,' he said.

'Nothing ever changes,' she said.

'It's only been a few weeks,' he said. 'Come here.'

He put his arm up on the sofa's back to receive her as she got up from the chair and she slid down next to him with her head on his shoulder – like teenage lovers in a movie, neither speaking. He turned his face to her and their open mouths met, grasping. Alternately, they sucked the air from the other's lungs, creating a vacuum in their merged mouths. Feeling no response in his penis surprised him.

Eventually, she unzipped his fly and worked it out through his underwear. It lay in her hand as limp as spaghetti. She didn't seem the least nonplussed. His gut fluttered. She shoved the table back from the couch and pulled his feet down and worked her way between his knees and took the soft cock in her mouth. Still no response. He was numb and dead. She tried milking it with her lips. Not to be denied, she undid his belt and slid his pants and shorts down his legs and cupped his balls in her hand, and nuzzled her face into the flaccid cock. Nothing. He was strangely embarrassed. Up to now, a word from her could stiffen it. Maybe she was cured of throwing bottles. He hoped that was the answer. He saw Anne, smiling, sitting in the corner. Holly got back on the sofa, and he pulled his shorts and pants up.

'Want some coffee?' she said.

'Decaf,' he said. 'I'll try some cream in it for a change, if you've got some.'

She went into the kitchen. He tried to put the limp dick out of his mind. He remembered how the evidence professor had made fun of judicial admonitions to jurors to 'disregard' a bit of startling testimony. One can't ignore a limp dick, can one? As the old professor had said: it was like un-ringing a bell.

She handed him the coffee, instant from the microwave, and sat down beside him. 'I'm sorry, I don't know what got into me.'

'Forget it,' he said, 'but we mustn't forget to clean up the mess in the fireplace.'

'Don't worry,' she said, 'Libby's maid will take care of it. How's Daddy's case coming?'

'Sweetheart, remember Carmine Castillo, your neighbor across the street. Was he ever in any kind of trouble?' He watched her eyes.

She looked away. 'I don't think so,' she said. 'Was he?'

'Don't you think you would have known, if he was?'

'I suppose so,' she said. 'What did he do?'

'I dunno,' he said.

He decided to let it drop.

They watched the dying fire. She took his wrist and pulled his arm around her shoulder. The burning cedar crackled. Fucking under Libby Cochrane's big quilt would soothe him more than watching this fire, but one needed a stiff dick for such pursuits. He loved the texture of her hair, and he pushed his fingers in among the thickness of it, and she turned her face up to him and for the first time that evening she smiled.

'Davey sent a deposit on that fancy condo in Palm Beach today,' Holly said. The smile replaced by a face ready to cry again.

'You knew he was planning to.' So that was why the tantrum.

'I guess I hoped he'd change his mind,' she said.

'Didn't you have fun last year? Besides, he must be committed to work in the Tripp office down there.'

'We've been all through this,' she said. 'You know I can't stand going away alone with him. We're supposed to leave the day after Christmas for three months.'

'I told you before,' Gunnar said, 'during those three months, and for another three months or more after, I'll be working night and day on your dad's case.' If there is a case. With Djilas out of town, he still had his doubts.

'I just want to be near you,' she said. 'I think I am going to tell him I won't go.'

'If you have trouble with Davey now, it could affect your dad's case,' Gunnar said. 'Your trouble is my trouble.'

'I don't want you to have trouble, my darling,' she said, 'but it feels good when you say my trouble is your trouble. I won't do anything to make any trouble.'

Gunnar returned her lovely open smile. Surely she would never lie to him.

21

Eddie Kerr's unhappy morning was worse than usual. He reread the letter from Dexter Epstein.

Dear Mr Kerr,
Thank you very much for the book you sent me. It might be a little over my head but I have plenty of time to work on it. Two years or more to be exact. They have been giving me some medication, to answer your question. They have also been providing a treatment program for my habit, sort of. I get a letter from my Mother almost every day but she is completely out of it as far as I'm concerned. My parents have been here already. I have made no friends but this big black dude is hitting on me to be his punk. I am scared of the S O B. Do you know what I should do? If I complain to anybody on the staff I think I might get killed. I don't know how I can hold this guy off much longer. They got me working in the license-plate factory, and this guy works there too. His name is George Washington. Can you beat that! He is about six-four, and he pulls his big black cock out and says he's saving it for me. The story is that almost everybody comes here straight, but a lot of them get tired of making love to their hand after a year or two. George Washington is doing ten for armed robbery and sodomy, both against the same victim I guess. I saw your firm's name in the paper the other day. Something to do with a big libel case. I told this guy I talk to that I bet you were working on it. I look forward to seeing you when you come to visit. I am counting the days. I have 675 left if I get out after two years. *Shalom*.
> Your friend,
> Dexter

In spite of his supersaturated work schedule, Eddie called to make an appointment with Barry Busch, dean of the criminal Bar. Barry was in trial and couldn't see him for two weeks.

Eddie felt helpless. Worse, Dexter was Eddie's failure and one he could not accept. He recognized his gross inability to cope with most problems he encountered outside the legal profession, but on the inside, where he lived, he must obtain the best possible result, whatever it required. There were no alternatives for him. He hoped Barry Busch would help him find the answer. Maybe he should talk it over with Gunnar. But what did Gunnar know about criminal law or prisons? Eddie was not ready to concede that Gunnar might be able to help him. Gunnar was too quickly willing to look beyond rationality for answers to questions that could clearly be reasoned out. Rationality was all Eddie had.

In air stinking stale sweat, Al Bergdorf took Tony's call in the locker room at the Athletic Club.

'I thought you were still out deer hunting,' Al said.

'I got back last night,' said Tony.

'Did you get your buck?'

'Does the Pope shit in the woods? I was raised in that country, every November I shoot my buck.'

'You didn't call here to tell me about the Pope,' Al said.

'No. They picked a developer.'

'Who got it?'

'Quentin Industries. Ray Flis and that redhead with the big tits.'

'Ruth Renken,' Al said.

'Yeah,' Tony said. 'I guess her Dad has got bucks. They're gonna clean up on this one. Shoulda been mine.'

'I know,' said Al. 'Did you call Gunnar?'

'They're taking my deposition today. I'm with him. They started yesterday.'

'Sure, I forgot.'

'Gunnar's got a special guy workin' on it. A course they been looking at everybody on the list. No reason to believe Flis and Renken are involved with those articles any more than the others. A course, they may know a lot we don't.'

Al asked how the deposition was going. They had spent all of yesterday going over Tony's early life and his career in the city. This morning they'd begun to ask him the details about the real estate transactions that he had been involved in when he lived in Florida, with some questions about Zilman interspersed. Tony had the idea they were going to get into the bank statements from the Bahamas in the afternoon. Gunnar thought they would be at it for at least two weeks.

'So far, so good,' said Tony, 'Call ya tomorrow.'

Al looked down at his protuberant belly. 'Hey Henry, let's throw that medicine ball around a while.'

Tony Djilas rejoined Gunnar and Eddie over box lunches in the small conference-room back at the office. 'Just reported in to the fat man,' he said. 'And Gunnar, about that bank-account shit you brought up while we were waitin' this morning. There's nothin' to it. It was like you askin' Eddie here to set up a bank account for you in some other state.'

Little did Tony know Eddie, Gunnar thought.

'And I never brought it up,' Tony went on, ''cause I just didn't think of it. At the time I figured it was some tax dodge, or he was workin' on some angle for a real estate deal out in the islands. Sure as hell, I didn't think it had anything to do with dope or I would'na hung my name on it.'

'For now, we'll have to put it away,' Gunnar said. 'I want to go back over some of these transactions Wood will be covering.'

Tony grinned affably, 'Sure,' he said, taking a swig at his beer.

22

Hot spray prickled the back of Anne's neck. Her hip joint ached as it always did when she ran the long way – just over six miles – but finishing the course in her best time, ever, lifted her spirits. Walking off the end of her run, she had seen Gunnar's car turn on to the main road, heading for downtown. Katie was sleeping in. Constitutional law had been cancelled.

Over the shower's hiss, she heard the telephone. Damn. She grabbed a towel and picked it up on the third ring.

'Mrs Larson?' It was a woman's voice.

'Yes, who is this?' To leave her hands free, she held the phone between her head and shoulder. She wiped her face with the towel and wrapped it around her body, tucking it into itself under her arm.

'I don't feel I can give you my name. Suffice it to say, I'm a neighbor, here at Preacher's Bay.'

'So what do you want?'

'I have some information I think you should have. I know if it were me, I'd want to know.'

Anne said nothing. A weight pressed on her chest. Water from her hair ran down her face.

'Are you there?'

'Yes, I'm here,' Anne said. She exhaled, not realizing she'd been holding her breath.

'Ever since last summer, your husband has been driving into Libby Cochrane's lane. Sometimes twice a week . . . usually on Tuesday or Thursday night. Sometimes both . . . very late in the evening. I've seen him go in there on Saturday, too, during the day.'

'Why are you telling me this?' Anne thought of nothing else to say. She remembered the row of smaller houses along Preacher's Bay Road near the turn-in to Cochrane's.

'Libby was divorced last spring you know. She lives alone, except for the help.'

Anne listened, said nothing.

'You know his license plate says 'lawyer'. It's been too dark to see, the last couple of months, but I know it's the same gray car . . . Cadillac, I think. He was there again last night.'

'Goodbye,' said Anne. But he's impotent, she had wanted to scream. She had met Libby Cochrane a couple of times, just casually. She was overweight and buxom, but a pretty face, close to her own age, maybe a little younger. Not the kind to worry a wife, except for her money. The Cochranes had legendary money. But Gunnar wouldn't be attracted by the money. Or would he?

She let the towel drop around her feet. Naked in the full-length mirror, a startled tear below her eye, at fifty-three, only the faintest lines showed in her porcelain forehead. Below the high cheekbones, the flesh sagged slightly to a nascent fold along the jaw. There was some excess skin under her chin, some extra tissue around her eyes. Eventually, she wanted a face-lift, and something done to her eyes and neck. Her fine blonde hair was abundant and always styled with flair. Her belly was almost flat, just a little extra flesh she couldn't make go away. Well-shaped breasts hung down more than when she was a girl, but not that much. Her upper arms were still taut, and she had darn good legs, everybody said that. Ten years of running had hardened her thighs. She turned so that she could see the mirror over her shoulder. A trace of cellulite clung to the back of her upper thighs, but her butt only drooped a little, and the curve of her hip ran smoothly into her upper leg. Five-six, a hundred thirty-five, Anne had always been secretly proud of her figure. Libby Cochrane would lose in any category of comparison.

They kept the heat low for sleeping and the December chill braced her damp skin. She wrapped the towel around her wet hair, crawled back into bed, pulled the pale-blue comforter over her head. Could Gunnar possibly have some legitimate business at the Cochranes'? The woman might be mistaken, or maybe making it up. But right down to his personalized license plate?

In a city known for beautiful women, why would he choose Libby Cochrane? Did the old money have some erotic appeal Anne couldn't understand? Libby's house was the largest on the whole lake. Could that cure his impotence?

Tap, tap on the bedroom door. It had to be Katie. Anne hesitated. Again, the tapping.

'Come in,' she said.

'Hi Mom, What are you doing in bed? I heard the phone.' Katie had a pink terry-cloth robe wrapped around her.

'I wanted to do some thinking,' Anne said.

Katie sat down on the edge of the bed. 'I know there's something wrong, and this morning *we* are going to talk about it.'

'I don't know if today is the best day,' Anne said.

'It's the only day we can be sure of. Today's the day. Move over.' With her robe still on, Katie slipped under the comforter, her back propped against the padded headboard. 'Who called?' she asked.

From the moment Katie walked through the door, Anne had been planning how to answer that question. No lie occurred to her. 'Someone who didn't give her name.'

'What did she want?'

'She told me your father is having an affair.'

'Oh Mom!' said Katie. 'In those words?'

'No, but she said he's been going to Libby Cochrane's house twice a week for months.'

'Oh Mom, do you believe her?'

'Why would she lie?'

'Couldn't he be involved in some business deal or legal work?'

'Cochranes are divorced as of last spring, and I know Gunnar didn't represent her.'

'Is this what's been wrong all these last months? Did you suspect him?'

You don't tell your daughter that her father is impotent, or at least impotent with you. You don't tell anyone, except maybe a doctor or professional of some kind. 'No, I didn't suspect,' Anne said.

'What could he see in her? I've been over there when her daughter Sarah had parties. She's nice enough, but far out of your league.'

'Maybe it's the money,' Anne said.

'Daddy's not into money, like that. Is he? Besides we must be rich enough.'

'Honey, we're not rich. Even if we were, your father would think of himself as a poor man with money – never rich.'

They spent an hour speculating on the reasons, and Anne said she felt they were steadily growing apart and she didn't know what to do about it. After Jack's death, Gunnar had never let her in. Both of them cried at different times, and then together, Anne with her head in Katie's lap.

Finally Katie said, 'I won't believe it until I see it, or he tells me.'

Katie suggested they go to the dining room. She could make tea while Anne dried her hair. A few minutes later they looked across the frozen waters of the bay separated from dark sky by the trees on the far shore. A foot of snow covered the lawn.

'Do you remember how the four of us used to lie on the carpet and watch TV, when I was about four or five, and Jack was nine or ten? You on one side and Dad on the other, and the two of you would lock your arms across our backs?'

'Of course, I remember. When Jack died, that was one of the images I saw most often.' Anne's mind raced through a jumble of disconnected thoughts and memories.

'Doesn't Daddy remember?'

'He remembers.'

Katie picked a lump of sugar from the bowl and popped it in her mouth.

'Uh uh uh, still stealing sugar lumps,' Anne said. 'I think you were less than a year old when I caught you the first time. You could have choked to death.'

'You won't leave him, will you?'

'I'm not even sure he's done anything, but no matter what he's done, I won't leave him. Not now, maybe not ever. But it may not be up to me.'

'He promised me,' said Katie, 'that he would never do anything to hurt me.'

She told Anne about the talk in the gazebo on the tenth anniversary of Jack's death. Anne said she didn't want to hang on to a man because of a promise he made to someone else, even Katie. Katie said she understood. Anne told her she loved him as much as she ever did, but she wasn't sure how he really felt. She wasn't sure he still loved her. Both of their faces were wet with tears.

'I know divorce isn't unusual,' said Katie. 'Two of my best friends have divorced parents. You know: Paula and Celia. And for that matter, old Winston, my erstwhile flame . . . the one who gave up the law for Wall Street. That was one of the things that made me nervous about him – the bitterness between his parents. They actually hated each other.'

'How could I forget Winston?' Anne said. 'I didn't feel bad when you two called it quits. He always had to find something wrong with everything.'

'But not you and Daddy,' Katie said. 'You two are a unit, indivisible. You used to sit one on either end of the sofa, looking into each other's eyes for the longest time. You didn't know I was watching, and you would start rubbing your toes together, and then one of you would slide your foot up the other's leg, way to the crotch and you'd either end up in a clinch or you would get up and go in the bedroom. Not just once or twice. It happened all the time. I started noticing when I was about ten and . . . oh Mom, all the way up until Jack . . . .'

Anne remembered. 'You know . . . he may never get over it,' she said.

They talked until almost noon when Katie had to run to make a one o'clock class. With the problem at least partially in the open, they could talk more.

Anne had her own memories. The best times of all were in the den. Gunnar used to sit in a big over-stuffed chair with his feet on an ottoman. She would kneel down between his legs and put her head on his lap and he would stroke her hair as long as she stayed. He never complained about the interruption. He just put the paper or book aside, and stroked her hair, and sometimes they talked for hours.

She could never tell Katie about one memory, seared into her flesh. The kids were at his parents. She had showered and perfumed and dried her long hair and brushed it out the way he liked, loose and fluffy. Naked, she'd crept up behind him in the living room. He was stretched out on his stomach, his chest on a pillow, propped on his elbows reading the paper. She walked over him, her feet on either side of his back, and crouched down on her haunches just above his neck, and he turned over, his face in her crotch, and she bent her head down and his head on the pillow was enveloped in her long hair, and she presented herself to his mouth and he eagerly accepted her offer. Oh God, her body ached for him, now as much as then. If only just his fingers enfolded in hers.

23

Every December the sun disappeared. Eddie Kerr followed the freeway north-west heading to Watsonville State Prison. Icy spots remained on the pavement from a light snow the night before. He drove cautiously, not having much experience with cross-country travel, and he harbored protective feelings for his yellow Mazda – purchased new, five years before. This trip should turn the odometer past 18,000. Beneath winter clouds that touched the swells in the plain, the drifts and swirls of white covered the open countryside like meringue on an uncut pie. Clusters of farm buildings hid out of the wind in ragged groves.

Dexter had been in Watsonville for almost three months, and Eddie had gotten one letter from him a month ago. Prisoners were allowed liberal use of the telephone, but Eddie was glad that Dexter wasn't calling. The current work schedule wouldn't permit it. Eddie had taken this day off grudgingly. But he thought of his miserable little client every day, and worry was mixed with fright. Barry Busch had said that Dexter could opt for PC, the protective-custody unit. Eager to relay the good news, Eddie left a call at the prison. When Dexter telephoned back, he was adamant: no 'Snitchville' or 'Fag Town' for him. Still, he said his problem with George Washington had not gone away.

Approaching Watsonville from the South-east, off to the right, the prison was set in a study of grays. Against gunsmoke sky, the dark wall made an even border above the lighter second-growth forest. Almost noon, Eddie decided to have a sandwich before meeting Dexter.

An hour later a guard led Eddie into a large room filled with pairs of chairs. They faced the front in rows with an arm in between. Augmented by long fluorescent tubes on the ceiling,

142

light filtered through barred narrow windows extending across the top of the sand-coated plaster wall in front. On a dais below the windows, raised about two feet above the floor, two blue-uniformed guards sat behind a table reading magazines. About half the seats were filled with couples of all races, two men in some, but a man and a woman in most. The pairs along one wall were separated from the others by short partitions. It was to one of these cubicles that the guard led Eddie. Dexter waiting, stood up and extended his hand. After the rubbery handshake and perfunctory greetings, Eddie placed his wide rump into one of the chairs and Dexter, jail-pale and even skinnier than when he was sentenced, sat down beside him.

'You're looking good, maybe a little thin,' said Eddie. 'I should try your diet.'

Dexter said he didn't think Eddie would like it. Too starchy. He thanked Eddie for coming. He said Eddie had been his only visitor besides his parents who had been there twice. The words were there, but they were flat, without expression. He looked even smaller sitting in the forlorn dark green prison-issue. His face was slack, a faraway sadness in his dark brown eyes.

For the moment, Eddie was intimidated by the subject of the letter. He had told him any good news he had on the telephone, the PC, and prospective transfers to other states. For openers he tried, 'Read any more of the science fiction?'

'I'm having trouble understanding it,' Dexter said, 'I can't concentrate in here.'

Eddie had forgotten the small package on his lap. They had unwrapped and inspected it in the office, and the guard had expertly rewrapped it in the green tissue with red ribbon. 'Here, I almost forgot. Happy Hanukkah.'

'Oh, thanks, thanks a lot.' Dexter put it on his lap.

'Go on, open it,' said Eddie.

Dexter tore off the ribbon and the paper. It was a micro-recorder, the kind businessmen and lawyers dictate letters and memoranda on. 'It's nice,' he said, 'but they'll steal it. They steal everything.'

'I thought maybe you could record your experiences and

thoughts. They might be of value to you someday,' Eddie said. 'Maybe you could hide it.'

'For a while, but then somebody will see it, and they'll steal it.' Flat words with no tone of anger.

'I understand the recreational facilities are quite good here?' said Eddie.

'Yeah, they're OK, but it gets you close to them,' Dexter said.

Eddie decided not to ask who 'them' was. Instead he jumped into the area he had been thinking about for weeks. 'What's going on with this George Washington character?'

'I'm his punk,' Dexter said.

'What does that mean? You know, I don't normally do criminal work,' Eddie said.

'When I first got in here I was scared . . . awful scared,' Dexter said. 'I didn't know who to talk to, and I was younger and smaller than almost all of them, and the blacks really scared the hell out of me. Growing up in New York and riding the subway and going to Coney Island and that kind of thing, I learned to be scared of blacks. One of my friends got shanked in the Union Square Station . . . . This place is full of blacks.'

As he listened, Eddie watched the side of Dexter's face. His skin was whiter and his lips protruded more than Eddie remembered.

'The Cubans are even scarier,' Dexter said, 'but that's another story. There are over a hundred of them in here. Anyway, this guy Foster, who turned out to be a friend of George Washington's, if you can call it that, came into my cell about a week after I got here. Told me he had some pot and he could get coke or ludes or whatever I wanted.'

'God, how do they get it in here?'

'Up their ass, women in their snatch – you name it. The guards sell it to certain guys. Anyway, he said I could have the stuff. Pay 'em some other time. He acted like he didn't care if he got paid. So, like a dummy, I never got around to paying him.' Dexter had smoked his first cigarette down to nothing, and he stopped to light a second. 'About a week later he came up to me out in the yard, and said, "Don't forget, you owe me." I said, "How much?" He said, "More'n you got mothfug. Sides I don't want no money, I'll let you know."'

'What did he want?'

'Sex. He and George Washington worked as a team. What I didn't know is that the population will support you against these kinds of guys, except when you owe them.'

'But you were willing to pay,' Eddie said.

'Made no difference.'

'You could have transferred out of here to Connecticut,' Eddie said.

'It wouldn't be any different anyplace else; if anything, worse. The old cons around here say this is some of the best time in the country. And my mother would have been there all the time. I can't stand her. She's wrecked my father's life. I don't want her in mine.'

For the first time Eddie detected some emotion in his client. He hated his mother worse than prison. He waited for him to go on.

'Anyway, a day later, George Washington walks into my cell and tells me that Foster had turned me over to him to be his punk. I told him Foster had no right to turn me over to anybody. Then he unzips his pants and lets them drop to the floor. I'm sitting on the bunk and he sticks his hard-on right in my face. I figured a guard would probably see him, but I learned later that he had Foster on lookout. That's one way they worked together.'

'I guess "punk" means sex partner,' Eddie said.

'Yeah, that's what it means. When guys like me come in here, the man tells you to scream your lungs out if somebody tries to force sex on you, so I told George Washington that I was gonna start screaming.'

'What'd he do?'

'He said if I didn't let him do it, he would see that I got raped the next day. And if I snitched ever he would see that I got raped . . . . I saw a guy get raped. He was a bigmouth. Five or six guys bent him over the railing on the third tier, and one of them shoved a rag in his mouth and two held him with his arms around the railing and they all raped him. It took fifteen – twenty minutes. I don't think that guy'll ever be the same . . . I guess I won't either.'

Eddie's stomach was fluttering. He didn't want to hear the rest, but he knew he had to. 'What do you mean, you won't either.'

Dexter wiped his eye. 'Right then I thought about what you said about PC again, but I figured I wasn't gonna get out of that cell without doing what he wanted anyway. Then he told me that he would protect me from everybody and everything if I would be his punk. You gotta understand what it's like for a guy like me to be in here. You're scared all the time. Once you're in PC, you're labeled a faggot or snitch for the rest of your term, and I didn't know what it was like in there. I still don't. I know a lot of them are queers, probably loaded with Aids.'

Dexter's reasoning didn't escape Eddie. He had spent his own life scared, in and out of the practice. He worked hard at not letting anyone know. He stopped looking at Dexter. They both looked straight ahead. Peripherally, Eddie felt Dexter glancing his way, every few sentences. Eddie had never heard anyone, queer or otherwise, tell about a personal homosexual experience.

'All the while he was standing there,' Dexter said, 'he had his hard-on aimed right at my face. He was trying to reason with me. I was afraid he wanted me to suck it, but then he took this tube of vaseline out of his shirt pocket and said if I would turn over and kneel on the bunk, I didn't have to worry about sucking him and he'd make sure he didn't hurt me – and he'd take care of me from then on. I tried one last thing.' Dexter put the cigarette out. 'Do you want me to finish?'

All Eddie managed was a quiet, 'OK.'

'I offered him five grand. I said I could get it from my dad.'

'No good?'

'No good, he said he had ten years to do; he wanted to fuck. Money was no good to him. So I turned over. He's been doing it to me three – four times a week, maybe more.' His tone had become absolutely flat again. 'And don't get the idea I'm the only one. I'm special, just his, but the population is full of guys who volunteer – they actually like it.'

Eddie Kerr looked at him, and waited until Dexter turned, and their eyes came together. He had never looked into eyes as deep and sad. 'I'm really terribly sorry,' Eddie said.

Dexter didn't look away. 'It's not as bad as it sounds, at least in comparison to what I'm really afraid of,' he said.

'What's that?'

'Aids,' Dexter said.

In room 2607, Downtown Hilton, Dov Levy prepared his first comprehensive report for Gunnar Larson on a laptop computer. Yesterday, Gunnar had completed Ward Chapin's deposition. The week before Suzie Cline had given hers. The anonymous caller had telephoned once more in mid-October, but he sounded scared and added nothing.

Many essentials of the target companies and individuals were provided by an information broker. Dov found the rest on his own. His training served him well. He had photographed hundreds of letters and other memoranda written and received by the people on the list supplied by Mayor Steve Carpenter. He made tapes of numerous telephone calls and other private conversations from their offices, none of them the wiser. In case of discovery, Dov had devised an elaborate cover story: the information was to be sold to the highest bidder, presumably somebody in the media interested in doing an exposé on the politics of city-development contracts.

Gunnar Larson didn't know how he did it, nor would Dov tell him, but bits and pieces Dov had transmitted had already broadened Gunnar's discovery horizons. The law office had served *subpoenas duces tecum* on each individual on the list, requiring them to produce correspondence and other documents, confounding to the recipients in the specificity of the demands. All of them suspected leaks in their own organizations. Inquisitions were held; some even preserved on tape by Dov's voice-activated recorders. Unfair firings occurred. The leaks remained unexposed, and the victims of Dov's diligence didn't dare ignore the subpoenas. Of course, none ruled out burglary, but to his knowledge Dov had left no clues. One thing was certain, playing strictly within the rules Tony Djilas' attorney would never have learned about the Pentecost correspondence, or the unlabeled envelope Dov had found under a ream of paper in publisher Carlyle Henning's drawer on one of his late-night visits to the *Times-Journal* offices. As he typed the last line of the section regarding the unlabeled envelope, Dov felt a swell of satisfaction. There was still work to do, but he knew he had provided Gunnar with at least the genesis of a case of malice.

24

Across the festooned room, in front of a stone fireplace burning four-foot long logs, Holly Tripp, in green silk and sequins, held forth within a circlet of young men. A rare gazelle, Al decided as he observed the abrupt little curve from waist to buttocks, ankles slender as fairies' wrists, all enhanced by the shimmering silk, taut across her thighs. A sprig of mistletoe hung down from the beam above her head . . . . There was a day . . . . Al went back to the smooth nutty smoke of the Havana.

Since coming home from World War Two Davey Tripp III's father, David Tripp Jr, had traditionally hosted a Sunday afternoon holiday open house. Every December Tripp and Company upper level employees, top accounts and close friends journeyed with their spouses and lovers to Chateau Tripp in the far south suburbs, solidly among an enclave of multimillionaires' mansions encircling sylvan Stratford Pond, all half-hidden in a forest even older than the portfolios supporting those venerable estates.

As part of the gloomy process not yet abandoned – though hope waned – of preparing Davey III for the helm of Tripp and Company, this year his father had decided to move the open house to Davey and Holly's eight-thousand-square-foot honeymoon cabin on the shores of Preacher's Bay. A snake of parked cars twisted through the woods from the house to Preacher's Bay Road where its split tongue strung out in both directions along the berms of bridal white snow, piled up by the plows.

Al Bergdorf was the only Jew invited. Everyone had to pass muster with old man Tripp, but Davey's marriage to Tony Djilas' daughter qualified Tony's best friend for the guest list. Stratford Pond, and the banks and businesses owned by its denizens, had

149

always been off-limits to the brethren. Between the wars, when the last conveyances were recorded, deeds to such living human beings as Albert Einstein and Sigmund Freud would have been void, not to mention Jesus of Nazareth who had passed away sometime earlier. Simon Bergdorf had no desire to enter the enclave as resident, but such affronts might have inspired him to surpassing achievement, cultural and commercial. He had probably accumulated as much wealth as most of *them*: those same snobs flocked enthusiastically to showings of Simon's art collection, understanding little and talking much.

Simon had started with nothing. Born in Russia, the son of immigrants fleeing to America from Czarist pogroms, he worked his way through college and law school, with side trips to Château-Thierry and the Argonne Forest with the Rainbow Division in 1918. In Paris, just before going home, the seeds of his passion for art were sown.

Aside from his profession at the Bar, Al had travelled a different road than his father. He saw nothing particularly interesting in art; business profits didn't motivate him – he was an heir to a fortune, unfortunately to be divided with three sisters – but he liked being a spoiler, making the unexpected happen. Sometimes devious, but always clever, he was known throughout the Bar for nothing as much as sheer effrontery. Not to say he didn't know the whole game, and well. After a short marriage, he had been lonely. Now, he sat alone, eating from a small plate heaped with canapés and other delicacies. Tony Djilas had not yet arrived.

Holly finally met Al's eyes, took her leave, and swung across the room to his rescue. 'Mr Bergdorf, so glad you could come. Don't you get up.'

'Al,' he said.

'Merry Christmas, or, should I say, Happy Hannukah?'

'Whatever pleases the most beautiful one at the ball,' Al said. 'Merry Christmas to you!' *Holy shit*. She sat on the arm of his chair. Her perfume spoke to him of better days. 'You know, I have it both ways, my son married a shik . . . Christian.'

'Wonderful, Al, it isn't the words anyway, is it? Are you getting enough of everything?' A waiter exchanged a full glass of champagne for Al's empty, and Holly turned down the offer of one.

'The buffet is great. Of course, as usual I've had more than my share. Where's your dad?'

She told him Tony would be there any minute, and took her leave, thanking him again for coming and suggesting he mingle. He declined politely, and before Al had finished his goodies Tony came in, blustering with greetings. When Davey heard father-in-law's voice he made it a trio.

Al held up his glass, splashing a little champagne on the suede armchair, 'To off-shore bank accounts.'

'Cut it out you schmuck,' Tony said, 'Gunnar believes me, and he's a real attorney.' A navy blazer emphasized the silver waves. 'And 'tis the season to be jolly,' and in a sweet tenor, 'Fa, la, la, la, la, la, la, laaaah.' Heads turned. 'Let's try some eggnog.'

Davey sent a waiter.

'I thought Gunnar was invited,' Al said. Tripling his chin, he examined the wine spots on his paisley tie.

'Holly says he couldn't make it,' said Davey.

Holly beckoned to Davey and he left the group, already not completely sure-footed.

'What's with Gunnar? This is the top invite in town,' Al said, 'I thought your daughter had influence with him?'

'My fat friend, that's worrying me. Might be something amiss. S'why he didn't show. Lives less than a mile; you can see his place from the boathouse.'

'Wasamatter? This looks like a nice setup.'

'She's been through a lot with men,' Tony said. 'This ain't the prize it looks like. A course, the money's unbelievable. Davey's old man is worth a hundred mil or more . . . speak of the fuckin' devil.'

Old man Tripp entered the room through a door in the far corner, patrician in every detail, tall and ramrod straight despite his seventy-five years: dark suit, small white mustache, white hair, perfectly trimmed, combed straight back from a forehead reaching to the top of his head. He began pumping selected hands; as he neared Al and Tony's corner, he noticed them, nodded, and went back to more selected hands.

'Hope he's seen a Jew before,' said Al.

'The sonofabitch, couldn't carry your old man's bag.'

'My old man never hit a golf ball in his life.'

'Details,' said Tony.

'Davey tells me he and Holly are heading for Palm Beach for three months,' Al said. 'They got an office down there, you know. Maybe that'll cool this Gunnar thing off.'

'Don't jump to conclusions, Counselor. I only said I have a feeling. I don't know when she'd see the guy. He and that Eddie Kerr work ridiculous hours, and Gunnar lives with his wife.'

'Hope it's just hero-worship, he must have twenty, twenty-five years on her.'

'Look at her,' Tony said. 'She's just a kid.'

'Some kid.' Al shoved a whole canapé in his mouth, wiped his lips with the back of his hand, and pulled a six-inch Havana out of his inside coat-pocket.

'Hey, there's the mayor! I'll get him.' Tony got up and pushed through the crowd.

A waiter arrived with three eggnogs. Davey came back, took one, handed Al another. 'To an early spring,' Davey said, holding his eggnog high.

'Whasadifference,' Al said, 'you'll be playing golf all winter in Palm Beach.'

A violinist with bushy hair in a burgundy tuxedo played 'Santa Claus is Coming to Town' quietening the room a little. Tony came back with the mayor and several followers.

'Don't get up Al, top of the season to you.' The mayor reached down and took his hand.

'Howarya,' said Al.

The fiddler joined Holly at the grand piano. They played 'Away in a Manger'. Everyone listened, some joined in. Al enjoyed it, but he had never learned the words. And then, 'Jingle Bells'. This one he could sing.

'Hey!' Tony yelled when the music stopped, 'My lawyer's got a great story, gather round.'

Al was caught off guard. 'Whaterya talkin' about?'

'You know . . . the guy auditioning for the big shot,' Tony said.

At least thirty people bunched up before Al's chair. Old man Tripp's face appeared in the back among the others. That was all Al needed.

'You see,' Al said in the silent room. 'There were three law firms trying for this big corporation's business, and they were all three going to get an audience with the CEO. The first was a hundred-man firm.' Al's delivery included elaborate gestures. 'They put on a real dog-and-pony show, brought in computers, accountants and everything, and made a presentation that took most of an hour. When they were through the old man said, "Just one more thing, what's two and two?" The lawyers were flabbergasted, surprised by the question. It must be a trick. They conferred among themselves, with the accountants, even ran the computer.' Al peered at his audience as if they were a jury. 'Finally, the senior partner says to the CEO, "It appeahs to be four."' Al sucked on the Havana and paused to enjoy.

'Next it was the two-hundred-man outfit's turn. Even more dogs and ponies. Took more than an hour. When they were through they got the same question, "What's two and two?" It took them twice as long.' Al gave them the time they needed. 'Finally, with consternation, the head man said, "Four, we're quite certain, sir."'

Al cleared his throat with a crude gargle. 'Now, it was my firm. I walked in alone, told the CEO we would do our best and I handed him a list of top companies our little thirty-man outfit had represented for decades.' Al kept coming back to meet old man Tripp's steely eyes. 'The CEO said, "Is that all?" I said, "We show instead of tell." He said, "'One more thing, what's two and two?" I backed away from the table looking at his associates, walked back across the room, opened the door, looked up and down the hall, and then I came back to where he was sitting, and I leaned across the table and whispered in his ear, "What do you want it to be?"'

The crowd roared, including old man Tripp.

Al took another suck on his cigar, and with a self-satisfied smile, he said, 'We got the business.'

'That's my lawyer!' said Tony.

Holly was back at the piano, the burgundy tuxedo behind her, richly polished fiddle at the ready. She motioned to her father. Tony walked to the piano with springy steps. Father standing in front, daughter sitting before the keyboard, both sporting their hundred-tooth grins, she and the violinist began to play 'Silent Night'. Tony sang it through in a glorious tenor. The room was as quiet as a Horowitz concert.

'Sleeeep in heavenly peeeeee-eace . . . slee-eee-ep in heavenly peace.'

Somehow, Al enjoyed celebrating the birth of history's most famous Jew.

Seventeen miles away in the Downtown Hilton, Dov Levy still labored on his report to Gunnar Larson. It had claimed the entire weekend, night and day. Just having completed the summary, he was typing page 47 – recommendations for further investigation:

Attorney Work-Product
Eyes of Gunnar Larson Only

1. Need dossier on Carlyle Henning, publisher, *T-J*, including exploration of spring '86 social event. Before deposing, suggest supplementary interrogatories pursuant to page 33 workup.

2. Suspect you have learned all you can re Chapin. I will continue to supplement dossier.

3. Suggest you take contractor Pierce Pentecost's deposition without revealing extent of our information. I will continue to supplement dossier.

4. I will renew investigation of Cline in connection with social event. As I have said she has thus far revealed nothing in that regard.

5. I am considering Miami trip in connection with Chapin. I will discuss this with you before leaving.

6. I am almost ready to eliminate the contract winners as factors. I intend one further step in supplement to Renken dossier.

Happy Holidays.

Dov submitted his report to Gunnar on a three-and-one-half-inch computer disk and kept one for himself. The bomb to blow Suzie Cline out of the witness box was already on the drawing board. Others would follow.

25

Al Bergdorf tucked the translucent beard under the ermine trim of the Santa Claus hat. Daughter-in-law Laura, blonde and chunky, climbed the open stair in the foyer to fetch Al's two grandchildren; Eric Allan, four and Betsy, two-and-a-half. To Al, the little boy's middle name was as important as his first. Laura insisted it be Allan. She was grateful to him, the only member of his son's family that didn't make war over the concession to raise the grandchildren Christian. Al had not gone to synagogue after he'd graduated from prep school. Ex-wife Ruth had raised son Simon Jewish but soon after his Bar Mitzvah, he, too, had abandoned religion completely; that is, except for the eighties' yuppie faith in the power of money.

Al heard them at the top of the open stairway: Eric Allan, dark like father and grandfather, already equipped with brown-rimmed glasses and wee Betsy, a towhead. When she saw Santa she screamed in C above high C. Eric Allan yelled 'Wow!' They bounced down the stairs to where Al stood with his big bag, mysterious in its bulk. Neither saw him as anyone but a real Santa needing no padding.

'Ho, ho, ho! Merry Christmas,' said Al, in the deepest tones he could manage, his voice well disguised. 'What have we here?'

Al dragged the canvas trove into the living room, where the maternal grandparents, vaguely gray, waited on the sofa with mustachioed Simon. A mammoth pine tree, veiled in silver, filling the whole corner of the room, grew out of a mound of treasure, concealed in holiday packaging. The two little persons followed him. 'Have you been good all year?' High-strung Eric Allan jumped up and down in place; giggling; Betsy copied.

'Yes, Santa,' said Eric Allan.

Betsy just giggled.

Al dug in the bag. 'Ho, ho, ho! Here's one for you.' He handed a big box wrapped in Christmas paper to Eric Allan. 'And for you, Merry Christmas!' Another, green with red ribbon, to Betsy.

Al loved the commotion. He emptied the bag, one item at a time. Laura made two piles behind each child: one, a couple of the larger packages; the other, all the rest. Al grinned under the irritating floss. Eric Allan tore the wrappings off an intricate plastic machine of destruction, first seen on his favorite Saturday-morning TV show. Betsy whooped over a sweet-faced doll with real blonde curls, dressed in a two-piece suit. The small piles unwrapped, it was time, by the negotiated terms, for Al to leave to make room for Grandma Ruth. He would come back in the evening to watch them open his personal gifts, and receive those for him.

With more 'ho-ho's' and exchanges of season's greetings Al took his leave. The last words he heard as the door closed behind him were Eric Allan's, 'Is Grandpa Al coming today?' His careful disguise had worked for three years in a row. It might be the last year to deceive Eric Allan.

He backed his Mercedes out of the drive in the clear sunshine, temperature still frigid. Driving slowly, he met Grandma Ruth in hers. Santa Claus waved out an open window. Ruth, looking straight ahead, ignored him. He drove on, alone.

Three degrees latitude north of the scene of Eric Allan and Betsy's excitement, a Canada goose, interrupted in its flight south, was Christmas dinner at the Kerrs'.

Mingled with the odor of roasting goose throughout the morning, the smells of sweet potatoes, dressing and biscuits had drifted through the old house. In her kitchen with sloping floor and cheap linoleum, creating a dinner for her three men was the high point of Mother Kerr's life. This year Eddie had added a new sewing machine to his praise of her cooking. Top of the line. She was ecstatic. During the meal, with her hovering over them seeing to their smallest need, father and the two brothers attended earnestly to the business of feasting. Later, waiting for the pumpkin pie, with real whip cream, and more coffee, they began the serious talk.

'You still workin' them long hours, Pudge?' Fred had never gotten over using the name he gave Eddie.

Eddie hated it. 'It's the only way to get the work done,' he said.

'I've been telling them down at the mill, Ed, you're always on the biggest case they got. Ain't that a fact?' His father had called him by his given name since he made partner, and apparently he was sticking with it. It had been over a year.

'Weren't you working on that Miracle Mills thing that was in the papers? I told them guys there's at least one person from this town gonna make a name for himself.'

'Yes, I worked on the Miracle Mills case,' Eddie said. He saw the headlines in the weekly *Argus*: 'Pudge Kerr's Imprisoned Client Succumbs to Aids.'

Mother refilled their cups. Someone was tipping over headstones at the cemetery; seven girls in the senior class had become pregnant; the Catholics actually had guitar players and folk singing in church on Sunday morning; the Pentecostal minister was caught in bed with the sixteen-year-old soprano soloist from the choir; the mill was laying off over a hundred after the first of the year.

Fred was moving up to senior loan officer. In spite of his robust body and handsome face with innocent eyes, he hadn't hooked up with another girl since Joanne Iverson called off the wedding seven years ago. At thirty-eight, Fred's face still sustained a perpetual smile. What Eddie couldn't do with Fred's looks at Lawson and Larson! Eddie made triple the money, but probably didn't save much more. Fred had somebody to cook for him, do his wash, make his bed, and he had time to read what he wanted. Not that his taste in reading was much: outdoor magazines and *Newsweek*. At least he reads some books. *The Hunt for Red October* was on his bedside table.

Eddie read himself to sleep on good writing, but his own writing style didn't change. He had not detected the secret. Eddie remained prolix, often circling the point like a vulture riding the air currents. Gunnar and others bitched, demanded cuts, rewrites, ignoring whole arguments. They said judges weren't interested. What did Gunnar know? He rarely wrote anything, at least not since Eddie knew him. Dictating memos telling people what to do was his specialty, but he had a bewitching talent to get people to agree with him. It didn't work with Eddie. He agreed with Gunnar only when they reached the same conclusion by coincidence. However Gunnar arrived, Eddie got there reasoning, applying a scholar's logical procedures. Exploring legal issues, he read the statutes, if there were any on point, and the comments and law review articles; he traced the cases, and read them beginning to end, digging for gems, immutable signals, leaving judges no choice but to agree. Reason was the basis of advancing knowledge. Choosing law, he could make a living reasoning. Gunnar relied too much on his guts – intuition, he called it. Intuition was another name for the lucky guess. Truth was something you worked for. You didn't find it lying around like a gold nugget. And at the culmination of a diligent search it was your property.

Eddie wondered if Dexter Epstein's parents had showed up as promised. Maybe he should call? On the phone yesterday, Dexter's voice had remained flat, as though he was partially sedated. He probably was. Qualudes proliferated in the prison.

Mother began to clear the dinner table. Father and brother gossiped on. Eddie saw Dexter as he had seen him two weeks ago: withered; dimly concave; victim, albeit of his own stupidity, but victim nonetheless, symbol of a lost case.

That evening Eddie said his goodbyes. His father shook his hand with a firmness that startled the son, totally new, actually transmitting affection.

'The boat and motor is the best gift I ever got, Ed,' he said.

'I'm glad you like it.'

'I hope you'll come up next summer and try it out with me.'

'Sure, Dad.' Eddie doubted that he would, but he felt satisfied. He had worked hard on the selection process, weighing many alternatives. His father's face told him he was right. The same for his mother, and the Browning Automatic was correct for Fred. Three for three. He had gotten a rod and reel from Fred, and a wool shirt from his parents. He knew his mother had picked it out. Over the years she had given him others, all in red and black squares like a checkerboard. Now, four hung in his closet. Father, mother and brother all said Eddie had to come in the spring so he could use both gifts out fishing. Perhaps they all loved each other, but nobody was saying.

With both of the Fleetham children out of town for Christmas, Gunnar and Anne invited Fleet and Rose for dinner. Having finished clearing the dishes from the blue linen with Rose's help, Anne pulled the drapes against the blinding sun, caroming off fresh crystalline snow.

'With that sun, you'd never guess it was below zero,' Fleet said, his big brown eminence dominating the end of the table opposite Gunnar.

The women's voices drifted to another part of the house. Gunnar and Fleet lingered over coffee. Gunnar hoped his unusual reticence remained unnoticed. Tomorrow Holly was leaving for Palm Beach. He might not see her for three months.

'How's that super-spy working out?'

With just the two of them in the room he had to get into the conversation. Be polite. 'Good,' he said.

'Don't want to talk about it?'

'I don't want to compromise you in your position,' Gunnar said.

'Are you saying he's breaking the law?'

'Heavens, no!'

'How would I be compromised if he's legal?'

'Frankly, Fleet, I don't know how he's doing it, but he's coming up with interesting stuff. Some very helpful.'

'Kind of mysterious for a civil case. Aren't you worried he could blow it for you?

'It's crossed my mind, but it's clear from our discovery-work that Terry Wood has no control over his clients. They've been holding back some vital stuff, correspondence and the like. How else would I deal with cheaters, and I've got nobody on the inside. There's some guy who calls, but he never delivers.'

'The old end justifies the means, huh?'

'Something like that.'

159

'Somewhere I learned that ain't supposed to be good enough in our wonderful system of justice.'

'Look who's talking, I remember when you held that pimp upside down off the Chrysler Bridge until he gave you a name.'

'I know *you* don't believe everything you read in the *Times-Journal*,' Fleet said. 'Besides that was before I learned . . . . What I do know is you're not yourself today. Really, you've been different lately. You've had big tough cases before. What's going on, partner?'

'Maybe it's age.'

'Can't kid the captain. We detectives don't miss anything. But I guess you ain't ready to talk about it. I can buy that. You know where I am. Ready for anything.'

'I know,' Gunnar said. 'Thanks.'

Having spent Christmas with her parents, Fleet's son and new daughter-in-law were arriving on an evening plane. Gunnar and Anne had attended the October wedding in Poughkeepsie. Katie said she was anxious to meet the new addition to the family. They all exchanged hugs, and Fleet and Rose headed for the airport.

Gunnar settled down in his den, stretched out in the leather recliner, field-testing the Icelandic sweater Anne had given him. He paged through his gift from Katie, a book of splendid pictures of Britain and Ireland. He saw himself with Holly looking out over the sea from the Highlands to the Hebrides. He remembered the British Museum and riding the double-decker buses to the end of the line with Anne. They had flown to London for a week in '75, the year before Colonel Jimmy Ray Starkweather delivered the message forever amending their All-American family.

It was a gay week, and he had marvelled at the way his marriage flourished as they'd neared their silver anniversary. They stayed in a small hotel on the Cromwell Road across from the Victoria and Albert Museum. They walked to Harrods, and on to Marble Arch, and listened to harangues at Hyde Park Corner, and spent money on Oxford and Regent Streets. And they had forsaken much of London to cling to each other in bed in the little room, and the love had been better than ever.

It had all changed. What was left were the bones, the flesh had disintegrated. For weeks before Christmas a new silence had displaced Anne's usually talkative nature. When she opened the box containing her new watch, she smiled and kissed him lightly on the top of his head, but she had moved an order of magnitude further away. Yet, she watched him with the eyes of a puppy as though he might do or say something to chase away their awful trouble.

Was fairness even an issue? Fair to whom? If your life reached a point where you didn't want to live it, did you have a right to take measures to restore, even Draconian measures? Or did you suffer through, nobly? Do what was expected of you. By whom? Anne said you change it. For sure, to try her way – counselors, psychiatrists, groups – he must forfeit his bond with Holly, give up the first fire he had found in ten years. Since that limp night in September he had been up for it whenever the opportunity arose. Jesus Christ. All questions, no answers.

Where did Katie fit in? On Christmas Eve, Gunnar had waited for her to open his present. In spite of the demands of the case, and the temptations to give her a check, he had visited a dozen shops, making sure she got the best. She had unwrapped it carefully as she did things, like her mother, saving the ribbon, folding the red paper, lifting the cover off the white box.

'Oh Daddy. It's wonderful. Alligator.' A couple of tears splashed out of her blue eyes as she held the attaché case up for Anne to see.

It was perfect, and she was perfect, and what more could he hope for than to have this one perfect child laughing and crying before his eyes. He got up from his chair and walked toward her with his arms spread wide. She sprung to him and hugged him around the neck, and for that moment nothing was missing in Gunnar's life.

26

By the end of February, Leo had been gone for five months.
No word other than postcards from Munich, Belgrade, Vienna,
Paris and other places on the continent. The subtle change
in the partner's attitude toward Gunnar was complete. They
didn't bother him with minor legal questions, crude small-talk,
or mundane mangement-decisions. He felt isolated. But it was
beatification, not exclusion. They recognized his present mission
of challenging the monolithic newspaper, but in their eyes his
major roll was filling the void created by Leo's leaving – not
in management or leadership, but in image. With Leo Lawson,
mentor to the important and powerful, gone, Gunnar became
the man on the hill overlooking the battle, the leitmotif the firm
projected to the Bar at large, as much as to ask, 'Do you have
a Gunnar Larson?' Associates treated him like students did a
visiting professor who had won the Nobel Prize.

In all other respects it was business as usual. This Saturday
morning was little different from any weekday. Bodies, in motion
and at rest, filled the office – support staff, associates and partners.
A public offering planned for early in the week occupied many.
Gunnar had told Shana to stay home. He was taking a day
away from the case. On Monday he would be back at the
depositions: Pierce Pentecost; then Carlyle Henning, head of
the whole damn newspaper, and the source of several pages of
Dov Levy's reports.

Judge O'Boyle had granted Gunnar's motion to advance the
Djilas case on the calendar, a date-certain in May, Monday the
eleventh. Dov was still working. Despite the documents which
he had miraculously produced, questions remained unanswered.
Long conferences with Eddie Kerr recurred almost nightly. Eddie

162

was gaining weight. The cold blue eyes in a face like a potato pie froze you, but the persistent challenge to tactic, strategy, legal nuance, expectation, even doubt, honed Gunnar's case. But on this Saturday, with blizzard winds driving ice crystals against the glass and swirling snow between the tall buildings replacing Corum Park and the streets below with vacant white, Gunnar decided not to work. He wanted, instead, to write a poem.

Holly had called repeatedly, too much, but he looked forward to the softness of her voice. Shana thought Mrs Hogan must be some kind of a nut, and wondered why they didn't open a file. The telephone didn't do it for Gunnar, nor Holly. She said she just had to see him. She was coming north. Her coming would jeopardize her father's case, Gunnar said, and she seemed resigned. He despised the image of her with Davey.

Naïve or simply blind, Gunnar had lived the first months of their relationship ignorant of one plain truth. In the lodge the night she had tried to persuade him to come to the Christmas open-house, they had lain naked under the comforter listening to the winter wind howl in off the lake.

'It's amazing,' he had said, 'that your husband is sound asleep by nine every damn night.'

'He wakes up early,' she said, 'he's in his office by seven. With eight hours sleep, his hangovers are bearable.'

'You'd think he'd miss sex?'

'Why do you say that?'

'At his age I suspect he gets horny on occasion,' Gunnar said. 'But I suppose the drink dulls it.'

'He gets it almost every morning.'

Strong hands squeezed the blood out of the top of Gunnar's heart. He said nothing, staring into the dark of the vaulted ceiling.

'What did you expect?' She sounded surprised.

'Not that, for sure.' A gust of wind across the roof muffled his whisper.

'Honey, after all I'm married to him. He gives me everything I could ever want.'

'He's fucking you every day?'

'Not every day!'

He let out a deep breath through puckered lips. 'Like today for instance!'

She didn't answer.

'Am I number two today?'

No sound, but the wind.

'I *am* number two today.'

'Gunnar, I'm married to the man. He has a right.'

He hadn't met her at the lodge for two weeks, and he had avoided her telephone calls for two days. He had always told his clients that jealousy was the hardest emotion to control. Businessmen should look at their result independently, not compare it with the other guy's. Looking at his ecstasy with Holly independently proved impossible. Davey Tripp's nose with the little purple lines insinuated itself in the middle. When they parted that night, she had said she was ready to leave whenever he wanted her.

He wasn't ready for her to leave. Obviously, he wouldn't jeopardize the Djilas case by injecting a new storm into his life. But even when the trial was over, he was far from sure of his course. The way she soothed his soul, he didn't know if he could ever give her up. He needed to write something to show her, for insurance, to hold on more tightly, to keep her from distraction in Florida, on the beach, around the pool, at cocktail parties. He didn't know if she was vulnerable to another lover. On the telephone her protestations of love and heat scorched the wires. She wanted him, to wait, to be there for her for ever. And then the picture of Davey's bulk oppressing her body. Jesus Christ.

In tenth grade in high school he had decided he was going to be a writer. He did articles for the school paper, mostly sports. He took journalism, and started out in college as a journalism major. Then he met Anne, and Jack was born. Gunnar's priorities were reshuffled. He needed a more practical career. He gave up his vision.

Thirty years later, behind the sheet of glass forming the desk top, separated from the aggressive winter storm by another, the muse crept back. This morning he needed to express himself eloquently, make her understand his passion, his retention of the sensations of their love. He thought of Dickinson's lines: 'Parting is all we know of heaven, and all we need of hell.' But only a poem of his own creation would do. He squeezed bits of learning from his memory, conjured the images and wrote, struggling with the words, crossing out, rearranging. He tore up a page of the yellow lined-pad and started over. An hour later it felt right, maybe not worthy of a poet, but adequate for a trial lawyer.

A VERY PRIVATE THOUGHT
FROM ME TO YOU
Thrusting myself past
tender yielding tissue,
Compelled by longing
to be one with you,
Essential as breathing
and heart beat,
A fleeting ecstasy.

Sweet,
But not as sweet,
As merely touching
the soft curve of your face,
Or my lips pressing
gently on your eyes,
Or, as you must know,
Luxuriant hair
captured in my grasp.

He posted it to her. General Delivery, West Palm Beach, Florida.

BOOK THREE
TRIAL

For a moment the lie becomes truth.

Dostoevsky

27

Press and spectators squeezed into the courtroom's eight rows of pews, except the one in front to the left of the aisle – protected by a red ribbon stretched across it like the places reserved for next of kin at funerals. Air-conditioning struggled with unseasonable May heat. Voices mingled like a noisy cocktail party. In front loomed the judge's bench, still unoccupied. O'Boyle always started at the appointed time, seventeen minutes from now at nine-thirty. Gunnar Larson, first out of seeming advantage, then out of superstition, like an outfielder stepping on the foul line, arrived in courtrooms early enough to choose the counsel table closest to the jury box – today to the judge's left.

Arranging file folders in three neat stacks on the yellowing oak table, Gunnar buzzed through a mental checklist with Eddie Kerr sitting plumply at his side. In twenty-six years, it would be Gunnar's first trial to a packed courtroom. Civil trials weren't sensational enough to draw spectators from the public at large: boring technical witnessess droned on; others struggled to articulate, often in monotones that, in spite of electronic amplification, barely reached the spectator area. There were no murder weapons, no detailed descriptions of rapes or other savagery, no blasé recidivist accomplices, promised freedom in exchange for their testimony, declaiming dramatic portrayals of the defendant in the act.

This time was different. The city's only newspaper was accused of defaming a prominent citizen. Over recent weeks rumors had spread across town, mutating with each telling into viler innuendo. Passes for all day admission were given to those first in line on the courthouse steps. Although lawyers knew it was one of the most important parts of the trial, only a few observers stayed for the morning jury-selection process. Chief Judge Simkins had decreed the use of the largest courtroom to Judge O'Boyle for this trial.

O'Boyle had once been Chief Judge, ideally suited to the job with his flair for order and devotion to the integrity of the bench. Selected by all the judges of some of the District Court in a democratic election, O'Boyle had for years stood valiantly against the merger of the inferior municipal court, of limited remedial jurisdiction, into the superior District Court with its broad powers. Like Gunnar, O'Boyle feared the dilution of judicial talent that must occur with the assimilation of some of the motley jurists from below. But as usual in such matters, forces of mediocrity prevailed, and the feared merger had become reality. The group photo of the new judicial hodgepodge evoked Goya's cynical portrait of the Spanish royal family: blank stares of incompetence, lower lips hanging petulantly, grins of status achieved without regard to talent or temperament.

Some lawyers, donning the magisterial black robe, are elevated – revealing wisdom and judgment beyond anybody's expectations. Gunnar had seen it happen again and again. But Kettle's misfits desecrated the flowing black symbol of authority. What makes a man worthy of the robe is his integrity, his ability to rise above his own prejudices, to represent the principles behind the symbol. The robe was for the best among us, or, at least, not the worst. The many Kettle appointees wielded the balance of power, and, of course, they removed O'Boyle as Chief Judge to make room for somebody political and manifestly representative of the mediocre majority, and thus, Governor Kettle, himself.

O'Boyle remained, dignified, judicial, learned in evidence and courtroom procedure, generally bucking the tide and likely to hold his seat on the bench as long as he wanted. Incumbent judges rarely succumbed to election-day challenges. When they retired, Governors appointed their successors.

At twenty-five past nine, Tony Djilas swung down the aisle, ever dapper in gray, flopping blue-print pocket-silk and blue tie, grinning wildly like he had been called to participate in 'The Price is Right'. He gripped each of his lawyers by the shoulder and sat down between Gunnar and Eddie. When Gunnar picked a jury, he allowed the prospective jurors to see him repeatedly confer with his client. Though Gunnar paid little attention to the client's advice, the seated juror got the impression the client had been instrumental in picking the jury.

Holly sat in the second row behind the empty pew. Gunnar had arranged for her pass. She had been back almost two months. The couplings at the lodge had resumed but, due to the approaching trial, never more than once a week.

For months Anne and Gunnar had only spoken as necessary, and cordially made small talk about the weather, or Katie's exams. They never touched, nor went anywhere together. Except for the few detours to the lodge, Gunnar went only to the office. This year nobody brought up the annual pool: ten dollars each from Katie, Anne and Gunnar. The one most closely predicting the time of the break-up of ice in the bay took the thirty dollars. Approaching the Djilas trial with a single-mindedness unequalled since his quest for the top in law school, Gunnar gave no time to the malignancy on his marriage.

Dov Levy had returned to town the first week of May, to check out loose ends, under instructions to remain, ready for anything. Spring Eddie had become more sour than Winter Eddie. The load oppressed even him. He worked the first ten consecutive days of May, logging 134 billable hours – a full month for many lawyers. He was trying to squeeze in some work on vital equipment – leasing agreements for Dan Blackmer. Eddie had plenty of help, but Dan did nothing important without first discussing it with him at length.

A couple of times lately Eddie had interrupted their trial preparatory conferences, mentioning to Gunnar that he was worried about his criminal client in state prison. Gunnar let the comments slide by, and directed the talk back to the Djilas case. He worried about Eddie's health. He must have gained twenty pounds on this Djilas file. He munched on pizza, and drank milk shakes and huge quantities of Coke. To the good, he neither smoked, nor drank alcohol.

Al Bergdorf was always a little embarrassed when he had to sit on a seat in a public accommodation like a train or bus, because his broad beam took most of the space normally used by two people.

171

But the courthouse was his domain, and he allowed his prodigious *gluteus maximus* to spread out with impunity. He had picked a spot in the back row. If Judge O'Boyle bore him animosity, he wanted to be as inconspicuous as possible. Still, it was like trying to hide a Mack truck on a merry-go-round.

One thing Al was sure of: Tony had the right lawyer. Sometimes desperate people went to faraway places hoping to gain an advantage by hiring a famous lawyer. Al had been on a business trip in Minneapolis when F. Lee Bailey's client was convicted after Bailey failed to convince a jury that a dead woman had strangled herself. In San Francisco, Patty Hearst was sent to prison after, as Bailey had advised, she refused to answer numerous questions on the grounds that the answers might incriminate her. With rare exceptions, Al was sure you were better off sticking with known quantities in your home state, rather than itinerants unable to live up to their reputations. And in spite of the great personal charm of Bailey and other talk-show lawyers, many local judges resented the intrusion of outsiders in their domain.

Of the six people taking seats in the pew protected by the red ribbon, Gunnar Larson recognized three – he had taken their deposition last winter – reporters Suzie Cline and Ward Chapin, and publisher Carlyle Henning. The court reporter with a bonnet of bounteous dark hair took her place at her stenotype machine in front of the bench, allowing a clear view of the witnesses. Gunnar watched the hand on the courtroom clock lurch ahead one minute to nine-thirty. A door in the corner opened, behind and to one side of the judge's bench, and a young red-head stuck her head through. 'He's ready,' she said.

The bailiff, in tan deputy's uniform, standing under the clock on the wall to the spectator's left, nodded and turned to face the crowd. The judge appeared in the door the girl had opened, and hurried to the chair behind the bench, black robe flopping around him.

In loud experienced tones the bailiff cried: 'All rise, O-yay, O-yay, this honorable court is now in session, Judge Michael O'Boyle presiding.'

The red-headed clerk sat down at the desk to the judge's right, and directly behind the witness box.

'Please be seated,' said O'Boyle. 'Good morning, Counsel.' His ruddy complexion extended over the top of his head through a few hairs. They returned the greeting in unison.

'Before we proceed, I have an announcement to make,' said the judge, setting a pair of half-glasses low on his Irish pug nose. 'I have reconsidered my earlier ruling on the public-figure issue.'

Had Gunnar been standing he would have had to sit. The first-day butterflies returned and he felt punched in the solar plexus. The judge was still speaking.

'. . . late last night. The clerk will deliver my memorandum to you at the noon recess if you choose to proceed today. I am changing my ruling to hold that the plaintiff, Anthony Djilas, is a limited-purpose public figure as a matter of law, as contemplated by the US Supreme Court in *Gertz*. Essentially, this means that being as the alleged defamatory statements occurred in a newspaper article, plaintiff Djilas must make a *primafacie* showing of actual malice, as well as falsity. I don't need to tell counsel the difficulties this could present to plaintiff. My memorandum includes all the case citations. I know this ruling may have a profound effect on the case, and plans of counsel, so I am prepared to grant plaintiff a continuance for a reasonable time if he should so move the court.'

Obviously, O'Boyle had decided that the major controversy surrounding the picking of the developer had made all of the bidders public figures. Gunnar had always known it was a close call for the court. He glanced at Terry Wood, lead counsel for the *Times-Journal*. A smile split Wood's broad fleshy face.

O'Boyle's reversal was a staggering blow, but not a knock-out punch. Good trial lawyers made swift assessments of new circumstances. Gunnar stood up. His voice was a major asset. It evenly filled every corner of the courtroom. 'May it please the court,' he said, feeling immediately in the swing, butterflies ancient history, 'of course, I am disappointed by the court's ruling and I object to it for the record, but, plaintiff is ready, I ask the court to call a jury panel.'

Terry Wood was on his feet. 'Your Honor, in view of your ruling, defendant has the right to prepare a new motion for summary judgment based on plaintiff's inability to prove actual malice. I object to proceeding at this time, and I respectfully move the court for a thirty-day adjournment, or whatever time the court deems reasonable.'

'Objection overruled, motion denied,' said the U-boat Captain, 'Mr Bailiff, bring us a jury.'

28

After six days of trial, Gunnar had completed his case for damages arising out of Tony Djilas' loss of the New City opportunity. It was like a routine breach-of-contract case – no mention of the defamation, or the newspaper article, other than in Gunnar's opening statement – until the afternoon of the sixth day.

By noon on day two, the pews were almost empty. There only remained Holly, Al Bergdorf and a couple of faces Gunnar didn't recognize, probably reporters. The spectators had been disappointed. They weren't alone. The jury looked bored. But the damage testimony went in smoothly. Eddie Kerr had done the preparation well. Terry Wood had argued in chambers that it was a waste of the court's time, that the plaintiff should prove he was entitled to damages first. But Gunnar had doggedly proceeded. The judge had succumbed to Gunnar's argument of weeks before: the damage testimony would give the jurors an idea of what New City was, avoiding much repetition later, and he could get it in a week. He had been off by one day, and he accomplished what he really wanted: let the evidence show the jury early on just how fucking big this case was.

Witnesses paraded in and out for six days: appraisers, architects, accountants, planners, economists, bankers, contractors and, lastly, an expert operating out of Denver – whose company had developed sophisticated computer programs to determine damages in construction-contract cases. Eddie had made a file for each witness containing concise summaries of their testimony and each question to be asked, typed out word for word. His back-up made Gunnar look like a genius.

All of the testimony tended to prove Gunnar's allegations in his opening statement to the jury: Tony Djilas, himself, stood to make $3.75 million had the more-than-$200,000,000 project become a reality. Terry Wood's skilled cross-examination made few inroads on the pronouncements of the experts. Finally, this afternoon Gunnar had called the city manager to the stand, and the president of the city council – both of whom testified that Tony's group was dropped from consideration because of the *Times-Journal* articles branding him a criminal. Further, both testified that the Djilas proposal had been on the verge of acceptance when the articles were published, subject only to routine bureaucratic procedures. The articles themselves were introduced when Helen Wilson, City Council President, was on the stand. With the damage testimony completed, it lay ahead for Gunnar to prove the falsity of the articles, plus that they were published out of actual malice – those responsible having known, or should have known, that what they wrote was false.

In February, Judge O'Boyle had ruled that Tony was not a public figure. He had also denied Terry Wood's motion for summary judgment on the basis of numerous affidavits attesting to Tony's law-abiding activities in Florida, and disputing the allegations to the contrary of Wood's key witness, Chucky John Waycross, a former Drug Enforcement agent. If the jury believed Waycross, Gunnar knew his client would lose. But Dov Levy's call from south Florida in late March gave Gunnar a grenade to throw at Chucky John when he showed up at the trial.

Even though the damage case had gone in smoothly, gloom pervaded the team. Eddie who never smiled anyway, looked as if his doctor had just told him he had six months to live. Tony's big grin had left him, replaced by a grim tight-lipped smile delivered only when his natural salesman's instincts told him the situation demanded it.

Six days ago, Gunnar, Eddie, Tony and Al Bergdorf had all met in Gunnar's office late in the afternoon after the first day of trial. Tony had wanted to start his bitching at the noon recess, but Gunnar, anticipating his opening statement to the jury after lunch, didn't have time to listen. Jury selection had taken all morning.

Even before he lit his cigarette, Tony was screaming: 'God-damnit, I knew that sonofabitch was gonna nail me! It was that fuckin' crap game! He can't forget I made a fool of him.'

'You can't be certain, Tony,' Gunnar said. 'They made good arguments that you thrust yourself into the New City controversy. There were a lot of people in this town opposed even to building it, important people. It was a controversy. I honestly think Mike O'Boyle thought he was going to get reversed if he let his first decision stand.'

Gunnar moved his gaze to the big man on the sofa. Al's face had a drawn look as if he had lost weight. His heavy eyelids drooped, but he was listening as he chewed on the cigar.

'Bullshit!' said Tony

'We're in too far to give up now,' Gunnar said.

'Give up, shit!' Tony said. 'Let's get him to change that ruling again!'

'Not possible,' Gunnar said.

'What do you mean, not possible?'

'Just what he said.' Al shook his cigar stub at Tony. 'Listen to him for Christ's sake. He knows the system. You broke your ass to get him. Now *listen*. You should be glad he doesn't want to pull out like the agreement says he can.' Al sank back down into the sofa.

Tony shut up.

'I'm going ahead with our case, as planned,' Gunnar said. 'I've got to talk to my lawyer here, so if you boys will excuse us, see you in court in the morning.'

When they were gone Gunnar smiled wryly at Eddie Kerr. 'What do you think?'

'It was a good opening statement.'

'That all?'

'You told them you were going to prove malice. I know your case for falsity, but I don't know your case for malice. Have you got one?'

'I got an angle or two.'

'Do you really think Tony's telling the truth?'

'My brilliant friend, do you think I would suborn perjury?' To Gunnar, trying to win the case on perjured testimony would be like Lincoln buying a slave.

'No.' And the Doberman stare.

'You're right. I wouldn't, and you wouldn't.'

Six days later Gunnar was still nagged by doubts about his chances, but he shoved those feelings into the background and proceeded outwardly as though the only question was the amount of money they were going to collect. He knew juries could pick up negative feelings, and this jury wasn't going to detect them in him.

Knowing her husband was in the trial of his life, Anne had been treating him well the past week – asking questions and listening to the answers. She even gave him a neck-rub every night when he got home – their first touching in months. His only contacts with Holly were smiles across the courtroom, the same kind he flashed to the few others he knew in the spectator area. He was anxious to get home to another neck-rub and at least seven hours of sleep. But first he had to stop at Dov Levy's hotel room and talk.

29

The *Times-Journal*, the city's monopoly press, buried the trial in the second section, but the TV news shows covered it in detail. Word spread that the numbers games were over; the trial that people were waiting for would begin on Wednesday morning. Scarce courtroom passes were gone by eight. The seats were packed when Gunnar Larson called Suzette Cline, *Times-Journal* reporter and party defendant, for cross-examination.

For two hours the night before, Dov Levy had meticulously reviewed the Hebrew script in his journal, chronicling the investigation of Suzie Cline's rôle in the libelous news articles. Gunnar Larson listened, questioned, and made last-minute memory-stimulating notes. On the stand this morning, Suzie was a different woman from the one Dov knew. She stood for the oath in a two-piece, gray checked suit. Rimless plastic glasses replaced her contacts. Her long loose hair had been cut and coiffed. With the dancing eyes distorted by the lenses, the dull-axe nose dominated her face – sexy reporter transmogrified to the virgin librarian that demanded quiet in the room when you were seven. With the preliminaries, name, address, occupation, education, previous experience and the like behind him, Gunnar moved to the issue of libel. Suzie Cline admitted that she was one of the authors; that she was assigned the project by Harold Jarvis, and worked under his supervision; that she and Ward Chapin shared responsibility equally, but that there was a specific division of labor.

Suzie's fingers, nails trimmed short without polish, toyed absently with a print handkerchief. The librarian image faded with the style of her answers – straightforward, no-nonsense. She sat erect, confident, the comically smart hoyden Dov had described – a ready-for-anything expression on her face. Telephoning Dov at his hotel last night and not reaching him, she must still believe that he was a grain trader, intermittently in the city on business. Gunnar felt no pity for her. So-called investigative reporters despoiled innocent people, and this little bitch was a past master. Besides, pity was an incurable disease, likely fatal to cross-examiners. He visualized her in tight-fitting leather. Suzie returned Gunnar's warm smile with one of her own, lips pressed together primly, magnified brown eyes meeting his.

'When did you first meet my client?' Gunnar leaned back in the swivel chair, knowing the answer, as he would to virtually every question he asked her.

'You mean Mr Djilas?'

'Yes.'

'I have never met him.'

'He offered to meet with you, and Mr Chapin, did he not?'

'Well we . . . .'

Sternly: 'He offered to meet you did he not?'

'He said that he couldn't make any of the suggested times . . . .'

Again, in the same tone, as though he hadn't heard the response: 'He offered to meet you did he not?'

'Objection!' In spite of his bulk, Terry Wood jumped nimbly to his feet.

'State your grounds,' said O'Boyle.

'He's not allowing her to complete her answer.'

'Overruled,' said O'Boyle.

'Are you ready to answer?' said Gunnar. Her pale skin reddened, almost matching the blush she had brushed on her high cheekbones.

'Yes, he offered to meet us, but . . . .'

'The decision to publish these articles was made by Carlyle Henning was it not?'

'I don't know.'

'You know it wasn't made by your boss, Harold Jarvis, do you not?'

'Yes.'

Gunnar returned to his smile. 'Henning is Jarvis' boss, is he not?'

'Yes.'

180

'You *are* friendly with Carlyle Henning?'

'Professionally.'

Gunnar decided to let Henning lie for a while; let Suzie think he was satisfied with her responses.

She answered a long series of questions establishing that in her interviews with Florida law-enforcement officials she had found nothing incriminating Tony Djilas, that she had learned that he'd testified before a grand-jury investigating Manny Zilman and others, but that she had discovered very little more about the grand-jury proceedings, except that Zilman escaped indictment. She managed to blurt out that Ward Chapin had spoken to some of the grand jurors. Gunnar assured her that Chapin would get his chance to tell his story very soon.

At ten forty-five, Judge O'Boyle called a short recess.

When Suzie Cline returned to the stand, Gunnar leaned against the front of the counsel table. Looking at Mrs Anita Lowery, middle-aged juror at the left end of the front row, he said, 'Earlier you testified that you didn't know who made the decision to publish the articles. I remind you that you are under oath. Do you care to reconsider your answer?' He came back to Suzie's eyes. They had narrowed. Her eyebrows moved up, slightly furrowing the vault of her regal forehead curving back to the highest of hairlines.

'No. I don't know.'

'Do you have an idea?'

'Objection, speculation,' said Terry Wood.

'Sustained,' said O'Boyle.

Suzie's self-confidence had thrived on the morning diet of bland questions, formulated in the kitchen of her inquisitor. He was ready to wean her on less tasty fare.

'Isn't it a fact that you attended a Memorial Day weekend house-party at the lake home of Carlyle Henning, just about a year ago?'

She must be fingering through her thoughts, recalling who was there, trying to guess what might have been leaked, and to whom. Nothing had come up in the depositions about the party. She looked directly at Chapin seated in the pew reserved for the defendants, then quickly away.

Gunnar moved in on her, close enough to see the fine down along the line of her jaw. He chided her. 'Could you have forgotten such an entertaining event?'

Wood stood up, then sat down, saying nothing. O'Boyle permitted himself an almost undetectable smile.

'I haven't forgotten,' said the witness. Her shoulders sagged and she seemed smaller in the black leather chair.

'Who attended . . . in addition to yourself?'

Pain covered her face. How quickly she had fallen. She had won so easily when he took her deposition. 'I don't know if I can remember everyone,' she said in a small voice like I want my mama.

'Just those you can,' Gunnar said gently. 'We'll work on the rest.' His tone contained a promise that their work would be exhaustive.

'Mr Henning,' she said, 'And Ward . . . Chapin, and . . . Cort Hamilton and.'

She stopped abruptly. Her face had gone white. She looked at Wood. His big face offered her nothing. Gunnar suspected Terry Wood had not heard about the party before he came to court today. Gunnar turned his back to the witness. In the seat at the counsel table next to Eddie Kerr, Tony Djilas – silver hair perfectly combed – held his lips in a sober line; Eddie's mouth hung slightly open. Gunnar looked over the room, allowing the silence its significance. Chapin smirked. Neither Henning, nor Pentecost were in court. Time to give them a little rope. Gunnar ignored Suzie's incomplete answer, and returned to his seat beside Eddie, whispering in his ear: 'The opening of my malice case, Mr Kerr. If we can stall a little here we'll get an offer over the lunch-break. Maybe nothing big, but an offer.' Eddie looked straight ahead. It was ten past eleven.

Gunnar walked to the left behind the tables and rested his hand on Terry Wood's wide shoulder. The seam was opening on his brown suit-jacket, and a bit of the gray padding stuck out. His red tie was pockmarked with pipe-tobacco burns. Many in the bar thought Terry's rags were a ploy, but Gunnar knew he was between marriages, and he just didn't get around to grooming. Gunnar put it to him in a low murmur. 'Care to join me in a motion for an early break? I think Suzie might want to talk to you.'

'Why not?' said Terry Wood.

'I'll have lunch sent in. You can call me . . . up 'til one o'clock.'

The three old pros, O'Boyle, Wood and Gunnar Larson got their heads together at the bench. 'Might save some time, your honor, if we break now and come back half-an-hour early,' said Gunnar.

Wood nodded his agreement.

'Fine with me,' said O'Boyle. Then he looked at Gunnar. 'Remember Counsel, if Car Henning is willing to put some real dough on the table just to keep his party a secret, you better listen.'

'You know me, Judge, I always listen.'

At one p.m. Angela announced Terry Wood's call.

'I've got authority for $500,000,' said Wood.

'You need ten times that, Terry,' said Gunnar.

'Aren't you going to run it by your client?'

'No need. Do you know who else was at the party?'

'I do now. But that proves nothing. Publishers know a lot of people.'

'Do you know what they were doing?'

'I've got an idea . . . do you?'

'Tell Henning I know what he was, or better, what they were doing. And tell him that the jury might wonder where Pentecost fits into this story, and tell him it's still his move. Five hundred K doesn't deserve a response. I'm still on five mil. You can tell me what he says in the courtroom. See you in fifteen minutes.'

Midwest May could be as lovely as tropical April, but Gunnar's cranky sinuses told him some alien pollen floated at large on the windless temperate day. Two wire-service reporters followed him across the courthouse plaza.

'What the hell's going on, Counselor?' one asked. 'Sounds juicy. How about a hint?'

Gunnar shook his head. Tony and Eddie trailed two steps

behind, looking straight ahead. Holly, already in the lobby, caught Gunnar's eye as he came through the revolving door. He let her see a tiny smile. Jesus Christ, she threw him a kiss. People would probably think it was for Tony.

Terry Wood waited by Gunnar's chair with the gentle grin of a man slow to anger and twenty years a friend. 'Henning stands on the $500,000. I'll quote him. "I'd come out of the closet for a million, let alone five." And, Gunnar, even if a jury infers malice out of this, your man was up to his ass in grass. The truth is still a defense to libel. I'd think about the 500 grand a while. You know nobody's ever nicked a newspaper for much over a million.'

'Don't forget *Tavoula-whatshisname v. the* Washington Post,' said Gunnar, 'and tell Henning I've already proved up three and a half million in actual, and he'll be out of the closet by two-thirty.'

They got the 'All rise' and a minute later Suzie was back on the stand, looking more miserable than ever. After Eddie opined that Terry Wood might be right, Gunnar went after Ms Cline.

'Do you remember the question that was before you this morning when we broke for lunch?'

'I do.' The fierce sparkle in her eyes of ten a.m. had given way to the guilt of a shamed spaniel.

'I'll restate it for the jury. Who was at the party besides you, Carlyle Henning, Ward Chapin, and Cort Hamilton?'

'Pierce Pentecost.'

'I'm not sure everyone on the jury heard that.' Gunnar fixed on Ralph Sullivan, second from the right in the front row, big intelligent eyes set in a chocolate-brown face. 'Would you repeat that name please.'

She did, a little louder, but there was nothing wrong with the PA system.

Gunnar plowed ahead. 'You were here yesterday when the city manager, Mr Gale, named all of the competitors for the development contract for Block 13, New City, were you not?'

'I was here.' Her voice sounded weak, almost breathless.

'The Pierce Pentecost who was at Mr Henning's party is the same Pierce Pentecost competing for the New City contract, is he not?'

'Yes.' Her face sagged. She smoothed the new hairdo, already frozen to her head.

Gunnar abandoned the leading questions. 'What did you do at the party?' They must have all talked during the break and agreed nobody could know what they had done; Gunnar must be bluffing.

'We drank a lot.' She tried a wistful smile.

'What else? You were there three days. It was pretty cold for swimming.'

'Car . . . Mr Henning has a heated pool.' Like an angleworm, Suzie wriggled to avoid the sharp point of the hook.

Gunnar turned his back on her and walked over to the jury box, the closest he had gotten to them since the trial began. Without looking back at Suzie he bored in, raising his voice slightly. 'Wasn't it odd that you were the only woman present?'

'Objection, irrelevant,' said Terry Wood.

'Sustained,' said O'Boyle.

Still with his back to the witness, Gunnar maintained his straightest face for the jury.

'Did you have sexual intercourse on that weekend with . . . .'

'Objection . . . .'

'. . . Carlyle Henning?'

'. . . Irrelevant.'

'Sustained.'

Without leaving the area of the jury box, Gunnar turned to address the witness, her eyes wide through the thick lenses, white visible all the way around the brown irises. She looked as breakable as a china plate. Gunnar returned to leading.

'You were in bed with Pierce Pentecost that weekend, were you not?'

Suzy turned to the right, toward Terry Wood. He jumped up.

'Objection, irrelevant!'

'Overruled,' said O'Boyle.

'You may answer,' said Gunnar.

Suzie bowed her head and covered her face with her hand like she was praying that her tormentor would stop. Gunnar felt neither pity, nor triumph. She had worked at her craft, now he worked at his.

'You may answer,' said Gunnar, stepping further to the side, so all the jurors could clearly see the witness.

She looked up, eyes wet. 'Yes,' she said quietly. Something more of her had shriveled away.

Gunnar turned back to the jury. Sarah Michaels, chubby face, pink-rimmed glasses, second from the left in the front row, opened her eyes as wide. 'At least once while you were in bed with Pierce Pentecost, you were having sexual intercourse with Carlyle Henning, were you not?'

'Objection, irrelevant.'

'Overruled,' said O'Boyle.

Gunnar stole a look at Al Bergdorf's broad face smiling in the back row; no doubt he was remembering Gunnar's praise of O'Boyle's knowledge of the rules of evidence. 'You may answer,' said Gunnar.

'Yes.' Her eyes showed nothing but ragged panic.

'And while you were in bed with Carlyle Henning and Pierce Pentecost, the two of them had homosexual relations, including but not limited to Carlyle Henning inserting his penis into Pierce Pentecost's anus, did they not?' Gunnar let his gaze rise just over the head of the jurors, holding his face in a neutral set. Their eyes all fixed on Suzie Cline.

'Objection, irrelevant, prejudicial!' Terry Wood stood waiting expectantly for relief from O'Boyle.

'Overruled,' said O'Boyle.

'Your Honor, may we approach the bench?' Terry Wood tried to break the pace.

'Not to argue my ruling on the objection,' said O'Boyle.

Gunnar began again, 'You may . . . .'

'The answer is yes,' said Suzie. There was ash in her voice. The surrender was complete. She looked prepared to raise her hands over her head and be led away.

'Isn't it a fact,' Gunnar again faced the jury, 'that homosexual relations occurred between these two, Henning and Pentecost, with Ward Chapin joining from time to time, repeatedly throughout the long weekend?'

'Yes.'

She was ready to admit to anything, but Gunnar'd had all he

wanted of the party for now. He walked across the room to a position beside the witness from where he was able to see the jury. 'And Ms Cline, isn't it a fact that from your own personal knowledge you, and I mean *you*, individually, have obtained no information from any source positively indicating that my client, Anthony Djilas, has ever committed a crime. Please answer yes or no.' Either was OK with Gunnar.

'Yes,' said Suzie.

'Objection, Form of the Question,' said Terry Wood.

'Overruled,' said O'Boyle. 'She appeared to understand it.'

'Nothing further,' said Gunnar. He would have another crack at Suzie Cline when they called her, as they must, in the defendant's case. He had humiliated one of Tony's antagonists and given the writers grist for their mill, but he had only established the tiniest of beachheads in the war. And he had lost all first-level settlement leverage – the two big-shots were out of the closet. You can't put toothpaste back in the tube.

30

After rave reviews on every TV news show, a clamorous full-house awaited day eight of *Djilas v.* Times-Journal, the toughest ticket in town. Ward Chapin had top billing.

Yesterday, after Suzie Cline had left the stand, stripped naked by Gunnar's cross-examination, he had changed the pace – calling Mayor Steve Carpenter as witness to Tony's good reputation. He hit Gunnar's every pitch where thrown: impressing the jury with Tony's honesty, loyalty, reverence, piety, generosity, intelligence, judgment, community spirit, citizenship, and, equally relevant to the proceedings, his business acuity, the capability of developing Block 13 for his own financial benefit, as well as the city's. Gunnar left the courthouse feeling what a bricklayer might feel having laid up the first wall of a building. With many yet to be built, he tried not to allow himself elation.

When Suzie Cline had described what Dov Levy characterized as her 'Mongolian cluster-fuck' – it came up in the context of her suggesting her German journalism professor friend join her and Dov in bed one night – she had belittled Car Henning's sexual prowess with women, suggesting that he had expanded his horizons to men because the preferred orifice was smaller. The ultimate irony was her belief that she had shared these intimacies with a grain trader, not an undercover Intelligence expert bent on her ruin. Yesterday, she must have realized that only Dov could have provided Gunnar with the information to humiliate and expose her. She had left a call at the Hilton, and first thing this morning at Miracle Mills. The staff at Miracle Mills and at the hotel informed callers that Dov was out of the city. Last night, to be safe, Dov had moved to the Marriot Central.

Now, Gunnar's big even voice filled the room. 'Plaintiff calls defendant Ward Chapin for cross-examination.'

One hand in his pocket, Chapin approached the witness box as though it were a throne. His square jaw elevated like a man with a vision, he held his right hand high and responded to the oath's question with a forceful *I do*. Well over six feet, his ample shoulders were draped in a steel-gray silk suit, not what Gunnar would have recommended for this jury, and not what one would expect of a newspaper reporter. Chapin's steel-rimmed aviator glasses completed an image of élan.

From his chair behind the counsel table, Gunnar charged through the preliminaries. Perhaps trying ineffectually, but more likely not giving a damn, the princely Ward did not hide his built-in smirk. His answers were quick, direct, confident – the answer to a cross-examiner's prayer. Witnesses were drilled to be direct, confident if possible, but never quick. Of thirteen years, his entire career, with the *Times-Journal*, he'd spent the last six as an investigative reporter. Chapin said he had a Bachelor's from Yale, Master's from Columbia, and he had grown up on New York City's east side. His father was a journalism professor at NYU, his mother a minor editor on the *New York Herald-Tribune* before it folded; and she was still writing feminist articles for women's magazines – the last volunteered proudly in an expanded answer. Listening to his loquacious client, Terry Wood, like a fly about to be swatted, face skeptical, jaw muscles twitching, processed every word instantly – Gunnar carefully avoided objectionable questions throughout the first hour. He wanted Chapin to remain confident. And so he apparently did.

'You heard Suzette Cline's testimony yesterday in regard to the Memorial Day Week party?' *Yes*. 'Did she leave anything out?' *No*. 'You knew Pierce Pentecost prior to the weekend at Henning's, did you not?' *Just casually*.

The jury got the idea that Chapin's digging in Miami was *not* motivated by an attempt to benefit a lover. Gunnar didn't give Chapin the satisfaction of denying whether he had a sexual relationship with Pentecost prior to the celebrated weekend party. Dov Levy's trip to Miami in January set up the next line of questions. Chapin was in tune with the moment, relaxed. At times his smirk even deliquesced to a warm smile.

'Isn't it a fact that you interviewed at least thirteen of the living members of the grand jury that had investigated Mr Zilman?'

'I really don't know how many.' His tone said, who's counting?

Gunnar's tone said, I am. He recited twelve names, waiting for Chapin's affirmative answer after each, and got it. Chapin agreed that, with Tomlinson, there were thirteen, if Gunnar said so.

'Isn't it a fact that, in one form or another, you offered to bribe each . . . .'

'Objection, no foundation and calls for a legal conclusion!' Wood was on his feet.

'Sustained,' said O'Boyle.

'Let's just say you offered to compensate each of these people to break the grand juror's oath of confidentiality, did you not?'

'I agreed to cover their expenses,' said Chapin, his expression less comfortable than before.

'You actually paid Cyrus Tomlinson, the man whose deposition I took in February, $10,000.00, did you not?'

'I didn't.' Chapin fiddled with imaginary errant hairs on his perfect dark-blond head.

'Defendant *Times-Journal* did, did it not?'

'I guess so.' Palms up, fingers curled, he examined his nails.

'There is an ongoing criminal investigation into your conduct regarding that grand jury as we speak, is there . . . .'

'Objection, irrelevant.'

'Sustained.'

O'Boyle had ruled months back that the oath-breaching grand juror Tomlinson could not testify in this case. Gunnar wanted to plant the seed in the jury's minds that Tomlinson wasn't called because his testimony would not have been damaging to Tony Djilas.

Anticipating a greater problem for Tony from Chapin's testimony than Suzie's, Gunnar had saved the next question for Chapin alone. There was a risk. Since giving his deposition, Chapin might have become aware of the legal problems of Tony's friend, Castillo.

'You didn't interview any of Mr Djilas' friends, did you?'

'I couldn't find any.' Chapin smiled like a knife.

Jesus Christ, he loves it. Gunnar got up and walked around the table toward the witness, his back to the jury, an irrelevant sheet of notes in his hand. 'Neither you, nor Ms Cline took the trouble to interview his closest neighbors, did you?'

Chapin eyed the paper. 'No.'

'You wouldn't want to spoil the makings of a good story, would . . . .'

'Objection, argumentative.'

'Sustained.'

A principal source of the information on which the *Times-Journal* articles had been based was Drug Enforcement agent Chucky John Waycross. Later, O'Boyle had ordered the defendants to reveal his name unless they wanted him out of the case for good. When they did, Gunnar had advanced Dov Levy twenty more thousand and sent him off to Florida.

Gunnar led Chapin through the Waycross connection. Chapin said he had located Waycross by running an ad in the *Miami Herald*. He had helped build the case against Zilman. Not long after he testified before the grand jury, Waycross had been fired – due to internal politics he had said in his deposition. To date, the *Times-Journal* had paid him over $25,000 for his 'contributions to the cause', Gunnar's words, which were allowed to stand in spite of an objection.

Gunnar had more, but he was quite certain neither Chapin, nor Terry Wood knew it. He would save it for later, let their star witness get a first-hand taste of Dov Levy's investigative acumen. But saving it was not without risk. Having to prove both falsity and malice, the possibility of O'Boyle dismissing the whole damn case without requiring the defense to do anything remained alive.

'It's fair to say, is it not, Mr Chapin, that without the information with respect to my client – obtained by you from Chucky Joe Waycross – you would not have made the claims of criminal activity on Mr Djilas' part that you did in the article?'

'I don't understand the question.'

Stating that he couldn't phrase it any more clearly, Gunnar

asked the court reporter to read it back. Picking up the paper tape from her machine, she did.

'I'm not sure,' said Chapin, again tampering with his high-priced hairstyle.

'You wouldn't have gone ahead on the arrest report and the bank account alone, at least not having even talked to Djilas?'

'I agree with that.' So what, his eyes added.

Now the jury must be wondering about the bank account. Sarah Michaels in the front row, in blue frames today, fixed her face in a frown of disapproval, but of what Gunnar didn't know. Jennifer Woody, much younger, second from the right in the back row, vividly made-up with her prominent cheekbones brushed scarlet, seemed intrigued by Chapin. She was not the only one to whom Ward Chapin was a curiosity.

At one point, Dov Levy had been truly startled by the man in the witness box. Suzie had invited Dov to a party at the home of one of Chapin's friends in the suburbs. They'd arrived late on a Saturday night. Dov's view of male homosexuality had not evolved beyond the stereotypical impressions absorbed over half a lifetime of hearsay. He envisioned men in bathhouses with strategically located cans of Crisco, raids by the police, furtive pickups in urban parks and men's rooms. For Dov, homosexual monogamy existed only among strange little men hidden from public eyes. Suzy Cline had led him that night into a luxurious salon filled with new knowledge.

First, he'd seen Ward Chapin lean back against the bar braced with one elbow. A much shorter man with dark wavy hair pressed his body full-length against Ward. The two wore matching tan jump-suits. Just as Dov spotted Ward, he planted a lingering open-mouth kiss on the younger man whose loving fingers ran through what had been neatly arranged hair. Around the room other male couples displayed similar affection. A man in his late fifties in perfect pinstripe, his head smooth and shiny, gazed raptly into the eyes of a man his own height and age in the embrace of a slow dance.

'The guy with the shaved head is Kenneth Johnson, president of the Cochrane department-store chain,' Suzie said.

Dov had hurried through the bar area, dragging Suzie behind

him. In the dimly lit area beyond people sat around randomly scattered tables. In one corner a black girl fronting a three piece combo sang 'Love for Sale' in a sultry voice. The drummer brushed a cymbal in slow steady rhythm for the dancers. The wares she was hawking would fall on a lot of deaf ears in this group, Dov thought. They sat down at an empty table. Minutes later, Ward and friend joined them. Dov jumped up.

'Jesse,' Ward said to Dov, 'meet my friend Andrew . . . Andrew, Jesse Katz . . . Andrew Levy . . . You know Suzie.'

Dov squeezed the pale little hand.

'Isn't Andrew lovely in his new jump-suit?' Ward said as they at down.

As always, Ward Chapin dominated the conversation. It had been mid-winter, and after bitching about the cold, he began bitching about the Djilas case. The waiter delivered two martinis to the matched pair and took Dov and Suzie's order.

'That bohunk Djilas is the biggest crook in this town, and he knows it,' Ward said. 'Such nerve, acting so fucking innocent.'

'I've told Dov about the case,' Suzie said.

'It seems your barristers can be induced to do anything,' Dov said sounding a little more British than usual. 'In the UK I think there is a good deal more restraint. Interesting though, Ward. What's really going on?'

Dov winked at Suzie as if to say, we might as well give him something to talk about. Suzie would think she and Dov had exhausted the subject. It was a good ploy. Wanting to show off for Andrew, and, four martinis into a weekend drunk, Chapin's mouth had played non-stop for two hours – urged on by Dov's innocent-sounding questions, Suzie none the wiser.

Now, facing Ward Chapin in the courtroom, every alcohol-soaked word from that evening was at Gunnar's disposal verbatim, though muddled with clinking glasses and the combo backing the lady singing the blues. Dov had carried a recorder. With the transcript of the tape, and the transcript of Chapin's deposition stashed on the counsel table, Gunnar tracked his game. Chapin pouted in the witness box.

'Incidentally, Mr Chapin,' Gunnar said, voice lower than usual, almost casual – in a tone as if to say, just as an afterthought – but looking squarely at the jury, actually Jennifer Woody's forehead, 'Have you ever said, "That bohunk Djilas is the biggest crook in town?"'

'Certainly not,' said Ward Chapin, cockier and quicker than ever.

'Objection, no foundation, move to strike,' said Terry Wood, not bothering to rise, protecting the record on this lose cannon, but not wanting the jury to make much of it.

'Overruled; he answered in the negative anyway,' said O'Boyle.

Surely, the judge must know Terry Wood's fears. The jury instruction you got without asking flashed through Gunnar's mind: if you determine that a witness has lied as to a material fact, you may disregard all of the uncorroborated testimony of that witness, should you so choose. And Suzie wasn't there today to refresh Ward Chapin's memory at the recess – if she even remembered. She had finished that party on Black Russians. But, to prove the lie, Gunnar would have to call Dov Levy as a witness to lay proper foundation for the admission of the tape. Only God knew what peccadillos Dov might be forced to admit in front of the jury. The whole case could fly apart.

Gunnar set out on a series of leading questions, hoping to bolster both the case of falsity and malice.

'Mr Chapin, it's a fact, is it not, that your source, DEA agent Chucky John Waycross, told you that before he was sacked he had built a criminal case against Manny Zilman?'

Terry Wood passed up the hearsay objection as Gunnar thought he would. Waycross was going to testify in Wood's case.

'That's a fact,' said Chapin.

'And he also told you that Zilman was not prosecuted because he made a deal with the US Attorney, correct.'

'Correct,' said Chapin. He seemed bored.

'And he also told you that Tony Djilas was protected by that very same deal, did he not?' Gunnar wanted the jury to first hear this damaging revelation from him.

'Correct,' said Chapin, with a knowing smirk at the jury.

'Waycross also told you that the terms of Zilman's deal were confidential did he not?'

'Yes, but . . . .'

'And because it was confidential you have no knowledge of the deal other than what Waycross told you?'

'Waycross was . . . .'

Loudly: 'You have no knowledge of the deal other than what Waycross told you?'

'No,' Chapin said, smirk gone.

'Even if what Waycross told you was correct, that doesn't mean Tony Djilas *needed*, and I emphasize *needed*, any protection does it?'

'He got me an arrest report on Djilas,' said Chapin. A self-satisfied look in the form of a close-mouthed smile returned to Chapin's face.

Nice and quick. He took the bait. Gunnar glanced at Terry Wood, then at his own table. Eddie was shuffling through a pile of papers. Tony Djilas stared intently at Chapin. Gunnar smelled the first drop of blood in the water. He moved in for the kill.

'And it's fair to say,' Gunnar said, 'that you based your allegations of my client's criminal activity on what Waycross told you about Zilman's deal *plus* the arrest report *plus* the bank records, is it not?'

'No, it isn't fair to say,' said Chapin, turning his head to look at O'Boyle, then at Terry Wood. Chapin's smile drooped to a frown. His eyes asked a question.

'May we approach the bench,' said Terry Wood.

'You may,' said O'Boyle.

The four of them, Gunnar, Terry Wood and his assistant, and Eddie Kerr, knotted tightly before O'Boyle – like puppies at a pan of milk.

'What now, Your Honor?' asked Terry Wood.

O'Boyle spoke too low for the jury to hear. 'I have ordered that there will be no reference to anything the grand juror Tomlinson said, and I meant it. That doesn't mean this witness can't answer a question put to him by plaintiff's lawyer requiring him to admit talking to the grand juror. He just can't tell what they talked about.'

Terry Wood broke in, 'But . . . .'

'No buts,' said O'Boyle. 'It would be hearsay anyway.'

Gunnar was getting a warm feeling in his gut.

'But, Your Honor,' Wood pushed ahead. 'It's not fair.'

'Come now, Counsel. It wasn't fair to get the grand juror to break his oath in the first place. Make no mistake, any attempt to tell this jury what that grand juror told your man will result in a mistrial and I will assess costs against you, Mr Wood, not the newspaper. You have the lunch-break to get it straight with the witness.'

Gunnar resolved to make the most of the ruling. Likely O'Boyle's vigor was acknowledgement of the near-impossible task he had set before Gunnar when he'd ruled that Tony Djilas was a public figure.

After the noon recess. Gunnar stood near the jurors, surveying all of their faces. As always, he looked for some sign and, as always, he found none.

'Mr Chapin, you testified this morning that you relied on more than Waycross, the bank account, and the arrest report. Please tell the jury what else you relied on to make the judgment that my client had been engaged in criminal activity' Gunnar looked directly into the long narrow face of juror Madge Meyers, second from the left in the back row, as if he were asking her the question.

'I spoke with one of the grand jurors,' said Chapin, betraying no feeling.

'One of the members of the grand jury that failed to indict Zilman, or anyone connected with this case for that matter. Correct?'

After a quick glance at Terry Wood, Chapin said, 'Yeah, that's correct.'

Another wall laid up, plumb, all the joints neatly pointed, but it was going to take a lot of bricks and more than four walls to make this building stand up. And now Terry Wood had the privilege of examining his client Chapin to rehabilitate him, if he could, from any of the damage inflicted by Gunnar's cross-examination. First, Wood took Chapin through a series of questions to establish he'd had no relationship or contact with Pierce Pentecost before or after Henning's party. He finished with a question ostensibly designed to summarize Chapin's motives or, at least, what clearly was not his motive. 'Mr Chapin, did Pierce Pentecost's interest in the New City project have any influence on you whatsoever in the preparation of the news articles subject of this law suit?'

In an instant: 'It doesn't matter, we wrote nothing but the truth!'

The answer zoomed by Gunnar like one of Fleet's service aces. Gunnar jumped up, realizing too late that it was not the time for a dramatic reaction. 'Objection, not responsive, move to strike the answer!' He asked O'Boyle if they might approach the bench.

The judge sustained the objection. 'The answer is stricken, counsel may approach the bench.' O'Boyle's face was screwed into a tight frown, a flood of red extending to the top of his bald head. Again, the knot of lawyers formed in front of O'Boyle.

In a hoarse loud whisper Gunnar said, 'Jesus Christ, Judge, I move for a mistrial!' Eddie squeezed his elbow.

'She's making a record, Gunnar,' O'Boyle said, referring to the court reporter craning her neck to hear the whispered conference.

'I apologize, Your Honor,' Gunnar said, anger subsiding.

'I don't want the jury to make too much of this,' said O'Boyle. 'I'm not calling a mistrial, but Terry you better not let it happen again, or I will; and I promise you I'll set the costs at twenty-five grand at least.'

'Your Honor,' said Terry Wood, 'I had no idea that the witness would blurt that out.'

'All the same it's your responsibility,' said O'Boyle. 'After I instruct the jury I'm calling it a day.'

The lawyers returned to their seats.

All eyes focused on the jury as O'Boyle admonished them: 'You will disregard the witness's answer to the last question, and I remind you that whether or not the newspaper's allegations about Mr Djilas are true will be for either you or me to decide, based on the evidence. If Mr Djilas is to have a fair hearing here, you must ignore remarks like the one just made by Mr Chapin.'

Consider the bell un-rung the judge told them, even as it continued to reverberate in their ears. The bastards got away with it. But they all do somewhere in the trial. And getting to

Chapin was like trying to kill a rattlesnake: even when cut in half, its teeth were still deadly, the tail still buzzed. With the cross completed on the two reporters, Gunnar had scored some points: a motive for malice might exist. Suzy Cline had found no evidence of Tony's criminality herself and she was capable of lying big. The jury had seen her caught in the act. And the evidence Chapin had relied on in preparing the articles had at least started to crumble. There was a long way to go, but a start had been made.

31

On day nine the judge was late. Around the courtroom door and inside, voices blended loudly. On his way in, Gunnar passed the defense group enclosing Terry Wood in the hall like fighters and their seconds listening to instructions from the referee.

Tony's wife had arrived from Florida. Terry Wood had taken her deposition in Fort Lauderdale last March when Gunnar had enjoyed a brief, but passionate reunion with Holly in his hotel room. Ila Djilas' deposition had been a waste of time. Most of Wood's questions were met with wide-eyed stares, shrugs, and a mumbled 'I don't know', or 'I don't remember'. Thinking a jury would expect it, Gunnar had asked her to testify at the trial. She sat in the second row, blue eyes blinking behind octagonal trifocals, her round face haloed with a kinky blonde permanent. In her husband's long absence she had evidently turned to food for solace.

Marvel Djilas, Holly's little sister, sat to her mother's left, probably an approximation of the girl Tony had married thirty-odd years before – excited blue eyes in a narrow white face framed with fine flat blonde hair to her shoulders – no hint of consanguinity with either Tony or Holly.

The bailiff gave them the 'All rise' and O'Boyle rushed in, robe flowing, apologizing for the twelve-minute delay. In chambers, he had just performed a wedding for a nephew and his bride.

'If you have nothing preliminary, Counsel, I'll call the jury,' he said, 'but let me say again, no more stunts like last afternoon.' He looked directly at Terry Wood's friendly face, so wide that his eyes looked like little hazel marbles.

'No, Your Honor,' said Wood. 'Again we apologize . . . .'

O'Boyle waved it off. 'Bring in the jury,' he said to the bailiff.

Last night, Gunnar and Eddie had spent two hours going over the proof. Eddie agreed with the strategy to back off the malice issue for a while, give the jurors a chance to get their breath. Gunnar would call Carlyle Henning and Pierce Pentecost later.

'Plaintiff calls Wright Maynard,' said Gunnar.

Maynard, born in Amarillo, Texas, now retired, had been a busy detective in the Broward County Sheriff's office from the mid-fifties to the mid-eighties, he said. He wore highly polished, black cowboy boots with his gray suit and, without a strand of silver in the dark brown hair, he didn't look anywhere near the sixty-six he claimed to be.

His identity and personality established for court and jury in Maynard's easy down-south twang, Gunnar moved ahead. 'Are you acquainted with Tony Djilas?'

'Not really,' said Maynard. 'But I know who he is.'

'How long have you known who he is?'

'Fifteen years or more . . . early seventies, late sixties, reckon.' His slightly sunken brown eyes were eager and observant.

He had become aware of Djilas through his real estate activities in and around Fort Lauderdale, Maynard said. He had also seen real estate ads Tony had run in the local paper.

'Did your responsibilities extend to drug law enforcement?' Gunnar asked.

Maynard's deep-tan Florida face smiled, showing good teeth. 'At's about all we were doin' then, seems like.'

'Was Tony Djilas ever involved in anything connected with drugs or marijuana, or the like?'

'Objection, no foundation,' said Wood in a just slightly pained tone.

'Sustained,' said O'Boyle.

'OK,' said Gunnar. Then, to the witness, 'To your knowledge?'

'Not to my knowledge. We never had any complaints and his name never came up on the job.'

'Never?' said Gunnar.

'Never,' said Maynard. 'Only thing was once there was a piece in the paper 'bout some kind of ruckus 'tween him and the city police. Some house he had for sale or rent, or some dang thing. That's years ago. I don't rightly know nothin' about it.'

'Considering your responsibilities in Broward County in the late sixties and early seventies, if Tony Djilas' activities in and around Fort Lauderdale had been under the scrutiny of agencies of other levels of government concerned with drug law enforcement, would you know about it?'

'Objection,' said Terry Wood. 'No foundation, calls for speculation, leading . . . .'

'Overruled,' said O'Boyle.

'Yep, I'da known about it. We all worked together,' Wright Maynard said calmly. All lawyers in earshot knew he had spent countless hours in the witness box. They also knew how hard it was to impeach a man like Maynard. He knew why he was there and what he needed to say to make the point, and juries loved him from the get go.

'Did you know anything about his reputation?'

'Good, furs I heard.'

'Objection,' said Wood. 'No . . . never mind, withdrawn.'

'Your witness,' said Gunnar.

Terry Wood got the witness to admit, reluctantly, that if Tony had something other than a good reputation, it was possible that he wouldn't know about it. And in his experience he had been surprised more than once by people he thought to be of good reputation. 'That's sure a fact, couple times anyway, but it still warn't such a big town in them days,' Wright Maynard added with an endearing grin for the jury.

You wouldn't forget John Koronis' big hawk-like nose. He was much younger than Wright Maynard, with a grim mouth and eyes like two lumps of coal set in leathery skin, well-done in the tropical sun. Buttoned tightly into a three-piece dark tweed and with a slight broadening of his R's, Detective Koronis summarized his twenty years on the Fort Lauderdale Police Department. He had first earned his detective's shield at about the same time Tony had come to town. His first cop's job was Providence, Rhode Island after getting his BS from Mass U. at Amherst in 1963. He met and married a co-ed from Florida. Linda's parents lived a few miles south of Fort Lauderdale in Hallandale. Anyone in the courtroom could tell Detective Koronis would not be satisfied until he was Chief Koronis.

Yes, he knew Tony Djilas. They had met at various civic and social functions in Fort Lauderdale. Both had been members of Kiwanis. And yes, Tony had an excellent reputation, and yes, he knew about Tony's phony arrest by the Fort Lauderdale cops. Terry Wood jumped to his feet.

'Objection, no foundation,' said Terry. 'Move to strike.'

'Sustained,' said O'Boyle. 'Stricken, as to the characterization of the arrest as phony. The jury is to disregard it.'

The witness frowned as though the judge had obviously lost his senses.

'I show you what's been marked as plaintiff's exhibit 113, Detective Koronis,' said Gunnar. 'Can you identify it?'

'Sure, it's an arrest report. The kind we used to use in the department.'

O'Boyle announced the morning recess. 'Let's keep it to ten minutes,' he added.

In the hall Tony said quietly to Gunnar and Eddie, 'Like I told you, this Koronis is a smart dick.'

Holly had joined her mother and sister standing beyond Al Bergdorf who was looking over the rail at the main floor fifteen stories below. They had agreed that he would not fraternize with the plaintiff's team in the courthouse.

Tony continued: 'Not only smart, but he don't forget a friend.'

'Not *too* smart, I hope,' said Gunnar.

The smallest member of the jury, Sarah Michaels, caught Gunnar's eye and smiled as she walked by.

'I think the jury likes him OK,' said Eddie. 'And they loved Maynard.'

'Koronis is trying too hard,' Gunnar said. 'I wish he would just answer the questions.

John Koronis emerged from the men's room and strode toward them. Gunnar's look and slight shake of the head discouraged him from joining the group; instead, he walked directly into the courtroom.

'Tony,' Gunnar said, 'this guy seems like he knew you better than he led me to believe last winter.'

'You know everything I know,' said Tony.

'Judge is on the bench,' said the bailiff through the open courtroom door.

Eddie had already started back. Gunnar stole a look at Holly and got the usual smile for his trouble.

Back on the stand, Detective John Koronis studied the document. All of the jurors looked interested. 'Please describe for the jury just what this particular arrest report is all about,' Gunnar said.

'Sure,' said Koronis. 'This report was prepared by Officer José Kelly. He was on stake-out at a house on Victoria Terrace . . . .'

'Objection, no foundation,' said Terry Wood.

'Sustained,' said O'Boyle.

'Detective Koronis,' said Gunnar, 'I want you to describe what the arrest report contains. Do not give your own opinion of what happened or describe anything beyond what is in the arrest report.'

'OK,' said Koronis. 'The report shows that on 13 December, 1972, Anthony Djilas was arrested in a dwelling at 599 Victoria Terrace that contained eight bales of grass, er . . . marijuana.'

'Did he own the dwelling?'

'It says on here that it was under his care and control.'

'Who was the arresting officer?'

'José Kelly, he signed the report, but his partner, Ralph Ek was with him.' Koronis shot the answers back before Gunnar completed the last word of the questions.

'Is José Kelly still on the force?'

'He was shot and killed in the line of duty in 1973.'

'What about Ralph Ek?'

'He's been gone even longer. He quit. I can't even remember what he looked like.' The witness rubbed his dark widow's peak.

'Were you involved in this arrest in any way?'

'Not until later, months later.'

'Are you able to remember any of the details of your involvement?'

'I checked my notes – I keep a daily log – before coming here.' The witness said he had brought the log with him, but he didn't need to refer to it to refresh his memory.

'How were you involved?'

'Like a lot of drug cases,' Koronis spread his hands apart, palms up, 'this one just hung there. The perp was out on bail. Finally, the defense attorney filed a motion to dismiss. Kelly was dead and Ek was gone, so the investigation was turned over to me. I met with Mr Djilas and his lawyer. They proved to my satisfaction that Mr Djilas was legitimately on the property to check it for the owner, some guy from Baltimore named Evans. Djilas' office managed the property as a rental. He should never have been charged in the first place. Lucky he didn't sue.'

'Then what?'

'I told the DA we had no case. They dismissed it.'

Terry Wood took over for cross-examination, the same brown suit as the first day with the open seam on the shoulder. 'Detective Koronis, are you familiar with the details of Officer Kelly's death?'

Jesus Christ, Gunnar thought, he's trying to make it look like Tony's involved. O'Boyle might sustain an objection, but not likely. Better not to show concern.

'I was on the investigation,' said Koronis.

'What happened?'

'Apparently he pulled a motorist over at the beach around three in the morning. The only witness was a drunk more than a block away. Kelly was shot once through the heart. His own gun was in the holster. The case was never solved.' Koronis looked at the jury and shook his head slowly from side to side. His drooping black eyes displayed sorrow. 'José Kelly was a hero in my book,' he added.

'Did you work hard on it?'

'Kelly was a cop. Almost everybody worked on it. We didn't have a lead.'

'How about Ek?'

'I thought somebody might ask me so I checked around. Found nothing. There was a letter in his personnel file, from San Diego, requesting a reference, way back in '75. I called the company. He never got the job.'

'Did you or your organization ever find out who put the marijuana in the house on Victoria Terrace?'

'Not for sure, but we had to assume it was the guy Mr Djilas had rented the house to. The owner had been in Baltimore all winter.'

'What was his name?'

'Smith,' said Koronis.

Terry Wood smiled. 'Did you talk to him?'

'We never found him. He broke his lease,' Koronis said with a straight face. 'I brought the whole file. You can look . . . .'

'Thank you, I already have a copy,' said Wood.

After the lunch-break, Gunnar called Mrs Ila Djilas to testify. He spent a gentle hour allowing her to tell the story of her marriage, from the time of meeting Tony to their move to Fort Lauderdale in 1969. The words trickled out in a brook of still-hopeful love for Gunnar's handsome client. Looking at the wistful heavy-set lady in the witness box, it was hard to imagine the two together: Tony lean and elegant; Ila worn out and beyond camouflaging with graceful adornment.

'Why did the two of you decide to move to Fort Lauderdale?' Gunnar asked.

'Just so Tony could work with Mr Zilman,' she said.

'Mrs Djilas, please speak directly into the microphone,' said O'Boyle.

'Do you have a clear memory of the time when you and Mr Djilas were living together in Fort Lauderdale?'

'Oh yes, we had a pretty house on a canal. The girls loved it. They spent a lot of time at the beach.'

'Did you see much of Mr Zilman?'

'Hardly ever.'

'How did your husband spend his time?'

'He worked a lot. Sometimes he played golf, but I think he mainly worked.'

'Did you go out together?'

'Hardly ever.'

Holly had shown Gunnar pictures of her mother. She had been a beauty. Perky breasts and blonde hair in a rich pile on top of her head.

'Did Mr Djilas talk about his work with you?'

'Yes, all the time.'

The jury's eyes were glazing over. Better get on with it. He wasn't sure calling Ila Djilas had been a good idea. It was just something you did in jury trials. Show the wife and husband together, a team, unity, all that shit, but these two were not a team. The question had been: what would the jury think if the wife *didn't* testify?

'To your knowledge, Mrs Djilas, was your husband involved in any way in the sale of marijuana or any illegal drugs?'

'Absolutely not.' It was the first time she'd spoken in much above a whisper.

'Now, as I understand it, Mr Djilas left Florida to come back here in 1973, right?'

'Yes.' Again, weakly.

'Why did you stay on in Fort Lauderdale?'

'Well the girls loved being there, and Holly . . . anyway Marvel was just starting high school. Tony thought it would be better if we stayed. He said he would bring us up here later.'

Gunnar wondered what she'd been about to say about Holly. Better let it alone. 'But you never did move here?'

'No.' Nothing more. Gunnar had hoped she'd explain so he could get her off the stand with just one more question. She stared at Tony with a pathetic look as if to say: what do I say now? Why did you throw me out like old clothes?

'Your husband and you remain separated to this day?'

'Not legally or anything like that. He's just never come back.'

Gunnar hoped the two divorced people on the jury would help the others understand.

'Are you aware of your husband's reputation in the community?'

O'Boyle sustained Wood's objection. The hell with it, Gunnar decided.

On cross-examination, Wood asked her if they had owned a boat in Fort Lauderdale. Gunnar felt the question like a straight left jab to the nose. Ila said they had, but she just couldn't remember much about it except that they'd hardly ever used it, and if anybody had borrowed it, she didn't know who it might have been.

Gunnar still had time to call Harold Jarvis for cross-examination. Boss to Suzie Cline and Ward Chapin, Jarvis admitted the decision to go with the articles came from above, and he had relied on the word of his reporters as to the truth of the allegations. He knew nothing beyond that. He had never had any discussions with Pierce Pentecost or any of the others bidding for the New City contract.

Gunnar's case was still on track. If Tony testified as expected, plus the stories of the cops, and the doubt enshrouding Suzie Cline and Ward Chapin, Gunnar thought he just might sustain the burden of making the case that the allegations against Tony were false. And he had opened the door on malice. If, tomorrow, he could tie Pentecost and Henning in a nice little lover's knot, O'Boyle might decide the question of malice was for the jury. He remembered what Tony had said to him last summer, 'If we had some eggs, we'd have some ham and eggs, if we had some ham.'

For the third or fourth time since the trial had started, Gunnar thought he might call and meet Holly at the lodge. As before, he thought better of it. If she could keep the bargain of no monkey-shines during the trial, he surely must. But every night as he tried to find sleep, Holly's lovely face intruded on thoughts of the next day's testimony.

32

Though absent since the first morning, when the jury was impaneled, Carlyle Henning's presence had been felt ever since Suzie Cline's description of the Memorial Day frolic in his bed. Today, in the witness box he held his chin high and locked eyes with Gunnar on every question. Bald as Eisenhower, his effort to look regal didn't quite make it. The expensive gray suit, in the faintest plaid, concealed the sagging flesh beneath, but his dewlap hung under his chin like a tom turkey's. After an hour's worth of questions demonstrating the plenary power Henning wielded at the *Times-Journal*, Gunnar got to the malice issue. He asked Henning how he had met Pierce Pentecost.

'I met Mr Pentecost on a trip to Paris a few years ago. We had adjoining seats on the Concorde.' Henning's replies were articulated precisely and in an evenly modulated voice with a touch of Harvard in it.

'Didn't you both stay at the Crillon?'

'Yes, but that was purely a coincidence. He was travelling with his wife.'

Henning had testified earlier that he had been divorced in 1970. He had one son.

'Did you agree to get together when you got home?'

'Yes, I had him out to my place a week or so after we returned.'

'Did you have sexual relations . . . .'

'Objection, irrelevant, prejudicial,' said Terry Wood.

'On that date.'

'Overruled,' said O'Boyle.

Henning looked at Terry Wood's face, grown pink with the moment. Wood said nothing. Henning said nothing.

Gunnar waited, no hurry. He used the silence as a weapon. Then he said, 'You may answer, Mr Henning.'

His dark brows knitted together, he looked at the judge. 'A man's life should remain private in some regards.' A flush had rushed over his face, continuing across his forehead and naked pate.

Courtrooms and bedrooms were two places you might see powerful people at bay and although O'Boyle betrayed no emotion, Gunnar knew the judge relished telling Henning: 'Please answer the question before you, sir.'

Henning changed his focus to the side wall, as if to ignore Gunnar. 'Yes,' he said.

'And this sexual relationship has continued on a regular basis since that date?' said Gunnar, knowing it would be easier for Henning to agree than to be questioned in detail as to what might have been irregular about it.

'You might say that,' said Henning.

'I take it that means "yes"?' said Gunnar.

Henning nodded.

'Let the record show the witness indicates the affirmative,' Gunnar said looking at the court reporter.

'Mr Henning,' said O'Boyle, 'you must answer the questions audibly. The court reporter only records sounds.'

'Yes,' said Henning still looking past Gunnar at a point on the wall just above the desk where the bailiff sat in his tan sheriff's uniform, and below the clock which indicated to O'Boyle that it was time for the morning recess.

The right schools, the right contacts, the right name protected men like Henning. In this courtroom this morning the forces from which he had been shielded all these years had breached the barricades. Tomorrow morning he would be further exposed in his own newspaper.

After a quick trip to the men's room, Gunnar returned to the counsel table. He wanted no conversation this morning, not even with Eddie. He had planned his line of questions to Car Henning precisely. Many would like to know more about the party and the titillating details of the relationship between Pentecost and Henning. But the fact that two people were fucking was established; further embellishment was irrelevant to his case. The next hurdle was to show that the fucking was somehow connected with the printed allegations against Tony Djilas. And Gunnar's comfort level wasn't high, exploiting these defendants' sexual preferences. Still, he knew nothing in this trial was more irrelevant than his comfort level as long as he stayed within the boundaries of the law. He was obligated to do whatever it took to win.

Carlyle Henning's chin had dropped a degree or two. His face was drained. In another hour, blocking the rich publisher's escape like a good boxer using the ropes and the corners, Gunnar established that Pentecost and Henning conversed several times a week – on the phone, at Henning's home, over lunch, at various clubs and parties. They had developed a close, caring relationship with many mutual interests.

Late in the morning Gunnar asked, 'When did you first begin discussing the New City project?'

'In what regard?' said Henning.

'In any regard.'

'As you probably know, our editorial policy has backed downtown renewal for many years. I presume Mr Pentecost and I talked about it from the time we first met.'

'Unfortunately the jury can't deal with presumptions, sir.'

'Then I have no specific recollection,' Henning said testily, the color returning to his face.

'Let me put it this way,' Gunnar said. 'It's fair to say that you and Mr Pentecost did talk about the New City project over a long period of time.'

'I'm sure we did,' said Henning.

'And is it fair to say that you talked about Block 13?'

'I couldn't say that for sure.'

'Surely you knew Pentecost was a general contractor?'

Henning nodded.

'Speak up,' said O'Boyle.

'Yes,' said Henning.

'And you knew he had been involved in major downtown projects before?' Gunnar waited for an answer. 'You have a question before you, sir.'

'I didn't think that was a question.'

'Trust me,' said Gunnar.

You could hear a giggle or two from the crowded spectator section. O'Boyle scowled. One juror smiled.

'Yes, of course, I knew he had built some buildings downtown, as well as many other places,' said Henning.

'And as close as your relationship was, you wouldn't expect this jury to believe you had not discussed the largest single project ever proposed in the city's history?'

Henning shrugged his shoulders.

'You did discuss Block 13 with Mr Pentecost, did you not?'

'I suppose so.'

'You did, did you not?'

'Yes, I'm sure we did,' said Henning, his face and bare scalp again totally flushed, 'but not in any specific way, or with any special purpose in mind.'

After more hedging and equivocating in the afternoon, the time arrived for Gunnar to play his ace. He had the reporter mark a document, and he dropped a copy on the counsel table in front of Terry Wood. He walked slowly back to a position in front of Henning.

'I show you a photocopy of a document marked "Plaintiff's 341"; are you able to identify it?'

'Just a minute, Your Honor,' said Wood, 'this document was never furnished to us in our continuing demand for production. We object to its use . . . .'

'Your Honor, I intend to use it for impeachment purposes,' said Gunnar. He had returned to his seat at the table next to Eddie Kerr and Tony Djilas.

'Approach the bench,' said O'Boyle.

The four lawyers, two lions at the bar and their assistants, clustered their heads close enough together to listen to O'Boyle speaking out of the hearing of the jury. 'What is it, Mr Larson?'

'That's what I was going to ask the witness,' said Gunnar. 'I think it is a compilation of notes in his handwriting.' Gunnar knew damn well what it was.

'What's wrong with that?' said O'Boyle to the serious face of Terry Wood.

'I don't like the smell of it,' said Wood.

'Off the record,' said O'Boyle, 'you know, Terry, I used to teach evidence, and I can't remember anything about an olfactory test for documents.'

'C'mon Judge, you know what I mean. It's only fair we get the jury out of here until we know what this is.'

'What about that, Gunnar?'

'Whatever you say, Judge.'

O'Boyle declared the mid-afternoon recess, and when they reconvened the jury box was empty.

Terry Wood, like a linebacker, big frame standing behind the counsel table in a stoop, was the first to address the court: 'Your Honor, it is defendant's position that plaintiff's 341 was obtained illegally, and is therefore inadmissable as evidence and cannot be used for any purpose in this trial.'

O'Boyle replied, 'Mr Wood, this isn't a criminal trial.'

'At least not yet,' Eddie whispered to Gunnar sitting next to him.

O'Boyle went on: 'I'm going to let counsel lay his foundation. If it is indeed the witness' handwriting it can be used for impeachment. Your objection is on the record.'

And, indeed, it was Carlyle Henning's handwriting, a fact repeated for the jury after they had filed back in. Gunnar noticed Henning's hand trembling when he held the document, as his own had in the exquisite excitement of the moment.

'Mr Henning, your notes on page one are cost projections for Block 13, New City are they not?'

'Yes.' Henning's eyes looked resigned, tired.

'And page two lists the likely prime bidders on the contract, correct?'

'Yes.'

Now Gunnar wanted to get the witness into the rhythm of a long string of yeses. Each question describing the notes on the four-page document was easily susceptible of an affirmative answer. Terry Wood, sensing the ploy interrupted with an objection: 'The document speaks for itself.' That O'Boyle quickly overruled. Gunnar was getting ready to take a gamble: break the cardinal rule of cross-examination by asking a question for which he didn't know the answer. There was little to lose and much to be gained. A couple more yeses. The time arrived.

In the same steady rhythm and matter-of-fact tone of voice Gunnar asked, 'And these notes were all prepared before 1 June, 1986, were they not?' He knew the whole case, and millions could ride on the answer.

'Yes,' said Carlyle Henning maintaining the easy give and take and removing any doubt that he had been considering the details of Block 13, New City before any of the defamatory articles about Tony Djilas were published.

Dov had earned his dough, and the bricklayer had built another wall, square and plumb. Gunnar supposed that Carlyle Henning had left the stand feeling relieved. If he was, his relief would only last over the three-day holiday weekend. The trap for Pierce Pentecost was baited and set.

33

Friday afternoon, Gunnar had found a pink telephone slip saying, 'Call Mrs Hogan at the lodge.' For weeks he had talked to Holly only infrequently, and he had not touched her for close to a month. He didn't miss what he didn't think about and, except for moments late at night, the trial ruled his mind. He wished she hadn't called. Maybe he wouldn't return it, but what if it was urgent?

Her voice revealed the urgency, 'Oh Gunnar I miss you; you know how I need you.'

She stirred him.

'How long have you been sitting there waiting for my call?'

'It's no problem at all. I love it here. It's full of my best memories.'

'Have you forgotten our bargain?'

'Of course not. I know you can't come out here.'

'It's been a long time,' he said. Gunnar had to see Dov before he left to spend the three-day weekend in London.

'There's a Baltimore Oriole building one of those hanging nests right in front of the bedroom window.'

'I've got to go,' he said.

'The bear says hello,' she said. 'And I love you.'

'Me too,' he said. 'Goodbye, now.'

Eddie Kerr tried Gunnar on the intercom. It was busy. He chased down a cheeseburger with a paper cup of Coke. After rereading Dexter Epstein's letter, he tried the intercom again. 'Gunnar, you got a minute to talk about a client of mine.'

'I'll come down there,' Gunnar said.

Shit. Gunnar never came into his office. He must want to keep it short.

If the mess shocked him, Gunnar didn't mention it when he came in the door. He removed a raincoat and a foot-thick file from one of the chairs and sat down.

'Dexter Epstein is having trouble in Watsonville. I got another letter from him today,' Eddie said.

'I remember – that criminal case you handled last year, dope dealer was it?'

'You know, he wouldn't take a transfer or protective custody. Now he's a punk for a long-termer named George Washington.' Eddie explained in some detail what a punk was.

For the first time since he had met him, Eddie allowed Gunnar to infer that there was perhaps a problem out there Eddie couldn't solve on his own. 'He sounds really desperate. I'm worried. I thought maybe you'd have some idea how we could help.'

'Have you talked to Barry Busch?' Gunnar said. 'I've had nothing to do with criminal in twenty years.'

'I've done that. Busch doesn't take the problem seriously. He suggested PC. Maybe I can get Dexter to reconsider.'

'I guess it can't be too big a worry if he's turned down PC.'

'I'm afraid it's a major-league problem,' Eddie said, letting his eyes hold on Gunnar's.

'Call Leo,' Gunnar said. 'He's in town. He'll call the warden.'

Leo was an angle Eddie hadn't thought of. 'OK,' he said. 'That might be the answer. I'll give it a shot.'

Gunnar headed for the door. 'Sorry, I couldn't help,' he said, and he was gone.

Eddie jumped up. Gunnar's back was already thirty feet away. 'Hey, Gunnar.'

Gunnar turned around.

'Thanks a lot,' Eddie said.

Gunnar was irritated with the interruptions, first Holly, then Eddie. But Eddie's human concern for his client was a pleasant surprise. Perhaps Gunnar had misjudged him. He decided to walk the ten blocks to Dov's hotel.

To start off the eleventh day, Gunnar called Pierce Pentecost. He had taken his deposition last winter, and with the transcript in hand he had convinced O'Boyle to declare him a hostile witness,

215

enabling Gunnar to examine him with leading questions, and impeach him if necessary.

Pentecost was smaller than Carlyle Henning, long narrow face with deep lines in sallow skin, like the people El Greco painted. He had come to court in a checked sport coat and an open-necked white shirt. He stood straight up for the oath, a narrow wispy figure with a thatch of dark hair going gray at the temples.

Gunnar started out benignly, merely introducing the witness and his business operations to the jury. Pentecost listened carefully to each question and waited several seconds in apparent thoughtful consideration before answering. Unlike Henning, Pentecost spoke directly to the jury with an air of confidence in a commanding resonant voice. He would be difficult to get into a rhythm. After Henning's debacle yesterday, perhaps Terry Wood had coached him.

Gunnar quickly changed the pace with a question the witness might really need to think about. 'Did you discuss your testimony with defense counsel since yesterday?'

Pentecost looked perplexed, then he glanced at Terry Wood as though he expected some kind of help. Wood was silent, face a blank.

'Yes, he told me to tell the truth,' said Pentecost.

O'Boyle cracked a smile. So did Gunnar.

'Perhaps. Did he tell you how to tell the truth?'

O'Boyle overruled Wood's quick relevance objection.

'You may answer,' said Gunnar.

'We talked a little about taking my time and speaking to the jury.'

At least he wasn't going to lie on a minor issue, but the point was made. Pierce Pentecost was clearly identified with the enemy camp.

A series of questions and answers confirmed most of Henning's testimony of the previous day regarding their relationship, sexual and otherwise. Then like a poison dart from a hidden blow gun: 'As a matter of fact you actually solicited Carlyle Henning's help in obtaining the contract for Block 13, New City?'

'No,' said Pentecost, taking no more time than the word. The fine broth of believability thickened with the lumpy lie.

Gunnar waited, giving the witness opportunity to think, perhaps amend his answer. Pentecost said nothing. Gunnar dropped a single sheet of paper on the table in front of Wood, handed another to the court reporter for marking, then took a quick look at the jury. From behind the grandma glasses, Sarah Michael stared raptly.

Pentecost, his mouth a straight line, took the paper with long thin fingers like spider legs with gold rings. The drab uneasy eyes scanned the single page, then shifted to Terry Wood, then back to Gunnar who stood directly in front of him. 'Where did you get this?' he said.

'I'm sorry sir, I can only ask the questions; it's not for me to answer any,' said Gunnar. The document's provenance would remained undisclosed, not that Gunnar could have provided an answer if he'd wanted to. Looking into Pentecost's eyes, Gunnar felt like asking him if he wanted a blindfold, or did he wish to see the guns when they fired. 'Do you recognize the document marked "Plaintiff's 342"?'

Terry Wood was on his feet going through the same litany of objections as last Friday when Gunnar had surprised them with Henning's notes on Block 13. Again, Gunnar reminded O'Boyle that the document was for impeachment purposes, and O'Boyle looked at the witness. 'Mr Pentecost, did you write this letter?'

'I guess I did,' he said.

'Objection overruled,' said O'Boyle. 'You may inquire, Mr Larson.'

The letter was typewritten, with no stenographer's initials below the signature. 'Mr Pentecost, did you type this letter yourself?' Gunnar asked.

'I think I did it on my computer . . . a laptop . . . in a hotel room in New York.'

'On the date stated, 15 May, 1986, more than a month before the articles defaming Mr Djilas were published?'

Wood objected.

'Strike "defaming". You may answer,' said O'Boyle.

'I have no reason to believe that wasn't the date I wrote it,' said the witness.

'Please read it to the jury, if you would,' said Gunnar.

O'Boyle overruled Wood's objection that the document spoke for itself.

Pentecost still hesitated, his face stricken. With his free left hand he rubbed his jaw like a man with a toothache. He looked at O'Boyle, apparently hoping for a miracle reprieve.

But, over the half-glasses, O'Boyle's glittering dark eyes showed no incipient signs of mercy. 'Let's move along. Go ahead and read the letter, Mr Pentecost.'

Pentecost cleared his throat and coughed. 'Dear Car, I have been sitting here thinking about you, and wishing you had come along. I took in "42nd Street" last night. All the tap dancing was marvelous. Made you think you were living in the thirties. Thelma Jones from the Chase Bank went along. On another subject altogether . . . .'

Pentecost's voice was steadily descending to a low croak. From his position standing in front of the witness and facing the jury, Gunnar caught O'Boyle's eye.

'You'll have to speak up,' said the judge.

Pentecost stopped altogether, his face down. His hands, holding the letter, dropped to his lap. His shoulders heaved. He was quietly crying. O'Boyle called the morning recess.

Gunnar felt a twinge of pity for the witness, then reminded himself of what Pentecost and the *Times-Journal* had done to Tony Djilas. Juries could be compassionate, however, so always avoid unnecessary brutalization of any witness he told Eddie Kerr as they were about to return to the courtroom.

Pentecost was back on the stand, composure apparently regained. All eight faces in the jury box were fixed in serious expressions.

'If the court and Mr Pentecost please, the clerk may read the letter and I will address specific questions to the witness,' Gunnar said.

Pentecost looked at Wood and got a nod back.

O'Boyle started to speak, 'That procedure is acceptable to . . . .'

'No,' said Pentecost, 'I'll read it.'

'Fine. Would you proceed from where you left off, please,' said

Gunnar standing directly in front of the witness with a copy of the letter in his hand.

'On another subject altogether,' Pentecost began reading. He had returned to the erect posture. 'I think I am getting the runaround from the staff at the Department of Development. I think I've told you that Kurt Hirsh doesn't like me. My friends on the City Council tell me that this Djilas character has the inside track. That might have something to do with his friendship with the mayor, and the Bergdorf firm has a lot of clout in City Hall as I'm sure you know.'

Gunnar watched the jury watch Pentecost.

He went on: 'Do you suppose you could help me in any way. I have invested close to a hundred thousand already in just front-end expenses. Think about it. I'll call you as soon as I get back to town, hopefully not long after you get this letter.' The witness stopped reading.

'Would you please finish,' said Gunnar.

'I did.'

'The complementary close,' said Gunnar.

'Love, Pierce,' said Pentecost.

By noon Gunnar had finished with the witness, and Terry Wood had completed his examination with only the feeblest attempt to rehabilitate Pentecost from his disaster. At the noon break Gunnar's face was confronted with the stainless-steel doors of the elevator. Behind him he heard Pentecost's voice.

'Oh, hello Andrew,' he said.

A male voice replied, whiny, with feminine intonation: 'It was a rough morning. I would think that some of it could have been avoided.'

That was all. The elevator was otherwise silent as is usually the case when courtroom combatants are encased together to descend to the street. The voice bothered Gunnar. He knew he had heard it before. He strained his brain. On the main floor he stepped aside to get a look. He recognized everyone else in the car, except the slight young man who got out with Pentecost and walked toward the atrium floor. He had thick black wavy hair, and a slim pretty face, slight hollows at the temple and well-formed lips the color of a dark rose. Gunnar listened to the voice again, faint and distant:

'I have never been so angry . . . .' it said, and then it faded into the babble of the busy courthouse at noon.

'Do either of you know that guy with Pentecost?' Gunnar said to Tony and Eddie.

Neither of them did, but Tony said, 'He talks like a girl.'

Gunnar knew he'd heard the voice before. It hit him! Of course, the fucking anonymous caller.

Back at the office he turned on the tape he had made of one of the calls. The voice came out of the speaker: 'I'll call again. I don't want to stay on the line any longer, but you can be sure I have information you can use.' Then the dial tone. He couldn't be positive, but to Gunnar's ear it sounded exactly like Andrew of the elevator.

It was worth checking out. Gunnar was convinced that with Tony's testimony beginning this afternoon, together with the cross on Cline and Chapin, plus the two cops, he had made a good enough case of falsity. And with little doubt left about the relationship between Pentecost and Henning, he had laid a foundation for malice. But as a matter of law, malice required reckless disregard of the truth or falsity of the allegations, or knowledge of the falsity. He knew he still had a problem there. Perhaps he could make it to the jury on what he had, but to win big and stand up on appeal, he needed to bolster his malice case. Dare he hope that the anonymous caller had something he could use? He picked up the phone.

34

Al Bergdorf sat down in the back pew at one-twenty. Even though he had a permanent pass, with Tony going on the stand, Al took no chance of not finding a seat when the court reconvened in ten minutes. After Tony had spent a couple of hours with Gunnar last night, Al and Tony had a late dinner at Maple Hills. They had both lamented the extent to which the trial had cut into their golf.

'Are you set for your day in court?' Al asked.

'Gunnar says I should perk up . . . act more like my old self. He thinks the trial's got to me.'

Al told the girl he'd have a stir fry and toast, no butter. 'Gunnar's right, you know, you got a lot on the line tomorrow.'

'This thing's gotta turn out right, Al.'

'If you tell the truth from beginning to end, Tony, it's *gonna* turn out all right. You'll see.' More likely O'Boyle would show up naked.

'You sound awful serious.'

'I am,' said Al.

Now, on the twelfth day, Grace North set up her stenotype in front of the judge's bench. As she leaned over her machine to adjust the paper, her wavy brown hair veiled her pretty face. O'Boyle came in, and the throng stood up, a procedure Al was finding easier with nearly twenty pounds gone from around his middle. He had been on the diet for six weeks. Maybe Grace North would give him a tumble if he dropped another eighty.

O'Boyle asked if Tony Djilas was Gunnar's last witness. 'One more, the Reverend Robert Goodspeed,' Gunnar replied. A murmur rippled over the room. Only Billy Graham was a better-known evangelist.

Tony looked splendid as he stood for the oath, like an admiral getting a medal from the president. The jury's faces brightened to Tony's smile. After he had affirmed that he would tell nothing but the truth, Tony, nodding toward Grace North, said to O'Boyle, 'Your Honor, that beautiful lady works harder than anyone in here.'

'I couldn't agree with you more,' said O'Boyle, ignoring the laughter.

Grace blushed as she typed the compliment in mechanical shorthand. He's got the guts of a burglar, Al thought. In the jury box little Sarah Michaels was beaming. Al and Gunnar had discussed how she might react to some of the raw testimony. It was always difficult to tell, but for the moment she seemed taken with Tony Djilas.

Gunnar began his examination from his seat at the counsel table. Al knew he would not take a lot of time. To minimize the cross-examiner's field of fire, plaintiff's attorneys want their clients to tell their story in detail, but without embellishment. Cut the chances for faux pas. Cases were often lost on cross-examination of the plaintiff. Besides, the articles themselves, and Ila Djilas' testimony had introduced Tony to the jury.

Tony did tell some of the more poignant episodes of his growing-up, the frequent moves, his father's alcoholism, and he spoke reverently of his mother's toil. But he never lost his humor, and the jury was barraged with extravagant smiles.

The tiny golden scimitar was easily visible on his dark blue lapel. Gunnar inquired about Tony's Shriner life. He was a member of the Patrol, a colorful marching unit. He spent hundreds of hours per year in fund-raising for crippled children's hospitals, much of it focused on the annual Shrine Circus.

He had been an active church member from the time he was married until he left Florida, and he professed still to attend on Sundays, when he could. In the back row, Al remembered their Sunday-morning golf games and smiled to himself.

At the recess, Tony approached Al at the rail overlooking the atrium. 'How'm I doing, buddy?'

'Never better, but Gunnar's not gonna like it, talking to me out here.'

Tony edged up closer, face to face. 'He sent me. See the guy behind me, the pretty boy with the wavy black hair. See if you can find out who he is.'

Tony pivoted and headed for the men's room. Gunnar followed him in.

Al edged unobtrusively toward Andrew, standing at the rail in a checked coat looking down on the crowded atrium floor. When Al reached his side, the young man seemed oblivious of the crowd and the cacophony of voices behind him. Al stuck out his hand. 'Al Bergdorf – takin' in the sights?'

'Oh.' Andrew looked startled. 'Oh, yes, I guess I am.' He reached for Al's hand. 'I'm Andrew Levy.'

His soft hand was as delicate as a sparrow's wing. 'Special interest in the case?' said Al.

'No, just curious.'

'Aren't we all,' said Al.

Before the courtroom came to order, Al handed Eddie Kerr a note. In large loopy hand it said: 'Tell Gunnar the nebbish's name is Andrew Levy. I am not sure of the spelling of his last name, but that's the way most Jews spell it.'

Back in session, Tony skimmed through the arrest in Fort Lauderdale on a breeze of smiling self-confidence, agreeing with everything Detective Koronis had said. 'It didn't surprise me that they had the place staked out when I went in and found the dope in the garage, but soon as the cops barged in I told them I was a Realtor, but they wouldn't listen. They just slapped the cuffs on me and read me my rights as though I didn't really have any.'

To Gunnar's next question, Tony replied, 'Of course, I didn't know the dope was there. I would have called the police. I couldn't afford such shenanigans in my business.'

'To your knowledge, did Mr Zilman have anything to do with the house on Victoria Terrace where you were falsely arrested?'

Terry Wood broke his silence. 'Objection, assumes facts not in evidence, calls for a legal conclusion. It wasn't necessarily a false arrest, Your Honor.'

O'Boyle paused for a moment. 'He may answer,' he said. 'Overruled.'

'Not to my knowledge,' said Tony Djilas.

Al saw only Gunnar's back encased in navy blue, seated at the counsel table. The ceiling lights illuminated his pinkish scalp through the thin hair on top. 'Mr Djilas, during Mr Chapin's testimony you heard mention of a bank account, did you not?'

Tony said that he did, and Gunnar asked him to explain to the jury just what the bank account was.

'I really didn't know,' Tony said. 'Manny Zilman asked me to do him a favor. He said I was the only guy he could trust. At that time I had no reason to suspect there was anything wrong with it. So I agreed to let him open the bank account in my name. He made deposits in it, and when he wanted money out of it I wrote the checks.'

'Why did he open it in the Bahamas, rather than in the United States?'

'To this day, I'm not sure. He told me it was for personal reasons. You gotta remember he was my boss. I tended to do what he told me. He said it wouldn't be for long, and it wouldn't involve a great deal of money. Later I found out he was depositing a lot more than I thought he had planned to.'

Al thought the testimony sounded like bullshit. But he knew Gunnar would rather have the jury hear it now, than when Terry Wood was cross-examining. It was the first hitch. The jury's faces were mostly fixed in frowns. Every case has a weakness, Al thought.

'You must have had some idea what Zilman was up to,' said Gunnar.

'To be honest, I thought he was planning some big real estate deal . . . maybe establishing credit in the Bahamas, or maybe some kind of a tax dodge. I thought what I didn't know wouldn't hurt me. We only had the account for a year or so.'

It was exactly what he had told Al. Al didn't believe it then, and he didn't believe it now. With all the clever deals in his own long career, Al Bergdorf still didn't understand Zilman's angle on the bank account. Obviously, Gunnar was too ethical to help his client build a more plausible explanation. But one thing was certain, as far as Sarah Michaels, sitting in the front row of the jury, was concerned, this bank account thing didn't compare with Car Henning putting his wee-wee in Pierce Pentecost's butt. And she was one of the six going to decide this case.

It was almost four o'clock when Gunnar asked Tony, 'Up until the time you were called to testify before the grand jury, were you aware that your employer, Manny Zilman, was involved in dope smuggling or selling, or any other criminal activity for that matter?'

'I knew he smoked grass on occasion. Other than that, to this day, I'm not aware of any criminal activity on his part. I know he was accused. People told me he was in deep trouble, but he never admitted it to me.'

'Mr Djilas, it has been alleged that the government made some kind of a deal with Zilman enabling him to avoid prosecution. Are you aware of such a deal?'

'Just what I've heard.'

'Have you heard that part of the deal was that you also wouldn't be prosecuted?'

'Big deal! There was nothing to prosecute me for.'

Terry Wood came to life. 'Objection, not responsive.' He ignored the obvious hearsay.

'Sustained,' said O'Boyle. 'The answer will be stricken.'

Gunnar asked Grace North to read the question back.

'Sure, I've heard,' said Tony.

'Did the deal indeed protect you?'

'Beats me. I don't even know for sure if there was a deal.'

'Do you think there was a deal?'

'Objection,' said Wood, 'irrelevant, calls for speculation.'

'Sustained.'

'Mr Djilas, when is the last time you had contact with Manny Zilman?'

'Sometime in late 1973, the year I quit and came back here. Could have been in early '74. There were loose ends on various real estate deals we talked about on the phone. Then he dropped out of sight. Somebody told me they thought he might be in that government witness program. You know . . . where they set you up somewhere with a new name, but I don't have any idea where he went.'

From his seat at the counsel table, Gunnar pushed on, 'Have you ever committed a crime Mr Djilas?'

First, Tony flashed the dashing grin at the jury; then he said, 'Is it safe to answer that?'

The six jurors and two alterates all smiled back.

Tony didn't wait for an answer. 'Yes, I committed a couple of crimes when I was a kid. Got in some trouble, too. We stole some beer. But since then, I don't think I've ever consciously committed a crime. Perhaps some traffic violations, I guess. I've had some speeding tickets.'

'Mr Djilas, you have, of course, read the articles published by the *Times-Journal*, and subject of this law suit, that allege you were involved in criminal activity in Florida – specifically the purchase and re-sale of marijuana?'

'Yes, I've read them.'

'Are those allegations true?'

'Absolutely not,' said Tony Djilas.

Gunnar turned to Terry Wood. 'Your witness,' he said.

Wood stood up behind the counsel table. 'Your Honor, due to the late hour, I would like to start my cross-examination of Mr Djilas in the morning.'

'Good idea,' said O'Boyle. 'We'll adjourn until nine-thirty tomorrow morning.'

Alone in the office, Gunnar got Dov on the phone. 'I've got a new name I need checked out. Maybe Fleet will help you.'

'Fine. I've taken to Phil Donahue on the telly. He's interviewing men who like to wear dresses and panty hose.'

They discussed Dov's two days in London; then Gunnar got back to business. 'The name is Andrew Levy, l-e-v-y. He's a slightly built . . . .'

'Just a minute! I know the bloke. Couldn't forget with the same last name as me. Of course I wouldn't have anyway.'

'You're kidding,' said Gunnar.

'No. He's Ward Chapin's friend . . . lover actually; or at least he was last winter. I met him at the party when I was wired for sound.'

'Jesus Christ, is his voice on the tape?'

'Just barely; you can't hear him. He spoke too low with all the background noise, and he said very little anyway. Chapin did all the talking.'

'I think he might be our anonymous caller.'

'Oy.'

'I heard his voice in an elevator. I believe it matches one of the tapes I made.'

'Lover scorned, or just greedy for some easy money, or maybe both,' said Dov. 'And then maybe he clammed up when he got back in Chapin's good graces.'

'Do you think you can do anything with him?'

'Suzie's the problem. She's still calling. She thinks I'm out of town. They told me at Miracle Mills that she asked for my number in Britain. Of course, by now she's convinced I'm the one who told you about the party at Henning's.'

'Think she's told Chapin?'

'It's possible. Not likely, though. Would you have?'

'I guess I wouldn't,' said Gunnar.

'Me neither.'

'I really could use something more,' said Gunnar. 'We've proved the motive, and made a fair case on the truth issue, but I've given the jury nothing definite on whether the bastards knew it was false when they published it. Of course, I think the jury could well believe they should have known.'

'Isn't that enough?'

'Technically yes, but it doesn't give me that warm feeling.'

'Barristers never get that warm feeling 'til the money's in the pocket. Eh?'

'True enough . . . and the whole case could go up in smoke tomorrow when they cross-examine Tony. I could sure use a little more. If that was Andrew on the phone, he might have what we need.'

'I'll get on it, tonight. You haven't got his number?'

'No. If he's not in the book, Fleet'll help. You've got his home number?'

'Right.'

'Tell him I miss the tennis.'

35

For the past week Eddie had done little at the trial except listen, and make detailed notes in a tiny unreadable hand. At times Gunnar would ask him to retrieve an obscure fact from memory, and he almost always obliged.

This morning as they assembled in the crowded courtroom to await the cross-examination of their client, Gunnar asked, 'Counsellor, did I ever pay you on that bet on the Series last fall?'

Eddie remembered vividly how happy he had been when the Red Sox blew it all in the sixth game; and then the Mets finished them off in the seventh. And he remembered Gunnar congratulating him over the intercom, and promising to pay when he saw him. But at the time he'd been so involved with Dexter's problems, and a million other things that just could not remember if Gunnar had given him the twenty-five bucks. He knew he had collected the two fives on the pennant races. But would Gunnar believe that he had forgotten? Eddie's penury was a standing joke around the office. Oh, what the hell, he must have paid. 'You paid me,' said Eddie.

'Ah ha, I got ya!' said Gunnar. He handed Eddie two tens and a five. 'I've been meaning to pay you for months, and somehow we are always talking about something else, and I forget.'

Eddie felt his mouth compress into his tight little smile.

'Anyway,' Gunnar said, 'my conscience is clear.'

They got the 'All rise', and in minutes Terry Wood had begun questioning Tony Djilas. 'Mr Djilas, what approximately is your net worth?'

He's not wasting any time, Eddie thought. Gunnar's objection on relevancy was overruled.

'Well I haven't really figured it out lately.' Spit it out, Eddie thought.

'Let me refresh your memory,' said Terry Wood, out from behind the counsel table, and looming before Tony with a document in his hand.

Tony told him he recognized the financial statements he had submitted in connection with the New City contract, and O'Boyle admitted them into the record. 'Looking at these, as of about a year ago, my net worth was $3,641,507.00.'

'Has it changed in a year?'

'It's less. The value of apartment buildings is falling because of the new tax law, and I've had some unusual expenses, mainly connected with this suit.'

'Are you paying your attorney's fees as you go along?'

Wood wants to tip the jury that Gunnar's working on a contingency, Eddie thought.

O'Boyle sustained Gunnar's objection. Then Terry Wood began the tedious task of getting Tony to establish where he'd got the money to acquire his assets, principally several apartment buildings located around the suburbs. But much of Tony's worth was in two forty-four unit buildings he had acquired in the mid-seventies. They had more than doubled in value. Wood had discovered in Tony's two-week long deposition that a couple of hundred thousand dollars of the seed money couldn't be accounted for precisely, but, as Eddie anticipated, it didn't come through for the jury. Djilas refused to change his answer to Wood's summarizing leading question regardless of how it was phrased, and Gunnar had made sure there were no accountants on the jury.

'Mr Wood, you're just not understanding the numbers,' said Tony. 'There is no missing thousand, let alone two-hundred thousand.'

Frustrated and red-faced, Terry Wood moved on. The onlookers shared his frustration. Many had slipped out at the morning recess. When they started up after the lunch-break, all had disappeared but the regulars. Holly had taken a seat beside Al Bergdorf.

Wood started a new tack. 'Before you went to Florida, you

and Zilman had become involved socially as well as in business, correct?'

'Some,' said Tony Djilas.

'More than some, correct?'

Tony's eyes narrowed, but he held on to the smile. 'Some,' he said.

'You played golf together, regularly at Olympic Greens, correct?'

'Some,' said Tony, smiling, eyes and mouth.

'You and your wife, and he and his wife took a trip to Europe together in 1966, correct?'

Eddie had interviewed Zilman's wife. They were divorced in 1968. She knew nothing. They were childless, and she'd got a property settlement of about $600,000.

'He had purchased a large quantity of kitchen ranges, Hotpoint, I think,' said Tony. 'The manufacturer had given him two trips for two. Ila and I went along.'

'When he decided to move his operation to Florida you were part of the plan, correct?'

'I told him I wanted to go along. It was like a transfer. If I hadn't gone, I would have been out of a job.'

Throughout the afternoon, Terry Wood stubbornly pursued Tony Djilas' relationship with Zilman. In the back row of the jury box, Richard Hayek's eyes, magnified by the thick glasses, dropped shut, and only popped open when his head flopped off-center in a move toward dangling repose. Other chins were supported by cupped hands wedged on padded arm-rests.

Terry Wood's first question the next morning reignited their interest.

'On direct examination your attorney raised the issue of an account at the Bank of the Indies in Freeport, Bahamas, correct?'

'Correct.' Today, in glen plaid, Tony looked as fresh and confident as he had the first morning.

Terry Wood had the previously marked bank statements admitted into the record. The checks themselves were long gone. He had Tony describe the statements, month by month.

'In fourteen months, according to your testimony, Zilman deposited over $1,200,000 into your account, is that correct?'

'I guess it is, if that's what they total up to, but remember, it wasn't my money. I did it as a favor for Manny.'

'Most, if not all of the deposits were made in cash, correct?'

'I have no idea.'

'Do you wish this jury to believe that you had absolute control of over a million dollars, and didn't have the slightest idea where it had come from, or what its purpose was?'

'I hope they believe it, because it's true,' said Tony, his face projecting utmost sincerity. 'And incidentally, don't those statements show that there were checks written out of the account almost as fast as the money came in. I doubt if there was ever more than a couple of hundred thousand in there at one time.'

'This whole scheme must have worried you, correct?'

Gunnar objected to the 'scheme' characterization. 'Overruled,' said O'Boyle.

'I'm not a worrier, but I did question whether I might get stuck with the income tax on the money. He told me I wouldn't, and if I did he'd pay it. Luckily, it never came up.'

Ironically, Eddie thought, the only people in the nearly empty court room who might believe Tony's story about the bank account, were sitting on the jury.

After a long series of repetitious questions regarding the bank account and which Gunnar could have objected to, Wood posited one last time-tested cheap shot from the cross-examiner's arsenal. 'If I told you that an employee of the Bank of the Indies says that you made several deposits in person in cash, what would you say?'

'I'd say he was a damn liar.' He let his face settle into the pout of the deeply wounded.

Gunnar didn't need to object. 'Let's move on to another subject, Mr Wood,' said O'Boyle. 'And unless you can prove the charge, I think you know how I feel about that type of question.'

Now Wood looked wounded. 'Very well, Your Honor,' he said. 'You owned a boat in Florida, correct?'

'I owned two,' said Tony. 'When I first got there I bought a twenty-foot open fisherman, and later, I traded it on a thirty-four-foot Chris Craft.'

'Where did you keep the Chris Craft?'

'In the canal behind our house on Ninth Street.'

'Did you ever lend it to anyone?'

'Manny used it a few times.'

'Zilman?'

'Yes.'

'How many times?'

'That was fifteen years ago.'

Eddie Kerr remembered from early interviews that when Zilman took the boat he sometimes kept it for days at a time, once more than a month.

'Enough so that he could have used it in smuggling operations?'

'I suppose so, but if he did, I didn't know what he was using it for.'

Terry Wood didn't have enough to win this case on cross-examination, and his face showed that he knew it. Eddie respected Wood's courtroom technique, but perhaps his investigation had not been thorough enough. On his next line of questions he proved he hadn't learned any more about the arrest on Victoria Terrace than Detective Koronis had related. Then, he gingerly inquired into Tony's family life in Florida, his decision to leave, and his life here since he had returned, especially his developing relationships with the mayor and other politicians.

With Tony Djilas' second day approaching its end, Terry Wood made a last attempt to discredit him. 'Isn't it a fact, Mr Djilas, that Ward Chapin called you on 12 November, 1985 in an attempt to discuss the pending articles with you?'

'I couldn't possibly remember a date like that.'

'Can you say he didn't?'

'No.'

Wood followed with a whole series of dates on which Chapin had allegedly tried to get Djilas to agree to an interview. Tony failed to remember any of them specifically, and after each he conceded that the calls could have occurred. He remembered that some had.

'Isn't it fair to say, Mr Djilas, that Ward Chapin and therefore his employer, the *Times-Journal*, gave you plenty of opportunity to discuss the news articles subject of this suit.'

Tony hit Wood's hanging curve over the center-field fence: 'No, it's not fair to say. You saw the cocky attitude of that jerk in this courtroom just a few days ago. He talked to me like he owned me, like I was some kind of a simp. Nobody talks to you like that and gets co-operation. He was just setting me up. He was . . . .'

Wood interrupted, heavy face gone maroon. 'Your Honor, move to strike, not responsive.'

'No, Counsel,' said O'Boyle, shaking his head. 'You opened the door.'

'Let the witness finish,' said Gunnar.

'No, I think he's made his point,' said O'Boyle, permitting himself his daily little smile.

36

From the dark booth, Dov eyed the front door. An hour ago Andrew Levy had picked up Dov's call on the first ring.

'I'm not sure you remember me,' Dov said in his most British tone. 'I'm Jesse Katz. We met at a party last winter. At Graham Garth's. You were with a boisterous newspaper reporter.'

'Yes, yes I remember the accent. You were that husky with Suzie.'

Americans had used that word on Dov before, but never as a noun. The voice coming out of the phone was unmistakably the same one Dov had just listened to on Gunnar's tape.

Andrew went on: 'How did you get my number?'

'I wanted to see you again so bad I had a butch I know at the police department find it for me,' said Dov.

'I guess nothing is sacred any more,' Andrew's soft musical laugh matched his voice.

'Would there be a chance we could meet somewhere tonight?' Dov crossed his fingers.

'Why not? Any place downtown is fine.'

'You name it, I'm from out of town, you know.' He hoped Andrew would pick a gay bar where Suzie Cline would never be. He wasn't that worried about seeing Chapin.

'Do you know where the Three-O Club is?' Andrew asked.

Might as well use the truth when it can't harm. 'I do, but there's a bitch that hangs out there I don't like, and there are so many drunks.'

'Oh sure, I understand,' said Andrew, and he gave the address of Sweethearts, the place where Dov sat, waiting.

'An hour?'

'An hour's fine,' said Andrew Levy.

Sweethearts was almost empty. Piano music came from a room in the back where the few male couples had immediately headed. A muscular black nude with an out-sized penis reclined in a faintly lit painting above the bar.

When he came through the door, Andrew quickly removed dark-rimmed glasses and stuck them in the breast pocket of his checked blazer. He is pretty, Dov thought as he held up his hand. Dov stood up and took Andrew's fragile fingers, and held them while he introduced himself.

'It was nice of you to call,' said Andrew. 'But right after you hung up I thought I should have invited you over to my place, but I didn't have your number.'

They both ordered Scotch rocks. Dov felt the solid weight of the tape recorder in his inside jacket-pocket. He asked Andrew about himself. He was a computer programer at Unisys. He wanted to get into acting, but one does have to make a living. Dov ignored the suggestion that they retire to Andrew's flat, and then led him to the trial.

'Knowing Ward Chapin, I suppose you've been following the trial in the papers.'

'The papers nothing, I've been there, right in the courtroom, three times. I had to wait in line . . . I used vacation time . . . . They ruined my friend Pierce. Pierce Pentecost, I met him right in here a couple of years ago. He's a very nice man.'

A couple in matching black leather came in the front door and stayed at the bar. One smoked a cigarette in a short holder.

Andrew's dark eyes appeared huge in his smooth spare face. He described the details of his days at the trial, reaching across the table and touching Dov's hand when he became agitated.

'It was a dreadful thing for Pierce to go through. At one point he cried.'

'It must be a mess,' said Dov. 'How is your friend Ward doing?'

'He's much stronger than Pierce. I think he did fine. He and I have been very close, you know.'

'So it seemed at Graham's party,' said Dov.

'Oh yes, that party! Wasn't it marvelous? Peggy sings so beautifully.'

The shvartzeh blues singer, Dov thought.

'And Graham has one of the finest homes in town. Isn't that cabaret room immense . . . . Do you know Ward, Jesse?'

'Not very well I'm afraid.'

Andrew said that he thought Jesse would know Ward better because Ward worked with Suzie. He and Suzie weren't that close, Dov said, and what was it Andrew was saying about Ward's trial . . . .

'Oh yes, the trial. I was there when Ward testified. He looked just great up there. They couldn't get to him like they did Pierce. Ward's proud of being gay. Too proud maybe, I don't think there are any gays on that jury, and Ward acted awfully cocky.'

'You and Ward are still close?'

'Well, I thought we were. At least until this trial started.'

'What makes you wonder?'

'There's been other times, too. Last fall and again right before that party at Graham's.'

When Andrew had anonymously called Gunnar, Dov thought.

Andrew went on: 'I got suspicious. He had said he wanted a monogamous relationship from the start. Over two years ago. Like I said, I was almost sure he was cheating on me last fall, and then I saw him kissing this leather queen in another bar where he knew I hardly ever went. But he convinced me he was just drunk; he does drink a lot you know. I hate it when he drinks.'

'I guess he does,' said Dov.

'And then it was all over television when Suzie testified. He was fucking both Car and Pierce, and maybe even Suzie for God's sake. Don't get me wrong, if you're bi, you're bi, like I suppose you are. But he was fucking other people when I was faithful to him, and he had promised. I don't know if I can take any more.'

Dov imagined Gunnar's reaction when he heard on the tape that Andrew thought he was bi-sexual. 'I suppose he's been quite good to you,' Dov said.

'He's given me some very nice things. He likes to dress me like him. But he's been spending money on coke lately, a lot I think.'

'That can be very expensive,' said Dov.

'You bet, and I can't stand the stuff. It hurts my nose, and I have so many allergies anyway. But . . . I'll say one thing, I like Ward better on coke than those darn martinis. They make him so loud. Well, *you* know.'

'Sure,' said Dov, looking straight into the deep-set dark eyes.

'And, the truth is I wouldn't mind playing the field a little, but he wouldn't hear of it. Says it's too dangerous. And then *his* fucking makes the papers. It wouldn't take much now, Jesse.' He reached across the table and laid his perfect little hand on the back of Dov's, and left it there.

'What would Ward say?'

'I simply don't care.'

Andrew used his hand to take a sip of Scotch. Dov decided to keep his hands in his lap when not in use.

Another short man stopped at the table. 'Hi, Andrew! New friend?'

Andrew didn't even look up. 'I'm busy Angie,' he said in a weak, but get-lost tone. Angie moved on.

Dov didn't know what to say next. Like the first night with Suzie, he had to make the decision. How much time did he have? Gunnar didn't know for sure when he would use Andrew, or his information, if he had any. Maybe, not until Tony's rebuttal case. That would be weeks yet. But just knowing what it was, now, might make the difference.

'Would you like to go up to my place,' said Andrew again. 'Are you into Wagner? I have the full Ring on compact disks, and I've got a great system.'

'No hurry,' said Dov. 'Let's have another Scotch.' He made the decision. Now or never. 'So I'm to understand you and Ward are no longer an item?'

'I think you could say that.'

Now, Dov reached across the table and laid his tan stubby-fingered hand, like a slab of bacon, on Andrew's pale wrist.

'Can I trust you completely?'

'Of course you can,' said Andrew, his eyes widening in erotic anticipation. With his rose-like lips he blew a kiss at Dov.

'I don't really like Ward Chapin,' said Dov. 'You see we have a mutual friend, a Brit named Trevor. Trevor and I have been close. Now Ward's fucking him, too. Seems the man has his dick in everybody.'

Andrew was stricken. All signs of energy left his face, but his eyes remained wide open. 'Are you sure?' he said. 'Are you sure?'

'I'm sure. I saw them.'

'You saw them.' The music went out of Andrew's voice. It receded to a mumble. 'Where?'

'At Trevor's. Andrew, my dear, dear friend I am so sorry to have to tell you this.'

'Ward was with *me* the night before last,' Andrew whined.

'If you can promise me absolute secrecy, I will tell you something *I* know that I think *you* should know.' Dov held his wrist again. 'Above all others, you must not tell Ward.'

'Jesse, you have my word,' he said, a hint of firmness in his small voice.

'I have a friend whose name I cannot divulge who is connected with this Djilas character.'

'The one who is suing Ward?'

'Yes. If you know anything about those articles, they might pay a large amount of money for your testimony.'

'Is that why you called me tonight?' Andrew sounded ready to cry.

'Well, I must admit I really want to get this bastard. Trevor and I had a good thing going, and now he's told *me* bye-bye.'

'Well, at least, you're honest. More than I can say for some people.'

Dov told him how sorry he was; that, of course, he knew exactly how he felt. Andrew said that he wasn't really surprised, especially after the news reports of Suzie's testimony, but the Trevor thing was for sure the last straw.

'Who shall I talk to?'

'You can tell me what you know,' Dov said, 'I'll pass it on.'

37

'Good! Daddy got the passes for tomorrow.' Katie found them on the dining-room table.

'You know I haven't seen your father in action for years.' Anne had been sitting alone drinking raspberry tea and looking out across the wrinkled bay into the fading light. 'He said he didn't like the idea of you missing classes to see Robert Goodspeed testify.'

'It won't be much you know, Mom. He's just a character witness.' Katie sat down and filled her cup.

'Much more interesting than those other characters.'

'You're *so* funny!'

'Comes naturally,' Anne said.

'Not like it used to.'

'Don't get serious on me. What are you going to wear?'

'I'm going to dress like a lawyer. My blue suit with a white blouse and red tie.

'I should wear a dress, don't you think.'

'Of course, an elegant dress. You're the wife of the star.'

'In name only.' As soon as she said it, Anne wished she hadn't.

'Oh, Mom! Not getting any better?'

'At least I don't think he's been spending Tuesdays and Thursdays at Libby Cochrane's lately.'

'How do you know?'

'I hate to tell you.' But she did. When Gunnar wasn't home by eight-thirty or nine on Tuesdays and Thursdays, more than once she had driven downtown and checked his parking space in the garage. His car had been there. One night he almost caught her. 'Am I awful?' she said to Katie.

'I don't blame you a bit. The way you must feel. But I think you should have asked him directly, when you got that call.'

'I just don't want to. If he wants me to know, he'll tell me. When he's ready.'

Katie's smooth hand holding the delicate pink cup made Anne notice her own. Purple veins stood out from the coarse surface on the back. Their slender bodies looked like sisters, but the difference told in the skin, especially the hands.

'Is it not getting any better?' said Katie.

'Not really. During this trial I've been rubbing his neck. I've never seen him this tense. It used to be second nature. I could hardly tell when he was in trial.'

'Oh, Mom.'

'Katie remember, I don't spend my every waking hour thinking about your father. I've got all my friends. And I've got my running. And I'm playing some tennis to let off some steam. I have to get on with my life, as best I can.'

'I know.'

'And you haven't heard my latest. You're hardly ever home, except to sleep. I've become an advocate and counselor, sort of, for battered women. On some of those Thursday nights I'm already downtown.'

'Battered women?'

'They need volunteers at the various shelters. To answer the phone and take them in when they come. And sometimes I go into court with them. Just for support.'

'That's wonderful,' said Katie. 'Are the lawyers any good?'

'I think they are. They're mostly women from Legal Aid.'

Behind Katie, Gunnar stepped silently through the kitchen door. Anne pretended not to notice him. Katie was talking about women lawyers and Gunnar put his hands over her eyes. She screamed, then let a huge puff of air out of inflated cheeks.

'Daddy, you scared me half to death.' She stood up and kissed him. Anne kept her seat.

'How are my two favorite blondes?' Gunnar said.

She must be a brunette, Anne thought.

* * *

240

Even O'Boyle looked impressed. Reverend Goodspeed approached the witness box like a knight striding to the round table. Salt-and-pepper hair with a curl flopping over a high flat forehead and a cleft chin, it was as if you were watching TV. The oath seemed unnecessary. After he was sworn, and had spelled his name and given his address for the record, Gunnar asked Robert Goodspeed his occupation.

'I preach the Gospel of Jesus Christ across the land.'

Jesus Christ, Gunnar thought. 'You have come all the way from Virginia to testify here today?'

'No sir, I am seldom home these days. I flew in from Southern California, and I am going to Mexico City tonight where we are opening our fourth Mexican campaign.'

Gunnar took Robert Goodspeed through a personal history that all but those who had been asleep for thirty years already knew. Sinners in a hundred countries had answered his mellifluous summons. His was a message of promise, not damnation. It worked. Millions took up his challenge and came forward.

Every January he listened to the State of the Union Address from a place of honor in the House Gallery near the president's family. On the nation's most momentous occasions Robert Goodspeed often prayed the invocation or the benediction.

'Reverend Goodspeed, are you acquainted with Mr Anthony Djilas, the plaintiff in this case?'

'I am.'

'And, Reverend, do you have some notion as to what the case is about.'

'I understand Mr Djilas has been defamed.'

Terry Wood just looked frustrated; he didn't bother to object.

'When did you first meet Mr Djilas?'

'In our South Florida Campaign in 1970. I was introduced to both Tony and Ila Djilas.'

'How did that come about?'

'Tony, er, Mr Djilas helped organize our revivals in Fort Lauderdale. The Lord provides loving local-church people to help us in the planning stage on all of our campaigns.'

'Have you had contact with Mr Djilas in the ensuing period?'

'Oh yes, we became friends. As all of you here must have learned by now: to know Tony is to love him.'

'How often have you seen him over the years?'

'Many, many times. He worked in our Florida campaign in the Tampa area in 1972, and when we came up here in the mid-seventies he worked very hard for us. We were able to spend a lot of time together. He's come to prayer breakfasts in Washington and New York where I have preached, and one of the most memorable times was when we made our campaign to Seoul, Korea in 1976. Tony was along the whole time. Oh yes, we are very good friends.'

'Reverend Goodspeed, have you had the opportunity to learn anything about Mr Djilas' reputation in the communities where he has lived?'

'Oh my, yes. You know we must be very careful who becomes associated with our campaigns. Before Tony became involved with us in Florida, we made certain background checks.'

'How about in this city?'

'Well, of course, since Florida, we've become personal friends.'

'Are you aware of Mr Djilas' reputation generally?'

'I certainly am.'

'And what is that reputation?'

Wood had to object for the record.

'Overruled,' said O'Boyle.

The Reverend smiled at the lesser mortal who would question his fitness to answer the question. Then loud and clear, in the loftiest of tones: 'He has a reputation as a fine Christian man, of the highest principles and integrity.'

'Your witness,' said Gunnar.

'Reverend Goodspeed,' said Terry Wood, not the least bit reverently, 'it is a fact, is it not, that Mr Djilas contributes large amounts of money to your organization.'

'I can't say for sure. I know he's been a contributor. Somewhere I got the impression that Tony tithes. Not to us, of course. I think much of it is to African missions.'

Gunner reflexively glanced at the one black on the jury, store-keeper Ralph Sullivan.

'No further questions,' said Wood.

Jesus Christ, did Wood think he was going anywhere with that. Might as well apply the *coup de grâce* to Terry's foot.

'One question on re-direct,' said Gunnar. 'Reverend Goodspeed, what do you mean by tithe?'

'To tithe is to give ten per cent or more of your total income to God's work.'

'Plaintiff rests, your honor,' said Gunnar.

'I'll hear motions right after lunch,' said O'Boyle. 'Court is adjourned until one-thirty.'

Gunnar walked up the aisle with Anne, her hand on his arm. Katie followed. Holly, still sitting with her mother, watched them from the corner of her eye.

'Who is that stunning woman?' said Anne.

'That's Holly Tripp,' said Gunnar, 'Tony's oldest daughter.'

Al Bergdorf smiled hello at the door, and pointed back into the courtroom where Terry Wood stood shaking Robert Goodspeed's hand.

'That's nothing, Al,' said Gunnar. 'O'Boyle told me this morning that the jury had sent a note with the bailiff saying they all wanted to meet the Reverend. The judge had to tell them no.'

Somebody, probably Shana, had left a copy of *Time* magazine on Gunnar's desk – open at the law section. A paragraph in the lower right-hand corner speculated that what currently appeared to be a serious problem for the *Times-Journal* should take on a new light next week when the newspaper presented its defense. The article said that First Amendment experts gave plaintiff little chance to prevail. They have a point, Gunnar thought. He had no idea what surprises might be in store – if Terry Wood was even required to mount a defense.

Last night Dov's excited telephone call had brought Gunnar back downtown. Minutes before midnight he'd listened to the tape Dov had made of his meeting with Andrew Levy at Sweethearts. Gunnar had decided against calling Andrew to testify today. It was too risky. Preparation was required. Besides, the damaging revelations would have detracted from the dramatic effect of the Reverend Goodspeed's whole-hearted endorsement of Tony Djilas' character. Andrew Levy would have to wait. The critical question was, would he? Andrew's mind could change again in much less time than Terry Wood would use to finish his case. And it wasn't until then that Gunnar could present another witness.

Standing behind the counsel table, Terry Wood made his argument to O'Boyle that plaintiff Djilas had not proved a *primafacie* case of libel and therefore the case should be dismissed. Freshly pressed navy blue had replaced the ragged brown suit. The jury had been dismissed for the arguments and Al Bergdorf sat alone in the back pew. Even the regulars in the spectator section had not returned to hear the boring legal locutions.

After fifteen minutes of pointing out the defects of plaintiff's case, Wood concluded: 'In closing, Your Honor, let me just say that if one were able to infer that somehow the falsity issue remained in doubt, it would still be logically impossible to infer that a *primafacie* case of malice has been made. Sure, a possible motive has been uncovered, but it is something else entirely to conclude that because a motive exists, the deed for which the motive exists has been done. Especially when you consider how precarious plaintiff's case of falsity is. How can we suppose that the defendant had reason to believe the allegations were false? Obviously, they bothered to check. The articles were in preparation for a year. This case should be dismissed.' Wood sat down.

They had come to the second most important point in a libel trial. Gunnar rose to make his plea to O'Boyle that the jury decide the case – after they had heard all the evidence. O'Boyle raised his right hand palm out. Gunnar quickly sat back down. He sensed the same empty fear as a half century ago in little Gunnar's flickering dark bedroom when an especially worrisome shadow moved without warning. Surely, O'Boyle would at least give him a chance to argue.

'Mr Wood,' O'Boyle said, 'although actual malice has been constitutionally defined, it still, in fact, is a state of mind. The letter sent from New York by Mr Pentecost . . . when taken together with the decision-making authority of Mr Henning

. . . and the admitted close relationship of the two, is just too compelling to take this case away from the jury on the issue of malice.' O'Boyle cleared his throat, then poured a glass of water from an insulated carafe sitting beside his gavel and downed half of it. 'I say all this in light of the evidence on falsity. If, when he decided to publish accusations as pointedly damaging as the articles before this court, all Henning had to go on was that bank account, the so-called arrest report, and the advice of Mr Chucky John Waycross, whom of course I have only heard up to this point by affidavit . . . vigorously rebutted by Mr Djilas, I'm not so sure a jury might not find Mr Henning to have recklessly disregarded the issue of truth on that ground alone. But throw the Pentecost question into the brew . . . that's what you have, a *brew*, a bubbling cauldron, susceptible of a variety of interpretations and clearly a jury issue.' O'Boyle stopped for a few moments. The wry smile indicated satisfaction with his metaphor. Again, he engaged Terry Wood's eyes. 'And I can't agree that plaintiff's case of falsity is precarious, as you put it. Perhaps the defendants' explanations will further enlighten the court. If so, this case might not go to the jury, especially if the evidence you present leaves the question of truth unresolved. In that event, I would be compelled to direct a verdict for defendants. Plaintiff has the burden of proving falsity. That burden does not shift. The US Supreme Court has spoken clearly to that issue. As it stands, until I have heard all of the evidence, I will reserve judgment and any further comment. The clerk will file my order denying your motion.' O'Boyle moved his eyes to Gunnar, opened his mouth and closed it twice like a goldfish in a bowl, and apparently decided to say nothing further.

The tension oozed out of Gunnar's body. Neither Wood, nor O'Boyle had mentioned the grand juror, Tomlinson. Terry Wood no doubt had his reasons. Of course, both Henning and his reporters had considered whatever Tomlinson told them when the decision to publish was made. But when the time came to pull the pin on that grenade, it never went off. The Tomlinson issue was one of those bar-exam questions unlikely to appear in the real world.

Gunnar leaned behind Eddie's chair and said to Tony Djilas,

'We're still in this case. That's all, just in it. There better be no surprises.' Except one of mine, he thought, let's hope Andrew Levy stays in the fold.

'We stand adjourned until nine-thirty tomorrow morning,' said O'Boyle.

38

Summer burned from day to day. By the middle of the seventh week, life had become the trial. Day broke and night fell on the trial. You slept only to rest for another day of testimony. Evenings and weekends were times of preparation and trying to understand what had happened that day and how it helped or hurt the case, and how it affected what was to come. The population of the world was the spectators, the court reporter, the bailiff, the clerk, the judge, the jury, the witnesses, the litigants, the lawyers and Al Bergdorf who, *sui generis*, fit no category. And only the lawyers were aware that this isolated society was not ruled by the judge. It was ruled by the facts, at least as the jury perceived them.

Gunnar had used only three weeks to present Tony's facts. Terry Wood needed more. Into his fourth week, he too, a master in the trade, had laid up some solid walls. First, he had called experts to opine that Gunnar's case of damages was far too high. Then he called the defendants. Only they knew their own thoughts, and Terry Wood had artfully drawn from them a reasonable story, an almost unassailable word-picture of responsible journalists doing their job. Each professed utter devotion to the truth. Ward Chapin, chin thrust forth like Mussolini, described his meticulous dedication to detail. He said he had double-checked everything. Suzie Cline had not been as forceful. Symptoms of shell shock suffered in her skirmish with Gunnar Larson, a month before, persisted. From a face flushed with fear, her unfocused eyes aimed at the floor or at the clock, or at her hands, but never at Gunnar or the jury. Still, her answers supported the substance of her colleagues' testimony. But she was too quick to agree to leading questions, too reluctant to resist the expert cross-examiner's challenge. She remained a serious problem to

Terry Wood's case for the defense. Following Suzie, Carlyle Henning, with an angry complexion, described himself grandly as completely misunderstood and he continued to protest his utmost good faith.

Because he truly loved Car Henning, Pierce Pentecost said he would not have wanted him to do anything unethical, even illegal, for money. Then, to an awe-struck jury, two of America's most venerated newsmen, Christopher Huntley and C. R. Stenborg vouched for Henning and for the *Times-Journal*'s national reputation for excellence.

The jury listened to much of it, but they tended to slip down in the soft leather chairs, and more than once Richard Hayek's head had started to dangle forward on his stump of a neck, only to be jerked back up, big eyes behind the thick glasses checking to see if anyone had noticed. But once Terry Wood had turned Suzie Cline over to Gunnar Larson, for cross, the jury came back to life.

'Isn't it a fact,' said Gunnar, 'that at a party last winter at Garth Graham's, Ward Chapin said, "That bohunk Djilas is the biggest crook in town"?'

Terry Wood jumped to his feet, incensed, 'Objection, what Chapin may have said eight months after the articles were published is irrelevant.'

'But, Your Honor,' said Gunnar, 'Chapin testified during the first week of this trial that he never said it. Period. Without regard to a time-frame. The answer to the question before this witness will show he was lying. It's fair impeachment.'

'Overruled,' said O'Boyle.

Suzie looked confused. Gunnar knew she was remembering how she had been nailed when she'd tried to lie about the Memorial Day party at Henning's. Without further prodding, she blurted out the answer Gunnar hoped for: 'Yes, he said it.'

'That Djilas was the biggest crook in town?'

'Yes,' said Suzie again. Her eyes asked, what more do you want of me?

At the recess that afternoon, Chapin swaggered up to Gunnar. 'So now, are you gonna sue me for slander, Counselor?'

Gunnar ignored him.

Chucky John Waycross, Chapin's reluctantly revealed source,

did not even appear. Dov's Miami investigation had borne fruit. He discovered that Waycross, married and the father of three, had been fired for engaging in sexual intercourse with an under-age girl while on a DEA stakeout. Somebody in the chain of command hushed it up on condition that Waycross resign and never show his face again anyplace that might embarrass the Agency. Waycross had informed Terry Wood that he was out of the case. Even if Wood could somehow reach him by subpoena, he'd take the Fifth, he said. Still, O'Boyle allowed certain portions of Waycross' deposition to be read in open court to show what Ward Chapin had learned from his frolicsome DEA agent. All the jury heard was that Zilman had insisted Djilas be protected in Zilman's plea bargain. Gunnar had exposed them to that a month before. Dov had come through again.

Otherwise, Gunnar agreed with the news accounts of the trial; Terry Wood's case had gone in quite smoothly. The jury could well conclude that even if the devastating accusations were false, the *Times-Journal*, after checking the facts over a period of a year, believed they were true. That was all that was necessary for defendants to win.

Terry Wood's own high-impact testimony was timed to go off this afternoon. The spectator area remained almost empty. Gunnar noticed that Al Bergdorf was losing weight. Beside Holly the ceiling lights ricocheted off Ila Djilas' trifocals; her sparse peroxide permanent remained unchanged. Daughter Marvel had long since returned to Florida.

Some sound drew Gunnar's attention to the back of the room. A young man employed by Terry Wood's office pushed an old lady in a wheelchair through the door. Gunnar poked Tony, 'Who the hell is that?'

'Holy shit,' said Tony, 'I think that's Emma Rosen.'

The name meant nothing to Gunnar.

'The wife of my neighbor on Ninth Street, Hyman Rosen. You know, your man in Florida found out he was dead.'

Jesus Christ! Wyman Farmer had offered to have Mrs Rosen interviewed in New York. Gunnar had forgotten her completely. 'Does she have an axe to grind with you?'

'I hope not,' said Tony. 'All I remember is, she was very

religious. Went to synagogue all the time. Hyman was a ren-egade. Played the ponies at Gulfstream. We got to be pretty good pals.'

'Was there anything between you and her?'

'Hell, we hardly ever talked. They were old *then*. I think she was ten years older than Hy. She must be pushin' ninety. They came over couple times. Once for an outdoor barbecue. Quite a few of the neighbors came. But hell no, we hardly ever talked.'

'You're sure it's her?'

'See that brown spot on her cheek. I'll never forget that mole. It had little black hairs growing out of it.'

Eddie Kerr listened over Tony's shoulder. Eddie would be wondering why they hadn't interviewed this old lady. It was Gunnar's fault. There were no excuses. Could a slip-up like this be the culmination of a year's worth of effort?

The young man had wheeled her up behind the other counsel table, and Terry Wood's big body leaned over, solicitously pumping her hand.

With judge and jury in place, Wood began. 'Your honor, if it please the court, we call our last witness, Mrs Emma Rosen.'

The young man pushed the chair to the front where O'Boyle could get a good look at its ancient cargo. Wood seemed nervously eager. He did his 'may-it-please-the-court' again, explaining to the judge that Mrs Rosen was confined to the wheelchair and, if there was no objection, he would question her from there. Once the clerk got a microphone set in front of her tiny gray face, Terry Wood asked her to state her name for the record.

'Mine name iz Emma Rosen, ee-em-em-a ah-o-es-ee-en. I liff et fi faw sebm Seckun Evenyuh, Noo Yawk Ciddy.' As she announced her address at 547 Second Avenue in New York, her English was enshrouded in the familiar accent of immigrant Jews raised in New York and speaking Yiddish in the home.

She was born in Poland in 1899, Her parents had brought her to the lower east side of Manhattan when she was ten. Only one leg protruded from beneath her long skirt, and what Gunnar could see of that was wrapped in an elastic bandage.

'Where were you living in 1972?' Wood asked.

'I liff wit mine Hyman, et one sebm nine fi Souteese Nint

Stritt in Fawd Lauduhdale, Fluhida.' Her head shook as she spoke.

'Hyman was your husband?'

'Yea'.'

'How long did you live there?'

'Hyman died en ninet'n sebnee sebm. I move beck ta Noo Yawk de nex' yea'. Fawd'n yea we liff dere.'

The court reporter must have understood. Her fingers automatically entered Emma Rosen's '1977' and 'Fourteen years' into the stenotype.

'Did you know Mr Tony Djilas when you lived there?'

'He liff righd nex' daw et one sebm nine one.'

'Did you become acquainted with him?'

'He liff nex' daw fuh fi yea, hiz wife lungga.' She sounded impatient, wasn't five years next door long enough to know someone?

Wood was having trouble laying his foundation and O'Boyle seemed amused. Gunnar saw little humor. He was scared of what this old lady might say, and a glance at Tony's face revealed the same.

'Mrs Rosen, I have to ask if you actually knew Mr Djilas.'

'I set we wuz neighbahs, awready.'

'But did you actually know him?'

'I didn ligem. Dot Zilman he woikt fuh, a good men he wuzn'd'.

'It shall be stricken,' said O'Boyle after sustaining Gunnar's objection. When Gunnar heard Zilman's name again he thought of the photo in the file: the handsome face, the greying hair.

'Did you know . . . .'

'Did I know em? I knew em, but ligem em, I didn.'

'Why didn't you like him?'

'Please, Terry,' said Gunnar. 'Objection, irrelevant.'

'Sustained,' said O'Boyle.

Gunnar didn't envy Wood. He'd had his share of stubborn elderly witnesses, both on cross and direct.

Wood tried again. 'Mrs Rosen . . . .'

'Dot im?' She pointed a stubby trembling finger in Tony's direction. She looked at her lackey who had retreated to the front pew. 'Hey you, weel me oveh dere. Lemme loogud em.'

O'Boyle nodded.

When her chair had been pushed up in front of Tony Djilas in his usual place at the counsel table, the little lady thrust her bewigged head forward. 'Dot you, Tony?'

Her eyes were huge behind the glasses. Gunnar felt compelled to stand, but that would have raised their faces further from her line of faltering vision.

'It's me, Mrs Rosen.' Tony leaned over the table and extended his hand.

She didn't take it. Maybe she didn't see it.

With his witness back in place, Terry Wood was ready. 'Mrs Rosen . . . did you know about Mr Djilas' involvement with Mr Zilman?'

'On . . . vulv . . . watzis . . . onvulv?'

'No, Mrs Rosen, involve – *ment*.'

Eight smiles radiated from the jury box.

'I dun know no onvulv *mond*.'

'Will counsel approach the bench,' said O'Boyle.

When they were knotted up in front of the judge and to the side of Mrs Rosen's wheelchair, O'Boyle spoke quietly to Terry Wood, 'Counsel, is this lady competent?'

'Bite yuh tungh, Judge,' the old lady squawked, 'I mebbe bline, bud I ain deaf.'

The whole assembly fell apart laughing, including O'Boyle. When the noise subsided, he said, 'I sincerely beg your pardon, madam.'

Emma Rosen ignored him. 'Gevalt! Did I know Tony un dot fancy-schmancy gunsel Zilman wuh in biznez togeddeh. Yea' I knew id.'

'Did you and your husband Hyman ever have business dealings with them?'

'Ai, yi, yi! Hyman lend im money.'

'Objection, no foundation,' said Gunnar.

'I'll lay it,' said Wood. 'Were you involve . . . strike that . . . was it your money?'

'Id wuz mine money. Hiz money, ah money, mine money, aw da sem.'

'How did this happen?'

'Zilman un Tony wuh en da dinink r'm . . . et ah house.'

'When?'

'July fi, nint'n sebnee two.' July 5, 1972.

'How do you remember the date so well?'

'How c'n I fuhged? En I still hev de check.'

'Who did the talking?'

'Who did de talkingk? Tony, dots who. En Hyman.'

'Where were you when they were talking in the dining room, Mrs Rosen?'

'W'ea wuz I? I wuz in da kitch'n lizningk.'

'What did Tony tell your husband?'

Gunnar's hearsay and foundation objections were overruled.

'Mrs Rosen, you may tell us what Tony told your husband.'

'I up so. I comm aw de way fom New Yawk Ciddy ta tell id. Id shdn' eppen ta a dog. Tony sez ef Hyman gib'm en dot gunsel Zilman one-hunded tousan dolleh, dey'll gib'm two-hunded tousan en tree monz.' In three months' time, $200,000 for $100,000.

'What did you do?'

'I come oudda da kitch'n. I tell em aw dot money didn' grow ona tree. Hyman sold hiz shoe-staw righd wen dey shod Kendy. I membuh, we wuz havink longe righd acrost da stritt fom da Foist Nashnul Benk. We god two-hunded en fifdy tousan fur dot staw . . . a nize staw, righd on Turd Evenyuh. He hed somm custumuhz fawdy yea'. We wen ta Fluhida un dot money, bud wen dey didn pay id beck, we'd aw we c'd do ta kip ah house.' When Kennedy was shot they were having lunch across the street from the bank where they closed their shoe-store deal. Then they almost lost the house in Florida when Zilman and Tony didn't pay them back.

'They didn't pay it back?' said Terry Wood.

'Nut a blintz, did dey pay. Da notinks paid notink. I esked Tony wen dey wuz gonna pay, un he siz da deal didn woik oud. Zilman siz ta Hyman, so sue me.'

In response to Gunnar's objection, O'Boyle said, 'Sustained, the statement attributed to Zilman is stricken as hearsay. The jury is instructed to disregard it.'

Unring the bell that pealed in the jurors' ears: *So sue me, so sue me, so sue me*. Gunnar felt the sudden emptiness of disappointment at the claims that Zilman and Tony had swindled the Rosens out of a hundred thousand of the quarter million they'd got for their shoe-store.

'Did you know what the loan was for?'

Gunnar leapt to his feet. 'No foundation. Objection, no foundation.

'Tony set et wuz fuh a reelahstay deal, bud, tanks a lod, I know betteh,' said Emma Rosen, and quickly added, 'Id wuz ta buy dobe.'

O'Boyle sustained the objection, struck the dope part, and admonished the jury to disregard it. 'We'll take a ten-minute recess,' he added.

There were two small rooms off the courtroom between the jury box and the rear wall. Gunnar led Tony into one, closed the door, ignored the small table and four chairs and remained standing.

Gunnar felt betrayed. 'If the jury believes her, this case is over,' he said.

'She's full a shit,' said Tony, 'That money *was* for a real estate deal. Zilman was taking an option on some beach front. He needed time, real time to make the deal. At least six months. The option cost a hundred grand. He painted a rosy picture to Hyman Rosen, promised him a third of all the action, plus a payback of his seed money in three months. Zilman claimed he had some big money coming in then. That could have been dope money, but I didn't know about it, if it was.'

Tony's gray eyes looked scared, but they pleaded to be believed, and Gunnar did. If only they had interviewed this woman, they could have been ready. He didn't have time to ask Tony why he hadn't mentioned the loan before.

'Remember,' Gunnar said, 'if this jury believes you were in the dope business, the game's over.'

To the extent the remaining five minutes allowed, Tony explained the details of the option deal Zilman had supposedly arranged.

Back in the courtroom Terry Wood showed Mrs Rosen a check that the court reporter had marked. His assistant handed a copy to Eddie Kerr.

'Do you recognize this check?' said Wood.

'Id wuz da one un ah accound et da Foist Nashnul Benk fuh da hunded tousan we gibm, Tony un Zilman.' Her and Hyman's check for $100,000 drawn on the First National Bank to Zilman.

Gunnar stood up. 'Your Honor, let the record show that it is made out to Emanuel Zilman only.'

'And let the record also show,' said Wood, 'that it was endorsed to Anthony Djilas by Emanuel Zilman, and that it was deposited in Djilas' account with the Bank of the Indies. Freeport, Bahamas.'

'Your witness,' said Wood.

Gunnar was stunned. Why hadn't those other neighbors mentioned this loan when Wyman Farmer had interviewed them? At least one of them must have known. Maybe that was what Mrs Castillo had been trying to say when Carmine had kept interrupting her.

Gunnar had to break this bitter old woman's story. Juiceless and brittle, Emma Rosen had been pressed between the pages of the book that was life without her husband Hyman, her sole reason to exist. Gunnar pushed his swivel chair from behind the counsel table to a position on one side and in front of Mrs Rosen's wheelchair, where he could see the jury. He sat down and looked into her parched face with its hairy mole and sunken mouth.

'Mrs Rosen,' he said, 'you probably despise Tony Djilas more than any living man, don't you?'

Crusty pus had accumulated in the corner of her left eye. 'A mentsch, hiz nut. I told ya I didn ligem.' He wasn't a nice guy. She didn't like him.

'And because that loan was not repaid your life has not been as good as it could have been, has it?'

'I told Hyman id wuz meshugas ta gibm dot money.'

Yes, it *was* crazy, Gunnar thought. 'I'm afraid some of us may not understand that word.'

'Hyman? He wuz m'huz . . . .'

'No, Mrs Rosen . . . strike that.'

'St'ike wot?'

'Never mind, Mrs Rosen.' Gunnar waited several seconds.

'Your life hasn't been as good as it could have been because you lost the money . . . .'

'Lose de money. Dot's wat you say. Dey stold id.'

'After he wrote that check to Mr Zilman, Hyman drove you by an old building on the beach near Galt Ocean Mile, didn't he?'

'I dun membah,' she said hastily, giving the impression she did remember.

'And he told you that Zilman was purchasing an option on that old building right on the beach, so that it could be developed into a fine hotel, didn't he?'

'Upshun, smupshun. Wot'm I, da booka knowletch.'

'You do remember, don't you, Mrs Rosen, and you do remember that your husband told you it was a risky deal, but if it worked out you could make more than half a million dollars. You remember that don't you, Mrs Rosen?'

'I sh'd live s'lung. Da goneff stold de money. Don' esk why mine Hyman gib id toom. Killed im ya know.'

'You do remember, don't you, Mrs Rosen?'

'Dotso? Dot I didn say, you did.'

'I have no more,' Gunnar said.

'Defendant rests,' said Terry Wood.

Mrs Rosen must have asked the young man to wheel her over in front of Gunnar on their way out. She peered at him through the heavy lenses. 'You w'dn't eppen ta be Dougluz Fairbenkz Joonya?' she asked. Gunnar smiled and shook his head.

'Do you have any rebuttal, Mr Larson,' O'Boyle said to Gunnar.

'I do.'

'Would you like to start tomorrow morning?' said O'Boyle looking at the clock, approaching four.

'No, Your Honor, I'd like to call Mr Djilas right now.' Gunnar didn't want the sparks from Emma Rosen's testimony to smolder all night.

Tony Djilas took the stand, looking tired but far from defeated. He turned the hundred-toother on the jury, and smoothed his perfect silver hair that didn't need smoothing.

'Mr Djilas you have listened carefully to everything Mrs Rosen has just said, have you not?' asked Gunnar.

256

'What I could understand.'

'Do you remember the transaction that was so upsetting to her?'

'Forget, I couldn't,' Tony said with a smile for the jury. Some smiled back. 'Hyman Rosen was a gambler, you know. I went to the track with him.'

Tony Djilas went on to describe the option deal in great detail while Gunnar watched the jury's faces, hoping for signs of acceptance. There were none. They were tired, too.

Gunnar thought he'd leave the last question for Terry Wood. He knew what it would be.

'Mr Djilas,' said Wood, 'you stood to benefit personally from the loan from Hyman Rosen, correct?'

'Manny promised me ten thousand if I could find him the hundred grand for the option, but he didn't get around to payin' me either.'

39

The dream woke Gunnar at three a.m. It was the same. The car slipped downhill in the snow and he pushed desperately and inside behind the wheel, Jack lived. It was as real as the present moment. When his awakened brain told him it had been a dream, tears came. Jack was as dead as ever. Anne heard him and turned over, and drew his head to her.

Her breast was warm and soft on his face, and she smelled faintly of flowers. Gunnar lay still, knowing he would not find sleep again. Perhaps an hour went by in thinking about Jack and Katie, about his relationship with Anne. The guilt ebbed and flowed, and made him draw away to his edge of the bed. Soon she slept. No words had passed between them.

The trial swirled around in the slowly receding guilt. Betrayal of Anne blended in with all the rest. In the blackness he saw the words in Dov Levy's reports submitted with the priceless evidence he had uncovered: *For sake of brevity the undersigned has omitted details of the source of the enclosed documents. Should you require more, please advise.* The clichés were the raisins in the dubious dough: fight fire with fire; all's fair in love and war; takes a crook to catch a crook; the ends justify the means.

The jury, or maybe even O'Boyle, might still find that Gunnar hadn't proven malice. But Tony would have no chance without the letter from Pentecost to Henning. Last night in the office, Gunnar had not decided positively whether to call Andrew Levy this morning. But he needed Andrew's testimony.

Andrew had been sucked in by Dov's tale of Ward Chapin's infidelity with the fictitious Trevor. For his revenge, he had agreed to testify. There had been no mention of money on Gunnar's visit to Andrew's apartment. Dov had suggested to him the possibility

258

of payment, but when he met with Gunnar, Andrew left no doubt about his appetite for revenge – whetted to its present ferocity by Dov's lie.

For the first time since Leo had returned from Europe, Gunnar was truly tempted to get his advice on an issue in the Djilas case. But he found himself unwilling to tell Leo the story of Andrew Levy, and ultimately, Dov. This decision would be Gunnar's alone. Didn't it come down to whether Andrew Levy was telling the truth? Gunnar was sure he was.

The light seeping in around the edges of the drape told him to get out of bed. In the kitchen he mashed the whites of two hard-boiled eggs together with some cottage cheese and put a cup of water in the microwave. He opened the front door to retrieve the morning paper. In the shadowless gray of early dawn a dove mourned, the softest sound of summer. As he drank the coffee, he read the account of yesterday's session of the trial in the *Times-Journal*. Emma Rosen's story was reported in every detail. Gunnar's cross-examination and Tony's rebuttal testimony were barely mentioned.

Andrew Levy's sleepy little voice answered on the fifth ring.

'This is Gunnar Larson. You may consider the subpoena served on you yesterday to be of full force and effect. I will expect you in Judge O'Boyle's courtroom at nine-thirty.'

'I'll be there,' squeaked Andrew.

Not knowing who might be appearing to testify, Terry Wood had brought all the major players to the morning session. When O'Boyle entered, Cline, Chapin and Henning stood as one in the front row. Pentecost stayed in the back, in the same pew as Al Bergdorf. Al's new lined face was emerging from the smooth ageless visage common among the obese. After O'Boyle asked them to be seated, Andrew, looking even smaller framed in the courtroom door, waited tentatively. Gunnar beckoned, and said, 'For plaintiff's rebuttal, I call Andrew Levy.'

Gunnar pointed to the witness box when Andrew, in a dark tailored suit, drew even with the counsel table. The moment gave Gunnar a chance to look quickly at Ward Chapin's face. It was utterly devoid of expression, an unusual condition for Chapin.

After the preliminaries, Gunnar asked, 'Mr Levy, are you acquainted with defendant Ward Chapin?'

'Yes I am,' Andrew said delicately, holding his hand near his full lips; a large gold ring encircled a slim finger.

'Would you describe your relationship.'

'We have been lovers for about two years.'

'Mr Levy, please speak directly into the microphone,' said O'Boyle.

'Has Mr Chapin ever discussed with you the articles he wrote about Mr Djilas?'

'Many times.'

Carefully avoiding eye-contact with Ward Chapin, Andrew's face followed Gunnar's slow walk from behind the counsel table to the side of the witness box furthest from the jury.

'Do you recall any discussion specifically focused on the question as to whether or not Carlyle Henning would approve the publication of the articles?' Gunnar finished, looking directly at Chapin on the aisle seat in the front row, his face frozen in narrow-eyed fury. Beside Chapin, Carlyle Henning stared straight ahead like a library lion.

'Yes, I do,' said Andrew, his voice adequately amplified by the PA system.

'And when did you have such a conversation?'

'Right after the Memorial Day weekend last year. Ward told me he had to go to his sister's in California. I didn't know he was with Pierce and Carlyle Henning.' A pulse throbbed under the white skin of Andrew's temple.

'Where did you have the conversation?'

'In his apartment . . . in bed. I stayed there all night.'

'And, in essence, what did Ward Chapin say to you?'

'He said Carlyle Henning had been vacillating about publishing the articles.'

'Did he say why?'

'Yes, he said that Car Henning didn't think the articles could be true, and he wasn't sure that Ward had enough evidence to back them up.'

'And?'

'Ward thought that the newspaper had nothing to worry about

because the articles were true. Ward really thought they were true, you know.'

Jesus Christ, thought Gunnar, am I being trapped?

But Andrew Levy went on: 'He said that it looked like the vacillation was over because Pierce had asked Car to help him get the New City contract, and by publishing the articles Car could help.'

'Objection, double hearsay,' said Terry Wood.

'Strike the quote attributable to Pentecost,' said O'Boyle. 'The rest may stand.'

Wood started to protest. 'But Your Honor . . . .'

'I've ruled, Counsel.'

In the jury box Anita Lowery turned and looked at Madge Meyers, knowingly.

'Did Mr Chapin say anything else?' said Gunnar.

'I asked him what if the articles weren't true. Ward said Car didn't care . . . if he could help Pierce. The two of them were very close, he said.'

'Your witness,' Gunnar said to Terry Wood.

'We'll take a fifteen-minute recess,' said O'Boyle, obviously appreciating the surprise that had shaken the *Times-Journal* camp.

Andrew Levy walked over to the counsel table. Almost tearfully, he said, 'Can I go now?'

Gunnar told him he would have to answer some questions for Terry Wood, but then he could leave. 'In fact,' Gunnar said, 'I think it would be a good idea.'

Gunnar and Eddie left the courtroom to stand at the atrium rail with Tony while he smoked a cigarette.

'*Deus ex machina*,' said Eddie.

'What the hell is that?' said Tony.

'Just a saying,' said Eddie.

'Latin,' said Gunnar.

'Legal hocus pocus?' said Tony.

'Not really,' said Gunnar. But it wasn't God that found Andrew Levy for us, he thought.

'How did you ever get that pansy to talk like that?' said Tony.

'Excuse me,' said Gunnar, 'Nature calls.'

'Don't ask me,' said Eddie Kerr. 'I have no idea where he came from.'

After the recess, Terry Wood posed a question to Andrew Levy who quivered on the front edge of the witness chair like a small rodent facing down a fox. 'Has plaintiff's counsel agreed to pay you for your testimony?'

'No,' said Andrew.

'Has anybody agreed to pay you?'

'Nobody has promised me anything.'

Just a 'No' would have finished it, Gunnar thought, but he had anticipated this line of questioning, and Dov was on his way back to London this morning.

'Has anybody suggested to you that you might be paid?'

'A person named Jesse Katz.'

Gunnar needed all of his willpower to keep from turning to look at Suzie Cline. And he ignored Tony's whispered, 'Who the hell is Jessie Katz?'

'Who is Jesse Katz?' said Terry Wood.

Andrew told of his meeting with Jesse Katz subsequent to the phone call. From there he began to tell what Jesse Katz had said to him. Gunnar sat transfixed like a man listening to the plan of his own murder. Eddie reached behind Tony and poked Gunnar sharply in the shoulder. Jesus Christ.

'Objection, hearsay,' said Gunnar, letting the rest of the breath he had been holding blow out between his lips.

'Sustained,' said O'Boyle, a ruling Gunnar knew closed the book for this trial on Dov Levy, alias Jesse Katz.

'Do you know anyone else who knows Jesse Katz?'

'Suzie Cline knows him,' said Andrew.

'May I have a moment, Your Honor?' said Terry Wood.

O'Boyle told him to take whatever time he needed. In response to Wood's look, Suzie joined him at the counsel table and whispered to his ear.

Gunnar said to no one in particular, 'She's telling him she doesn't really know Jesse Katz.'

'How do you know that?' Tony said.

'Trust me,' said Gunnar.

'No further questions,' said Wood.

'The witness is excused,' said O'Boyle.

'Plaintiff rests,' said Gunnar.

'Defendants rest,' said Terry Wood.

'We are adjourned until Monday morning at nine-thirty a.m.,' said O'Boyle. 'We'll take up the instructions in chambers and any motions. Then you each have an hour and a half to argue to the jury. I hope you all have a nice weekend.'

No matter what happened from here on, Gunnar was glad he had drawn O'Boyle whose mind worked logically and quickly. He was decisive and suffered delays with great impatience. Lesser judges might have taken three months to get through this case. The end was in sight. Except for Memorial Day they hadn't missed a week-day since the eleventh of May. The jury should be deliberating on Tuesday. Gunnar would use the weekend to compress seven weeks of testimony into an hour and a half's argument. He knew it could make all the difference.

40

In O'Boyle's wood-panelled chambers, redolent of brewing coffee, Terry Wood and two assistants lounged on a leather sofa. Gunnar and Eddie sat in chairs pushed away from the desk.

'You know, guys,' O'Boyle said, 'this trial has been hard on my golf game.' Rumors were that last year O'Boyle had turned in more registered rounds than any other member at Westview. 'But, kidding aside, you tried a damn good case. There's usually so much acrimony in libel. Not that I didn't feel some of the undercurrents in there, but you know what I mean.'

The five lawyers nodded.

'I assume you have a motion you want to put on the record,' O'Boyle looked at Terry Wood. Gunnar knew that O'Boyle's reference to the record was his way of saying he would deny the motion.

'Yes, I have a motion, Your Honor,' said Wood.

'Get Grace in here,' O'Boyle said to the clerk, 'And keep these gentleman supplied with coffee . . . . Wasn't that old girl from New York something? When you've heard as many witnesses as I have, there aren't many you remember. But, "Bite your tongue, Judge" . . . that's one for the book.'

Grace North, chestnut mane brushed a million strokes, set up her machine between Eddie and the clerk's chair.

'You may proceed, Counsel,' said O'Boyle.

From his place on the sofa, Terry Wood moved the court for a directed verdict for all defendants. Grace's fingers silently struck the keys on the stenotype like she was fondling the ears of a poodle sitting at her knee. Wood argued that plaintiff had failed to meet the Constitutional requirements to prove a libel case against a newspaper. O'Boyle denied the motion without further comment.

'Let's get to the jury instructions,' he said. 'I've read through all your proposals . . . more than thirty each. Actually I have forty-two from defendant. Frankly, I like the way plaintiff has tied them all together.'

Gunnar thanked Eddie Kerr with a glance. His pulpy face remained impassive.

A chaos of arguments and counter-arguments filled the morning. The judge's pronouncements of measured finality moved them from issue to issue. At twelve-fifteen O'Boyle told them they were finished; they should be back in court at one-thirty, ready to make their final arguments to the jury.

'And so, ladies and gentleman of the jury, I thank you for your kind attention throughout this long trial. My clients: Ms Cline, Mr Chapin, and the *Times-Journal* Company represented here in court by Mr Carlyle Henning also thank you. I leave you with a final thought: the Constitutional right of the free press and the Constitutional rights of individuals are of value only to the extent that juries like you enforce them. Newspapers written and edited by people running scared wouldn't be worth reading.'

His final argument finished, Terry Wood returned to the counsel table. Sweat, like drops of rain, ran down his wide forehead. Two young men sitting in the back commenced clapping.

'Remove those two on the aisle,' said O'Boyle, crashing his gavel to the bench. The bailiff strode quickly to where they sat in the rear. One started to argue.

'One more word, you'll spend the night, maybe the month,' said O'Boyle.

They walked quietly to the door where one whirled and yelled. 'Long live the free press.'

'Arrest him, Darrell,' said O'Boyle to the bailiff. 'We'll take a ten-minute recess.'

Court reconvened at three-fifteen. Not all of the seats were filled, but at least fifty listeners had joined the regulars, among them, Anne and Katie. And Leo Lawson. It was the first time Gunnar had seen him in more than a month.

No one ever guessed Gunnar's summations were memorized.

He deviated only to answer unanticipated points raised in the preceding argument. Yesterday, in his air-conditioned bedroom, drapes drawn against the blistering July sun, Gunnar had rehearsed to a full-length mirror, and then to Anne and Katie, who offered a couple of suggestions.

Gunnar thought the informal effect of beginning while still seated behind the counsel table had a certain charm. Besides, the tension that would have made his knees tremble were he standing subsided as he began to speak. 'This has been a very long trial . . . jurors are rarely asked to sit on civil cases in the summer, but it was spring when we began.' He got up and moved around the corner to the end of the table.

'May it please the court . . . members of the jury . . . Counsel. There has been talk today about Constitutional rights, principally a newspaper's right to print whatever it wants. We don't quarrel with that right. We endorse it. But this case is about another right, an American's right to be compensated for injuries caused by others. This case is about just such an injury.'

Gunnar was up and running. No fear, no trembling; instead, laser-like concentration on the moment. The feeling he got from doing what he did best, and knowing his best was extraordinary. Something special, like a Ray Robinson left hook, or a Horowitz mazurka.

'This case is about a false statement in a newspaper that caused injury to Tony Djilas. The newspaper may have had a right to print it; Mr Djilas has a right to be compensated if he is injured by it. The court will tell you that Tony Djilas has the added burden of proving malice, that the newspaper knew it was false, or at least should have known.'

From the end of the counsel table fifteen feet from the jury, Gunnar moved one step closer, and contacted each pair of eyes for an instant. The alternates had been dismissed. Six pairs of eyes remained.

'Your job is to decide whether we have proved both falsity and malice, and when you do decide that we have, to then decide what is a fair amount of money to compensate Tony Djilas for the terrible wrong that has been done him.'

He reminded them of each witness by name and the significance, or lack of it, of their testimony. He reminded them of the ringing support of the mayor, and the personal tribute to Tony's integrity from Robert Goodspeed, one of the foremost churchmen in America.

As the first hour eroded, Gunnar led them through each element of Tony's loss. Then he moved forward another step. His familiar little shoulder stoop bent a degree closer to the jury as he recalled Iago's lines from *Othello*. 'A great poet wrote

> "Good name in man and woman, dear my lord,
> Is the immediate jewel of their souls;
> Who steals my purse steals trash; 'tis something, nothing;
> 'Twas mine, 'tis his and has been slave to thousands;
> But he that filches from me my good name
> Robs me of that which not enriches him,
> And makes me poor indeed."'

Gunnar moved to the left, so he could see the jury and with a turn of his head look back at Tony. '*Poor indeed*. The *Times-Journal* has made Tony Djilas poor indeed. Only you can return that good name to Tony Djilas. And when you do, you can't return it whole.' Gunnar waved his arm in the direction of the defendants. 'They have forever impaired it! The point is, even if you fully compensate Mr Djilas for the monetary losses he has suffered, neither you, nor anyone else, can return his good name intact. It is forever tarnished. Some who have heard the awful accusations will never know what you do here. And many who do, will still wonder and doubt. Such is the consequence of defendants' ruthless act. To mend malicious conduct, such as the willful destruction of a good man's good name, the law provides yet another means: punitive damages.'

Punitive damages – the tort lawyers dream – the key to the counting house, Gunnar had always said; the earth-size boulder teetering over the head of insurance companies; the capital punishment of giant corporations. Recently, Penzoil's punitive damages verdict had bankrupt Texaco.

'Yes,' said Gunnar, 'punitive damages are designed to punish those whose appetite for instant gratification blinds them to the rights of others. This is the perfect case for punitive damages.

'It is by making a large award of punitive damages, in addition to compensating Tony Djilas for his money losses, that you can do justice.' Gunnar allowed his voice to jump up a level. '*Punish them for what they have done!*'

He dropped back to the mellow tones of reason and understanding. 'Imagine the anguish they have caused in robbing Mr Djilas of his good name . . . and punish them accordingly. Once you have determined compensatory damages are justified, you may award punitive damages in whatever amount you see fit. Much evidence has been presented proving the millions of dollars that Mr Djilas would have earned on this project, and so Mr Djilas needs you to see that he is compensated for his enormous losses.

'But how do you measure punitive damages? Judge O'Boyle will tell you that punishment is meaningless, unless those punished can feel it. You don't spank a bull with a fly swatter . . . . When I was a boy, we had a neighbor who kept a breeding bull; one morning his wife came running and told my dad that the bull had Rudy down – in the barn. By the time we got over to their place, Rudy had gotten out of the barn, and the bull had walked out into the corral. No sooner had we jumped out of the car, than Rudy was crawling over the fence to get in that pen with that same mean bull. Only this time, in his hands he held a two by four, four feet long. That bull made another move toward Rudy, and Rudy hammered him right between the ears with that two by four. The bull just stood for a minute rocking his big head back and forth, and then he took off like a bird in a windstorm for the far end of that corral . . . . Now, to make this half-billion dollar newspaper feel it, you're going to have to hammer it right between the ears with a two by four. They might feel ten million; they won't feel much less. Ten million is only one fiftieth of their worth. One fiftieth.'

Gunnar let the big number sink in. The silence grew, second by second. Wide eyes behind slightly tinted glasses in the front row told him Sarah Michaels, her mouth in a tight little crimp, hands folded around her hanky, was spellbound. Could she possibly understand money in these amounts? Her husband, a machinist, had worked for the same company for thirty-seven years.

Gunnar didn't need to look at his watch. He had nine minutes left. He moved near the center of the jury box, standing in front of Sarah Michaels.

'It's only right that the punishment fit the crime. You have heard the man who, for all practical purposes, totally controls what you and I read in the newspaper. Now, we know he will print whatever will benefit his friends and lovers regardless of its truth or falsity, or regardless of who is harmed, or even ruined by it. But far worse . . . the evidence in this case shows that his decision to publish not only recklessly ignored the high probability that the allegations were false, but he did it deliberately to ruin Tony Djilas. And why? Because one of the people with whom he was promiscuously engaged in homosexual intercourse had asked him to . . . . *Make the punishment fit the crime.*'

Gunnar poured himself into their eyes. They must each feel his outrage. The judge would instruct them that emotions must not be involved. But if this was to be his career case, emotions must be involved, his and theirs.

He was where he belonged: arguing to a jury and the exhilaration was exquisite. It was like playing a great fish, using all he had learned to subdue it, the thrill of the battle, knowing any second the fish might be gone, knowing you'd never see it again. Sometimes it passed close to the boat, close enough to see his silver sides and his great bulk. These last few minutes before jury, Gunnar saw the silver sides, and he had known all along what a giant it was. It only remained to bring his prize to the gaff.

Now, his knees felt the rail in front of the jurors, his face only a foot or two away from those in the first row. 'What is malicious?' he said. 'It is malicious for the head of a big city newspaper to publish an allegation that a person, a truly good person is a dope dealer. Not just that he wasn't fit, or qualified for the responsibility of building Block Thirteen. No, he was a dope dealer, that lowest of creatures among us, poisoner of our children, corrupter of our nation.

'And what did the big city newspaper have to support their accusation? Mr Djilas had once been arrested in a house he managed in his professional capacity as a Realtor. Never mind that the charges were dismissed without trial, almost with the apology of the police force. Remember Detective Koronis said: "We were lucky he didn't sue us."

'And, Mr Djilas had allowed his employer to open a bank account in his name. Never mind that there was no evidence of where the money came from that went in to the bank account, save and except the check that Emma Rosen brought to court, that no one, not even the newspaper, contends was the product of the dope business. And then they had Chucky John Waycross the fumbling, fired former DEA agent who didn't even show up in court. That's the basis for an article calculated to ruin a man. And without your substantial verdict, he *is* ruined.'

He was down to four minutes. The last four minutes of a year's work. 'Of course, you remember, two well-educated, fine-looking young newspaper reporters testified at great length that they were convinced the articles they had written about Tony Djilas were true . . . . Before you put too much weight on their anguished pleas for your understanding, remember there is no question that they both lied to you on two material issues. Ms Cline tried to misrepresent what happened at Carlyle Henning's infamous party. She later admitted she lied, and Ward Chapin denied having said at another party that Tony Djilas was the biggest crook in town. His own colleague, Ms Cline, later told us that he had indeed said it. You know they will lie when they think it's to their benefit to do so. And Henning lied trying to conceal the plea for help from his lover Pentecost, and Pentecost lied trying to conceal the same pathetic letter.

'This case is about a lie, a monstrous . . . festering . . . ugly lie. And to save their skins, the liars lied again and again.' Gunnar waited and savored the silence. 'The only defense against a lie is the truth, the whole truth and nothing but the truth, so help you God. You heard the newspaper crew take that oath right here. Now' – he paused, the six pairs of eyes were riveted on his – 'are you going to look to them for the truth?' Gunnar's head moved slowly, side to side; his eyes said, of course you're not.

'Think about it,' and then with a plea like a child's, 'Please . . . return to my client . . . his good name. And, please . . .

compensate him for that which you can't return. I believe punitive damages of ten million dollars would be fair, and compensatory damages of another ten million dollars would be fair.'

Now feel my passion, Gunnar thought, as he paused for a last moment; I believe what I am telling you. You must feel with me. He wrung the closing from his gut and his heart and his brain. He opened his arms wide to them: 'We have choices we make in our lives. I chose to fight to save Tony Djilas' name – that a huge newspaper corporation chose to ruin. Now you must choose whether to restore that name, or to leave him lost . . . and alone . . . and without justice. Thank you.'

He had used his time to the last second; and he had used his energy to the last erg. He wondered if he could make it back to his chair. When he sat down he took one last look at their faces, and could he believe it? Sarah Michaels winked at him. He allowed his mouth to reveal only a tiny part of the smile he felt.

41

O'Boyle took the morning to put the finishing touches on his jury instructions, and he had them delivered to the lawyers at eleven-thirty. Both Gunnar and Terry Wood opened the Tuesday's afternoon session by making formal objections to certain inclusions and omissions in the instructions O'Boyle was about to give to the jury. Eddie commented that Bergdorf, sitting in his usual spot in the back, had been in court for at least half of the trial. Holly and her mother sat in the front pew behind Gunnar's counsel table, and Suzie Cline, Ward Chapin and Carlyle Henning sat in the front on the other side. Nobody else showed up.

'Bring the jury in and lock the door behind you,' said O'Boyle to the bailiff. Interruptions were not tolerated during the charge to the jury.

The worry had already set in. Gunnar knew the good feeling at the end of his argument yesterday would wear off an hour or two later. He had declined Tony's invitation to dinner with him and Al. Holly's eyes had pleaded for a call as they were walking out.

But Tony persisted. They hadn't dined together for weeks. Besides Al was dying to talk to him. Al had stuck to his bargain. He hadn't meddled once, and doesn't he look good, losing all that weight. Gunnar had finally relented on the condition he bring Eddie Kerr along. Al suggested they meet at Shinbashi where they sat around a huge chopping block with a griddle, and a young Japanese in a white chef's hat did tricks with a meat cleaver. Al had ordered for them all, some kind of chicken. He was taking his diet very seriously.

Tony was ebullient. Every sentence contained a new word of praise. 'Sensational! You were sensational,' he said.

Trial lawyers never tire of panegyric from their clients, but

272

Gunnar's capacity to feel much of anything hadn't returned. But he still secretly relished the wink from Sarah Michaels. 'Don't count your chickens,' he said to Tony.

'Whadaya mean!' said Tony. 'They're in the barn, or wherever they go at night.' He turned to Eddie. 'You are a lucky young man. You can learn from a master.' Then to Al: 'Have I got a lawyer, or what, Al?'

'I gotta admit it, Gunnar. By a country mile, that's the most time I've ever spent watching somebody else try a case. But I gotta admit it; I learned something. You did a helluva job.' Al stuck out his hand.

Gunnar felt a little surge of warmth toward Al, the first in a lifetime. 'Thanks,' he said, grabbing the big lawyer's hand and holding his eyes for an instant. Then to all three he said, 'The case would never have gone in as well as it did without Eddie here. This has been a two-man effort. But, Jesus Christ, it's way too early to get happy. Terry Wood made a fine summation, and all our problems haven't gone away.'

Eddie's face shared his anxiety, but he had told Gunnar in the cab that his argument had been 'powerful'.

'Now maybe you guys can tell an old friend how in the hell you got your hands on that letter,' said Al.

'Don't look at me,' said Eddie. 'He never told me either.'

'Me, neither,' said Tony.

'Sorry, I'm sworn to secrecy,' said Gunnar.

'What about the pansy?' queried Al.

'Sorry, gentlemen, same answer,' said Gunnar. 'And we should pay more attention to our host here,'

Strips of chicken, and green and orange and yellow vegetables crackled in the hot oil. The tall Jap flashed the wide enamel smile and asked if they wanted more tea.

'When that girl comes back I'll have another martini,' said Tony.

Gunnar just couldn't talk about the trial any more, and Al Bergdorf picked up on it, and steered the conversation to small talk over the great food. They broke up early.

Now, on Tuesday morning, O'Boyle droned on, giving the jury a course in libel law, and evidence. Whenever a plaintiff's lawyer

273

hears the instructions in a complicated case he is convinced that the jury couldn't possibly make all of the necessary findings required in order for them to render a verdict for his client. But they often do. Each time O'Boyle repeated the phrase 'By clear and convincing evidence', Gunnar felt a needle in his gut. In most trials the burden for plaintiff was a preponderance of the evidence, a mere tipping of the scales, but 'clear and convincing' sounded insurmountable as Gunnar listened to the judge.

O'Boyle neared the end, 'The assessment of damages for libel is the province of the jury and because there can be no definite standard to measure the amount, your award, if any, is entirely within your discretion. You may consider more than out-of-pocket losses in determining compensatory damages.

'In arriving at the amount of your verdict you may take into consideration the extent of defendants' publication, the aggregate number of readers of the publication . . . .'

A media expert Eddie Kerr had hired testified that the front-page article was read by close to a million people.

'. . . and its tendency and probable effect upon the plaintiff's standing in the community.'

O'Boyle had come to the last page. 'When you retire to the jury room, you will chose a foreman who will preside over your deliberations. If your deliberations extend beyond six hours, five of the six of you may agree upon a verdict, otherwise your verdict must be unanimous. If the verdict is unanimous only the foreman need sign it. If less than unanimous the five who agree must all sign it.'

He read the verdict form aloud. Then the bailiff led the jury out in single file.

On the way home Gunnar stopped at a phone booth and listened to ten rings at the lodge. Of course she wouldn't be there now.

Anne had heard his car and met him at the front door. 'Were you pleased with the charge?'

'It was OK,' said Gunnar, 'but with the Constitutional defenses in a libel case the charge always sounds like a directed verdict for the defense. But I can't complain. At least I don't think it's likely to be a good basis for a defense appeal.'

He told her about the dinner at Shinbashi the night before and the nice things that had been said.

'You know Gun, at the arguments I talked a little to Al Bergdorf. He doesn't seem so bad,' she said. 'In fact he's really proud of you, and grateful that you took the case. I was proud of you, too. You were awesome.'

'Thanks sweets,' he said. 'The jury went out about four. I don't know if they deliberated at all today, but we could get a verdict tomorrow.'

'You must be so excited, and anxious. I know I am,' she said.

'You know,' he said. 'I think I'll watch television . . . if it still works.'

He went into his little den. From the leather recliner he watched the picture form on the tube. My God. Andy Griffith as Ben Matlock trying a case. He flicked the channel to a rerun of 'All in the Family'.

Anne brought two glasses of ice tea. She put hers on top of the TV, and knelt down and untied his shoes. His shoes off, she went around behind Gunnar's chair and began to rub his neck. But he had already canted forward in eager anticipation. The phone rang in the kitchen, and Anne left the room.

'Stifle,' said Archie to Edith.

Anne was back in the door way. 'For you . . . a woman,' she said.

Gunnar picked up the phone. To his 'Hello' he heard: 'Waited at the lodge until eight.'

'That's about when I called,' he said.

'Shit!' she said, 'I wish I had waited. Tomorrow?'

'I don't know. Not while the jury's out. I'll be at the office in the morning.'

'OK,' she said, 'but it's been so long.'

'I know,' he said. 'I know.'

Anne was waiting in the den. 'Who was it?'

'A juror, she said for a hundred grand she'd see I got a verdict.'

'Oh, go on.'

'No, it was just business, sweets. New case. I told her to call the office.'

'What kind?'
'Libel,' he said.
Mixed with his guilt, he heard Anne say, 'Word travels fast.'
I wonder if she meant anything more by that, he thought.
'Where's the meathead?' said Archie.

42

Sarah Michaels wished Jennifer Woody wouldn't smoke in the tight confines of the jury room. But she was too polite to say anything.

Madge Meyers wasn't. 'Jennifer, I'm sorry, but I just can't stand second-hand smoke. I'm sure you understand.'

Jennifer's face was made up perfectly, as usual – maybe a little too much, Sarah thought.

'Oh sure. I'm sorry,' Jennifer said. 'But if we take a long time deciding this, I don't know what I'll do. I get so nervous.'

'I'm sure the bailiff will let you out for a smoke,' said Madge, equine face looking pained and ugly in every other possible way. 'And anyway, this shouldn't take so long. We can't start trying to tell people what they have to write in the newspaper. After all, we do have freedom of the press.'

Good heavens, thought Sarah Michaels, she's for those awful people. Yesterday afternoon they had decided to have an early dinner, and not talk about the case at all until this morning. Over their steaks, they had elected Ralph Sullivan foreman. He owned a hardware store and was the only black among them.

This morning Ralph suggested they take a paper ballot, just to get the sense of how we feel at the outset, he had said. After he picked up the folded slips he reported that three had voted for the defendants and three for the plaintiff. We have our work cut out for us, he said. That was when Madge complained about the smoke.

'Let's each of us state why we feel like we do. Would you like to begin, Dick,' Ralph Sullivan said to Richard Hayek.

'Like Madge says, this freedom of the press thing is real important.' A tiny image of the window reflected from each of the lenses of Richard Hayek's thick glasses. 'Like that Wood fella said, if we pay big money to this guy, they may be afraid to print the things we oughta know about. Like this big development downtown. There's enough crooks in the government without giving crooks the big plums. I'm not sayin' this guy Djilas is a crook, I'm just sayin' if he was, we wouldn't want the paper to be afraid to print it.'

Madge has been working on him, Sarah thought.

'I think the newspaper was way out of line,' said Anita Lowery. 'They've got too much power. If we let 'em get away with this, they'll print anything. Besides, Tony Djilas is a good man. You wouldn't see Robert Goodspeed speaking up for a crook.'

'We do hafta consider all those Constitutional rights they have,' said Ralph.

'That's right,' said Jennifer Woody, 'That judge as much as told us we couldn't favor Djilas. I voted for the paper. I don't want to sit here for ever. I'll go bananas without my Marlboros.'

'Jenny,' said Ralph, 'I don't think the judge meant you to think you couldn't favor Djilas. You're mistaken on that.'

'All the same, I don't want anybody telling me what I can read in the paper,' said Madge.

'Neither do I,' said Sarah Michaels, 'that's why I voted for Mr Djilas. As Mr Larson pointed out, this pervert, Carlyle Henning, decides what we are going to read based on which man he's sleeping with. And I think Mr Larson presented the evidence the judge told us was required for Mr Djilas to win. He showed that the accusations were false, and he showed that Mr Henning didn't care whether they were false or true. He wanted his friend Pentecost to get the job. What about you Ralph, what do you think?' It was Sarah Michaels who had suggested Ralph for foreman.

'Well, I voted for Djilas because, as you just said, I think he fulfilled the requirements that the judge spelled out. And I tend to believe 'em . . . and those cops. If everything the newspaper people said was true, maybe we'd hafta side with'm. But I really don't trust'm. They lie when it suits'm. And that last little guy, Levy . . . he seemed real sincere to me. And there's the letter. I mean this guy Pentecost axed for help. Course he didn't axe him to print lies about Djilas, but it's not Pentecost who got sued here either. I think Djilas deserves to win. What's he gonna do if we don't back 'em. The rest of his life everybody's gonna think he's a crook. It'll be a lot harder on him to lose, than the newspaper.'

'Don't forget the clear and convincing part,' said Madge.

We better work on Jenny and Dick, Sarah Michaels thought. 'Jenny,' she whispered, 'I don't really think it hurts if you smoke in here.'

'Madge wouldn't like it,' said Jenny.

'Why don't you ask her again?' said Sarah Michaels.

Jenny did.

'If you light another cigarette in here I'm calling the judge,' said Madge.

'I'm sorry, I won't ask again,' said Jenny, her pretty face on the verge of tears of embarrassment. She looked at Sarah Michaels as if to say, that wasn't very smart advice you gave me.

43

On Thursday morning at nine, Gunnar took a call from Leo.

'Yeah, they're still out,' Gunnar said, 'startin' their second full day. At least two of them must want to give us something.'

Shana stuck her head through the door, 'Terry Wood is on the line.'

After assuring Leo he'd call him when he'd gotten a verdict, Gunnar took Wood's call. 'I give at the office,' said Gunnar.

'Aren't we light-hearted today?' said Wood. 'But you can't fool me, your guts are doing more acrobatics than mine.'

'Ain't it the truth.'

'I will tell you one thing, I saw that old broad wink at you.'

'She just had something in her eye. Besides I gotta get five of them.'

'Whatever, I've got some authority,'

'I'm listening.'

'One big one.'

'She winked at me, not you.'

'Better run it past your client.'

'Don't need to.'

'Don't you think it's your responsibility to at least let him in on it.'

'If you insist, but only to get a number from him. He ain't about to take one million, Terry. I'd be surprised if he took five.'

'Call me. They may come in any minute.'

Shana found Tony Djilas in Al's office. 'You were right,' he said, 'you didn't have to call me.'

Again, Gunnar pointed out all the pitfalls in the case. 'And they've been deliberating for at least eight hours,' he said. 'That means that there are at least two against us, and God forbid, maybe four. I don't think you should refuse to negotiate. I guess I wouldn't want to turn down three, but I doubt if they'll pay three. If they get hit big, they know they have a good chance on appeal.'

'Lemme talk to Al a minute.'

Gunnar held the line. The more he thought about it, the better three million sounded. With a million cash, after taxes, invested, he'd never have to worry and if the marriage didn't work out, with the house and the pension plan and their reserves, there would be twice that much for Anne.

'Tell 'em we'll take four,' said Tony.

'They won't pay it, but I'll tell them.'

'Maybe they'll come back with three,' said Tony.

'I doubt it.' Gunnar hung up and called Terry Wood. He promised to call Gunnar right back.

Terry Wood didn't call back until two in the afternoon. 'Henning didn't want to go past one-point-five,' said Terry Wood. 'But I told him I was nervous about how long they're staying out.'

'Don't feel like the Lone Ranger,' said Gunnar.

'Anyway, he just agreed to two. That would be a record in this state. Make you even more famous. And, best of all, no appeals.'

'I'll run it by Tony.'

Tony turned it down, and said he wanted to stick on four million. Gunnar suggested a counter-offer of three, and Tony still said no. He agreed to think about three and a half over night. Gunnar reminded him the jury could come back any minute with nothing. The thought made Gunnar shudder.

'OK,' Tony said, 'try 'em at three and a half, maybe that'll get them up to three.'

'I'll try,' agreed Gunnar, 'but, like I said, that jury could have decided to give us nothing as we speak.'

'I saw that lady with the pink glasses wink at you,' said Tony.

'Oh for Christ sake, that doesn't mean anything!' But Gunnar prayed it did.

At four-thirty Terry Wood called back and rejected the three and a half. 'You and I would settle this at three, wouldn't we?' he said.

'Maybe,' said Gunnar, 'but our clients won't.'

Gunnar called the clerk at five, and she told him the jury was going home for the night.

44

Holly had called from the lodge just after five on Thursday afternoon and begged Gunnar to come to her. No, he said. Couldn't she understand? Today, the verdict meant everything. Once it was rendered he could become a normal human being again. He promised to see her as soon after the jury returned as possible. That would probably be another week, she had grumbled.

When Gunnar arrived downtown on Friday morning, Terry Wood sat in the lobby smoking his pipe and reading the morning paper. Gunnar shook his hand and brought him to his office. You could see for miles through the glass into the clear sweet summer morning, which would soon become a muggy bitch of a July day.

'I think they're hung,' said Terry Wood.

'You don't really, or you wouldn't be here to try to settle this thing,' said Gunnar. 'I think they'll be back today. They want to get free of it just like the rest of us.'

'What if they are hung?' said Terry.

'Then we'd have to try the miserable sonofabitch over again, that's all,' said Gunnar, 'and I would wish I had gotten Djilas to take the two mill. Have you got any more for me?'

Terry Wood shook his head with a guileless smile, hazel eyes bright and beady in his big face. Gunnar felt real affection for this broad-shouldered man who had fought through the courtroom wars for twenty-five years.

'I can't come up with anymore,' said Wood. 'Oh, I'm sure if it got down to a couple of hundred thousand extra, I could put it to bed. But no more than that . . . you?'

'Nothing. He won't even come down to three.'

They made a little small talk, and Terry Wood told Gunnar that he had done a hell of a job for his client. Someday he would like to know how Gunnar got that letter and those notes. And, by the way, who the hell was Jesse Katz? Gunnar assured him that he could never tell him any of those things, and that Terry, too, had done a great job for his client.

'Nothing like you did, I'm afraid,' said Terry Wood. 'But one thing you can be sure of: I didn't know about that letter. Hell, I didn't even know Henning was a switch hitter!'

They both agreed that defense was a different ball-game, and then Terry got up to leave.

'If anything comes up, I'll be across the street all day.'

'Sure,' said Gunnar, 'thanks for stopping by, Terry. But I'm afraid this one's out of our hands.'

With Terry Wood gone, Gunnar thought he would take a crack at Al Bergdorf. He hadn't actually called Al directly in fifteen years.

'Hey Gunnar, what can I do for ya.'

'Bring that jury back.'

''Fraid that's outa my control, big fella.'

Gunnar spelled out his concerns to Al. 'We could be leaving two million on the table, or even two and a half.'

'I know, Gunnar, I've told him the same as you have. Last night I even told him to take the two mill. I figured he could push them up a little further, but he said to forget it. He's got chutzpah, that guy! I gave up. It's no use, he's not gonna settle this case for under three million. He wants at least a million clear for himself after expenses.'

'Just thought I'd try, Al.'

'People have different ways of looking at money,' Al said. 'To me the main thing is winning the case. I'd consider a two-million settlement a win. Maybe it would have to be three million for you to consider it a win.'

Gunnar wasn't sure the win meant anything right now. But at his age a million cash for backup would mean a lot.

Al went on. 'For Tony, winning's got nothing to do with it. He's got a specific purpose in mind for that money. I'm not sure what it is. And he says his good name is important to him, and to his kids, but I'm not so sure it's all *that* important. I can say it now, Gunnar, I haven't felt that good about this case. You know, like something's missing, something big.'

'I hope the jury doesn't feel that way,' said Gunnar.

'No big deal,' said Al. 'Hey Gunnar, whadaya say we get together for dinner when this is over. Just the two of us. Kinda bury the hatchet. I gotta say again, you tried a helluva case.'

'Sure Al, I'll call you.' But he wouldn't. The thought that maybe he had somehow misjudged Al Bergdorf darted in and out of Gunnar's mind.

Just past noon on Friday, convict Dexter Epstein was able to return Eddie Kerr's call.

'Thanks for calling, Dexter,' Eddie said. 'I've been worried about you.'

'Everything's the same.' His voice was flat, like the recording telling you to hang up and try your call again.

Eddie had gotten a worried letter from Dexter's father, and Leo Lawson had been unable to do anything right now but he had said, due to the crowded conditions at Watsonville, early parole was possible; perhaps as soon as this October when Dexter would have served a year. The warden still offered protective custody.

'What about PC?' said Eddie.

'Nah.'

Eddie had been unable to decide whether to tell Dexter about the possibility of parole in a couple of months. He was worried about the letdown if it didn't come through. Leo had said it was just a chance, that's all.

'Our big case is almost over. The jury's out.'

'I've been reading about it in the papers,' said Dexter, still without a spark of real interest.

'Dexter, I'm going up north to visit my folks in a month or so. When I do I'll come over to Watsonville and see you.'

'OK,' said Dexter.

Dexter's plight possessed Eddie's mind and his gut churned in frustration. Even the Djilas case was subordinate. If only they would parole him in October, it would be as if it had never happened. Dexter could go back to slipping around a cityscape somewhere, jumping from one solutionless problem to another like he always would, and Eddie would be no part of it. But for now, Eddie Kerr sat alone with the cancerous ache of his doubt and for a while he even forgot the jury was still out.

At three-fifteen Gunnar was on the phone telling Fleet there was still no verdict. Angela came running through the door.

'Judge O'Boyle's clerk just called! They'll wait for you for fifteen minutes. The jury has reached a verdict,' she said.

'Get Eddie . . . gotta go Fleet.' Gunnar headed for the courthouse.

The clerk had been asked to notify Tony separately, and Tony and Al met Gunnar and Eddie at the courtroom door. Al sat down in a back pew, and the other three hurried to the counsel table. Terry Wood and his assistant were at the other table, and Suzie Cline and Ward Chapin sat in the front row. Two other women were with them, reporters Gunnar supposed. Carlyle Henning hadn't come.

'All rise,' said the bailiff.

O'Boyle swept in. The crowd outside the courtroom indicated that he had cleared another trial out to take this verdict, a procedure rarely practiced in civil cases.

'Please be seated . . . bring in the jury,' said O'Boyle

Gunnar had never seen six more non-committal expressions, except he noticed that Jennifer Woody's mascara had run a little as though she might have been crying. They all looked tired.

'Have you reached a verdict?' said O'Boyle.

'We have, Your Honor.' Ralph Sullivan's brown face glistened.

'Please give the verdict form to the clerk.'

The redhead took the paper to O'Boyle. He read it without expression and handed it back to her.

'The clerk will read the verdict,' said O'Boyle.

Gunnar drew in his breath.

'We, the jury, duly empaneled and sworn, upon our oaths, do find in favor of plaintiff Anthony Djilas, and against defendants Suzette Cline, Ward Chapin and the *Times-Journal* Company, and we assess damages as follows: for compensatory damages: against Suzette Cline, $1.00; against Ward Chapin, $1.00.'

One Dollar. Gunnar let out all his breath. He felt the beginning of tears behind his eyes. The clerk kept reading.

'Against *Times-Journal* Company, $4,500,000.00 . . . . For Punitive damages: against Suzette Cline, $1.00; against Ward Chapin, $1.00; against *Times-Journal* Company . . . .' The clerk hesitated as though she wanted to make sure. She began again; 'Against *Times-Journal* Company, $7,000,000.00.'

Different distant sounds filled the courtroom. On top of everything was Al Bergdorf's clapping, and Tony pounded Gunnar on the back hard enough to hurt. He must have heard right.

The clerk handed the verdict form back to the judge.

'Let the record show,' said O'Boyle, 'that all of the jurors except Madge W. Meyers have signed the verdict form. The jury is dismissed with the court's thanks.' Then he looked straight into Gunnar's eyes. 'Have a nice weekend,' he said, a tiny smile twitching around the corners of his mouth.

Gunnar looked at the jury and Sarah Michaels gave him another wink. He quickly got up and went over to her, and grabbed her hand. Madge Meyers and Richard Hayek were already headed out the door, but he managed to shake hands with the others, thanking them 'Very Much.'

The defeated remained seated, their necks twisted toward the retreating jury. Back behind the counsel table, Tony threw his arms around Gunnar and said, 'It was you. You were the difference.'

And Dov, Gunnar thought. But those were the words a lawyer liked to hear, and so seldom did: You were the difference.

45

'We gotta celebrate,' Tony had said. 'Terrific, we gotta celebrate!'

But Gunnar had told him there were calls he had to make, that he and Al should go ahead.

'We'll be at the club . . . you know, Maple Hills. Come on out later, on your way home.'

Just to end the conversation, Gunnar said he would if he could. But he wouldn't. First, he needed to be alone. Then he had to make the calls. In which order would he make them?

On the way back to the office he had decided to try Leo first. He was home.

'We got a verdict twenty minutes ago,' Gunnar said.

'I know, I know, they cut in on "Jeopardy". I can't believe it.'

'Something huh?' said Gunnar.

'Something is right,' said Leo. 'Congratulations, I must say, this is the first time since I left that I wish I was back there, sharing a little of the excitement. Those young guys are going to want to kiss your hem.'

'Yeah, my hem,' said Gunnar.

Next, he had to decide who first, Anne or Holly? Suddenly, he felt ashamed of himself, and dialed his own number.

'I heard,' said Anne. 'Katie just called, it was on the radio. Lotta money, huh?'

'Lotta money, but they'll appeal, and O'Boyle might cut it down. I'm glad it's over.'

'I predict,' she said, 'O'Boyle won't cut it, and you will win the appeal.'

'Every press organization in the country will be submitting *amicus curiae* briefs.'

'Gun, I'm so proud of you. You've been making me proud of you for thirty-five years. This reminds me of the time just before graduation, when you found out you were ranked number one. We went to that award ceremony, and you got a standing ovation from your classmates. You remember?'

'Yeah.'

'Let's enjoy this, right now, like we did then.'

'Tony wants me to celebrate with him.' He had no intention of going to Maple Hills; he was hedging until he tried reaching Holly.

'Maybe you could spend some time with him, and then come home for a late supper,' she said. 'I could poach some salmon steaks.'

'Let me call you back,' he said.

'Soon?'

'In just a few minutes, no more than an hour. OK?'

'OK.'

Even if Davey was there, it was safe to call Holly at home. She had as much interest in this trial as anyone, except Tony himself. She picked it up on the first ring.

'We got a verdict,' Gunnar said.

'Oh my God,' she said.

'Eleven and a half million.'

'You lie.'

'Serious.'

'Oh my God, my father must be ecstatic!'

'He is.'

'I'll meet you at the lodge in an hour. I just want to take a bath.'

'Holly, I can't.' He listened to his own decision-making process. 'I need to savor this one for a little while for itself. I want to feel it. It probably will never happen again. One verdict like this every quarter century is all I can expect. I'll meet you tomorrow afternoon.'

'Davey just called. He's meeting Dad at Maple Hills. They wanted me to come too, but I told them my head was splitting – so I could be with you.'

'You knew about the verdict?'

'Yes, but I wanted to hear you tell me. You don't want me to sit here all alone do you? And I'll make you so glad you came to me. Just imagine it: it's been almost three months. I'll do strange things to you.'

He felt the heat. 'I'm sorry, sweetheart. You can still go to Maple Hills. Tell them you're feeling better.'

'Gunnar it's still "us", isn't it?'

'Of course. I'll be there tomorrow.'

'I need you . . . where are you going tonight?'

'Home,' he said. 'This is my biggest verdict ever . . . she's been there all the way. I hope you understand.'

The line was quiet for a few seconds. 'You're right,' she said, 'this must be a big moment for Anne, too. I just want to see you, for us, not to celebrate a jury verdict. I will see you tomorrow won't I?'

'Sure.'

'I love you.'

'Me too,' he said. A wave of shame chilled his feeling of elation. But he faintly felt his fingertips tracing the line of tiny hairs down across the satin of her belly.

As soon as his line-light went out, Angela was on the intercom. 'There's a guy from the *New York Times* waiting. He's been holding for fifteen minutes. Lubeck or Lubosh, something like that, and we're getting a steady stream of calls from reporters. Winnie is helping me take down all the numbers and messages. Just so far, we've heard from newspapers in Washington, Philadelphia, Chicago, Cleveland, St Louis, Denver and Minneapolis. She just handed me another list: Boston, Pittsburgh, Louisville and Dallas. What should I do with them?'

'I don't know,' said Gunnar.

'Do you want the guy who is holding? And Len wants to talk to you.'

'I'll talk to the guy if he's waited that long. Tell Len I'll get to him as soon as I'm done on this call . . . . Hey, can't Eddie take some of these calls?'

'He left fifteen minutes ago,' said Angela.

'I'm Arnold Lubasch, legal reporter for the *New York Times*,' said a voice on the line. Gunnar had heard the name before.

'What can I do for you? I'm really very busy,' said Gunnar.

'Are you planning a press conference?' said Lubasch.

'Not really. Frankly, I hadn't thought about it.'

'Can I have your reaction to the verdict?'

'It was fair,' said Gunnar. Oh, so goddamn fair, he thought.

'Do you expect an appeal?'

'No,' said Gunnar.

'You're kidding, of course?'

'Yes,' said Gunnar.

'Have you spoken with the jury?'

'No,' said Gunnar. 'Listen, it's getting late, and I have a lot to do. See you in church.'

Next, he buzzed managing partner Len Pettibohn. 'You called?'

'Yeah, I called, congratulations. I'm green with envy. Carlyle Henning must be jackin' off to the *Flight of the Bumblebee*.'

'You're nothing, Len, if not colorful.'

'We gotta do something, Gunnar. Angela's swamped. A written statement or something. Maybe a press conference. That's it, I'll set up a press conference for noon tomorrow. That'll give 'em all a chance to get here.'

Gunnar remembered the astonishingly generous deal Leo had cut for him on the fee; it was only fair to help the firm get as much publicity out of it as possible. 'Maybe you should make it Monday.'

'It won't be news, Monday.'

'Whatever you say.'

'We'll get them all in the building auditorium tomorrow. I'll call the manager now. There won't be anyone using it on Saturday.'

What price glory? Gunnar thought. Finally, he called Fleet. Then Dov.

It was late in London and Dov was excited. He wanted to hear the details of Andrew Levy's testimony. They were on the phone for close to half an hour.

'Anyway, my friend,' said Gunnar, 'I doubt if we would have gotten anything without Pentecost's letter and Henning's notes, not to mention Andrew.'

'Now you will have enough money to come to England,' Dov said.

*　　*　　*

Inside the front door, Anne clung to him. This was the biggest moment in his career. He wanted to share it with her, and he squeezed her back, the hardest he had in a year, maybe two. All the way home he kept telling himself: Don't get carried away. Something usually went wrong with the big ones, and you expected it in libel. The Constitutional issues often wound up in the US Supreme Court. At least with one this size, you had incentive to fight them all the way. But this was tonight, and he didn't want to lose the feeling that had bathed his soul when the clerk read the verdict.

'Sit down, let me work on that neck,' she said.

It felt wonderful. After a while she kneeled in front and spread his knees apart and laid her head on his lap. He let his fingers wander through her fine blonde hair.

'Like old times,' she said.

'Yeah,' he said, 'and you're still as beautiful as ever.'

She remained quiet after that. His thoughts ran over their lives together, and he did remember that standing ovation. He had delivered as expected in the courtroom. None of his problems were her fault. Was an erection so goddamn important? The brew of guilt, shame, embarrassment, anger, and fear coagulated into a momentary amalgam of self-loathing. On a night like tonight, he should be feeling much better than he was. There was nothing else in trial practice to achieve. The toughest thing was beating a newspaper. Few even got public-figure libel cases to the jury. The losers were legion.

'Should I put the salmon on?' she said.

'Sure,' he said.

'I love you,' she said.

The salmon was wonderful, and later they watched the ten o'clock news together. Gunnar's verdict was the lead story. There was speculation that Carlyle Henning was on his way out. Of course, the *Times-Journal* announced their intention to appeal.

The evening passed quietly, and the two of them touched more than usual, but Gunnar didn't allow her to break through his shell. He was too scared to take the chance. He relished the thought of taking the *Times-Journal* on in the US Supreme

Court, but getting too close to Anne tonight was just too frightening.

Later, as Gunnar tried to find sleep within an explosion of thoughts and feelings, Al Bergdorf's image crept in. His behavior from day one left nothing to be desired. Why was he uneasy? What could be missing? Something big, he'd said. Surely Dov would have found it.

46

Six months ago Al Bergdorf would not have fit in the seat he had slipped easily into at the back. In the small auditorium a crowd clogged the center aisle. In front of him a dozen rows upholstered in maroon and separated by darkly stained wooden arms sloped down to a proscenium stage. Apparently admission was denied no one, but the front five rows were reserved for people with media credentials. Al recognized the faces of some of the local reporters, and a blonde he had seen on CNN, but he didn't know her name.

Several microphones were mounted on a speaker's stand to the left side of the stage. Sitting in folding chairs arranged in a line across the center were Len Pettibohn, Gunnar, Tony and Eddie Kerr. Gunnar seemed subdued. Tony effervesced in his glen plaid.

Captain Franklin Delano Fleetham nodded and dropped into an aisle seat in Al's row. Leo Lawson sat further down in front. Captain Fleetham got up to let Davey and Holly pass.

'We would have been on sixteen or seventeen by now,' said Davey. 'I got a new tee-time for two-thirty. We'll have to leave here by one-thirty.'

'No problem,' said Al.

'Steve had to cancel,' said Davey. 'He can't play this afternoon.

'I know, he called. Tony wanted to invite Judge O'Boyle,' said Al.

'You're kiddin'!'

'Maybe so, but he sounded serious.'

'He's some joker,' said Davey.

Al saw one of Terry Wood's assistants take a seat in the back

294

row. He needn't have bothered. Four TV cameras were set up on the sides.

Len Pettibohn, still looking like the All-Big Ten tackle of 1965, identified himself at the speaker's stand. 'On behalf of Lawson and Larson, I welcome you all to our fair city. Those of you who haven't been here before now know that it does warm up in the summer. Ninety-six is forecast for this afternoon. This press conference was necessitated by the unusual number of telephone calls coming into our office from the media – well over a hundred, yesterday afternoon and evening.'

He had Gunnar and Leo Lawson stand when he introduced them as the co-founders of the firm. Then he set some ground rules for the questioning, and turned the speaker's stand over to Gunnar. Tony and Eddie stood as Gunnar introduced them.

'As most of you must know,' Gunnar said, 'this case is not a closed matter. There will no doubt be motions and appeals in the future. No one can possibly predict the ultimate outcome. Therefore, there are many questions that I will not be able to answer, probably most of them. But I will try my best to answer some of them, so your trip here will not be a total waste.'

Gunnar pointed at a woman in the front row. Al recognized her as a reporter for the *Times-Journal*.

'Mr Larson, how were you able to obtain the letter from Mr Pentecost to Mr Henning?'

'That is the type of question I will not be able to respond to. I suggest you not waste your turn.'

Gunnar was in command, chairman of the board. He pointed at one of the frantically waving hands in the fifth row.

'It appears that someone on the inside of the *Times-Journal* assisted you. Would you . . . .'

'You're wasting your questions,' said Gunnar, and pointed again.

A shrill voice said, 'Don't you believe in the First Amendment?'

'The first amendment to what?' Gunnar smiled, and pointed.

'Are you aware this could be the largest libel verdict against the press in history?'

'How about Miss Wyoming?' said Gunnar.

'That was overturned,' said the voice.

'Would you consider settling this case for something less?' said another voice.

'That would be up to my client,' said Gunnar.

'Will he be taking questions?' said the same voice.

'No,' said Gunnar.

Thank God, Al thought.

Davey leaned over, 'But I bet he'd love to.'

Al watched the backs of the reporters, wondering if any of them would think of an interesting question that Gunnar could answer.

One did. 'How did this libel case differ from others you have been involved in, or might be aware of?'

'The compensatory damages were easier to measure,' said Gunnar, 'because the plaintiff was deprived of a specific piece of business due to the defamation.'

'Whom do you consider the outstanding trial lawyers in the country?'

'I really have no basis for such a broad statement, but I would have to say any such list should contain names like Spence, and Haynes, and I would think Meshbesher. But I'm just talking about my heros, there's no way of knowing. It could be some hard-working assistant DA someplace. Fame often goes to the loudest mouth, and there are plenty of those in our profession.'

'Who might they be?'

'You know, as well as I do, probably better,' said Gunnar.

'Is this the most important case you've ever handled?'

'No.'

'What was?'

'An adoption, many years ago.'

'Do you think the judicial system works well in this country?'

'No,' said Gunnar.

'What's wrong with it?'

'It doesn't work well,' said Gunnar.

'Why not?' said the same voice.

'That's three questions,' said Gunnar. 'You're only supposed to get one,' and he pointed at someone else.

'Seriously, Counselor,' said the woman Al had recognized from CNN, 'what is the system's biggest fault?'

'Probably, that most people don't have access to it because of the high cost.'

'What will your fee be in this case?'

'I don't know,' Gunnar said, and pointed.

'Was this an intelligent jury?'

'Yes,' said Gunnar and pointed.

'What will be the principal issues on appeal?'

'We're not going to appeal,' said Gunnar. Everybody laughed but the questioner.

'Who's Jesse Katz?'

'Did you come by that letter legally?'

'Is the judge an old friend of yours?'

'Do you disapprove of homosexuals?'

'Did only the other side lie?'

'Would you have won if the grand jury proceedings hadn't been confidential?

'Do you have a personal bias against the press?'

Again: 'Who was the insider at the *Times-Journal*?'

Al said to Davey, 'They don't care if he answers or not. They just want to use their own loaded questions in their reports.' In a mimicking voice Al went on, 'He refused to say whether or not he came by the letter legally, or whether he disapproved of homosexuals.'

A few more questions and Gunnar thanked them and it was over.

'Let's go play golf,' said Al.

Back at the office, Gunnar found a note on his desk from the producer of ABC's 'Night Line'. There were also notes from the producers of all three network morning-shows. He told Shana to tell them he could be reached at home tonight. The afternoon was slipping away and Holly was waiting at The Lodge.

Anne thought it strange that he had asked her to watch the press conference on television, but she complied without argument. Anyway, she thought it would be fun to see him on TV. The minute Gunnar said thank you to the reporters, she put a sweatband on her head and was out the door. She ran down the curved lane through the woods to the main road in a slow gait to accommodate the oppressive heat. She crossed and headed south-east against the Saturday-afternoon traffic toward the intersection with Preacher's Bay Road.

She dropped into a slower trot as she covered a mile of the black top on Preacher's Bay Road. Last December she had supposed that the anonymous call originated in one of the row of small houses on her left. Just beyond Cochranes' lane she slowed to a walk. There were no cars in either direction. She quickly ran through the roadside ditch, dropped down and rolled under a barbed wire fence. Beyond the fence in a dense stand of trees, she picked a spot behind a windfall, and waited, watching the entry to Cochranes' lane. Neither embarrassment nor guilt allayed her resolve, but given enough time the heat might. She had brought along a pair of small binoculars – 8 x 30 – the kind used at football games. Drenched in sweat, Anne settled down to watch for the car she hoped would never come.

In less than a half hour a burgundy Mercedes slowed down as it approached. Through the binoculars she saw the unforgettable face she had seen in the courtroom – Holly Tripp. The car turned into Cochranes' lane and disappeared into the woods. She must be a friend of Libby's. She lived in the next place east on the lake.

At least ten cars had gone by, their drivers shielded from the intense heat by air-conditioners. After an hour sitting on the soft grass among buzzing flies, she gave herself fifteen more minutes. With less than one of those minutes gone, she saw the gray Cadillac come over the rise. In seconds the binoculars told her it was him. He turned into Cochranes' lane.

Holly Tripp. He's fucking Holly Tripp. She got up and walked slowly out of the trees. Now it all made sense.

Holly stood in the door, creamy-soft naked. His penis was suddenly hard, and their mouths came together, hungrily sucking the air from each other's lungs. He closed the door with his foot, and they ran to the big bed under the open rough timber-beams.

She helped him undress and she sucked him into her throat.

Scrambled all over his body, kissing as she went. He drew large nipples from hiding, and she fed him from each breast. There were no words. In the past, he had been in command, driven to enter her absolutely, radically, to invade every element of her person, to deprive her of will, to come to her, to become her, to be her – perhaps to prove his penis, to put away doubt. Now she was him. Her will ruled, she meant to possess, to suck the entirety of him within in her, to make him her tenant – reward and punishment for separating from her flesh too long. Her need so obsessive, she became larger than him, an amazon of sexual energy. She rolled him on his back – a nanosecond of fear, but then his cock, monarchal, met her onslaught – and she mounted him from above in a squat like an Eskimo woman begetting on the ground, moving her body rhythmically with vigorous thrusts of her knees. Powerful peristalsis transported all of him into her primal vacuum, lustrous gray eyes boring into his, saying look how much pleasure I can give you, look how much I love you.

The draught of semen, exquisitely expelled, left him helpless beneath her, a de-energized rag. She stretched out on top of him and kissed every inch of his face, and then she lay still with her mouth on his ear whispering over and over again, I love you, I love you, I love you.

Just his eyes moved toward the clock on the dresser. It was four – only twenty-four hours since the verdict. In one day, two ecstasies. But no abatement of doubt, no diminishment of questions, no replenishment of answers.

BOOK FOUR
ANSWERS

Being entirely honest with oneself is a good exercise.

Freud

47

Gunnar Larson had scattered Sunday's *Times-Journal* across the dining-room table. Supposedly, he was walking on Sunday morning for the first time since the trial began. Anne thought he might have headed straight for the Cochrane estate and his beautiful young lover – if that is what Holly Tripp was. Anne couldn't be absolutely positive, but the idea made far more sense than an affair with dowdy Libby Cochrane. And his face last night had all but confirmed it in writing.

Sails dotted the lake like little puffs of cotton moving before the slightest of winds. Yesterday, she had decided to confront him when he got home. But the weekend of the verdict wasn't the time.

'Good morning, dear Mother,' said Katie. Her head was wrapped in a pink towel and a bikini, hardly more than two black cotton belts, barely concealed the required precincts.

Katie was getting too skinny, Anne thought. 'Where on earth would you wear that?' she said.

'To the beach, of course,' said Katie. 'Mom, you were never a prude.'

'Hardly the garb of a lion at the Bar.'

'Which, of course, I'm not – yet, anyway. Besides, we women must always play multiple rôles. Mine will be lawyer and *femme fatale*.'

'This is something new, I take it.'

'No, I admit it's been a bit recessive, but with this suit on, I can no longer hide it.' Katie picked up the front page of the *Times-Journal*. 'Isn't it exciting! Can you believe it's happening? I'm sure I'll be deluged with attention in school, Monday.'

'No more than at the beach in that get-up.'

'Where's Daddy?'

'I just got back. I presume he has started his Sunday walks again, but now I'm not sure he's actually been doing that much walking in the past.'

'Oh, Oh. What now?'

'I don't think it's Libby Cochrane.'

'Who then?'

'Holly Tripp.'

'That beautiful thing we saw in court! Djilas' daughter?'

Anne told Katie about her run down Preacher's Bay Road in yesterday's heat.

'I was on the verge of following him to the house when I returned to my senses.'

'Jesus,' said Katie. 'I'll bet they're meeting at the Lodge. Cochranes have this big cabin in the woods. That's where Sarah had that slumber party when I was in high school . . . but you can't be sure.'

'I'm sure . . . almost, anyway.'

'How?'

'Besides what I saw, I could feel it when he came home last night. It was in his eyes, and the way he moved and talked . . . I made grilled cheese-sandwiches – you know how he likes them – and when I brought his into the den, he looked at me like Trendy used to when he'd had an accident on the carpet.'

'Are you going to tell him that you know?'

'I'm not sure.'

'You may be jumping to conclusions,' said Katie.

'You didn't see his eyes . . . . You're the law student. Is there any other reasonable inference from the evidence?'

'Something's up, there's little question about that. But you can't be sure there's a sexual relationship, or anything emotional for that matter.'

'You didn't see his eyes.'

'Mom, you're just going to have to ask him.'

'Katie, remember I don't *have* to do anything . . . I want to do the right thing.'

'He's not doing the right thing. He's being a sonofabitch. My own father, a goddam adulterer.'

'Please, honey, don't you become his judge. Don't let your relationship with him get wrecked just because mine is. And,' Anne quickly added, 'I'm not sure mine is.'

For an instant, Anne had thought of telling her about their sexual impasse.

'I think you should confront him,' said Katie.

'I know. You've been my only advisor on this. You must never hint to him you know.'

'I'm tempted.'

'I need to be able to trust you.'

'Of course . . . you can,' Katie said. 'I need the same from you.'

'You for me, and me for you.' Anne reached across the table and took Katie's hand. 'I love you, darling daughter,' she said.

'Me too, Mom.'

Anne felt a tear spill down her cheek. 'I'm not ready to give him up.'

'I'm glad of that,' said Katie. 'Men can be so fucking stupid.'

'Stupid is going to be on "Night Line" Tuesday night.'

'Oh wow! Is he going to Washington?'

'They wanted him to, but they agreed that he could go to the local ABC studio. Ted Koppel is going to interview your father and two other experts on First Amendment freedom-of-the-press issues. Can you believe it?'

'Who are the others?'

'Bob Woodward of the *Washington Post* – not your father's favourite individual – and some journalism professor from Yale, I think.'

'I'm afraid Daddy will be outnumbered two to one.'

'That's what I said, but he said there will be no sides because he's for freedom of the press, too.'

'Freedom for them to pay him eleven and a half million dollars,' said Katie.

'You don't think that's wrong, do you?' said Anne.

'In law, Mom, only losing is wrong.'

Katie left for the beach and Anne went in to shower. Looking for a bathing cap in her vanity, she happened on the poem she had been working on months ago.

> He could charm a bird from a branch.
> He could coax a cat from a tree.
> But he couldn't say one sweet thing to me;
> He couldn't say one sweet thing to me.
> Forget to listen. Forget to see.
> Next, he'll be forgetting me.

She liked the meter, but the self-pity shocked her. She had sunk further than she recalled. Since writing the verse last spring, she had found new strength. Discovered a talent for living with herself. Awareness that she was not dependent on Gunnar freed her spirit. She loved him, but she loved herself as much. Not that she was ready to give up on the marriage. The strategy that Katie doubted so much was just that: a strategy – to preserve it. But if it failed, she would be OK. She wasn't so sure he would. She decided to bide her time. No confrontation, for now.

Between the drawn drape and the bedroom window, a fly buzzed and tapped the glass. Naked, Anne took an inventory in her full-length mirror. Libby Cochrane was one thing, Holly Tripp quite another. She turned to inspect her profile, and held up her breasts with cool palms, squeezing out her inverted nipples – brown and thick and yummy, Gunnar used to say, his favorite chocolate-creams. She flexed the muscles in her butt, then raised on her toes, appraising the graceful curves of the muscles in her calves.

'Not too bad,' she said out loud. 'If I can hold it all together.' She didn't miss the unplanned double-meaning.

48

Gunnar sat behind his big desk on Friday morning, the last day of July. He had already agreed to study the possibilities of two new libel cases – one against the *Times-Journal*, the other against the plaintiff's former employer. He had referred three more to Eddie Kerr.

In the past, he would have been looking for reasons to accept the retainer; but now, his scrutiny was aimed in the opposite direction. He didn't really want the cases. For the first time in his career he understood what his old friend had meant.

Homer Reach had claimed that one case had sucked him dry of the will to litigate. Homer had taken on a divorce file he didn't want in the first place. He didn't handle divorces, but an admiring colleague had prevailed on him. There's no one else who can protect this beautiful woman, he had said.

The husband had hired a New-Age lawyer – Homer's term. In his opinion: a rude, whining, advertising sonofabitch, with a mouth like a mad gander. Other than that he was OK.

The husband was determined to keep his millions and leave a few dribbles for the wife, and the mad gander meant to help him. Homer became obsessed with preventing such a perversion of the system. He forgot about his other files. He used every trick he had learned in thirty years of litigating. Hired the best experts; created ingenious investigative ploys in a part of his mind he didn't know existed; studied the judge like a murderer planning the perfect crime; forced errors from the mad gander like a Wimbledon champion. The hate Homer's dedication engendered in the husband blinded him to reasonable defense or compromise. His bitter attitude alienated the judge and Homer routed them like the US Navy destroyed the Japs at Leyte Gulf.

After five years and two trips to the Supreme Court, Homer's client ended up with almost all of the twenty-million-dollar marital estate. The husband was left with about what he had planned for the wife in the beginning. Hearing of his victory, other bellicose spouses sought Homer out to fight their internecine wars. And Homer took on a couple of their cases. He soon realized that his combat with the mad gander had used up his reservoir of litigating juice.

Sure, he had won. Sure, he had collected a million-dollar fee. But like Von Paulus at Stalingrad, Homer had spent too much, reached too far. He faced defeat. So he surrendered.

Homer tried alcohol for solace and excitement, then an affair with a twenty-five-year-old receptionist in his office. When his wife left him, he made a try at a comeback, but soon turned the case over to a younger colleague. The last time Gunnar saw him, Homer said his client, to whom he devoted the five years, was spreading the word that he had overcharged her. A few weeks later, Homer tried to fly from his window on the twentieth floor. Gunnar wondered what his last thoughts had been. Did he remember that the mad gander was still going strong? Recently, he had been elected chairman of that gaggle who refer to themselves as matrimonial lawyers. There actually are people who have to be Marvin Mitchelson, or the equivalent, 365 days a year.

In the four weeks since the verdict, Gunnar had appeared on 'Night Line', Henning had been fired, and O'Boyle had denied Terry Wood's motion for a judgment notwithstanding the verdict, or in the alternative, a new trial. Wood had thirty days to file his notice of appeal. Both *Time* and *Newsweek* had devoted a full page to the case, and Gunnar and Holly had clung together at least a dozen times. They had to make up for months of privation she said.

The call he was waiting for came late in the morning.

'How ya doin' this fine day?' said Terry Wood. 'How about I buy ya lunch on short notice?'

Gunnar was lunching with Leo, but he would cancel. 'Why not?' he said.

'Athletic Club at twelve-thirty,' said Wood, 'It'll be fun to be seen with a celebrity.'

'My fifteen minutes are over,' said Gunnar.

In mid-July Gunnar and Anne had attended Terry Wood's third wedding. The reception had been a blast. Three decades' worth of trial lawyers comprised much of the company. And with the verdict only a week old, Gunnar could have stolen the show. In deference to the occasion he refused to discuss the Djilas case. Instead they all talked about halcyon days when you could trust the other guy, and you could afford to handle a case with less than a million at stake.

At the Athletic Club, the hostess took Gunnar to a private dining-room panelled in cherry wood. Bride Nancy had already made Terry over. He smelled of good cologne and aromatic tobacco. His broad shoulders filled a new navy blazer, and his fingernails were clean. They ordered iced tea and turkey sandwiches, and talked about the wedding and the heat. And Gunnar's notoriety.

'I thought I should have had my say on "Night Line",' said Terry, 'but there's no time for losers.'

'You didn't miss anything. I just uttered platitudes,' said Gunnar.

'Like everybody else in town, I saw it. You were marvelous. I suppose next you'll be running for governor,' said Terry. 'Or there's a senate seat coming up next year.'

'Cut the bullshit. You know what I think about politicians.'

'Some guy on CBS called you "laconic". What the hell does that mean?'

'Beats the hell out of me. You better hope it's not catchy. We've been together a lot lately.'

'You want to talk money, huh?' said Terry.

'If you've got any to talk about.'

'I've got a little.'

'That's what I'm afraid of. By the way, where you getting your authority these days?'

'Carlyle Henning's replacement, the new man from Bahston. He wants to clean up this mess as fahst as we can. It's gone way too fah already . . . . What'll it take?'

'C'mon Terry make the offer.'

'You're the big winner, what's your demand?'

'Eleven and a half million.'

'Let's get serious. I got three million.'

'You got more than that. Djilas wouldn't take that before he had a verdict.'

'Have you told him how appeals courts tend to reverse verdicts against newspapers?'

'Both Bergdorf and I have gone through the whole drill with him.'

'Getting chummy with big Al?'

'He's not so big anymore. You should have invited him to the wedding. He's not such a bad guy.'

'Wow, have you changed your tune. Age is mellowing, I take it. It couldn't be that he referred you the case that made you famous.'

'C'mon, you're supposed to be seducing me to accept your paltry offering.'

'To tell you the truth, and if I say it's the truth, you know it's the truth. Right?'

'I hope so.'

'I got four million. Take it to Djilas.'

Gunnar couldn't help it; the figure sounded wonderful. And he thought of the two million it meant for him, but he knew Tony Djilas wouldn't take it.

'Now, I'll tell *you* the truth. This Djilas ain't an ordinary guy. There's no way he'll take four. Never. *Ever.*'

'What do you think will crack him?

'He says nine, but I think eight. That's bargain basement. Tell C. Ross Wingate that he's saving three and a half million, and the mess will disappear. And the people of this town will begin, right now, to forget the more sordid aspects of his newspaper.'

'I'll take it back to him.'

They finished a pleasant lunch, talked about what an asshole Governor Kettle was, and what a good case O'Boyle had tried. Two weeks later they settled for 6.75 million.

49

TIMES-JOURNAL COMPANY   **August 19, 1987**

Pay to the order of:
Anthony Djilas and Lawson and Larson Ltd $6,750.000.00
Six million seven hundred fifty thousand and no/100 DOLLARS
FIRST NATIONAL BANK

Gunnar held the check in his hand – a lavender deed to eternal bliss. He couldn't afford to fondle this little baby too long. The interest on just his half was $750.00 per day. In six days, forty-five hundred. More than his father had ever earned in his best year baking crackers.

Before retiring in 1958, Carl Larson had worked in the same bakery for more than forty years. To Gunnar's knowledge, his father had never considered an alternative to his toil in front of the ovens. Peeling sheets of crackers from an endless, never-stopping belt kept his legs bare of hair, his narrow body devoid of fat. When the allotted time to qualify for retirement was served, no younger person could be found to do the job. Presumably, soda crackers would have disappeared if automation hadn't arrived. Gunnar's father was making $28.00 a week when they'd moved to the distant suburbs.

Today, the size of the check in Gunnar's hand made him laugh. Mommy and Daddy had taught him the importance of being secure: saving money for a rainy day; filling the potato bin; not wasting anything. Debt was your greatest enemy. Leo said power and money were one and the same, but Gunnar didn't understand the essence of large accumulations of wealth. For Anne, money was a way of helping those without it, but Gunnar hadn't learned charity. He believed in it as an abstraction, but money had come so hard in the early years, he was loath to let go of it.

Fleet's view of money made more sense to Gunnar. Fleet equated money with time. He said you could measure it in minutes, hours, days, months or years. Money bought you freedom. If you had it, you escaped the slavery of reporting to work every morning.

One thing Gunnar knew for sure: once spent, it was gone for ever. He had Shana process the check through the firm's trust account, deliver Tony Djilas' share, and invest $3,250,000 in one-year United States treasury notes – the safest investment in the world, as far as Gunnar knew. He would take care of the taxes later. About a hundred thousand would go to the firm to cover Eddie Kerr's time, and the other twenty-five, the promised bonus, would go directly to Eddie.

Eddie Kerr saved *his* money, too. But the balance built up slowly. His salary and bonus had edged up to about a hundred thousand. Over the years he had stashed away more than that in savings and investments. He saw the twenty-five-thousand-dollar bonus from the Djilas case as a windfall, and he decided to spend part of it. He fished the telephone book out of the debris in his credenza and dialed a travel agent.

'I would like to tour Great Britain the last two weeks of September,' he said. 'I want to rent a car and go at my own pace.'

The travel agent agreed to deliver airline tickets and itinerary by week's end. Eddie decided he would discharge his obligations to see his parents and Dexter by taking an extra day on the Labor Day weekend.

That evening, the money safely stored away, Gunnar leaned back in the soft leather chair. Beyond the glass wall, city lights flickered. His eyes found Jack's picture on the credenza. He felt the same old pain like a rusty nail lodged in his lung. Perhaps he should put the picture away. Must he hold on to his grief? By what right did *he* survive, to skirmish in courtrooms over who was buggering whom. During the trials, anger stood second in line – behind a guile nurtured over twenty-five years of managing the system. When anger cheated ahead, Gunnar was at the mercy of his opponents. Homer Reach had said not long before he died, 'Gunnar, I can't come back because I am pissed off all the time!' And the anger was there before Jack died. It had always been there.

The shadowy fear of being alone eclipsed the palpable joy of this morning's check. His relationship with Anne was slipping through his fingers like dry sand and although Holly had revived his passion, fucking a married woman did little for loneliness.

His father had been gone for fifteen years, his mother for six, and his brother had consigned himself to oblivion somewhere in southern California; was it Torrance or Whittier or Van Nuys? Gunnar could never remember. Dickie moved around so damn much. He felt a twinge of guilt about Dickie. Mother was their common ground while she lived; with her gone, they seldom talked.

Eleven years ago a helicopter crash in Germany had torn a gash that didn't heal. You must let it go, Anne said. How ever the hell you did that. Tonight, the picture awakened his memory to Duck Creek, and the trip west the summer between Jack's second and third year at West Point.

They'd discovered Duck Creek, a friendly serpent of a stream in which Charley Brooks, an author living in the woods nearby, had claimed that brown trout as big as cocker spaniels dwelt under the overhanging banks. Gunnar and Jack had one more night left to fish together that summer. It would be their last, ever. They started out from the parking area early. Still high above the peaks of the Hebgen Range to the west, the sun blazed through thin mountain air. Instead of approaching the creek directly, they angled off into the pine woods on a path that would lead them a couple of miles upstream. Scattered puffs of clouds crawled across the sapphire mountain sky, occasionally occluding the sun to produce stark shadows moving across the landscape. The valley below the parking spot was completely open for a mile upstream, save for one twisted cedar in the center. Beyond, trees along the bank became more frequent as the dense woods converged with the flowing water. Through the trees to the left, tall meadow grasses luminesced golden light like a plain of autumn corn. Bear scat on the trail had given Gunnar mild qualms and on past nights when they'd come back out they'd sung and yelled to each other and shaken bells, imagining giant grizzlies in every clump of brush they passed.

One night, weeks earlier, a Park ranger had been waiting at their car when they'd emerged from the woods. 'You guys are out awful late,' he'd said to Gunnar as they stood by the car. 'It can be dangerous back in there at night.'

Repeating the conventional western wisdom on avoiding confrontations with bears, Gunnar said, 'We make as much noise as possible, so they will hear us coming.' They discussed the fishing and the moon. Then came back to the bears.

'What is really the best way to protect yourself from the grizzlies when we're fishing way up Duck Creek?' Gunnar had asked the ranger.

'Always go with someone slower than you,' he answered. On that last day, at the point where smaller, shallower and slower Richards Creek joined Duck Creek from the South-east, they'd cast streamers into the pool formed by the confluence. They both hooked trout in that first pool: Gunnar, a husky brown; and Jack, a rainbow. From opposite banks they held up their fish, lips stretched wide by grins under the shadows of broad-brimmed hats.

As Gunnar thought back on that day so long ago, it seemed that either one or the other was hooked up all afternoon. They cast big fluffy grasshoppers fashioned of deer hair and pheasant feathers on number eight hooks into the current right up against the bank. After sunset, they worked back down to a pool behind a beaver dam, almost as tall as Gunnar.

Father and son quietly approached in dim light. You could just see the outline of the opposite bank. The rotten-egg smell of hydrogen sulfide gas escaped from the muck as Gunnar's waders sunk in over the ankles. Swimming along the glassy surface a beaver was etched in black and white at the point of a wide wake.

Upstream, Jack cast in the shadows, his fly rod waving in the gloom like a sorcerer's wand. A coyote barked, not more than a hundred yards away. Sandhill cranes warbled hoarsely, some on the ground, some gliding overhead, long necks and bills silhouetted in the failing light.

Gunnar worked out some line, and cursed as he dropped his muddler minnow on the edge of a beaver's lodge. Abetted by luck more than skill, he jerked the fly from the tangled branches. Beyond his vision in the dark, the muddler minnow, greased to float, plopped into the quiet water. A splash in the murk quickened his heart. Gunnar heaved back on the rod, his line taut to something hidden in the blackness along the far bank. He shrieked Indian-like in the night.

'What happened, Dad?' Jack yelled.

'I'm in to something big! Maybe a goddam beaver.'

Jack splashed across the shallow end of the pool. 'I'm coming over. I've got a light.'

The line suddenly cut through the water toward the dam. Gunnar had hooked a big night-feeding brown. The fish changed direction and ran upstream, through the middle of the pool. Gunnar gained some line, yard by yard. Jack plodded through the mud, flashlight in hand.

'Turn the light off, it's blinding me,' Gunnar said, too abruptly.

Steadily, he eased the fish toward Jack's ready net. Then a desperate run to deeper water. The line went slack. Gunnar's breath rushed out. He had lost it. In a second, he took up the slack on the reel and felt the weight of the trout. 'He's still on!' Gunnar yelled.

'Good!' said Jack, 'he must be a monster!'

This time as Gunnar eased the fish to the bank, the flashlight beam focused on the big shouldered brown, tired, but still shaking his head, frantically contending for freedom. Jack deftly slipped the net under him. He was theirs. They moved back from the bank and played the light on the splendid creature lying still on a bed of flattened swamp grass. Slick brown sides covered with red and black spots along the back glimmered in the beam like oils on a painter's palette.

'He must go six pounds or more,' Jack said.

It was one of the best moments in a long and a short life. On their way back to the car through the night woods, phantasmal grizzlies lurked among black trees as Gunnar sang loud and off key, 'I'll sing you one ho!'

'What is your one ho?' Jack sang back.
'One is one and all alone and ever more will be he so.'
Together, 'Green grow the rushes ho.'
Then Jack, 'I'll sing you two ho.'
'What is your two ho?'
'Two, two, little white boys, clothe them all in green, ho!'
And together, 'Green grow the rushes, ho!'

The brown hung on the wall in Gunnar's den, a reminder of their moment. Now, as the images filled his mind as they must when he was alone with the picture, his eyes watered and the passages in his nose thickened and stung. But tonight he wasn't going to cry; what he was going to do, was go back to Duck Creek. Tomorrow.

50

'We are beginning our descent into Bozeman. Please replace all trays, and bring your seat-backs to an upright position.'

Gunnar pushed his head up against the glass. To the South, like an obscene finger, the Grand Teton poked above the horizon, and closer, Yellowstone Lake spread out – pale blue blob on blue-black. Beneath the plane the Yellowstone River poured out of Paradise Valley through the canyon known as Allenspur.

The plane dropped lower over the mountains cloaked in deep pine green. With the harsh scraping sound of the low-ering landing gear, a broad valley came into view, quilted in squares of golden yellow, and various shades of green and brown. They descended over the small city midst the quilt-ing, laid out orderly in the center but with tentacles following little canyons out from the edges. Gunnar remembered the football stadium and the white-domed field house at the uni-versity. The end of the runway crosshatched with arcane white markings preceded the sharp squeak of the tires striking the pavement. Gunnar had returned to Bozeman for the first time in a dozen years.

As they taxied back toward the terminal, the Bridger Range towered above them to the North. Gunnar remembered the peaks, Sacajawea, Ross and Baldy. Ninety miles to the South, he could still get to Duck Creek well before sunset.

Anne hoped he would have fun, but she'd said little else when he'd started digging out his gear last night. He called Holly from the airport this morning. She pleaded with him not to go. She wished she could go along. She could, you know. There's nothing Davey could do about it. He prob-ably wouldn't miss her any way. What if Gunnar didn't come back? Her life would be over. He had promised her he would be back in a few days. He told her he had to go. There was no choice in the matter. He would only be gone a few days.

The drive through spectacular Gallatin Canyon in his rented jeep evoked earlier times. Huge slabs of rough tan rock walled him in. The river rushed along the highway in the opposite direction. Around every bend, trout fisherman stood waist-deep in fast water. Gunnar remembered standing in some of the same places; Jack close by, Anne and Katie scrambling over the steep slopes above. Twelve years since he had tried, he wondered if he could still cast a fly. Traveling the treacherous road, you had to watch for cross-country semi-trailers on their way to and from California. It was five o'clock when he got to the parking area at Duck Creek.

He quickly stuck his rod together and headed for the path through the woods. From the low bluff, he could see out across the meadow to the lone twisted tree. The vista was altered. The once brimming creek had dropped two or three feet. Unlovely banks of mud were exposed below the sere August grasses. Perhaps, much further upstream, beaver dams might still hold the water level up, where it belonged.

He followed the trail through the woods toward the pool where he and Jack had landed the big brown. Stark black print on white paper nailed to trees guarding the path warned that he was entering an area frequented by grizzly bears. Old news.

It took him three-quarters of an hour. Only a few brittle sticks remained on each end of what had been a grand dam. A slow trickle of muddy water parted the parched grass that had once been the bottom of the deep pool. But even so, he remembered where he had stood, and where Jack had stood. And he played the whole scene over again in his mind just as he had done last night, but this time he was right there, and not only was Jack gone, the whole goddam pool was gone, and the fish, and the whole goddam world was changed to something ugly, and he dropped to his knees and then to his face and cried into the dry grass.

*   *   *

The sun had dropped through an hour's worth of sky and the glare gave way to softer evening light. Gunnar snuffed the mucus out of his nose and pulled himself up into a sitting position with his elbows hooked around his knees. From that level he couldn't even see what was left of Duck Creek.

He had let it all slip away when his son slipped away. Not only fishing, he had loved mountains and the oceans and the canoe country up north and flying in the quiet new jets and golf and baseball and basketball and boxing and skiing and hunting and, Jesus Christ, there was no end. He shared with pals or with Jack or even with Anne and Katie.

Sonofabitch, sonofabitch, sonofabitch, sonofabitch. Oh Jesus Christ, when will it be over. I need him. I need him. I need him. There's nothing else I need. I want him. I want him. I need him. I never run out of tears. Never. Never. Never. I can't cry for anything else. Nothing else is sad. He shared with no one. *What's to share.* He heard everybody's stories of jumping fish, of home runs and royal flushes . . . and *he* had verdicts. When you landed that seven-pound brown or the even made a hole-in-one, or wrote a book or had a son, there was no fucking appeal. It was yours to keep. Or so Gunnar had thought. He looked up into the trees and reached way down inside for a scream, but nothing squeezed through his throat. He was so fucking afraid he would never be done with the fury, the unforgiving determination somehow to make the account balance – when some sonofabitch had absconded with all the assets.

Then Jack said to him. You're not crying for me; you're crying for yourself. I would never have spent my whole life in a courtroom if you had died.

'But it was in the natural course of things for me to die first,' Gunnar said.

Either way, we would have been without each other, Jack said.

A few minutes later Gunnar started back for the car. 'I'll sing you one ho,' he croaked.

The woods were silent. The summer wind barely moved the lightest branches.

Green grow the rushes ho. One is one and all alone and ever more shall be he so.

51

In downtown legal circles, Gunnar's fee arrangement had become common knowledge. Some junior partner at Lawson and Larson had probably leaked it. Ultimately, it found its way into a *Times-Journal* article covering the demise of Carlyle Henning. The phrase 'set for life' became tedious. Gunnar wondered what the hell it meant anyway. Nothing had changed but his bank balance. Was one ever 'set for life'? He sat behind the same desk. The same bodies swarmed busily through the same office. Files were piling up again. He had agreed to pursue the two libel cases, and Len Pettibohn pressured him to take on a major new defense file for Miracle Mills. Demand for his presence as a speaker mounted. And Gunnar felt more obligated to the firm than ever before.

Three weeks ago he had hurried back down the trail from the dried-up beaver pond at Duck Creek. He had missed the last flight out of Bozeman. He couldn't stand the thought of being alone in a motel that night, so he'd driven all the way to Billings and caught a red-eye home. He called Anne from the airport, so she wouldn't be scared when he came in the front door in the middle of the night. When he crawled into bed he told her that it just hadn't been what he'd expected, and he didn't want to stay.

'It used to be your favorite place in the whole world,' she said, her eyes half-shut with sleep. 'Gunnar, where is your favorite place now?'

'I don't know,' he said. 'I guess I don't have one.'

When he awoke from his exhausted sleep, she was gone, running he supposed.

In the weeks following, Gunnar had lunch with Leo, Len, Fleet

– whose swollen knee prevented him from resuming their tennis – and Tony Djilas, who brought Al Bergdorf along – he had lost even more weight – and with Terry Wood, who was being mentioned as a possible appointee to the state Supreme Court. Terry didn't have a chance; he was too competent for Governor Kettle.

Everybody assumed that even though Gunnar was set for life, he was ready to resume his litigation chores, although to a man they told him to take a vacation. He deserved one they said, and he looked tired.

In some ways he *was* ready to resume his chores. After all, that's what he did for a living. He could prepare and try a lawsuit by rote, better than the best efforts of many of his colleagues at the Bar. Back at work, he dictated assignment memos for the preparation of summons and complaints, and a Rule Twelve motion in the new Miracle Mills anti-trust case, and research assignments for them all. But something was different, something he couldn't specifically identify. Homer Reach's image lurked in Gunnar's office where he and Homer had chatted so many times in the years before. Homer had died. You only have so much juice, it said. Some have more than others, but each one has a finite amount. After Homer had won his big case, lawyers had said, Old Homer, yep, he's set for life. If my juice is drying up, at least I have the money to see me through, Gunnar thought.

Holly wanted to see him on Tuesdays, Thursdays, Saturdays and Sundays. Even though he felt sometimes that there was renewal for him in their love-making, he could only handle so much. He tried to make Saturdays a lunch, then hand-holding in some remote park, or driving in the country; and he said he needed the walking exercise on Sunday morning, like always. Tuesday and Thursday nights were for sex at the Lodge. And when the air conditioner broke down – until Libby got it fixed – Holly took him out on the boat twice.

Despite the booze, Davey worked hard and played five rounds of golf a week, late afternoons and weekends. Anne seemed to ignore Gunnar's comings and goings and, once or twice, Gunnar thought of the old adage: Give him enough rope, he'll hang himself.

After delivering the bonus check, Gunnar hadn't seen much of Eddie Kerr. His preoccupation with his criminal client's fate in the crowbar hotel in Watsonville seemed out of character. It must somehow tie in with a sense of failure about the case. No one knew better than Gunnar, Eddie's obsession with being right. And Gunnar was again considering capitalizing on Eddie's obsession by bringing him into the new Miracle Mills case. He had been indispensable in *Djilas v. Times Journal*. The bonus had been a bargain. But such employment must wait. Eddie was on a two-week vacation in the British Isles.

Winnie Slaught, Eddie's secretary, tapped on the jamb of Gunnar's open door. 'Can I come in for a minute, Mr Larson?'

She hadn't broken the habit. Unlike most of the attorneys in the office, Gunnar didn't like being called 'Mister'. For the moment he overlooked it. He liked this slim, energetic young woman, with her thick bob of dark brown hair. He told her to come in and sit down, but instead she walked around behind his desk and laid a newspaper in front of him, open to an inside page.

'Have you read this yet this morning?' she said, putting her finger on a one-column headline that stated simply: PRISONER SUICIDE.

Sometime Tuesday afternoon, Dexter Epstein, 22, a native of New York City, was found dead in his cell at the state prison in Watsonville. The medical examiner concluded that Epstein had hung himself with a belt. He is survived by his parents, both of New York City. Warden Alphonse Ricci said that Epstein very likely would have been paroled next month. He pled guilty last year to a charge of possession of a controlled substance with intent to sell. He was in the first year of a three year sentence.

Through his compressed lips, Gunnar blew out a puff of air. 'Do you think I should try to get a hold of Mr Kerr?' said Winnie.

'Can you?'

'He's driving around Scotland someplace. I do have a number for him in Edinburgh. But he's not due there until tomorrow night.'

'This could . . . no *would*, ruin his trip. Maybe you should let it go. He'll be back in a week.'

'And then *this* came in the morning mail.' Winnie handed Gunnar a single handwritten page. 'And this was with it.' She held a microcassette between her thumb and forefinger, the kind used in pocket recorders. Gunnar had one in a drawer.

Gunnar read the short note written in scrawly hand.

Dear Mr Kerr, I thought this might interest you. I was sort of bragging about your big case when it was all over the papers a couple of months ago. This guy, Malcolm Edwards, laughed and said he'd been following the case in the paper. He said it was all jive. I asked him what he meant and he said he'd tell me sometime. I got together with him last Friday. He didn't know I was recording our conversation on the recorder you gave me. The tape is enclosed. If I don't see you again, I want you to know there is no one who has ever treated me better than you have. Love, Dexter.

The last sentence made Gunnar shudder. He looked up into Winnie's eyes, wide behind her rimless glasses. 'Let me handle this, Winnie. I'll explain to Eddie when he gets back. That we didn't want to wreck his trip. OK?'

'Sure, Mr Larson, whatever you say.'

When she had left, Gunnar put the cassette in his recorder, and hit the play-back button. Outside his glass wall a light September rain fell on the city. Some of the maples in Corum Park were turning yellow.

Because his recorder ran too fast, the voices came through in a slightly high pitch. But one, laced with 'motherfuckers' and 'you knows', was unmistakably a black male – apparently the Malcolm Edwards referred to in Dexter's letter. The other must have been Dexter Epstein. A radio or television in the background, and other occasional unintelligible voices, made the conversation hard to follow. Gunnar listened until the tape went blank thirteen minutes later. Then he got up and locked his door.

After he had told Shana to hold his calls, he rewound the tape and listened through again, stopping and rewinding in places to hear a third and fourth time.

MALCOLM. Fuckin' Jillus act so lily white. You know. Bigga muthfuckin' crook as anybody. You know.

DEXTER. How would you know?

MALCOLM. My man bought from that muthfug Zilman in Miami. You know. Shee-it, I was th'onliest kid in the deal. You know. Bout sixteen. You know. Them muthfugs kilt them po-leece in Fort fuckin' Lauderdale. You know.

DEXTER. What do you mean, *your man*?

MALCOLM. Big fuckin' Ed, my uncle. Shee-it, He killed my ol'man with a muthafuckin' axe when he ketchem with his girl fren. He surprised the mothafuckin' judge an made bail. Couple weeks later he stuck his muthafuckin' girl fren with a fuckin' ice pick. He be's on death row in Florida. Shee-it! You know. His own muthafuckin brother. Shee-it!

DEXTER. Who killed what police?

MALCOLM. Ain't nobody ever knowed. You know. But Big fuckin' Ed kilt them cops for that Muthfug Zilman. You know. He sposta get the fuckin' chair for axin' my ol'man, and killin' that whore. If they knowed he kilt them muthafuckin' cops. You know. They'da fried his muthafuckin' black ass by now.

The tape became garbled in a mass of muthafuckins and a Tide commercial. Cleaner, whiter without bleach, muthafuckin' cunt. Shee-it. For the sheets that feel good on your skin. You know, we want muthafuckin' grass. Gunnar stopped it, then rewound.

MALCOLM. We want muthafuckin grass, we know where it be. You know. Can't nobody get a better deal from Zilman and that muthafug, Jillus.

DEXTER. How do you know Djilas was involved?

MALCOLM. Are you stupid muthafug? This Jillus muthafucka. You know. He had some muthafuckin' cop in his pocket. You know. These other muthafuckin' po-leece checkin' this Zilman out and they ketch that muthfug Jillas. Them guys't ketch Jillas, you know, thems'a ones Big Ed kilt. Zilman give Big Ed six bales ta kill 'em.

DEXTER. Who'd he kill?

MALCOLM. Two muthafuckin' po-leece. One right in his muthafuckin' black and white. Ain't nobody ever even find the other muthfug. You know. My muthafuckin' uncle took him way out in the Everglades.

Gunnar snapped the recorder off. That other cop, Ek his name was, had applied for a job in San Diego. At least there was a letter from some company that said they had gotten an application from him. Jesus Christ. This guy can't be right. Only in one place did he actually single out Djilas. Gunnar was letting this voice, probably that of an habitual liar and criminal, get him concerned. He fast-forwarded the tape to a spot near the end.

Out of a progressively worse garble, one exchange was surprisingly clear. Dexter's voice, mixed with the background noise, said something about Djilas and Eddie Kerr. Then came Malcolm's words.

'Jillas, that muthafucka had sixty bales in a mothafuckin' garage in Dania. You know. Big Ed and this other mean muthafuckin' nigger bought all of it. Big Ed had quarter million fuckin' dollars in a muthafuckin' suitcase. Gave it all to Jillas. I didn't see no Zilman on that deal. This other big Jew-boy, Dean or Don, alus hangin' out wit Jillas. You know. He's alus holdin' this muthafuckin' Uzzi. Kill yo ass as soon as look at it! You know. Yeah that muthafuckin' Jillas, some muthafuckin' cat. Alus dressin' like he be's on the avenue. You know.'

Gunnar shut the recorder off. If he had heard the truth, his client Tony Djilas had repeatedly committed perjury on the pivotal issue being tried. And he might be an accessory to murder. Gunnar put the tape and the letter in his top drawer and locked it. He had agreed to meet Holly at the Lodge early that night.

52

On trips to the Lodge, Holly filled Gunnar's consciousness. During the half-hour drive, anticipating the passion, and her smooth skin and his quick and complete response to her body, he was ready before he turned his car into Cochranes' lane. In the last weeks of their loving, he had become as potent as a herd bull. She cajoled, and playfully whined like a pup begging at the table, but she never argued with him. She worshiped the solid icon between his legs. Apparently, she remembered what fighting did to it.

But, today, behind the wheel of his car, after listening to Dexter Epstein's tape, no anticipation of ecstasy intruded on the wellspring of new thoughts and dark hypotheses. The first question: With whom should he share the information on the tape? He recollected how tapes had destroyed Nixon. But this wasn't a question of destruction, at least not his; unless a stalk of suspicion grew from the doubts of cynics, suspicion that Gunnar had suborned false testimony.

He tried rationalizing. All significant trial testimony is doubted. Cases without doubt are not tried; they settle. The function of cross-examination is to uncover perjury, freshen stale memory, or recover information once conveniently lost. Tony's testimony had withstood Terry Wood's cross-examination and the scrutiny of judge and jury.

None of Gunnar's contrived analyses worked. The new and terrible variable had already claimed its own place in his mind, like a tumor before the biopsy. Jesus Christ, how much those reporters would love to get their hands on that tape!

In a lifetime of trials and guileful negotiating, Gunnar had perfected certain proven routines and safeguards. Often he had later decided that the favorable result was due to his disciplined adherence to the drill. When he'd parked his car behind the Lodge, he decided to use the one that always made sense because there was no downside. He would mention Dexter Epstein's tape-recording to no one until at least twenty-four hours after making the decision to do so.

In the vestibule Holly hit him with the beam of her irradiating smile. 'My God, honey, what's the matter? You look like a lost dog. Where's my smile?'

He made excuses and kissed her, and they began and finished the ritual, but the herd bull had been replaced by a tired day-laborer dutifully servicing his wife in a room shared with four children.

The next morning Gunnar had put all other work aside, and behind his locked door he had listened to the tape several more times. By ten, his twenty-four-hour rule in mind, he had called Leo and asked him to have lunch the following day.

Now, Leo sat across the desk from him, chewing on the turkey sandwiches from the box lunch Shana had set before him. The temperature had dropped into the thirties overnight and steel-gray clouds hung low over downtown. After Shana brought in the coffee refills, Gunnar got up and closed and locked the door.

'That,' said Leo, 'is the only time I have ever seen you lock your door. This must be big.'

'I hope not,' said Gunnar. 'But I am worried, very worried. I had to talk about this. There was no one else.' He took the tape recorder out of the drawer. 'You'll soon see what I mean.' Gunnar hit the playback switch.

Neither of them spoke during the whole time the tape was playing.

At the end Leo said, 'Foul-mouthed bastard, isn't he?'

'That's the black dialect of prisoneese,' said Gunnar.

'Is that it? The source of your door-locking worry?' said Leo.

'Yeah, that's it. It gives one the impression that Djilas is a perjurer, the worst kind. A fucking plaintiff committing perjury. He came to court on his own.'

'Did you think he was lying when you interviewed him?'

'Of course not.'

'How about when you examined him before the jury?'

'No, not then either.'

'How about on cross?'

'I thought he might know a little more about that bank account than he owned up to. But, otherwise, even on cross . . . I believed him.'

'Apparently the jury did, too,' Leo said, 'and Mike O'Boyle had his means, if he thought their verdict was unfair.'

'Yes, all that's true.' said Gunnar.

'Then, what in God's green earth are you worried about? The case is settled. You've got your money. And Djilas has got his. And regardless of whether this convict is telling the truth or not, you did this city a great service in exposing Carlyle Henning and his yellow rag.'

'Quite a speech.'

'Well that's the way I feel. What's more, I don't believe the bastard on the tape.'

'You make it all sound so simple.' And Leo's unambiguous sentiments did assuage Gunnar's anxiety. 'But let me ask you something. What if you did believe the guy on the tape?'

'If the belief was founded on hard evidence, I might ask the client for an explanation. Just in case the thing could explode in my face. But that isn't the case here. I'd flush this tape. Where the hell did you get it anyway?'

Gunnar told him.

'One thing's for certain,' Leo said, adjusting his dark-rimmed glasses, and pointing his finger at the little recorder in its black leather case, 'You can't give this thing to Eddie Kerr. You don't need any loose cannons.'

'Jesus Christ, it's first-class mail.'

'I don't care,' said Leo, 'if it was hand-delivered from Ronald Reagan. Don't let him listen to this tape.'

For two days, Gunnar had been thinking about Eddie's bearing of ethical superiority that put off every lawyer in the firm. 'I'm not sure the guy is lying,' he said.

'Of course, you're not sure. You'd have to be God to be sure, but you have no basis for believing it.'

Gunnar wondered if Leo remembered how reluctant he had been to take the case in the first place. But his reluctance has been associated with Al Bergdorf. And Holly. Gunnar had liked Tony Djilas from near the beginning, but who didn't? 'To know Tony is to love him,' the all-hallowed Reverend Goodspeed had said in open court.

'And one thing you must promise me, old partner,' said Leo. 'You will not let anyone else hear this tape, including Eddie Kerr.'

On his first day back on the job, Eddie Kerr actually said 'Good morning' to the surprised Angela when he plucked the fistful of telephone messages from his box, and again to Winnie Slaught as he entered the door of his windowless office.

'Mr Kerr, Mr Larson told me to make sure you talked to him the moment you got back. I'll tell him you're here.'

'OK,' said Eddie, with his usual emphasis on the K.

He had shed five pounds on his tour, and he felt wonderful. Travel agreed with him, and on the Pan-Am flight home from Gatwick, he had already planned a new trip for next year. To Scandinavia, the homeland of his ancestors on his mother's side. There was a note on the seat of his chair from Gunnar – the same message that Winnie had conveyed. The debris on his desk and credenza had been arranged in squared-off piles and the usual boxes were stacked neatly in the back corner.

Gunnar came through the door and slid into a chair. 'Welcome back. Did you have a good time?'

When Eddie had finished describing his trip in detail, interspersed with Gunnar's perfunctory questions, Gunnar told him about Dexter Epstein's suicide. Eddie felt the tears rush to his eyes in the sudden realization that he had no closer friend.

'I'm sorry,' Gunnar said. 'I know you and he were close.' He handed the letter and cassette to Eddie. 'I didn't want to spoil your trip. I took the responsibility of waiting 'til you got back. You were out of touch, and I didn't think you could make it to the funeral anyway. I'm doubly sorry if I did the wrong thing.'

'That's OK,' Eddie said. He wished he *had* been able to attend

330

the funeral. In a less expansive mood than this morning's, he would have been filled with resentment.

'Let me know what you make of that letter,' said Gunnar. 'I should tell you there's nothing on the tape, nothing at all.'

After Gunnar left, Eddie read the letter several times, but his grief submerged any analytical thought. Anyway, maybe he would talk to Malcolm Edwards and find out what he might have said. Eddie got up and closed his office door. Returning to the letter, he read the last line again: If I don't see you again, I want you to know there is no one who has ever treated me better than you have. Love, Dexter. Eddie laid his head on his crossed arms and cried.

Ten minutes later he inserted the tape in his dictaphone. He had Winnie hold his calls and for the next hour he listened to the coarse purr of the blank tape, his mind filled with the events of his past year with Dexter, and the mindless sonofabitches who had driven him to kill himself. He reread the short newspaper article and the letter.

He would call the Epsteins in New York, but first he called the prison. Some clerk reported that Malcolm Edwards had been released last Friday and gone home to Miami, Florida.

One more thing before he attacked the mass of work that awaited him: he replaced Dexter's tape in the dictating machine with a fresh one and dictated an official-sounding letter to Warden Ricci asking for a complete report on the suicide of Dexter Epstein. Finished with the letter, Eddie picked up the microcassette. The label displayed the Maxell logo. Eddie remembered that the recorder he had given Dexter at Christmas was a Sony, and he had given him six Sony cassettes with it. They used Maxell in the office.

Later, during the tearful conversation with Dexter's father, Eddie asked him if the recorder had been found in Dexter's cell. Mr Epstein said it had, and they had gotten it back with five tapes, all blank. But, for the moment, the anomaly of the tapes was buried beneath Eddie's anger and profound sense of loss.

53

Knowing Dov Levy's sub rosa investigative techniques must have crossed the line teased Gunnar's conscience. Betraying Anne was worse. Even so, he refrained from harsh moral judgment of himself. In the Djilas case he'd thought he had been fighting a righteous battle against a ruthless conspiracy of deceit. And Holly had revived a dying spirit, no good to Anne or anybody, including himself. But lying to Eddie Kerr about the tape bathed Gunnar's soul in shame. Like most children of his generation, he had been trained on guilt, but he had never mixed up a potion of vinegar and wormwood like the one he now tried to swallow. The thought occurred to him that Winnie Slaught might have listened to the tape before she brought it to him. Shame and guilt were one thing; exposure was still another.

Shana stopped him as he entered his office. 'Gunnar, Marvin Linden wants you to call him right now.'

He closed his office door behind him – a new habit – and got Linden, chairman of the Bar Association Ethics Committee, on the phone.

'Gunnar we need you Wednesday, the thirtieth. The Committee is acting on the bill of particulars against Kindred Diamond. I need your experience. Can I count on you?'

Diamond had been accused of bribing an insurance adjuster to arrange unfair settlements for his own clients. Gunnar groped for words. Jesus Christ, what could he say? 'I'll try, Marv.'

'Gunnar, I need your commitment. This is major league. I want to try to disbar the sonofabitch.'

'You can imagine the load I . . . .'

'You're talking to me, Gunnar, I know about loads. You're not in trial are you?'

'No, I just . . . .'

'Gunnar, you're the past chairman. I need your clout.'

'I'll be there, Marvin. But I'm not prejudging this thing.'

'Heaven forbid,' said Marvin Linden.

As perverse as the judicial system had become, its true masters observed certain boundaries of behavior. Like government bureaucracies, the judicial system benefited those who operated it far more than those it was supposed to serve – that is, except professional criminals; they were served well by the intricacies of the system. When you played the game, you developed techniques that adhered to the rules, especially if you wanted to run up consistently big scores. Gunnar compared it to pin-ball. Do anything, but, for Christ's sake, don't tilt it. To decide whether or not you had tilted it, the legal community had promulgated a code of thou-shalt-nots within which were buried little blades sharpened on both edges to be used against players who insisted upon making their own rules.

One thing was clear to Gunnar: under the *Code of Professional Responsibility*, just hearing the allegations on the tape, that his client had committed perjury, with nothing else, didn't require him to respond in any way. But he wasn't so sure how those rules applied to withholding the tape from Eddie Kerr, its rightful owner. Of course, the point was moot, because Eddie would never bring a charge against him. Knowing his position was safe provided no solace, no relief of any kind from the guilt or the shame.

A call from Conway Frietag followed Linden's. Frietag was the chairman of next year's State Bar Convention, and a thirty-year friend.

'But, Jesus Christ, Bunkey, that's nine months away!' said Gunnar.

'I know, I know, but we always line up the main speaker early, and it's always some fucking appeals-court judge. You remember when we had an hour of Warren Burger . . . telling us in stentorian tones how fucking incompetent we were. Enough to gag a maggot. Next year we want to hear from the guy who kicked the shit out of the monopoly press.'

'Let me think about it, Bunkey,' said Gunnar.

'I have the assignment to nail you down by the twenty-first. That's today.'

The twenty-first, *today*. Since listening to the tape, Gunnar had lost track of time. He had forgotten. Neither Anne, nor Katie had reminded him. They must have gotten their heads together.

'Bunkey, I've got to call you back.'

'Gunnar, don't pull that on me.'

'Goodbye, Bunkey.'

He hadn't had the dream. *He had forgotten*. For the first time in eleven anniversaries, he had forgotten. He whirled in his chair and looked at Jack's picture. His eyes brimmed over in apology.

He took a half-hour trying to make some sense of the morass in his head. He turned down three calls, including one from Holly. Then, he dialed his own number.

'Hello, sweets,' he said. 'It's me.'

'Is something wrong?'

'Not really, I just needed to talk a minute,' said Gunnar. 'You know what day it is?'

'I know what day it is.'

'I forgot,' Gunnar said.

The line was silent. He sensed her preferred response, that he was making progress. But it wouldn't sound right. Not today.

'I'm surprised you didn't remind me,' Gunnar said.

'Dear, I never would have thought you needed reminding. Anyway, the last few days I thought it was written all over your face. If you wanted to talk about it, you would.'

At that moment he set the twenty-four hour clock running for telling Anne about the tape. 'I'd like to eat together tonight. The three of us.'

'Gun, Katie's not coming home 'til late. She has a moot court meeting. Do you want to try for tomorrow night? It's been ages since you've been home for dinner during the week.'

'Tomorrow's OK.' Gunnar said. He felt relieved that he wouldn't be able to go to the Lodge this Tuesday.

He pulled an envelope out of his desk and wrote on the front: 'In the event of the death of Gunnar Larson, my executor is instructed to destroy the contents of this envelope.' He placed the cassette in the envelope, folded it in thirds and put it in an identical envelope that he marked Personal on the front and back. Finished, he walked his secret over to the First National, and locked it in his safe-deposit box. On his way out of the office he passed Eddie Kerr and found himself unable to say anything, but their eyes met for an instant, and Gunnar tried to make his face muscles smile.

When he got back to the office there was a call slip in his slot from Conway Frietag. Gunnar had forgotten how abruptly he had cut him off.

'Sorry, Bunkey,' Gunnar said into the phone, 'something came up.'

'I need your commitment, Gunnar. Don't let me down.'

His being featured speaker at the State Bar Convention would be great for the firm. He had nine months to prepare. But what could happen in those nine months?

'Gunnar, are you still there?'

'You want me to talk about *Djilas v*. Times-Journal, or can I pick any subject.'

'Of course, everybody will expect you to talk about the Djilas case.'

Gunnar saw room for leverage. 'Let me pick the subject, and I'll commit today.' It wasn't his style to say 'Otherwise, no.'

'Tell, you what old college-chum, old law-school buddy, you pick the subject, but the program committee's got to approve your choice. OK?'

'OK,' said Gunnar.

In the middle of the afternoon, having accomplished nothing so far this crisp autumn Monday, Gunnar decided it was time for the pluses and minuses. He pulled out a yellow pad, drew his customary line down the middle, and captioned each column with his customary $(+)$ on the left and $(-)$ on the right.

On the minus side he tried to write 'ignominy', wasn't sure of the spelling, and substituted 'reputation'. For no identifiable reason he wrote 'Katie' on the minus side and then 'Holly'. Then he wrote '$3,000,000' on the plus side. An uneasy embarrassment made him delete the money from the analysis. Two entries later he realized his old decision-making drill wouldn't work. Everything came up minus.

Another approach: this guy Malcolm Edwards only directly

implicated Tony Djilas once – the sale of the sixty bales for a quarter million in cash. If that were Djilas' only personal profit-making deal in the dope trade, the articles were still technically a libel. The newspaper's allegations were much broader, or at least a reasonable man could infer they were much broader. Even so, that didn't change the fact that Djilas might have perjured himself on material facts at issue in the trial. But so had the others. How much would be gained by talking to Tony one more time? Or maybe even Al Bergdorf?

Gunnar decided to check a detail. He got Wyman Farmer on the phone and asked him to find out if there was a guy named Edwards on death row in Florida, and if there was, why was he there? Wyman Farmer promised to get back to him by noon tomorrow. If there was no uncle on death row, maybe Gunnar could just walk away from the whole issue of the tape. Take Leo's advice.

Before she left the office for the day, Shana stuck her head in the door. With a wide smile she said, 'I forgot to tell you. Yesterday, Gregory Gunnar took his first steps.'

'Give him my congratulations,' said Gunnar, and he promised himself to get the kid a present. Within an hour, he forgot.

54

Wyman Farmer hadn't waited until noon. His call from the eastern time-zone arrived in the office before Gunnar. The message: Edward Edwards had been on death row in Starke, convicted of killing his brother and a woman, allegedly a girlfriend, in separate incidents. But the Supreme Court had saved Edwards. Now, he was serving two life-sentences.

Malcolm Edwards hadn't got those facts straight, but the essence was there. Either he was confused, or prison bragga-docio kept his uncle in the shadow of a phantom electric-chair. Gunnar took no comfort from the minor discrepancy. His own sentence loomed. He wished desperately for commutation, but the Supreme Court wasn't about to save him. Maybe Tony Djilas could. Like a desperate patient searching for a miracle cure, Gunnar called Tony and made an appointment for lunch, tomorrow. No, he shouldn't bring Al. He would like to get together, just the two of them.

Over a centerpiece of red roses they clinked the crystal together. 'To Jack's memory,' Gunnar said.

'To his memory,' said Anne and Katie.

'Oh, it's wonderful to get together like this,' said Katie. 'Let's do it every year.'

Gunnar and Anne faced each other from the ends of the dining-room table. Katie sat on one side facing the bay, now hidden in the darkness.

'It occurred to me today,' said Anne, holding Gunnar's eyes, 'that this is the way we *should* celebrate Jack's memory. Pick out a day just for him. And then concentrate the rest of the year on living our lives as best we can.'

'Good idea,' said Katie softly.

Gunnar conceded in silence, but he wondered whether he could heed the advice. In Gunnar's fantasy at Duck Creek, Jack's words had sounded the same injunction.

Katie told the story about Jack, holding up his big fish, coming to the dock with smiling father and grandfather; and Anne remembered when Jack had packed a bag to run away when he was five. They reminisced about his growing up, and his excellence in school. Gunnar recounted Jack hitting a tree with the old Plymouth when he was learning to drive, and Katie remembered another tree and a girl in a bikini. For an hour of lobster tail and chocolate mousse they clung together in a tent of memories while the beast that was Dexter Epstein's tape lurked somewhere outside in the dark. After Katie had kissed them both and begged her leave, it charged back into the light, ruthlessly replacing Jack's memory and everything else, as it had from the moment Gunnar first deciphered Malcolm Edward's prisoneese.

'Anne, can we sit in the living room? I need to talk.' He rarely called her by her name.

Once routine, he hadn't confided in her in years. She knew things even Leo didn't. On occasion, out of frustration, he had even breached the sacred attorney-client privilege. Yet nothing compared to his present dilemma. Leo, friend and partner of more than a quarter of a century, clearly the man he admired most, saw no issue. The course was clear, he said; you flushed the tape. And you moved on.

Anne put The New World Symphony in the stereo and brought coffee to the living room. There was space beside Gunnar, but she chose the big chair forming a right angle with the sofa. He rinsed his dry mouth with the hot fluid, and set the cup on the intricately etched cocktail-table.

'Sweets, I'm up against it.'

Silent, she waited, with a look that said I already know what you are going to tell me. But, of course, she couldn't know.

'I got hold of some information,' he said, 'not particularly reliable, but still it's bothering me.'

The set of her face became more quizzical. But she said nothing.

'I think Tony Djilas might have perjured himself.'

'Don't they all . . . to a degree, anyway.'

'This is different,' he said. 'This goes to the very heart of the case . . . whether or not he was a dope dealer.'

'Do you know for sure?' Her brows narrowed.

'No, not for sure, but I'm feeling pretty queasy about it.'

He told her about the tape, and the substance of Malcolm Edwards' allegations. From the stereo, a solo flute evoked vast desert vistas, and distant lines of Indians on horseback.

'I'm sorry,' Anne said. 'I suppose you've talked to Leo?'

'Yeah, he doesn't see a problem. Just flush the tape, he says.'

'Are you considering that?'

'Of course, I've considered it. But that would change nothing.'

'I know,' she said.

'First,' said Gunnar, 'there's a question of legal ethics. I can avoid that by doing nothing, but I would spend the rest of my life wondering if this verdict,' he spread his arms out palms-up, shaking half-closed fists, 'was based on goddamn perjury.'

When he paused, she remained silent, her face sagged, sharing his pain.

'I'm having lunch with Tony tomorrow. See if I can get a clue. There's a couple of names that might startle him. But I'm not going to tell him about the tape.' He stopped, looking for something, he didn't know what, in her brown eyes.

'There's no doubt is there, Gun?'

'Sure, there's doubt.'

'No, I mean about what you must do.'

She got up from the big chair, and slipped in behind the table beside him. She reached out and held his face with both of her hands.

'Of course there's no doubt, my darling Gun. You must find out the truth, no matter what it takes. That what trials are supposed to do, aren't they?' She let her hands fall back to her lap.

Devoutly to be wished, Gunnar thought. Not truth, trials are about winning. 'What if Tony was a doper. What if that's what the truth is?' he said.

'Then, you'll know what to do,' she said.

He didn't look at Anne, instead he stared at a pencil drawing on the opposite wall next to the stone fireplace: a little girl with long hair and a full skirt holding a bouquet of yellow flowers. She had huge round eyes. They had bought it at an art fair twenty years ago because it reminded them of Katie.

'There's something else I need to tell you,' Gunnar said. 'It has nothing to do with the case, at least not directly.'

'I know,' Anne said.

He looked at her open face; he felt goose flesh on his upper arms and it felt like the hair moved on the back of his neck. 'You know?'

'I've known for a long time,' she said. Her eyes were moist, and she bit her upper lip, an old habit.

First shock, then relief. 'I had no idea,' he said.

She just waited. Her face said, but now you will have to tell me, yourself. The coffee cooled in the cups.

'Do you know who?'

She nodded, two barely perceptible jerks of her head.

Already he felt a lightening of the load. He told her about Holly, not in any great detail, and she asked him for no more than he volunteered. She told him about her anonymous caller, and Libby Cochrane. He forced a smile at that. And she told him she'd seen Holly turn into Cochranes' drive the day of the press conference.

When he had no more to say about Holly, Anne said, 'And now, what are you going to do?'

'I don't know,' he said. He tried to say he was sorry with his eyes. At that moment he thought the words would sound ridiculous.

55

The hardest part of getting ready to leave for Florida was telling Eddie Kerr about the tape. After yesterday's lunch with Tony Djilas had left Gunnar with no proof or satisfaction of any kind, only more doubt, he'd decided to fly to Miami the next day. Leo pleaded with him to forget about the whole thing, to get on with his life. He even hit him with a low blow. 'Don't you think you owe it to the firm to get back on track, especially when they need you for this new Miracle Mills thing?' Gunnar had told him that what he suggested was impossible. He would if he could, but he couldn't. Surely Leo knew there were some things you had to do. As Gunnar expected, Leo finally wished him luck and wondered out loud how in the world he had ever gotten Gunnar to fix that game.

Gunnar abruptly whirled around in his chair. It had been the same every day since he'd got back from Duck Creek. Looking at the picture of his son in the silver frame, the smiling eyes were alive and talking. We have settled the matter, they said.

Gunnar worked out a loose plan. First he would track down Malcolm Edwards, and speak with him, face to face. If that didn't resolve the issue, he would talk with Mrs Crossman, Tony's old neighbor. According to Wyman Farmer, she disliked Tony. She wouldn't likely protect him. Then, he would try to find the widow of either one of those cops, if Officer Ek's wife indeed *was* a widow. After that, if the issue still remained in doubt, he would go to Starke, and talk to Big Ed Edwards himself.

The plan was optimistic, perhaps even naïve. The *Times-Journal* had spent hundreds of thousands preparing their case. If the information Gunnar sought was available, they should have found it. To return from Miami with no more than they had, with all doubt resolved in Tony's favor, was Gunnar's earnest prayer.

Tonight was his Thursday evening with Holly. He hadn't decided how much to tell her. It was possible that she knew the answer. Not just possible: if Malcolm Edwards' story was true, Holly must have known all along. That was perhaps the strongest argument that the allegations on the tape were false. Holly wouldn't do it to him. She couldn't. There was too much tenderness between them. The thought of the tape induced a flush of embarrassment. The heat in his face triggered a replay of that morning's scene.

Gunnar had walked into Eddie Kerr's office, closed the door behind him, cleared off a chair and sat down.

'I've come to apologize to you.'

Eddie's little mouth showed a couple of teeth, part of a faint smile. 'For what?' he said.

Gunnar handed him the cassette he had retrieved from his safe-deposit box. Eddie turned on the Doberman stare.

'That's the tape that was with the letter,' said Gunnar.

'You're kidding. That was US mail.'

'I know, I did get it from your secretary,' Gunnar said, 'but I'm not offering that as an excuse.' Warmth spread out on the skin of Gunnar's face. 'It was inexcusable.'

'What was so important?' Eddie asked.

Gunnar told him what was on the tape. Then, he said he was going to Miami to check it out.

'Why not just let it be?' said Eddie.

'I can't. Maybe the same reason I couldn't keep the tape.'

Gunnar apologized again, stood up, and offered his hand. Eddie reached out, tentatively Gunnar thought, and let him squeeze his limp fingers.

'Forget it,' Eddie said, his chubby face without expression.

'Let me know what you think when you listen to it,' said Gunnar from the door. 'And if you decide to reveal it to anyone, would you give me some warning.'

'Sure,' said Eddie.

Even with the 'forget it', the apology had been neither accepted, nor rejected, and no other hint of forgiveness was offered. Gunnar questioned his own reaction had the rôles been reversed, but he was further chagrined when he realized that Eddie Kerr would never have withheld the tape, under any circumstances.

When Al Bergdorf arrived at his office directly from the airport, he found three telephone messages from Tony Djilas. Tony had to see him immediately, they said.

Al's trip to Minneapolis had kept him out of touch with the office, and he had left no indication with the staff where he could be reached. He hadn't gone on legal business. A plastic surgeon planned to remove the folds of loose skin that drooped from Al's shrinking belly. He had lost 109 pounds, and his waist size had contracted to thirty-eight from fifty-four.

He gave much of the credit to Gunnar Larson. Watching him handle the Djilas case was Al's inspiration. He doubted that Gunnar knew any more law than he did. He was sure Gunnar didn't make as much money – he spent all of his time in court and you couldn't make real dough in a courtroom. Nevertheless, Al's admiration for Gunnar continued to grow. Gunnar did what he did with grace. Al had vowed to find the graceful self that lived within his cocoon of blubber.

He remembered the caption under the picture in his high-school year book: A man of great face value. And he remembered the face, even then, a problem with the shadow of dense beard beneath his darksome skin. But he was as handsome as any boy in that class. His black hair shone in thick waves, and his large well-cut nose ruled a face with darkly bright eyes and full sensuous lips, ready to smile. In high school and college, practical jokes were his game.

With great excitement, over the past months Al had watched the emergence of his real face. Among the lines flaring out from his nose and running down from the corners of his mouth, and the folds along his jaw, the image from his year book came through. Al liked what he saw. And the skies rained compliments. With that extra belly skin gone, he was going to call Ruth Renken for a date. He could offer her sound advice on Block 13. But, first, he had to deal with Tony Djilas.

*   *   *

'Al, you won't believe what I'm gonna tell you.'

'You got an ace on the fifteenth.'

'Sure, a three hundred yard par four. I got an ace.'

'What gives, moneybags?'

'Cut it out, I'll trade it for a year's interest on yours,' said Tony Djilas, a new fall-plaid jacket draped perfectly from his broad shoulders. 'Where the hell were you? Hey, I love the suit! You look super, pinstripe, just like Gunnar.'

Al wasn't about to tell Tony where he had gone. More grist for Tony's put-down humor-mill.

'Thanks,' said Al, 'Now what's the big urgency?'

'My case should be history, right. Settled. Put to bed. Right?'

'People are gonna talk for a while,' said Al.

'Gunnar invited me to lunch yesterday,' said Tony. 'Over tea and fucking crumpets he wants to talk about the case some more. He asked me about some names that never came up before. And he wants . . . .'

'Slow down,' said Al. 'What names?'

'A guy named Big Ed. Edward Edwards. Fucking worst kind of nigger. He's a lifer, got a lotta ink in Florida, years ago. He was supposed to get the chair. Then the fucking Supreme Court let 'im out of it. And he asked about another guy named Malcolm Edwards, must be some relative. I never heard a that guy.'

'What they got to do with you?'

'Beats the hell outa me.'

'What'd you tell him?'

'Nothing. Just that I didn't know 'em. I told him I heard a Big Ed. Everybody down there has.'

Tony lit a cigarette. Al felt a grab of nerves. On the plane from Minneapolis he had decided to give up the cigars. Four hours into that plan, he thought again. Maybe he should wait until his weight stabilized.

'Did he say what he was driving at?'

'I dunno. He kept hem-hawin' around, comin' back to the Edwards guys. I asked him what'd he think I was, some kind of a nigger-lover? He said he didn't want something to jump out and bite us? I never did figure out just what the hell that meant.'

'I'll call him,' said Al.

'I dunno, maybe not. Let's let it lay.'

'Then what was so urgent?'

'Well, Al . . . I got ta wonderin'. When I said history. I meant history. They can't start this thing up again . . . can they?'

'You ain't telling me there's something laying around you didn't tell me about, or Gunnar, for that matter?'

'Hell no! But I can't help wonderin' when he starts talkin' like that. I don't need no more bullshit.'

'Well I'll tell you, my silver-haired buddy, if you held out something big and the other side gets a hold of it, you bet your life this case ain't history.'

'I told ya there's nothin' n'that's what I told Gunnar.'

'Well if he thinks the other side's got something, he's sitting right up there now.' Al pointed out the window at the upper stories of the glass tower of the Finance and Commerce Building, 'Right up there, stewing about it. He's got even more than you have on the line. They can take the whole wad back if you were lying on the stand.'

'Listen buddy, don't get your shit hot. I told you the whole story from the beginning. The dope was Zilman's bag. I had nothin' to do with it. Nothin'. *Capice*?'

'Then you got nothing to worry about,' said Al.

'After all we went through, you can understand I'd be wonderin'. Right. By the way, how would they go about gettin' the money back?'

'If they had new evidence they'd make a motion to set aside the judgment that was stipulated to when you guys settled. It ain't easy. O'Boyle wouldn't do it on somebody's say-so. Not a chance. No judge would. They'd have to have the hardest evidence. It happens once in a blue moon.'

'Never,' asked Tony, 'on somebody's say-so, huh?'

'Never,' said Al. 'Except on yours, of course.'

'Ya know, there's always somebody out there wantin' to take potshots at somebody else.'

'Don't worry about that. Judges know that. Everybody knows that.'

'Well, I feel better. I'm glad I talked to ya.'

'Gunnar must have said the same thing, didn't he?'

345

'I didn't really ask him. I got a little pissed off, but I don't think I showed it. He was nice enough about it.'

Al understood how Gunnar might feel, with so much involved. But even if Tony was lying, there wasn't much to worry about. The conversation turned to golf. Al hadn't played much lately, because he was embarrassed by how he looked in the shower. Worse, he felt too weak most of the time to take a good swing at the ball.

Before Tony left he returned to the subject. 'I can't help thinkin',' he said, 'even if they re-opened the case, or whatever you call it, how would they ever get the money back?'

'Well,' Al said, 'if they got the whole process reversed, and they entered a judgment for the defendants, and you didn't give them the money, they'd get the DA to charge you with perjury and you could get a trip to the slam. That is, if the DA hadn't already charged you on his own. And knowing O'Boyle, he'd see to it that they did.'

'How often does that happen?' Tony asked.

'In a prosecutor's office the size of ours, I imagine they always have a perjury case or two moving through the system,' said Al.

'I'll get going,' said Tony, 'I got a late lunch with Holly.'

'Say hello,' said Al. 'You sure you don't want me to call Gunnar?'

'Nah, he just had a bug up his ass. He'll forget about it.'

56

Gunnar relished plunging into steamy Miami-International. A hint of intrigue hung in the air with spates of foreign words, mostly Spanish. Lines of dark skinned people waited for tickets on airlines with strange names.

He caught the shuttle bus to Avis, rented a white T-Bird and checked into the Marriott about a mile from the airport at 836 and LeJeune. He hung up his coat, and threw his damp shirt on the dresser. The air-conditioning chilled his moist skin. Three stories below, bikini-clad young women frolicked in a huge pool. Holly would put them all to shame. But she could never fit those marvelous tits into one of those suits.

His session with her last night had been strained. His first thought was that she was upset because he was leaving, but that wasn't it. She wanted to know what could be so important in Miami. He told her it was business; he couldn't talk about it. After half-hearted kisses, she said her dad had told her he'd had lunch with Gunnar. Just some follow-up details, Gunnar said. She wanted to talk more about the lunch, but he didn't respond. She failed to hide her frustration.

A fall rain battered the roof of the Lodge. The cold damp air had prompted a fire, left to die on the hearth in the bear's room. They snuggled under the heavy quilt, like spoons. She dropped her hand down behind her and gently fondled his penis. Though less than staunch, she soon worked it into her and he held her tightly to him, his hands cupping her breasts, twisting her nipples, and he pushed his mouth into the thick mass of her hair. His hips worked in slow motion and he lasted a long time. The image of Anne holding his face in her hands mixed with Malcolm Edwards' muthafuckas and flew madly around in his brain like wild birds trapped in a cage.

Eventually, Holly turned in his arms to face him pressing full length on his body. She kissed him more than he wanted and, soon, she steered her little love-talk back to her father.

'He seemed worried,' she said.

'Did he say what about?'

'Could it have anything to do with your trip to Miami?'

'Honey, I told you that was business. I can't talk about it.'

Back in the Marriott, Gunnar took some fresh light clothes out of his bag, then placed a call to Wyman Farmer at his home. He gave Gunnar two addresses and telephone numbers: one for Edna Romero, the widow of slain cop José Kelly; the other, Malcolm Edwards' apartment in Liberty City.

'The only Eks I found never heard of the lady you're looking for. Maybe Mrs Romero can help you. And if I were you, I wouldn't go to Liberty City alone,' said Wyman Farmer.

'Hasn't it been pretty peaceful lately?'

'Maybe, generally, but just a week or two back some salesman from Toronto pulled off at the Ninety-fifth Street exit of I-95, just to ask directions. Two guys stabbed him to death in broad daylight for his Rolex. The cops nabbed them the same day when some pawnbroker got suspicious. Of course, they were higher than a kite.'

'I'll be careful,' said Gunnar.

'Famous last words,' said Wyman Farmer.

The behavior of veteran litigators perplexed Eddie Kerr. They seemed to depend on a cryptic reasoning system, unintelligible to true scholars. Winnie Slaught had told Eddie there were voices on the tape, but that the language was so absurd she didn't try to listen to the whole thing. While the work piled up, Eddie had spent most of a day pondering his next move. But, thankfully, when Gunnar had delivered the original tape and admitted his deception, Eddie's immediate problem was solved.

Last night he had gone to the county law library to study the *Code of Professional Responsibility* as interpreted in the indexed rulings of the American Bar Association. In minutes, he found it. The comment to Rule 3.3 was clear: Even though a lawyer is required to act when he discovers false evidence was presented at trial, the obligation ends with the conclusion of the proceedings. Gunnar hadn't heard Dexter's tape until after the case had been settled, and judgment entered accordingly. The proceedings had concluded. Surely, Gunnar was aware of the rule? Maybe not. The research compelled Eddie to call Gunnar before he carried this thing too far. He simply had no obligation to go running off to Miami. Didn't he realize the mess he might create?

From the library, Eddie called Shana at her home and asked how he could reach Gunnar. She told him the number was in her desk drawer and Eddie headed back to the office to find it.

Seven miles away in the law library at State University Al Bergdorf – still with no idea of what was troubling Gunnar – performed the same research ritual, and came up with the same answer. What the hell was Gunnar up to? As he sat pondering the question he noticed a slim young blonde with a pretty face poring over *Davis on Administrative Law*. He recognized her from the trial or some place. Yes, she'd watched the preacher testify.

'Weren't you at the Djilas trial?' Al asked.

'You're Mr Bergdorf, aren't you?'

'Yeah, Al Bergdorf.' He stuck out his hand and smiled into the ingenuous face.

'I'm Katie Larson, Gunnar Larson's daughter.'

'Sure, that's it. Small world. How about I buy you a cup a coffee.'

'Sure,' she said, 'there's a machine in the lounge.'

Al was elated to break the monotony of the evening. And maybe he could learn a little more about her old man.

'Come on in,' Anne said to the faint tap on her bedroom door.

'I thought you might be reading,' said Katie. 'What is it?'

'Joseph Campbell,' said Anne.

'Oh Mom, you have to tell me all about it. But, listen, you won't believe who I've been talking to tonight.'

Anne put her book and reading glasses on the bedside table. 'I have a feeling you're going to tell me,' she said.

'Mr Al Bergdorf, senior partner of Bergdorf and Ratner.'

'The firm your father refers to as "Bag and Rat",' said Anne.

'I know Daddy doesn't like Al,' said Katie, 'but after talking to him for over an hour tonight, I just can't understand it. He's a sweet man. He's nuts about his two grandkids. And he thinks my father is the best trial lawyer he has ever seen. And, Mom, he said that very matter-of-factly. He wasn't saying it just for my benefit.'

'These lawyers can be pretty clever, you know,' said Anne.

'No, this wasn't anything like that. And do you know that man has lost over a hundred pounds already this year.'

'You sound like he really impressed you.'

'He did. And he invited me to see his father's collection of paintings.'

'He's twenty years older than you, or more.'

'Oh Mom, don't be silly! He wasn't coming on to me. You could tell, he was just lonesome.'

'I don't know how well your father would like it.'

'I have judgment,' said Katie. 'I don't care whether he would like it or not. More to the point, I think he's wrong about Al Bergdorf . . . . But what's going on with you, gorgeous lady.'

'It's out in the open.'

'Daddy and Holly Tripp!'

'He told me about it Tuesday night after you left.'

Anne described the scene word for word, but she didn't say anything about the tape or why Gunnar had gone to Miami.

'What are you going to do now?' said Katie.

'Nothing, nothing at all,' said Anne.

'Well, you know what you're doing, Mom, I've no doubt of that. I've got to get to bed now, my study group meets first thing in the morning. So goodnight, and by the way, I'm going to view those paintings on Sunday afternoon. Let me be the one to tell Daddy about my new friend. OK?'

'Of course. Goodnight, my darling baby.'

57

When Gunnar returned from the hotel dining room at ten, the light on his phone was blinking. The front desk told him to call Eddie Kerr. Eddie said he had listened to the tape and he shared Gunnar's anxiety over Malcolm Edwards' allegations about Tony.

'But the rules don't require any action on our part,' said Eddie.

'What rules?' Gunnar asked.

'*The Code of Professional Responsibility*,' said Eddie. 'As you know, it has force of law. The comments to three-point-three say . . . .'

'I know,' said Gunnar.

'Then why the trip to Miami?'

A surge of impatience. Perfect adherence to the law was important to Eddie Kerr, but didn't he realize there were issues, not necessarily legal?

'I can't explain right now, Eddie,' Gunnar said. 'We'll talk about it when I get back. I'm aware of three-point-three.' After the tape-exchanging episode Eddie must think he's a raving lunatic.

'You've lost me,' said Eddie.

And so I have, Gunnar thought. 'I'll be back soon,' he said. 'There's a couple of things I want to look into. I appreciate the call.' Anything to get off the line. The issue wasn't for argument.

'Whatever you say,' said Eddie. From two thousand miles away, the Doberman stare.

On television, J.R. Ewing leered at a half-naked blonde. Gunnar flicked through the channels. An over-enthusiastic face rhapsodized about the amazing Minnesota Twins. The telephone startled him.

'I miss you,' Holly said. 'I can smell you on the pillow.'

He had told her he was staying at the airport Marriott. 'You've got to be careful,' he said.

'Davey . . .? If he isn't drunk at the club, he's home in bed.'

He still hadn't told her Anne knew about them. He didn't think the day before he was leaving town was the time.

'What's that voice?'

'The television,' said Gunnar.

'I thought maybe you had a girl in your room.'

'Rest assured.'

'Did you get started on your business?'

'Tomorrow morning,' he said.

She kept him on the line for an hour. He was uncomfortable, but he had no plausible excuse to hang up. She returned repeatedly to the same questions: 'What could be such a big secret in Florida?' or 'Why was my dad so upset by your lunch?' Finally, Gunnar said he had to get an early start and needed his sleep. She loved him more than she ever thought she could love, she said. He hung up. She was going home to sleep the night with Davey, and be at his service in the dawn's early light. But, she'd told him again last night, she would move out. Anytime Gunnar was ready for her.

In spite of the miasma of thoughts, the fatigue of travel would bring sleep. How quickly Anne had known what he should do. Leo was just as fast to decide. A brand new three-million-dollar T-Bill, reward for his greatest achievement. What would Dov do? Dov and Leo thought alike. You get a job done, and you go on to the next one. Let the judges do the judging. What would Jack think? Same as Anne. Katie, too. Mother and Dad. Grandpa. Forty years ago. How did he put it? It's no better to have the right answers to the wrong questions, than to have the wrong answers to the right questions.

At nine o'clock the next morning Gunnar pulled the T-Bird on to the 103rd Street exit ramp off I-95. He turned left under the freeway on 103rd. Liberty City wasn't the least ominous on a Saturday morning. All of the faces on the sidewalks were black. They walked purposefully in the intense sunlight, past vacant store-fronts, oblivious of the white interloper in the white T-Bird.

The address Wyman Farmer had gotten from the Miami police was on NW 11th Avenue. The terms of Malcolm Edwards' release from Watsonville and, presumably, Florida law, required him to register when he returned home to Miami. When Gunnar called the phone number Malcolm had given the police, he got a recording stating the line had been disconnected.

The address turned out to be a pink stucco two-story that appeared to consist of four apartments, two up, two down. Some one had written 'fuck you' in black spray-paint on the front of number one, the apartment on the lower left. On the end of the building an outside wooden stairway, devoid of paint, led to number three, Malcolm Edwards' putative home.

The one-story building next door on the left had plywood nailed over the windows and the guy with the black paint had expressed himself on all visible surfaces. To the right, on the vacant corner-lot, only the burned-out body remained of a recent model Lincoln.

Gunnar gingerly made his way up the dubious stairs. Somewhere down the block a baby screamed as if it was being dismembered. On the landing he pushed on a broken doorbell. Hearing no sound, he pounded on the door covered with flaking pink paint. He waited. Pounded again. Many old dwellings made you think of better days, when the building was new and had made someone a good home. This one had always been depressing.

He waited two or three minutes. Pressing against the door window, he cupped his hands around his eyes and looked in. The sun glowed on a shade pulled down over the only other window in the room. Empty Budweiser cans covered a white metal table.

Back home, he would have tried the door knob. Liberty City stories made him hesitate. He looked down at the sidewalk and the empty street. The neighborhood seemed deserted. His shadow fell over a rusty brown heel-print on the bare plank. Gunnar sucked in a breath and twisted the knob. The door wasn't locked. He knocked again, loudly. He knocked once more.

He waited at least a minute. Then he turned the knob and pushed the door open. Dark soapy water filled a dirty sink. He stepped into the smell of old garbage and stale beer. The only sound, a steady drip from the faucet. The dirty arm of a gold sofa protruded in the door to a room facing the street.

'Anybody home?' he said in a normal tone of voice. A little louder, 'Anybody home?' Nothing. He walked slowly across the kitchen floor, its pattern long since worn away. He stepped into the room with the sofa.

'Christ . . . . Oh Jesus Christ,' he whispered.

On the long sofa a black man lay, eyes staring at the ceiling, white T-shirt soaked with bright red blood. The throat was sliced open all the way across, giving the impression that the head might fall off if the body were moved. The white cartilage of the trachea showed through the coagulated blood. Movement caught Gunnar's eye. On the arm of the sofa near the man's feet sat an emaciated-looking calico cat with spots of blood on its white face. The cat watched him, motionless. Nausea fluttered through his gut. He ran back into the kitchen, and heaved his breakfast into the gray water in the sink. The amorphous brown muffin enveloped in slime sunk slowly in the opaque water as he gripped the sides of the dirty sink. His knees threatened to fold up under him. He wasn't sure whether it was the revulsion or the fear that made his whole body shake.

When his legs would hold him, he walked back into the room with the corpse. He recognized Malcolm Edwards from the picture Fleet had gotten him. *Café-au-lait* skin with a Fu Manchu mustache. Muscular upper arms. A step at a time, Gunnar walked through the bedroom door beyond the end of the sofa. The cat followed and rubbed up against Gunnar's tan slacks leaving a faint streak of red. On a table he found a black dial telephone. As he expected, the line was dead.

Gunnar headed back to the stairway. He felt light-headed, sick, like he was coming down with the flu. Cops and criminal lawyers were used to scenes like this. But it was new to Gunnar. Violent death was as foreign to him as space travel.

Parked at the curb back on 103rd, Gunnar gave the cops a few minutes to respond to his 9-1-1 call. His breathing returned to normal and the thump of his heart subsided in his chest. The murder's impact on his plan occurred to him. Jesus Christ, had he been the cause of it? Did someone want to keep Malcolm

Edwards from talking to him? Hardly likely. Eddie, Leo and Anne were the only people who knew what was on that tape. He had mentioned Malcolm Edwards' name to Tony Djilas, but that idea was just too far-fetched. Malcolm Edwards had simply returned to become a cipher in the Miami milieu of narcotics and murder.

Four black-and-whites had answered Gunnar's alarm. Two were parked right on the scraggly grass in the front yard. Gunnar told the cops exactly how he had happened to find the body. He was investigating a case that Malcolm Edwards might have some information on, Gunnar said. He had touched the door, the sink and the telephone in the bedroom, nothing else. His prints were available if they needed them. They took his number at the Marriott and back at the office, and told him he was free to go.

Too tentative for talking, Gunnar went back to the Marriott. After a light lunch he napped, made appointments to see Edna Romero and the Crossmans on Sunday, and spent the late afternoon by the pool. Rejuvenated, he took an evening drive to Coconut Grove and walked along the harbor front admiring the sailboats and thinking about Malcolm Edwards.

58

Edna Romero greeted Gunnar from the front door of a low Spanish-style stucco almost hidden in the dense flora of old Fort Lauderdale. She was reluctant to see him at all. On the phone she had said, 'Let bygones be bygones.' But when Gunnar told her he thought he might know who had killed her first husband, José Kelly, Edna agreed to give him a few minutes first thing Sunday morning.

She led him around the back to a red-brick patio set among several live oaks and lush shrubbery. She walked erect like a runway model, one foot directly before the other, and her red and pink tie-dyed smock left her long tanned legs completely uncovered. Strands of gray in her close-cropped dark hair, cut a little longer on her neck, and a thickening of the flesh under her chin, said forty-five, but she was one of the most elegant women Gunnar had ever met. Her eyes were hidden behind dark glasses with a golden chain dangling around the back of her long graceful neck.

After they'd sat down, she poured steaming coffee from a carafe that was waiting on the white, ornate iron table.

'I have a good life now,' she said. 'It's been years since anybody but Joey has talked about Joe's death.'

Joey, now eighteen, was the only child she'd had with José Kelly, killed in the line of duty fifteen years ago, less than a mile from where they sat. Why was someone from way up north so interested in her first husband's unsolved murder?

Gunnar briefly described the trial, and told her that afterward he had fortuitously come upon some information pointing the finger at José Kelly's killer. But he didn't think it was in her interest to know the specifics now, if ever. She understood.

Gunnar told her how Detective Koronis had testified that he had taken over the investigation José Kelly was working on, and had later exonerated Tony Djilas.

'Everybody knows John Koronis was on the take,' she spoke in a low smooth tone. 'Joe told me about it, more than once. He had offers himself, all the time. I think he ended up dead because he turned them down.'

'Not unlikely,' said Gunnar.

'Second time around, I married an accountant.' She smiled wryly.

Earlier, when Gunnar had described the trial, Edna Romero said she had heard of Tony Djilas, nothing more. 'Do you remember the name Zilman?' Gunnar now asked.

'Sure, I remember that name, Djilas was supposed to be connected with him, and Diane Ek talked about him too, after her husband disappeared.'

'The wife of Ralph Ek?' The sensation of satisfaction at having found something he was looking for quickly gave way to the anxiety that it might lead to disaster.

'Yes, Ralph was Joe's partner.'

'Are you still in touch with Diane?'

'Christmas cards. She had three kids to raise. Got an office job at Burger King and moved to Kendall.' Reddish lights in Edna's dark brown hair caught the slanted rays of the morning sun.

'What happened to Ralph Ek?'

'He disappeared. Fell off the face of the earth. Of course a lot of people thought it was tied to Joe's murder. But nobody ever proved a connection.'

'No trace at all?'

'He quit the police department maybe a month before Joe was killed. That's one of the reasons Joe was alone that night. They were short-handed. Supposedly Ralph applied for a job in San Diego, but when Diane checked, the company said they had no record of it. Eventually, she had him declared dead, so she could collect social security and remarry. But the marriage plans fell through.'

'She still single?'

'Yes, I'll give you her address and phone number.'

'Do you think Ralph Ek is dead?'

'Dead or scared to death. He's ignored a growing son and two daughters for fifteen years. The family lives as though he's dead, I guess,' said Edna Romero. 'Can you tell me exactly what you hope to find out?'

'I just don't know.' Gunnar's voice trailed off to barely audible. 'If I'm lucky . . . nothing.'

Hidden birds twittered in the thick back-yard branches. She took off the dark glasses and her calm brown eyes asked if she could do any more.

'I've taken enough of your time,' Gunnar said, getting to his feet.

'One thing,' she said, 'Diane'll tell you the same. There was a guy Joe said was the worst rotten apple of all. He was some kind of public official name of . . . mmm. Warren Cress . . . no, Loren Cressick. Joe hated him.'

As instructed, Gunnar called ahead to confirm his meeting with the Crossmans. Peter was sorry he had to cancel, but his wife, Clemmie, he said, just wasn't up to it. Perhaps Gunnar could call back in a few days? Gunnar said he would, and dialed Diane Ek's number.

'Sure,' she said, 'it'll break up another boring Sunday afternoon.'

Gunnar ate a sandwich in a small restaurant on the beach. Squinting into the reflected sunlight on the Atlantic, he had never seen so much dazzling female skin in one place. But he was preoccupied. Before leaving Fort Lauderdale, he called Wyman Farmer at home in Coral Gables and asked him to find out what he could about Loren Cressick first thing Monday.

I-95 south to Miami was already filling up with Sunday-afternoon traffic. Where the elevated freeway passed along the eastern edge of Liberty City on his right, skyscrapers, like random fence posts loomed ahead. He saw the slashed open throat of Malcolm Edwards, and mulled the terrible coincidence of the grisly event. If, indeed, it was a coincidence.

From the end of I-95, just past downtown Miami, Dixie Highway carried him along in three lanes of breakneck traffic to Kendall Drive and Diane Ek's condo complex. Gunnar walked up to 311. Diane ushered him into a small living room furnished with pieces much too large. Unlike Edna Romero, dark-haired Diane had lost her race with time.

She dropped into a big chair opposite the matching sofa that she assigned to Gunnar. Her thick middle bulged in a flimsy faded dress. Following her in, Gunnar had noticed that considering her bulk she was narrow in the hips and buttocks. When she reached down to gather up the Sunday paper, a dipping neckline revealed her udder-like breasts to the nipples.

The blue eyes in the pretty, carefully made-up face of many fat women explored Gunnar's body.

'Welcome to our humble digs, Mr Gunnar.'

A framed photo on the avocado wall revealed that Diane had once been as beautiful as Edna Romero. Her skin still looked soft and creamy, pale for Florida. She winked and told him he could smoke if he liked, but she had quit three and a half months and ten more pounds ago. He thanked her and told her he had never smoked.

'Then how about a beer, or I got some Calvert's?

He didn't drink either, hadn't for a very long time.

'I hope you do something that's fun.' She giggled and bent over again to remove some invisible impediment from the floor.

'Sometimes,' he said, but he really didn't want anything now. Maybe they could talk a while.

'Be my guest,' she said.

As Gunnar's story of the trial and his talk with Edna Romero unfolded, Diane slid further down in the big chair, all the time gazing raptly into his eyes with a faint smile on lips she periodically moistened with the tip of her tongue. Eventually she crossed her husky legs, sliding her skirt up so he could effortlessly see the broad white of her thigh to where it met the green tweed of the dated chair.

With all the windows open, Gunnar spoke against the groan of traffic along Kendall Drive. The cross-ventilation and the breeze of ceiling fans tempered the humid afternoon. Someone turned on a television or radio in the other end of the apartment.

She interrupted to tell him that her son was in his room. But her two daughters had taken an apartment together in Coconut

Grove. Jeffy, she said, had a serious learning disability – a great memory, but he couldn't do the simplest arithmetic or write anything at all. He was twenty-one years old.

As Gunnar recounted John Koronis' testimony, Diane picked some pins from the lamp table and began to pile her shoulder-length hair on top of her head. It gave her a cooler, fresher look but her raised arms exposed the stubble of her underarms. He asked her if she had ever heard of Tony Djilas.

She sat up straight, and the thigh disappeared. 'Oh yes,' she said, 'I've heard of him all right. When Ralph arrested him. That was the beginning of the end for us.'

'Did he tell you anything about the arrest?' The beginning of the end, Gunnar thought. What kind of man had he represented? What kind of man was Holly's father? How much did Holly know?

'Sure, the Djilas arrest was a main topic of discussion for months. People were pressuring Ralph and Joe Kelly to back off.' Diane's pleasant smile vanished. Her eyes glittered. 'If only they had. But they were honest cops,' she said. 'This guy Djilas was associated with Manny Zilman.'

'Do you know how they were connected?' Gunnar asked.

'This Zilman was a big dope-dealer, and Ralph said Djilas was kind of his connection with the cops and politicians.'

Gunnar thought of the three-million-dollar T-Bill. But, of course, all of this was hearsay, fifteen years older than Malcolm's. Two people saying it didn't make it true.

'Did you ever meet any of these people?'

'Not until after Ralph disappeared, I was home taking care of three little kids. But I know Ralph met with Zilman before quitting the force.'

'Did he tell you what they talked about?'

A voice behind Gunnar said, 'I didn't know we had company.'

Gunnar twisted around to look at the smiling face of what looked like a six-foot-two chubby ten-year-old.

'Kenny, this is Mr Larson,' said Diane.

Gunnar stood up and shook his hands.

Kenny looked pleased. 'If you could be anybody in the world for one week who would you choose?' he asked.

Gunnar looked sheepishly at Diane.

'You better tell him,' she said. 'He won't quit until you do.'

Gunnar pondered. Ronald Reagan would be the easy answer, but he couldn't stand the simple-minded clown.

'Does it have to be someone alive?' said Gunnar.

'You don't want to be dead do ya?'

Kenny's uncomplicated logic was inescapable.

'Jack Nicklaus,' said Gunnar. 'I guess I'd like to hit a golf ball like he does for one week.'

'Good choice,' said Kenny, 'I watch him on TV. He's the greatest that ever lived.' The low voice went with the big body, but not the young boy's face.

Her husband actually met with Zilman, Gunnar thought.

'Who's your second choice?' said Kenny.

Diane seemed to enjoy Gunnar's new conversation more than the old.

'I really don't have a second choice,' said Gunnar.

'Who ever heard of not having a second choice? Don't tell me that!' said Kenny.

'Ted Williams,' said Gunnar

'He's an old man,' said Kenny. 'That's not a good choice.'

'When he hit four-o-six,' said Gunnar.

'That's against the rules. You gotta play by the rules!'

He was out of touch with baseball. When Jack was alive, Gunnar knew every big league player. 'Pete Rose,' said Gunnar.

'Now, that is a good choice,' said Kenny. 'Do you wanna ask me?'

Diane's lips formed a lopsided you-better-do-it smile; and her eyes said, this is a big event for my little boy. Gunnar felt like a chump for hesitating. He asked Kenny to sit down next to him, and he reached up and rubbed the fresh blondish crew-cut and put his arm around Kenny's shoulders. Holding his face only inches away from Kenny's he said, 'Who would you choose to be?'

'He-Man,' said Kenny, 'but forty-times stronger.'

'Wise choice.' Gunnar said. 'And who's your second choice?'

Kenny squinted like he was looking into the sun. His lips drew back tight revealing his upper teeth, yellow with tartar, and his eyes closed tight. 'Oprah Winfrey,' he blurted.

A spray of saliva struck Gunnar's face. 'But she's a woman,' he said automatically.

'Then I'd know what it was like to be a woman,' said Kenny.

'The first man ever,' said Diane, puckering and throwing a kiss to whoever wanted to catch it.

They went through seven more choices each. Kenny reverted to cartoon characters. Gunnar stuck with athletes. The boy-man's mind intrigued Gunnar and fought for dominance over the penumbral intelligence that he suspected Diane had been about to reveal when Kenny had walked in. He pulled Kenny against him playfully and felt a special warmth, associated only with Jack – one of the treasures he had been robbed of that he valued the most. When Jack died he had thought of that touching, so different from touching a female. There hadn't been much after Jack was in junior high school, but it was there on deposit when Gunnar needed it, perhaps not until he lay dying – but his account to draw on. Then the bank failed.

Kenny whispered in his ear. 'Ask Mom one.'

'OK,' said Gunnar. 'Diane, what's your first choice?'

'Today,' she said, 'that's easy, I'd choose to be your woman.'

Gunnar felt the heat in his face, but nowhere else. Kenny flopped his big head on Gunnar's shoulder, the fuzzy crew-cut rubbing Gunnar's ear.

'He's asleep,' Diane said. 'This happens whenever he gets excited. He goes out like a light. It's like he uses up all of his energy. The doctor says it's nothing to worry about.'

Kenny's eyes were tightly closed and his chest expanded with deep breaths. Gunnar looked at Diane for instruction.

'Just ease him down on the sofa. He'll be like that for a couple of hours,' she said.

Gunnar tugged at Kenny's big body until he had him stretched full-length on the big green sofa. He looked as though he had tripped and sprawled headlong on the run, and his body twitched like a dog does in its sleep.

'He'll be fine now,' Diane said. 'We'll go into the den.' In spite of the excess weight, she rose with alacrity and took Gunnar's hand. The first door in the hall opened to a small room with a short sofa and small desk and chair.

'When the girls moved out I made this into a den,' Diane said. 'When they come home, they can pull this sofa out into a bed.'

Before she sat down she turned to face him, moving up close enough so he could feel her gigantic bosom through the thin fabric of his shirt.

'Do you know how long it's been since I've been with a man like you?'

Gunnar's uncomfortable stare was answer enough.

'Almost fifteen years,' she said. 'Ralph was a thinker, and strong like you.'

Gunnar brought his hand up and touched her cheek. 'I'm committed, Diane,' he said.

'I don't get my first choice today?'

He tried to smile the smile of duty. Committed to whom? he thought. The simple unguarded open face made him draw her to him, and he kissed her on the forehead. 'It just wouldn't be right,' he said.

She reached both arms around his waist. 'Am I too fat?'

'No, no, no. You're attractive.' Her weight had nothing to do with it. He could sink into her softness, and let her mother him and it would feel good and soothing. And, perhaps, it would even be good for her. But he wasn't going to do it. The lines had become too blurred already. He squeezed her tightly to him, and then stepped back. 'It wouldn't be right,' he said.

She dropped her eyes and turned and sat down; then he, beside her. She let out a long sigh and rubbed her eyes with the back of her hand.

'What did you ask me?' she said.

'You mentioned your husband had contact with Manny Zilman.'

'You know, Gunnar,' she said. 'Even after all these years, you've gotta promise me you won't drag me into anything. I've still gotta worry about the kids.'

Gunnar promised and told her that she could trust him. The sexual tension was ebbing, and it seemed OK with her.

'For a while it was an ongoing thing,' she said. 'Let me tell you what happened.'

'Good,' said Gunnar.

'It wasn't long after the Djilas arrest. Zilman asked Ralph to meet him somewhere down in Hallandale. I don't know what he said, but whatever it was made Ralph believe that our kids wouldn't be safe if he didn't do what Zilman asked.'

'Which was?' said Gunnar.

'He had to quit the police force. First Ralph thought we should all pack up and leave. But Zilman told him he would see we had some money. The second time he met with Zilman he came home with five thousand in cash. I figured Zilman was giving him a job.'

'Did Djilas' name ever come up after the arrest?'

'I guess it came up, but I don't know in what way. Not then, anyway. But the Feds were after Zilman. Ralph got a subpoena to appear before a grand jury. That's when he disappeared. At first I wasn't so worried because when he left he said he'd be gone for a few days. He also thought the Feds might have tapped our line, so he said he wouldn't be calling. He said I should never let on to anybody that I knew anything at all. I should play dumb housewife. I guess it wasn't that hard a rôle for me.'

Without thinking, Gunnar squeezed her forearm, shaking his head at her self-disparagement.

'I never heard from Ralph again,' she said.

Gunnar suspected that Ralph Ek might have gotten in much deeper than his wife knew. 'What about Djilas,' he said.

'After Ralph was gone for two weeks, I panicked and called Zilman's office from the Tom Thumb on the corner near where we used to live in Fort Lauderdale. They said he wasn't in. I called a couple more times and left messages to get a hold of Mrs Ek.' Diane moved her head from side to side, the pain of recollection on her face.

'Finally, after about another week, I went to Zilman's office on the beach, E.Z. and Associates, they called it. They told me he was out of town, but I saw this real handsome guy in the back. The girl told me that was Mr Djilas, so I asked to see him.'

Her skirt had slipped way above her knees again, and she absently tugged at the hem. Gunnar hung on each word as if he were listening to a crucial opposing witness in a courtroom.

'He took me into an office in the back and asked what he could do for me. I told him who I was, and that I was scared for my husband. He said he had no idea what I was talking about, but that he would try to get a hold of Mr Zilman and tell him what I'd said. That I should meet him at a Big Boy's on Highway One in Dania at a certain time. He said I should tell no one, and I didn't.'

'Did he show up?' said Gunnar, his adrenaline taking over again, tense jaw muscles anticipating the words he hoped he wouldn't hear.

'Yes, he was very nice. He gave me a package. He said he didn't know what was in it, but that it was from Ralph, and he said Ralph said if I told anybody about it, I would never see him again, and there'd be no more packages. I asked him when I'd hear.' Again, her head began moving from side to side as she spoke. 'Djilas said he didn't know. He was just delivering the package.'

Gunnar let out a breath of relief, daring not to think he was kidding himself. 'What was in the package?'

'Ten thousand in cash,' she said.

'Did you ever see Djilas again?'

'No, but I talked to him on the phone. About a month later. I broke down crying, and he was real nice, but he said he didn't know anything. He just happened to work for E.Z. and Associates. Not long after, I called again and the phone was disconnected, and information told me his home phone was unlisted. You gotta remember I was frantic. I didn't know if Ralph was alive or dead. Then I got it into my head he had run out on me. A few times that year I'd got suspicious that he was running around. One time he'd been drinking, and he smelled of some kinda ladies' cologne or something.'

Diane looked down at her body, then into Gunnar's eyes. 'I wasn't heavy like this. Ralph loved my boobies, but I think he strayed now and then. Cops do, ya know.'

Gunnar was edgy. He didn't want to hurry her, but he was embarrassed by the intimate detail. Already, this kind woman had let him get closer in some ways than Holly had. He still knew nothing of Holly's relationships before Davey Tripp.

Finally, without telling them the truth, she'd sought advice from some other cops' wives, including Edna Kelly, Diane said. They'd told her that if anyone knew what was going on, Loren Cressick would. *The name again*. Cressick told her that Zilman was gone for good. Left town. But she'd thought he was lying. Gunnar said he thought she might have been right.

'Somewhere along the line,' she said, 'I reported Ralph as a missing person. The cops said I didn't have to because there was a federal-bench warrant for his arrest after he didn't show up for the grand jury.'

'Did you hear about that job application in San Diego?' Gunnar asked.

'I checked it out, both by letter and phone. They said they had no record of it. They wrote me on a fancy letterhead, and that letter the Fort Lauderdale police have in Ralph's file was typed on a piece of plain paper. I think it's a phony. In 1981 I had an attorney get Ralph declared dead. Of course, long before that, I knew he was. I think I knew he was . . . right from the start. He loved his kids. He wouldn't stay away without getting in touch. Zilman must have had him killed.'

She reached over to the desk and handed Gunnar a picture of a darkly handsome man.

'That's Ralph . . . not long before he disappeared.'

'A nice-looking man,' Gunnar said.

'Sometimes we kid ourselves too long,' Diane said. 'It's very destructive. My two girls believed their father was dead long before I would admit it, and they were just little kids.'

All Gunnar could do was nod his head. In the serious blue eyes set wide apart in the plump pretty face he got a glimpse of absolute truth. In his nostrils he got the first faint sniff of the putrid smell of self-delusion.

At the front door, Gunnar thanked her and hoped to see her again, and he asked her to tell Kenny goodbye for him. Diane raised on tiptoe and kissed him on the mouth.

59

'This is one of my father's favorites,' said Al Bergdorf. 'Matisse painted it early in the century. It's worth millions now. In the 1920s my father met an agent of the famous Russian collector S.I. Shchukin in Paris. The guy had the Matisse you're lookin' at. My father traded him a huge canvas by some Dada painter long since forgotten. Of course, at the time the guy was supposed to be going places. Some make it, some don't.'

'It's thrilling to see a painting like this in someone's home, especially someone you know,' said Katie. 'And the walls are covered with so many . . . so much color.

'My father is partial to vivid color . . . especially over the last twenty years, as his eyes got worse. No Rembrandt palettes in here. I wish you could meet my father. He's past ninety. He and mother have already left for Florida for the winter. He's blind now, you know.'

'No, I didn't.'

'He still wants to keep his favorite paintings in the house here as long as he lives. Even though he can't see them, he says they are his friends. Sometimes he touches the brush strokes lightly with his fingertips. He says the images are still clear in his mind.'

'I can understand. One wouldn't forget this painting easily. Or any of them.'

'I have to admit that I never really understood the abstract stuff, but it's still pleasant for me. Like the Pollock I have in my office. I've never had the least idea what was in the artist's mind, but I'd never want to be without it. My father finally gave it to me officially, just last year after he lost his sight completely.'

'I suppose all of these paintings will be yours someday?'

'Not on your life. He's already lent out more than he has here

to museums. When he dies they all come back. The city fathers
have agreed that the house can become an art museum. His will
funds its operation in perpetuity. It's to be called The People's
Museum of Twentieth Century Painting. That's a mouthful,
isn't it?'

'Exciting! It's a perfect place. Right here, across the street from
the lake, and it's walking distance to downtown.'

'Yeah, I grew up in this house. Pop was forty-six when
I was born. I have two sisters older, and two younger. We
each have one painting and our wills give those back to the
museum.'

'His name should be on it.'

'He didn't want that. He's dedicated it to all the Jews who
died anonymously in the twentieth century. Anyway, Bergdorf
would be a hell of a name for a beautiful museum. It's as bad
as Guggenheim. Pop says that if you conduct your life with
honor, you don't need to have buildings named after you when
you die.'

'He sounds like an amazing man.'

'He is, and he was a great attorney in his day, too, like
your dad. By the way did you tell him you were coming over
here?'

'By the time I got home Friday night, he had left for
Miami.'

'Little vacation?'

'I think it was business, but Mom didn't tell me, if she
even knew.'

'I don't know if he would approve of you being here.'

'Why in the world not?'

'I don't think he likes me very much.'

'You must have misunderstood him.'

'He's not one you misunderstand. But maybe he has his
reasons.

'Hattie, you need something?'

'Mr Al. There's a phone call for you. Some man. Do you want
to take it in here?'

'No, Hattie. Thanks. I'll take it in the office.'

* * *

'For Chrissakes, Al! I've been tracking you all over town.'

'You sound agitated. All confused over how to spend your three million?'

'Cut it out. Do you know what that fucking Gunnar has done now?'

'Flown off to Miami.'

'How the hell did you know?'

'His lovely and brilliant daughter is here, right now.'

'You're kiddin'!'

'Not on your life.'

'What the hell is she doing there?'

'If it's any of your business, looking at the paintings. You oughta try it some time. Now what's the big urgency?'

'Is this a safe line?'

'Unless Hattie's listening in. She's been with my parents for forty-eight years.'

'Gunnar had an appointment to talk to Pete Crossman – my old neighbor when I lived on Ninth Street in Fort Lauderdale. For this afternoon. Has the sonofabitch gone crazy?'

'I have no idea what's stuck in his craw. It must have something to do with that Big Ed thing you were telling me about. I'll talk to him as soon as he gets back.'

'That could be too late.'

'Tony, for Christ's sake . . . too late for what?'

'Don't get your shit hot.'

'Too late for what, Tony? What the hell do you know that I don't. On second thoughts, don't say anything. I don't want to know. I want to talk to Gunnar.'

'You got it all wrong, Al. Simmer down.'

'This ain't for the telephone, and I got company. I don't like the sound of this. I don't want any part of what it sounds like. I'll talk to you tomorrow.'

'Are you enjoying yourself, Katie?'

'Oh Al, for sure. They're all so wonderful; especially this one, the flowers.'

'Yeah, women like the Chagall. That's my mother's favorite, and my sister Barbara's, too. My father has owned it for fifty years.'

'Al, while you were gone I remembered reading about the museum idea in the paper. Didn't some of the neighbors object to the zoning variance? I was still in high school.'

'Schmucks. Oh Katie, excuse the expression. Please. I got carried away. I handled that case.'

'I couldn't agree with you more.'

'Mom, someday you must come with me to see the Bergdorf collection. It's breathtaking.'

'I can't wait to hear your father's reaction.'

'He's got Al Bergdorf all wrong. I don't know if I've ever met a nicer man, except Daddy, of course. We talked for hours. I can tell, he's so lonely. When his father dies, that great old house will become a museum.'

'That's what I heard. By the way, Katie, some man called today. Wanted to know where you were. He said his name was Jones. I told him I couldn't give out that kind of information to a stranger over the phone. He said he'd call back. He had a high-pitched voice, kind of Hispanic, I think.'

'I don't know any Jones. Maybe it's got something to do with law school. Whatever, it's been a perfect Sunday. I wonder what Daddy did today way down there in sunny Miami. Oh my God! He is alone, isn't he?'

'I think so. I doubt if they travel together. She's pretty married you know.'

'I don't know how you stand it, Mom.'

'I'm doing fine. And it's getting late, little girl. I'll probably be out running when you get up in the morning.'

'Sweet dreams, Mom. I love you.'

'I love you too, Katie dear.'

60

Somebody had shut Peter Crossman up. On Monday morning when Gunnar called him for a new appointment, he said he had decided not to talk. He was fed up with the Djilas business. What the hell more do you want, he said, you won millions.

Tony Djilas had good reason to ask Crossman to maintain his silence. Same as Leo and Eddie, Tony would see no point in digging up old trouble, or creating new where none existed. Especially if three-point-three explicitly absolved you of the obligation. Even without three-point-three, Gunnar had found no competent evidence clearly implicating his client. To Diane Ek, Tony had said he was merely delivering a package for Zilman. Just as he said he'd merely opened the bank account for Zilman. But Ralph Ek had told Diane that Tony was a go-between for Zilman with the police and politicians, and poor dead Malcolm Edwards had seen him make a quarter-of-a-million-dollar dope sale, or so Malcolm had said. All hearsay. Clearly inadmissable shit. Yet, in spite of how badly he wanted otherwise, the empty pain of doubt rose in Gunnar's chest and his confidence in finding a winning way out eroded by the minute. More than just a dope dealer, Tony Djilas might be an accessory to the murder of two fathers, leaving behind two little boys and two little girls.

Kenny Ek's days were vacuums of fantasy. Cared for by strangers while his mother struggled to earn their keep and his father lay rotting in some Everglades bog, Kenny had been deprived of what he needed most. Gunnar had recognized the risk of talking to the widows. Even if they offered no solid evidence, they sucked him into the stink of the crime. Victims, fifteen years later, as much as the torn-throated corpse he had seen on

372

Saturday. And Gunnar might be in league with their tormentors, however unwittingly.

Or was he? What had happened to the presumption of innocence? Proof beyond a reasonable doubt. Jesus Christ, he was ready to pronounce sentence. Both Tony's and his own. If only he could find something or someone to make him believe in his client again. But you couldn't prove a negative. He had known that from the start. He had known that since Philosophy 1. The jury had decided that clear and convincing evidence exonerated Tony Djilas. But they hadn't heard Dexter's tape, nor had they talked to Edna Romero or Diane Ek.

Gunnar had two trails to explore: Loren Cressick and Big Ed Edwards. The prison at Starke was three hundred miles north. He hoped Cressick was closer. He dialed Wyman Farmer's number.

'I've already located him,' said Wyman. 'He lives at 199 Ocean Drive. That's on Key Biscayne, only twenty, twenty-five minutes from where you are.'

'Anything else?'

'Not yet, but my source in Fort Lauderdale said that he remembers Cressick was involved in some kind of drug investigation in the early seventies, but he came out clean.'

'Can you connect him with Zilman in any way?'

'Hey Gunnar, this is only nine o'clock Monday morning. You just called me yesterday.'

'Sorry, I'm a little over-eager on this.'

'Do you mind telling me what's going on?'

'Ideally, I'm hoping to find something that clears Djilas.'

'I thought you won the case. Are they opening it up again?'

'Nothing like that, Wyman. It's hard to explain.'

'Forget it. Mine is not to reason why.' Wyman told him that he should have Cressick's unlisted telephone number by noon, and he would get back to him in twenty-four hours on his criminal record and any other police data, maybe sooner.

After he had finished his call to Wyman Farmer, Holly had kept Gunnar on the line for an hour, asking a hundred questions, few of which he answered directly. She must understand that in his line of work he was obligated to maintain confidences. She should get used to it, he had said, and no, it didn't look like he would make it to the Lodge on Tuesday night. Perhaps Thursday. No perhapses, said Holly. Tony wanted Gunnar to call him tonight at home. I'll talk to him soon as I get back, Gunnar had told her.

Loren Cressick had agreed to see him fifteen minutes from now at ten p.m. Gunnar tossed four quarters in the toll basket as he headed the T-Bird on to the Rickenbacker Causeway. From the main span of the causeway bridge, hemmed in by racing traffic, he dared a look over his left shoulder at the spectacle of the city. Mirrored in the stillness of Biscayne Bay, lights from the tall condos along Brickell Avenue enlivened the night.

At the first traffic light at the end of the palm-lined boulevard through Crandon Park, Gunnar turned left on Ocean Drive. At the entrance to the Commodore Club, an Hispanic guard approached the car.

'My name is Larson, to see Mr Cressick in the east building.'

Back in the booth, the guard picked up a phone. Seconds later he nodded and pointed toward the white tower, furthest back on the grounds among a cluster of three. The zebra-striped gate rose.

In the marble and plate-glass lobby, another Hispanic guard checked him through to a bank of elevators. One tap on the door of 1301, and it opened.

'Larson?' asked a man of seventy or more, wearing a bright yellow sports-shirt unbuttoned to the waist, revealing a snarl of white hair. His waxen head was hairless, and he wore steel-rimmed glasses.

Gunnar stuck out his hand. 'Gunnar Larson.'

'Cressick.' He sounded like he had a sore throat and he shook Gunnar's hand indifferently. His eyes were small, like a rat's, and he had no lips. 'Follow me,' he said.

From an opulent living room, through open sliding-glass doors, he led Gunnar out on a long terrace. Toward the end nearest the sea were a table and two chairs. Seven or eight feet beyond, the shadows enshrouded a seated figure.

'Sit down,' said Cressick. 'That's Dirk. He looks after me.'

Dirk looked as though he had been cut from black cardboard. From behind the silent form, you could hear the gentle tide running along the beach below.

Cressick filled a water glass half-full. 'Help yourself.'

Gunnar declined.

'You should know you can cause trouble poking around down here,' said Cressick.

Gunnar started to tell him about the trial.

Cressick interrupted: 'Not interested. You know, Larson, your problem is you can't tell your friends from your enemies. That can be costly.'

'Perhaps,' said Gunnar, 'and I'm the fool if it's true. But I have to do what I think is right. Do you know my client, Tony Djilas?'

'I let you come up here, so I could do you a favor. You could hurt a lot a people. Some bad.'

To the North above the tops of the renegade Australian pines, Miami's skyline radiated red and blue light across Biscayne Bay. In the East, over the Atlantic, lightning raged inside a mountain of black cumulus like an apocalypse beyond a range higher than the Himalayas. But on the terrace the tropical air was still.

'Of course,' Gunnar said, 'I don't want to hurt anybody, especially my client Mr Djilas. There have been allegations . . . .'

'From Sonny Romero's wife.'

Edna Romero. He already knew Gunnar had spoken with José Kelly's widow. 'Certainly not,' said Gunnar. 'I went to her for information, but she had none to give that I didn't already know.'

'Who gave you my name?'

'I can't reveal that.'

'You want me to talk, but you don't want to talk.'

Cressick got up and replenished Dirk's invisible glass.

'I thought perhaps you could help,' said Gunnar.

'I am helping you by telling you to go back home. Get on with whatever it is you do . . . . You have a family.'

When Gunnar first considered taking the Djilas case, the welfare of his family had skipped through his mind. He had dismissed the qualm as absurd. Now the threat was as real as the trembling in his hands. 'Are you threatening me?' he asked.

A movement of the head in the shadows caught a wandering spark of light. Dirk's hair was gray.

'Why would I threaten anyone?' said Cressick. 'I'm an old man. Comfortable. No time for threats, or need, for that matter.'

'But you have friends,' said Gunnar. The rules had changed. The reference to family unsteadied him, blurred his mission.

'I had heard you weren't a stupid man,' said Cressick.

Its glowing tip indicated the man in the shadows had lit a cigarette. Gunnar hadn't seen the flare of match or lighter.

'At times, we are all stupid,' said Gunnar. When his emotions revealed themselves in the courtroom, trouble soon followed. The emotion was usually anger; the trouble, deviation from carefully laid plans. In the warm wet air on the dark terrace high above the sea, fear and distant panic dried his mouth, like he had been running in a desert.

Cressick was as still as the man in the shadows. The silence prickled with hostility.

Gunnar took a last shot. 'I have heard you were involved with Emanuel Zilman.'

'I thought lawyers didn't deal in hearsay. I know nothing of any of this,' said the words. But the sound of the croaky whisper, like the hiss of a snake, had another meaning. Lives, it said, are on the line if you fuck with me.

On the way back across Rickenbacker Causeway, Gunnar hardly noticed the spectacular city with its vantage-point on the bay. He hadn't even learned if Cressick knew Tony Djilas, or Zilman for that matter. Cressick had told him nothing. It was Gunnar who'd been interviewed, and then advised. Of course, Cressick had some kind of a stake.

After midnight, he returned Wyman Farmer's call. 'Sorry for the hour, I just got in from my meeting with Mr Cressick.'

'No problem. I was up watching Carson. Do any good?'

'Not really. What'd you have for me?'

'I thought you'd want to know right away. We found two deeds for large tracts of commercial land in Broward County running from Zilman to Cressick. Late 1973, another in 1971. He eventually broke them up and sold them off over the next ten years. That's all so far.'

'Good work,' said Gunnar.

'When you heading back north?'

'Soon. I have a meeting on Wednesday afternoon.' Gunnar was tempted to call Marvin Linden and beg off. He didn't feel like sitting in judgment of anyone right now, even that prick Kindred Diamond.

Gunnar thanked Wyman Farmer and headed for his pillow, but sleep didn't come. Instead, he replayed the scene in Cressick's penthouse in slow motion, word for word. The second time through, it hit him like an electric shock in his spine, goose flesh prickled his upper arms, and he felt a tightening in his sphincter. Even though the air on the terrace had been dead calm, Dirk had turned away so that the flare of the match wouldn't illuminate his face. There was only one person, only one person anywhere, who would take pains to hide his face from Gunnar Larson.

61

With morning already diluting the dark, sleep had come. Gunnar's last thought had been of Kenny Ek. If you could be somebody else for one week who would you choose? Then fitful sleep and dreams: Cressick's waxen head and rat eyes, and the figure in the dark. Zilman. And shapes beyond memory. Menace – enough to wake him. A line of light around dark drapes. Alarm surged into the void that comes with the first moments of wakefulness. Cressick's lipless croak: *You have a family*. Gunnar called the airport and booked the first flight home. Big Ed would have to wait. Gunnar needed to be home. Now.

The 727 sliced through the stratosphere at five hundred plus, but time passed like a twelve-year-old's last hour of school on a spring day. *You have a family*. Did you ever know the true value of what you hold dear until you lost it? The prospect or expectation of the loss was the next best measure. Gunnar was in unfamiliar territory. For the first time in eleven years he could not definitely shape the outcome of an issue that mattered. But he could. He could back off. Keep his three million. Look no further. Notify Djilas. Tell your friends they have heard the last of me. They have nothing to fear.

The cabin was only half-full. Gunnar moved over to a window seat. The plane's shadow rushed across clouds layered to the horizon. A rift revealed a tiny Tennessee village – a place for them all to hide. In seconds it was gone. *You have a family*. There were two people besides him in that family. Neither would want him to ignore the new evidence. Neither would be impressed by the niceties of three-point-three. When the cause was right, cunning techniques to liberate concealed truths were one thing,

378

but to overlook perjury on the principal issue in the case required resources Gunnar could not locate. If he did, where would he go from there? He loathed the system, but it was a system. However grotesque, it had a distinct form. And form fosters predictability. Gunnar's talent could only have developed and flourished in predictable circumstances. He came back to the proposition: there was no hard evidence that Djilas had lied.

What about cross-examination? Leading questions revealed the truth, freshened memory, exposed falsehood – now, perhaps, they could be an antidote for the poison of self-delusion. Isn't it true Mr Larson, that you made only the most cursory investigation before you agreed to represent Tony Djilas, and isn't it true that you learned of the off-shore bank account from the defendants, not Tony Djilas, and isn't it true that you learned of the arrest on Victoria Terrace from the defendants, not Tony Djilas, and isn't true that neither you, nor anyone else, believed Tony Djilas' explanation of the bank account, and isn't it true that you learned of the transaction with Hyman and Emma Rosen from the defendants, not Tony Djilas, and isn't it true that you learned of the death of José Kelly from John Koronis, not Tony Djilas, and isn't it true that you learned about the package of cash delivered to Diane Ek from her, not Tony Djilas? Those were the right questions. Gunnar must answer yes to every one. For the thirteen days since hearing the tape, the reasons and the will to believe in Tony, like summer twilight had dimmed by degrees to finally vanish at this moment. At the first dusk of doubt more than a year ago, Gunnar had forsaken the chance to correct his course. Now it was too late.

Did Holly know? She had been in high school at the time. Tony might have shielded his family. Gunnar needed to believe so, as much for Holly as for his great verdict and his three-million-dollar T-Bill. Did Al Bergdorf know? What about the mayor? What about the Reverend Robert Goodspeed? No matter who else knew before, Gunnar knew now. *Djilas v.* Times-Journal, his great white whale, stinking brown and rotted through, floated on a putrid sea. Dead of natural causes.

He took the little dictating machine out of his attaché case and pushed the record button. He held the recorder close to his mouth, jet engines humming in the background: 'To Terrance J. Wood. Re, *Djilas v.* Times-Journal *et al.* Dear Terry, since our settlement, and indeed since Judge O'Boyle's entry of judgment in the above-referenced matter, I have discovered information that leads me to believe that the verdict was obtained on the basis of materially false testimony. Said information is clearly hearsay, and inadmissable, nor would it, I believe, lead to the discovery of evidence that was admissable. Paragraph. My client maintains that my belief is erroneous. Nevertheless, it is my belief. Therefore, I enclose a check payable to your client in the sum of $3,375.000.00, the entire amount collected by my firm. Of course I have no control over the half paid to Anthony Djilas. Be assured that throughout the prosecution of my claim, I believed that all material evidence adduced at the trial in support of my case was nothing but the truth. Very truly yours, Gunnar Larson. Copies to Anthony Djilas, Judge Michael O'Boyle and Al Bergdorf.'

He tilted his seat back. A cabin attendant with Holly's face asked him if she could get him anything. 'Home,' he said with a forced smile. He let his eyelids fall closed and he felt the tears seep out from beneath. He remembered Homer Reach talking about running out of juice. Gunnar never wanted to enter a courtroom again, but what the hell else could he do? He rubbed the sleeve of his blazer across his eyes.

He thought of Jack. Duck Creek had helped. Gunnar saw Kenny Ek's pudgy face, and then a collage: elegant Edna Romero; Kenny's mother Diane, croaking Loren Cressick, the dark cardboard figure on the terrace, Holly, Tony Djilas, and Anne and Katie and Al Bergdorf. If Al had known all along, he had set Gunnar up.

He would call Tony Djilas first thing in the morning. Tony's next move would be up to him. But he could call off his dogs because the letter was in the messenger's hands, Gunnar would say. And Tony didn't know the tape existed. Fleet would get the tape tomorrow. *You have a family*. Then nothing could be gained by threatening Gunnar's family. Katie and Anne would be safe. Or would they? Jesus Christ. He saw the corpse of Malcolm Edwards. Of course Cressick was involved.

* * *

It seemed like he had just fallen asleep when he heard the announcement that they were beginning their descent. Anne waited at the gate. She had gotten his flight number from Shana.

'I have been dying to hear what you found out,' she said after she kissed him, harder than she had in a long time.

She persuaded him to go straight out to the lake with her, skip the stop downtown at the office. He was too tired to resist. On the way Gunnar described each detail of his trip, even Cressick's comment about family – Anne had a right to know – and the feelings Kenny Ek had evoked.

After they'd turned into the curved road along the lake, leading through the tall trees to their own drive, he told her about the letter he had dictated on the plane. 'We were rich for a month,' he said.

'We'll manage,' she said.

Grinding the gravel of the driveway, the wheels rolled to a stop in front of the garage. He didn't tell her he was out of juice, but he felt it more than ever, as though there was a hollow spot where all the information had been stored that told him how one goes about the practice of law. In the dusk, Katie stood on the shore throwing pieces of bread to a hen mallard. He had never been so glad to see her.

She waved. 'Welcome home, traveler!'

With Gunnar in bed and asleep at nine, Anne went to Katie's room. In bra and panties, she sat on the edge of the bed curling her hair.

'You didn't tell him about my new friend?' said Katie.

'Of course not, that's up to you.' She wished Gunnar had told Katie about his decision to send the letter.

'Al *is* my friend you know. I haven't told you the latest. He's giving me a job. We're going to talk more about it, but I think it's a sure thing.'

'Clerking?'

'Yes. In their municipal law and zoning department. After that I hope to get a taste of real estate development-finance. Bergdorf and Ratner is a top firm in that field. Even Daddy says so.'

'When are you going to tell him?'

'Before I officially agree to take the job. Anyway, Mom, they have a nepotism rule at Lawson and Larson, you know.'

'I know, but your father has told you he can get you a good part-time clerking job in litigation whenever you're ready.'

'I've decided I don't want to litigate.'

'Since when?'

'Oh Mom, since Sunday.'

'Baby, you aren't falling for that old man?'

'No, but I would love him for an uncle; besides, it's not important . . . . Anything new on Holly Tripp? I've been thinking about it, Mom. How long are you going to just sit there? It must be a year.'

'Your father once told me that when he was trying a case and he was unsure of what to do, he tried to put off the decision as long as he could. Often as not, he said, the right course would present itself.'

'But this isn't a courtroom, Mom,' Katie said. 'There's feelings involved, and right and wrong.'

'I know,' said Anne, 'I know.'

They kissed, and she told Katie to call home tomorrow afternoon around three.

'You're so cryptic,' said Katie.

'Just make sure you call,' Anne said, as she closed the bedroom door. If Gunnar hadn't told her by then, Anne didn't want Katie learning about his letter in the media.

62

Wednesday morning had one purpose: deliver the letter, kill any incentive for evil motive toward Gunnar's family. Get *Djilas v.* Times-Journal behind him. Gunnar drove downtown ahead of a line of thunderheads stalking the city from the West. Shana had just taken off her raincoat when he handed her the tape.

'First priority,' he said. 'Get this ready for hand delivery in fifteen minutes, and have the bank transfer the funds from my T-Bill account.'

Beyond the glass wall, the storm front crept closer. He swiveled around in his chair and looked Jack right in the eye.

'Time for you to rest, my son,' he said. 'I've bugged you enough.' He took the picture from the top of the black-lacquered credenza and held it for a while, hands resting on his knees, his eyes fondly on the face he would love until death. His throat closed and he found he couldn't talk. But that was OK. From a drawer, he withdrew a large brown envelope and slid the silver frame inside. On the front he wrote: Photo, Jack Larson 1975. Storage. He put the envelope in the out-box and turned back to the desk. Shana came in holding the letters.

'Gunnar, I'm so sorry. I'm in shock. You must be devastated.'

'Honey. I have no choice. But promise me you won't discuss anything about this letter or what may come up later with anyone, even Greg.'

'Of course.' Then her tears came and she sat down in one of the chairs in front of his desk.

Gunnar got up and walked around to stand beside her and stroke her hair. 'I love your loyalty, Shana. I hope I deserve it.'

She stood and wrapped her arms around his neck. 'I'm so lucky to know you,' she said.

He signed the letter to Terry Wood, and the check Shana had prepared. The copies to O'Boyle and Djilas would go out unsigned.

'Now, dear, if you would. Oh, forgive the "dear".' Shana hated the term. She thought it was sexist.

'Don't be silly,' she said.

'Anyway, Shana, would you listen carefully to the call I am about to make. I would like as close to a verbatim transcript as possible.'

Wind-driven rain plastered the glass wall. The taller trees in Corum Park bent before the gale.

'Hello Tony, this is Gunnar.'

'Have you come to your senses?'

'Finally, I have,' said Gunnar.

'Good,' said Tony. He sounded offended.

'Within fifteen minutes of the time I hang up this telephone, the letter I am about to read to you will be delivered to Terry Wood, attorney for the *Times-Journal* Company, with copies to you and Judge O'Boyle. My secretary is monitoring this call and making a transcript from her notes.'

'What the fuck are you talking about?'

Gunnar read him the letter, slowly and distinctly.

'You are out of your goddamn mind. Why should I pay because my fucking lawyer goes crazy! Listen to this, you too, Shana. I am ordering you not to deliver that letter.'

'The decision is made. It's irrevocable,' said Gunnar. 'But don't worry. As the letter says, I have no admissible evidence proving you breached your oath.'

'Then what the fuck are you doing?'

'I said I had no admissible evidence. But I know you lied, just as you know you lied.'

'But I didn't lie.'

'I am asking Terry Wood to call you the minute he receives the letter. So you will know it's too late to try to coerce me by hurting anyone in my family.'

'Listen to me, Gunnar! Listen to me! You're wrong! Why would you think I'd hurt your family?'

Gunnar told him about his talk with Loren Cressick.

'I barely know Loren Cressick,' said Tony.

'But you know somebody very well who is tight with Cressick.'

'And who the hell is that?'

'Manny Zilman.' The line was quiet for several seconds. 'Stay by your phone until you hear from Wood.'

Gunnar hung up and handed the letter to Shana. 'Hurry,' he said.

He turned down two calls from Djilas in the next five minutes. A strange calmness subdued him. He made up his mind not to talk to anyone on the outside about his decision. No press conferences, no nothing. The one exception would be Al Bergdorf. If Al was aware of the deception, Gunnar had to know. He asked himself if Holly was on the outside or the inside? He wouldn't tell her anything, but he would listen to her. He had learned something of divided loyalty. How would she react to his giving up the money? Between Palm Beach and eight thousand square feet on ten acres of lake shore, she lived the good life. The fall to a divorced Gunnar's brand of austerity would be precipitous.

Gunnar looked at the file jackets on his desk as if he couldn't possibly ever understand of them. He took Terry Wood's call. Gunnar assured him the letter and check were genuine. It was no joke. Terry said he had quickly checked the rules and, in his opinion, Gunnar's action was unnecessary. 'Terry, I am aware of three-point-three,' Gunnar said and thanked him for his concern.

'OK,' said Terry, 'I'll call Djilas as instructed, and tell him I have the letter. Mind letting me in on what that's about?'

Gunnar told him he couldn't discuss it, and answered Terry Wood's final question with, 'No, I have no idea what my former client will do now.'

He turned down a call from Holly, and tried to focus his mind on the afternoon's Ethics Committee meeting. His eyes rested on the Mondrian, lines forever straight, uncomplicated blues and reds and yellows, ordered as the painter had discovered they must be. It wouldn't make a bad flag for the right army.

Before leaving for lunch he dictated a letter. To Kenny Ek, care of Diane Ek: Dear Kenny, I am sitting behind my desk this morning thinking about the good time we had together last Sunday. Today, my choice to be someone else for one week is to be your father. I am sending a check so that when your mother has the time off, she can bring you to see me and stay at my house. Who would you choose to be on your next turn? Have your mother write me a letter, and tell me. Love Gunnar.

While examining and sorting his feelings for Katie Larson most of Monday and Tuesday, Al Bergdorf had savored his Sunday afternoon with her and the paintings. Tony's call intruding on his bliss was the sole sour spot. He had called again on Monday. That time Al was succinct:

'Listen, Tony, I want you to understand something.'

Tony interrupted.

'No, you listen to me,' Al said. 'Davey Tripp brought you in here three years ago for help on New City. And you and I got along great. You're a nice guy. But I've had this practice for twenty years, and my old man for forty before that. In sixty years we have not been involved in one scandal or any kind of hanky-panky. Sure the top guys are all Jews, and there's going to be people around taking pot shots, but we know, we all know, we're on the up and up.

'Now, people know you and I have become good friends, and if you've been pulling some bullshit, the stink is gonna rub off on me, and worse yet, on my old man, and all the others. I'm gonna do whatever I have to, you can bet your life on it. Do you understand?'

The line was silent. Then, 'You got it all wrong, Al.'

'I hope so. But like I told you Sunday. I don't wanna talk any more about this case until I talk to Gunnar Larson. Then I'll call you.'

Tony had maintained his silence for forty-eight hours. Now, the switchboard operator said he had pleaded with her to get Al to take his call. He said he needed help. Bad.

'Whasamatter now?' said Al.

Tony read aloud his copy of Gunnar's letter.

'I knew the guy had class, but I would never have figured him to do this. He hasn't got that much dough. If it were Leo it wouldn't make that much difference. But Leo wouldn't give back the money anyway. Wow!'

'Al, who the fuck's side are you on?'

'I never hearda this before. The only other guy I know who'd do it, is my old man. Holy shit!'

'Al, will you listen to me!'

'What'd he find out Tony?'

'He talked to a buddy of Zilman's, and I don't know who else.'

'When you fucked Gunnar, you fucked me too, and Steve Carpenter and all your friends in this town.'

'But I didn't . . . .'

'Cut the bullshit, Tony. I'll ride this out. I'm glad my old man can't read the papers, and Gunnar'll be an even bigger hero, but you ruined the mayor. Steve Carpenter's political career is over. Bye Tony.'

When Al called Lawson and Larson, Angela told him Gunnar was out. Al wondered if Katie knew what Gunnar had done. What guts! He's playing the game by the old rules. When lawyers trusted each other. When they actually saw themselves as officers of the court. When law was a profession. But why now, with the stakes so high?

Al would ride it out, but it could be a rough ride. Speculation would make him Tony's mentor. Clever Al Bergdorf of dubious ethics, a sharp Jew lawyer, hit on the idea of hiring a white knight to champion a phony claim. Jewish lawyers were always suspect. Not-so clever schmucks like to say, get yourself a good Jew lawyer, you can't lose.

We keep our skirts spotless for sixty years and they call us 'Bag and Rat'. Old Simon Bergdorf never acknowledged it. Avron Ratner, Simon's younger partner, dead last year of cancer, knew it and was embarrassed by it. A man didn't choose his name, he had said; what I should be proud of is now a laughing matter. Al resented it. Friends told him it was better to be the bag than the rat. Not so funny, he would say.

His father taught him. 'We are Jews. It is our lot to be persecuted, but better to be a rich Jew than a poor Jew.' Al wasn't so sure.

387

He had become a cynic at thirteen. Cindy had white hair, so fine he could hardly feel it between his fingers. He had thought he loved her, and she once said to him 'You are the cutest boy I ever met.' He had lived on that for weeks. And then she told him that her parents had forbidden her to see him, except in school. 'Are you really a Jew?' she had asked.

He thought Cindy would have looked like Katie Larson when she grew up. He wondered if Gunnar would forbid Katie to see him. He doubted that she would listen. The office manager, David Fink, had set up a work program for Katie. Al was excited. He would show it to her this afternoon. They were meeting on the front steps of the law library at two.

Kindred Diamond slouched through the door behind his lawyer, Barry Busch. Nine blue suits sat around the long table in the windowless Bar Association meeting-room. Busch, who wore a red plaid vest under his navy blue, and Diamond, in a black pin-stripe, took seats in the middle of one side across from chairman Marvin Linden. Gunnar sat where he always sat, at the end furthest from the door.

Marvin Linden began to read aloud the bill of particulars against Kindred Diamond. After Barry Busch's reply, the nine of them would batter the cornered Diamond with questions and then vote on whether they should refer the matter to the Supreme Court for disbarment proceedings. The chairman's monotone elaborated Diamond's offenses one by one, and Marvin Linden didn't resist raising his voice to bespeak the most egregious sins. On this solemn occasion Gunnar still felt empty of any kind of legal wisdom. But he would try his best.

Al Bergdorf had just gotten back to his office from lunch. The thunderstorm that had invaded the city had given way to a soft steady autumn rain. He would need an umbrella when he went to meet Katie. In spite of the shock of Gunnar's letter, he was buoyant over the prospect of another afternoon with Gunnar's daughter, their third get-together in six days. He would leave in ten minutes at one-thirty. He gave himself a half-hour to make the three miles to the State campus through congested traffic. Katie said she would be crossing the Mall from her one-o'clock class in Gumble Hall.

Tony Djilas had called twice while Al was at lunch, but he ignored the messages when he got back.

'It's Mr Djilas again,' said the switchboard operator.

'Tell him I'm not in,' said Al.

Her voice was back in seconds, 'He says Katherine Larson is in danger.'

'Gimme the call.' Al looked at his watch and picked up the phone. It was one twenty-five. 'Tony, what the hell are you talking about?'

'Somebody just told me that Gunnar's daughter is gonna have her face cut today.'

'My God! Who? Where?' He saw her perfect skin and the wide inquisitive eyes. Then he saw her walking, a lone figure, on the vast Mall.

''At's all I can tell you. I got nothin' to do with it. You gotta believe that.'

Al hung up, grabbed the umbrella and ran for his car, parked in the basement. He stopped at the receptionist's desk. 'Call the university and tell them to get a message to Katherine Larson to stay in her one-o'clock class in Gumble Hall until I get there. Then call the police and tell them there may be a criminal assault on the Mall around two o'clock.' It was already one thirty-one.

In the elevator Al decided a cab would be faster. He stood at the curb for two or three minutes helplessly watching three lanes of traffic creep along the one-way street in the rain. No empty cabs. Everything stopped when the corner light turned red. In the far lane, a cab waited with a passenger in the back. Al ran into the street, threading his knees between bumpers, and opened the front passenger door.

'Cabbie. I got an emergency. Life or death.' He reached toward the driver with a hundred-dollar bill. In the back, behind the glass, an old lady, black straw hat pinned on her blue hair glared, horrified.

'Sorry, mister, I got a fare.'

The light turned green. Al jumped in and fished two more hundreds out of his wallet and threw them in the driver's lap.

'Take me to the footbridge over Jefferson Avenue in front of the student union at the university. If you make it in ten minutes. I'll give you two more C-notes.'

The cab lurched forward, fishtailing on the wet asphalt, tires screaming through the intersection, while the old lady pounded on the glass. Emergency! Al yelled. Apparently appeased, she settled back for the ride. It was one-forty.

At Fowler, blocked by a mass of cars across all three lanes, they killed at least a minute and a half at a light.

'Can you get anything on that radio?' Al asked.

'Nah, it's on the fritz,' said the driver.

At the stoplight on Oakdale, the cab driver bumped over the curb and, watching his chance, shot through the red from the sidewalk amid a cacophony of protesting horns. Running the red on Fourteenth, they squeaked in front of a UPS van by inches. Traffic thinned out the second mile and they sped down Nineteenth Avenue at seventy, running two more reds. Where are the cops when you need them?

Al glanced at the old lady in the back seat. Her bag of small parcels had spilled on the floor. Her head was thrown back and she was laughing. Their tires whinnied around the last corner on to Jefferson Avenue. The hospital towers rose above the Dillon Student Union building on the right, six blocks ahead. They could see the footbridge connecting the union with the Mall, arching over the six lanes of traffic, inching through the drenching rain. A red light held them three blocks short. One minute seemed ten, and they were moving again. Classes broke ten minutes before the hour. At one fifty-one Al threw two more hundreds in the cabbie's lap and said, 'Please send the police to the Mall.' The cab stopped at the right curb under the footbridge, and Al jumped out and ran up the stairs.

From the top of the arch under the sinking sky you could survey the tree-lined mall. Al knew it well. Ahead to the right was the law library, attached by a tunnel to the main law school building beyond, with its Grecian columns like the Supreme Court. Next was the monolithic Chemistry Building, four stories of red brick, topped by a mansard roof. Beyond it, Administration. Each of the four buildings on the east side had a counterpart structure on the west side, three or four hundred feet away. From an elevation on the north end, Waldorf Auditorium, like the Parthenon, overlooked the whole scene. Four sidewalks leading from the buildings on one side, to those on the other, divided the Mall in five sections.

Domed Gumble Hall stood at the far corner. Katie had told Al that she walked diagonally across the Mall from Gumble to the law library. If he got there first, he should watch for her from the steps, she'd said. Catching his breath, Al scanned the broad expanse of dark green, broken by patches of autumn brown. After three weeks of dry weather, the grass willingly absorbed the steady rain. It was unlikely that anybody would attack Katie in front of the hundreds of students clogging the sidewalks, but maybe they would rely on the anonymity of the crowd. If she cut across diagonally she would be alone for several hundred feet. God, what if the bastards had already struck?

Because of the rain, she might stay on the sidewalk out of the wet grass. Al hadn't opened his umbrella. The drizzle soaked his hair and ran across his face and down his neck in the back.

Then he spotted her. She emerged from the mass of moving umbrellas in front of Gumble Hall, and started walking directly toward the law library, a good nine hundred feet away. She had on the same purple coat she'd worn on Sunday, and shiny black boots. A red umbrella obscured her face, but it was her all right.

Katie crossed the sidewalk between Chemistry and the Business School. From behind one of the big maples forming a line along the Mall's west edge, a dark figure came into view walking through the rain on a course that would intersect with hers. God, is that him? Al moved forward. He hadn't run for years. Three-hundred-pound lawyers don't run. Even with a hundred pounds shed, his legs felt like bricks were tied to his shoes. Frustration and fear formed a fist in his stomach.

Katie and the stranger in rain-soaked fatigues drew closer. Al ran on, biting for larger chunks of air, long-dormant muscles painfully pumping his knees. The pursuer's steps quickened. Al had less than two hundred feet to go, the man in the fatigues less than a hundred.

'Katie, Katie, hurry, run to me!' Al ran on, yelling.

The red umbrella moved back and he saw her smile and she waved.

'Run Katie, *run*.' He waved his closed umbrella. She didn't understand. The stranger in the fatigues did, and broke into a fast trot, a mindless force impelled by some absurd promise. Then, Katie turned and saw the man running and she began to run to Al, only fifty feet away. Al saw the glinting claw of a knife only a stride behind Katie, and the sonofabitch kicked her feet out from under her and grabbed her hair and drew the knife back as Al threw his body against him, ripping the atrocious hand from the fine blonde strands.

'Run Katie, run!' Al felt a sting under his ribs on his right side. The attacker struggled to his feet in a second. Deep-set black eyes glittered in a grimace of ugly purpose. He stuck Al's midsection again and then slashed at his face, missing when Al jerked his chin to the left, but the blade sliced through the flesh where neck meets shoulder. Al clinched like a stunned fighter, then slid down the man's squirming body, finally clutching one ankle. One booted foot smashed Al's head and the other pulled free. He lay still, his face pressed into the sod. Jesus, his neck hurt.

'God,' he said out loud into the wet grass, 'let her get away.'

Screams of frightened girls blended with the sirens and Al Bergdorf's tears mingled with the fallen rain.

Gunnar formulated one question for Diamond: Did he feel any obligation whatsoever to the system, and if he did just exactly what was it? Gunnar waited his turn, the efforts of the other inquisitors a distant murmur like voices in another room. Linden wanted him to go last, really nail the shyster. A bright-faced girl with glasses in her hair and a pencil behind her ear came through the door.

Marvin Linden barked at her. 'You know there are no interruptions in these hearings.'

'I have an emergency message for Mr Larson.'

Gunnar jumped out of his chair and went to the door.

'Captain Fleetham said you should come immediately to operating room number five at University Hospital.'

University, it must be Katie. 'Nothing else?'

'No, I'm sorry,' said the girl.

Gunnar left the meeting, ignoring Marvin Linden's concern. 'I object,' said Barry Busch.

In the cab, Gunnar's mind raced back to the bird colonel in the lobby. Was it starting all over again – this time, Katie? No message, but Fleet summoning him to the OR. She must still be alive. Oh God, make her be OK.

63

Gunnar rushed down the polished hall, side-stepping a crew in blue-green scrubs pushing a patient on a cart with an IV bottle hanging over him. Just beyond, Fleet got up to meet him.

'Fleet, is it Katie?'

'She's fine,' said the big brown man, with the tightly shorn salt-and-pepper curls.

'Oh, thank God!' Gunnar threw his arms around him. Then, stepped back and took a deep breath of the medicinal air. 'What happened?'

'Al Bergdorf is in pretty bad shape. He's in surgery now.'

'Did *he* try to hurt Katie?'

'He may have saved her life, for sure saved her from getting cut up.'

'How was he involved?' Gunnar's gratitude was mixed with embarrassment.

'I only know what Katie told me. You might as well hear it from her.'

She was in the ER, Fleet said, an ankle sprain. He had expected her back by the time Gunnar got there, and he had hoped to get a word in with Al Bergdorf before they wheeled him into surgery. Anne was on her way.

'Sit down, Gunnar. I want to hear Katie's story again anyway. We got the perp. I think he's bilingual, but he's only spoken Spanish so far. He made a long-distance call to some law office in Miami.'

A forlorn little woman came down the hall, taking short precise steps. Towering over her, Fleet asked if he could help.

'I'm Barbara Weisenstein,' she said, pronouncing the W as a V. 'Al Bergdorf's sister. Do you know where they have him?'

Fleet introduced himself, then Gunnar, and told her that Al was in surgery, had been for most of a half-hour. She asked nothing more, and sat down in a chair across the hall with her own thoughts.

In minutes, Al's son Simon joined the waiting group. His black coat was streaked with rain and his dark curls shined wet. His frantic face was dominated by a wide mustache like a piece of mink fur. Behind him, his wife Laura led a little boy and girl by the hands. Last was Al's ex-wife Ruth, with the face of an owl and the voice of a traffic cop.

'What's he gotten himself into now?' she said to son Simon. The little boy pulled at her skirt demanding candy. 'Shush Stevie,' she said, 'this is a hospital. There are sick people here. If you don't behave you'll go to the morgue.'

'What's the morgue?' said dark-haired Stevie, pushing his glasses back up on his nose.'

'Never mind,' said Ruth Bergdorf, who, like Al, had never remarried.

Gunnar saw Katie get out of the elevator and hurried to meet her. She swung toward him on a pair of aluminum crutches. Gunnar wrapped his arms around her shoulders pinning the crutches to her side.

'Daddy, have you heard the horror?'

'Very little, just that you have a sprained ankle, and Al Bergdorf is seriously hurt. Let's sit down right here.' Gunnar motioned to Fleet.

When Fleet had gotten a chair, Katie began, tense, cords standing out on her neck. She spoke fast, straining as though she was trying to lift a heavy object. 'I had an appointment at the law library with Al and I was walking across the Mall in the rain when Al came running toward me – waving his arms and umbrella and yelling for me to run.' She pushed strands of disheveled blond hair away from her blue eyes. 'And then I saw someone running after me, and this man knocked me down and grabbed my hair and Al knocked him down and I ran away. And the police came and the paramedics, and crowds of students. I couldn't walk. Al lost enormous amounts of blood. If he dies I don't know what I'll do. Where's Mom? Is she coming?' Katie pressed her face against

Gunnar's shoulder. A fit of sobs seized her, shaking her whole body. Gunnar wrapped his arm around her head.

A nurse came through the swing-doors at the end of the hall where the others were seated. Gunnar left Katie with Fleet and got there in time to hear the nurse ask if Mr Bergdorf was allergic to anything.

'Nothing,' hooted the owl.

'OK,' said the nurse, 'this is going to be a long surgery, and it's rather hectic in this area. If you follow the next hall to the right before you get to the elevators, it runs right into the hospital chapel. It might be a good place for some of you, or all, to wait.' And you better pray your hearts out, her eyes said.

The chapel occupied two levels of the end of a wing. Inside, young Simon Bergdorf's family, and Ruth and Barbara, took seats on the right in the front row of six wooden pews.

In the standing area at the rear, Gunnar dropped his voice. 'Who'd believe there was such a place in here?'

'It's dark,' said Katie, taking jerky breaths between the residual sobs still shaking her chest, her eyes adjusting slowly from the bright hall.

The rainy afternoon's light filtered through panes of blue, and red and green stained-glass in abstract patterns above the dais. Gunnar slipped into the back row on the left, and helped Katie take a seat beside him, leaving room for Fleet next to her on the aisle. They sat silently, except for the sound of Katie's shaky breathing and faint organ music – Bach from a hidden loudspeaker. Gunnar prayed for Al Bergdorf's life and gave thanks for Katie's.

Two vases filled with elaborate bouquets of cut flowers were perched on metal stands at the front corners of the dais. A speaker's stand with a microphone stood beside the one on the left. A whiff of a cigarette drew Gunnar's eyes to the right. Between drags, Ruth Bergdorf bitched pianissimo into son Simon's sorrowful face. Al's sister Barbara sat quiet as a nun.

The door opened at the rear. It was Anne. Gunnar raised his hand as though they were blended in a crowd. She smiled quickly through her worried look, walked up behind Katie and bent and kissed her on the mouth.

'Oh Mom,' Katie said.

Fleet stood up to let Anne pass. As she sat down between Katie and Gunnar, she handed Gunnar a newspaper. Gunnar's own face smiled up at him from the center of page one. Underneath was a picture of the check he had delivered to Terry Wood that morning. Headlines ran to the right and left of his picture: LEGAL EAGLE DROPS PREY and IF DJILAS IS A LIAR, WHAT'S THE MAYOR? Gunnar didn't bother to read the text.

Anne interrupted the beginning of Katie's story to turn and kiss Gunnar's cheek. The story had brought Katie's sobs back. 'I think maybe she needs to be sedated,' Anne said to Gunnar in a whisper.

The door in the back opened again. Tony Djilas, trained grin replaced by a face of utter despair, stood beside Holly, splendid, even in sadness. Gunnar's emotions agitated one into the other like dirty clothes in a washer; reason not just subordinate, but gone without a trace. His legs pushed past Anne's knees, his feet trampled Katie's tender sprain and led him past Fleet before he could react, and carried Gunnar to Tony. With doubled fist on the end of a taut forearm club, Gunnar smashed Tony Djilas' mouth. A second blow knocked him to the floor. Gunnar dived on Tony, crossed forearms over his face. But Holly's scream brought Gunnar to his senses and he felt himself lifted by the shoulders and the throbbing began in his broken right hand.

'Stop it! Stop it!' Katie yelled.

Fleet pushed Gunnar behind him, as Tony wobbled to his feet, nose and mouth bleeding. 'I had nothing to do with this.' he said.

The Bergdorfs assembled in the aisle.

'Goy assholes,' said Ruth Bergdorf.

Fleet gave Gunnar a gentle push, and he sat back down next to Anne again, lifeless as cooked meat. Katie's sobs drowned out the organ.

'I am going to take her out of here,' said Anne.

After a quiet argument, Anne and Katie, on her crutches, passed through the door. Holly stood apart from her father and looked to Gunnar for a sign. He couldn't give it. He couldn't get organized and his hand ached.

Fleet herded the Bergdorfs back to their front pew, at the same time watching Tony and Gunnar over his shoulder. He came back and took Tony by the arm and led him to a seat across the aisle from Gunnar. Then he motioned to Holly to sit in front of Tony. The rose-petal flesh of her face was fixed in a frown. In the front, the Bergdorf heads were all swiveled around watching like birds on a wire.

A uniformed campus cop appeared in the door behind Tony. 'This is under control,' said Fleet, reaching for his wallet.

'Never mind, Captain,' said the cop. 'I know who you are.' He slipped back through the door.

Fleet sat down beside Gunnar. 'Let's all just sit calmly for a while,' said Fleet. Then quietly to Tony: 'I want to hear your story as much as you want to tell it.'

Tony held his blue pocket-square to his bleeding mouth. Trance-like, Holly stared straight ahead. Gunnar watched her profile and felt a need to comfort her. Fleet restrained him with a gentle hand on top of a tense thigh.

Half an hour later, when Anne returned, the tableau hadn't changed, except that the Bergdorfs had long since lost interest in the transactions at the rear.

'They sedated her and put her to bed, out like a light.' Anne said.

When Fleet made no move to let her pass, Anne sat down in the seat in front of him, across the aisle from Holly. From Gunnar's seat off to the side, he saw the profiles of his women, juxtaposed. He still had never told Holly that Anne knew. He visualized the pale vaccination scar under the gray silk covering Holly's upper arm, his thoughts strewn about like old car parts in an untended junkyard. Minutes later, the Bergdorfs filed up the aisle and through the door: to the coffee shop, young Simon said.

'Al Bergdorf is the best friend I ever had,' said Tony, his throat rasping like too many cigarettes. 'A real class guy. I love him so much I joined his Jewish country club. I was the only Gentile in the whole club. He never knew about any of this bullshit.'

The room was silent, save for the faint strains of music. Tony had shoved the gory hanky back in his breast pocket and blood encrusted his mustache. He faced straight forward, at the back of Holly's head, his face full of sharp angles and angry knots.

'My old man taught me to lie,' he said.' It's the only thing he ever taught me.'

Anne turned her head to look at Tony. Gunnar leaned forward so he could see past Fleet. Holly sat still as a marble goddess.

'There's a lot a liars,' said Tony. 'Ya buy a car, they lie to ya. I barely got my first one home. Ya buy a house, they lie to ya. Everything's a good deal. I can give you the best deal. Special this week. I learned fast, then I met the master. Real big time. He used to call me his hired liar, and laugh like hell. But I'm not gonna lie with Al in there dyin'. Not on your life, like he says.'

The tape was back to the Bach. Gunnar felt subdued, lucky, no vestige of anger. His life had been filled with favors granted, none within an order of magnitude of the one Al Bergdorf had granted him today.

'I called Al to tell him Gunnar's daughter was going to get cut,' said Tony, 'I hoped he could do something. I knew they were friends, sorta.'

Gunnar's biceps tensed and he clenched his fists. The pain in his right hand almost made him yell.

'I found out from Florida by telephone,' said Tony.

The dormant spot inside that energized Gunnar's brain for the practice of law came back to life. Maybe he should warn Tony that he might be incriminating himself to a cop?

'It had nothing to do with me or the *Times-Journal*, or the verdict,' said Tony. 'Zilman was afraid Gunnar was getting too close.'

'Too close to what?' said Fleet.

Holly turned around slowly in her seat. Her face drained of blood. Her eyes held Gunnar's, asking if he remembered where they had been together.

'Too close to murder,' said Tony. 'Those cops. Zilman had Big Ed Edwards kill both of 'em, and I knew it. I've known it for fourteen years. The Feds put Manny in their witness program even though he never had to testify. The guys he fingered all pled guilty . . . but he went back to Florida. Spent most of his time in Jacksonville. But their deal with him didn't include killin' those cops, and there's no statute of limitations on murder. But I'm through carrying it. I don't hurt people. I'm no hood.'

'Do you know where Zilman is now?' said Fleet.

'I lied to that jury. I should have known from the beginning, but I guess I thought if he could make the big score, Gunnar wouldn't let a little bullshit bother him.'

The last tiny doubt stuck in some cerebral synapse in Gunnar's head dissolved. He felt free for a moment. But just a moment. Holly's stricken face and frightened eyes brought him back.

'Do you know where Zilman is now? said Fleet again.

'I think he had that young Edwards killed too. Just last week. I should never have mentioned his name to Manny. He was afraid he would help Gunnar.' Tony let out a chest full of air and stopped talking.

Holly chewed her lovely lower lip. A movement inside the door at the rear drew Gunnar's eyes to the stout figure of Davey Tripp.

Fleet tried again. 'But where is Zilman now?'

'Ask her.' Tony sounded groggy and out of control. He waved his left hand, loose at the wrist, in Holly's direction and sank back in his seat. 'She knows. She loves the sonofabitch.'

'No, Tony,' Holly said. 'No, please, *no*.' Her anguished look said, these are secrets. She turned back to the front of the chapel and dropped her head into the V of her hands, elbows on her knees. Her head moved, just slightly, from side to side.

'She traveled with him for six years,' Tony said. 'From when she was seventeen 'til he dumped her for another teenager. She couldn't get enough of the sonofabitch. She knew he offed those cops.'

Holly keened like a squaw over her dead brave. '*No, no, no.*' Anne crossed the aisle and slid into the pew beside her and drew Holly close, whispering into her curly hair.

'Oh, no, no, no, no.' She was dying of despair.

Gunnar fought for air. Not Holly, not his sweet adorable Holly. She had breathed life into his dead body.

'Hell, Manny told me he slept with her twenty times in Palm Beach last winter. I knew someday I'd have to turn him in. But

I wanted to win the trial first. I wanted the money. I wanted to never have to run out on the landlord.'

Lungfuls of air burst through Gunnar's closed lips, the same sensation as when Colonel Jimmy Ray Starkweather had walked out of his office leaving him alone with Jack's death. He leaned his forehead on the back of the pew in front of him and tears fell to the floor.

At about six o'clock a nurse came in and told them that Mr Bergdorf was out of surgery, in intensive care. Gunnar headed down the hall and found one of the surgeons.

'He's got a chance. We can't get his pressure to where we want it, but he's got a chance, that's all.' The surgeon was a bear of a man with a fine square face. A blue muslin cap covered his hair. 'We removed his spleen, but not before he lost a lot of blood. And we resected the liver. We tried to stop all of the bleeding in there, but I don't know. The laceration was extensive. Very chancey. The cut at the base of his neck is OK. He must have run into a madman. Ironic, you know. Mr Bergdorf has lost a lot of weight recently, especially around the abdomen. If he hadn't, that knife might not have done so much damage.'

'When will he come out of the anesthetic?' Gunnar asked.

The surgeon glanced at his watch. 'He should wake up eight-thirty, nine.'

Laura and Barbara Weisenstein took the children to the main lobby. Ruth Bergdorf went home. Anne shuttled between Katie, sleeping in a room on the floor above, and Holly stretched out on the pew in the empty chapel. Gunnar sat outside a room in the intensive-care unit, waiting with Tony Djilas and young Simon Bergdorf – who said his grandparents were flying in from Florida in the morning. At eight forty-five a nurse came out and took Simon back through the doors with her.

He was back in minutes, crying. 'He says he's dying and he wants to talk to you, Gunnar, alone.

'You mustn't excite him at all,' said the nurse, 'but we think he'll be more agitated if we don't let you in.'

Gunnar walked over to the bedside. Al lay under a profusion

of tubes and wires, surrounded by hanging bottles, and numerous arcane devices, beeping and buzzing. His face looked deeply lined. With his left hand, Gunnar squeezed Al's hand gently. It was cold.

'Hi, Gunnar.' Al's voice had one tenth of his old power. 'Simon tells me Katie's OK.' He looked out of bottomless eyes tucked deeply into their intricate pouches.

'She's fine, thanks to you,' said Gunnar, still unaware of what might exist between his daughter and Al. 'I didn't know the two of you even knew each other.' The knot in his throat restricted his voice.

'I know. She'll tell you about it. I'm afraid I might not have time. I'm kinda scared, Gunnar, but I gotta tell you two things.'

Gunnar pressed harder on Al's cold hand.

'First,' Al said, 'I always thought something was missing, but I never knew Tony was lying to you, and to that jury. I wouldn't want you to think that I did. You know a dying man wouldn't lie about something like this. He would just let it alone, or even admit he's wrong.'

Gunnar nodded his agreement.

'And second, you had the idea I was some kind of shyster. You're wrong Gunnar.'

Guilt oozed from Gunnar's pores as he looked into the creased face shaded by incipient beard.

Al went on weakly, 'People believe hearsay, especially about Jews.'

'Will you forgive me, Al?' Gunnar said.' And Al, I wish I could repay you for what you did today for Katie . . . and for me.'

'Sure . . . I just don't want you to think . . . .'

'I think you're the best.' Gunnar bent over and kissed Al's brow. 'I'll never forget it. Ever . . . . They told me I should only stay in here a couple of minutes.'

'Sure Gunnar . . . but one more thing. Get Simon.'

Gunnar went out and was back in a minute with Simon at his side.

'Simon,' Al said, straining to be heard. 'I want you to be a witness to this . . . Gunnar, write this down on something . . . I hereby give my Jackson Pollock painting to Katherine Larson.'

Gunnar wrote it down on the back of a business card and dated it. Then put the pen in Al's hand. Some kind of monitoring device was connected to Al's fingernail, but he managed to scratch a signature on the card. Then Simon signed it and handed it back to Gunnar.

'You see she gets it, Simon,' Al said.

'Sure Dad, but you're going to be able to give it to her yourself when you get out of here.'

'Simon, give me a little time with Gunnar. Then bring the kids and Laura and Barbara in.'

Simon went out and a nurse nervously mopped Al's brow.

'My feet are getting awful cold,' Al said, 'hands too.'

The nurse went out.

'Katie told me how hard it was on you, losing your son. I think I know how you feel. I'm losing a son, and a daughter, even though I've only had the daughter a week. And two grandchildren. And Laura. Dying's losing everyone, all at once. Send Simon and the kids in, will ya. Tell Katie how glad I was to get to know her. Goodbye, Gunnar.'

'Goodbye, dear friend,' said Gunnar.

Gunnar was determined to wait outside Al's door all night. Son Simon stayed by Al's bed, and Tony sat in a corner like he was waiting to be arrested. Admitting to the Chief of Detectives that he'd lied under oath, arrest was a definite possibility. He told Gunnar that Holly had gone home with Davey.

There is no guilt like guilt for an act that cannot be rectified. Gunnar vowed some kind of atonement. It was his fault. How badly he'd wanted to believe Tony Djilas. How big those millions had looked, but Al had never been as sold as Gunnar on his pal's story. Al and Gunnar could have become friends. If they had, the tumour of guilt somewhere below his heart and above his stomach wouldn't be so heavy or seem so permanent. But Al was a Jew. And just as Tony's father had taught him to lie, Gunnar's father had taught him that you couldn't trust Jews. They're in for themselves, whatever that meant. They stick together. They protect each other. They've got all the money. They own all the banks. *They*. Jesus Christ. There is no *they*.

If there was, they had just saved Katie's life. But they didn't. Al did.

Laura came back into the hall. 'He's going back down to surgery. I heard the nurse say his blood pressure had dropped to eighty over twenty-five.'

Shortly after midnight, Simon Bergdorf walked blinking into the lobby waiting area and with ragged red lines in his eyes, he ended the everlasting day. To Gunnar and Tony he said, 'My father has just passed away.'

Except for Al's funeral, Katie didn't leave the hospital for two weeks.

64

In the month following Al Bergdorf's funeral, Gunnar's unexpected act of honesty fascinated the country. Columnists speculated on his motives. Articles entitled 'There's Still Hope', and 'Take a Lesson, Yuppies' proliferated. All the while, Gunnar stuck by his decision to talk to no one outside.

Katie took the job at Bergdorf and Ratner. Old Simon Bergdorf insisted she take the Pollock home, so she hung it on the dining-room wall opposite the picture window on the bay. She had a long recovery ahead of her. Few nights passed without the awful dreams. Being named president of the Law Review was a boost, but she confided in her parents that maybe the law wasn't for her.

Gunnar got a letter from Diane Ek saying she and Kenny were coming next July. Kenny said his first choice was still He-Man. He'd got so excited after the third reading of Gunnar's letter that he'd fallen asleep for four hours. And don't forget my first choice, she said, I've already lost ten pounds.

Tony's confession in the chapel brought his arrest for perjury and, upon reading the indictment, Terry Wood reopened the *Times-Journal* case. Barry Busch represented Tony in both matters. Fleet said Busch was already bargaining, offering Tony's testimony against Zilman for probation.

In spite of Holly's contrition, Gunnar never went back to the Lodge. She had loved Manny Zilman, but now she hated him. A kid fell in love with Zilman, but a woman fell in love with Gunnar, she said. What about last winter? he asked. She was desperate without Gunnar, she needed warmth, she said. Read *sex*, Gunnar thought. But she was sorry. There would never be another man. It's over, Gunnar said. Her daddy had taught her to lie, too.

He wormed it out that Davey had forgiven her, was standing by her. Memories of her softness and the heat tempted Gunnar, but he would not give in. To succumb would be his ruin. She wept and pleaded through daily phone calls. Just yesterday, a clinical account of her plans for him should he come back to the Lodge – just one more time, she said – had interrupted his labors at the office. He was delegating duties and deferring obligations before leaving for two months. He and Anne had decided to try a reprise of their European trip – London, motoring in Scotland and on to Paris – just the two of them. For opening night he had booked that same tiny hotel on Cromwell Road across from the Victoria and Albert Museum. And he looked forward with confidence to bedding his favorite blonde. Somehow he knew for sure it was going to work there, even though he hadn't yet had the courage to try at home. He still wore a heavy overcoat of sadness for Al Bergdorf, but Gunnar was OK. You know when you're OK, especially when you haven't been for eleven years, one month and seven days.

Two days after the *Times-Journal* had run the picture of Gunnar's check, Eddie Kerr had walked into his office.

'This belongs to you,' he said, and he handed Gunnar a check for twenty-five thousand dollars written on Eddie's personal account.

'Oh no you don't,' said Gunnar, 'you earned every dime of that. Keep it.'

'No, the bonus deal was subject to covering our costs, and obviously we didn't,' Eddie said. 'I will consider it a personal insult if you refuse to accept my check.'

Gunnar got up from behind his desk to stand face to face with Eddie. Eddie's startled look was replaced by the Doberman stare. Gunnar wrapped his arms around him and drew him up close, patting Eddie's plump back. 'You're a big man, Mr Kerr, and a damn good lawyer.' Gunnar stepped back, and Eddie stepped back even further, and Gunnar said, 'I just don't know why you insist on hiding that soft heart. You know I've known about it for quite a while now, and I don't intend to keep it a secret.'

'I don't know what you're talking about,' said Eddie.